Peggy Eaton Omnibus

Silver Joey
Daughter of the Downs

Peggy Eaton Omnibus

Silver Joey
Daughter of the
Downs

PEGGY EATON

A *Time Warner* Paperback

This omnibus edition first published in Great Britain by Time Warner Paperbacks in 2004
Peggy Eaton Omnibus Copyright © Peggy Eaton 2004

Previously published separately:
Silver Joey first published in Great Britain in 1998
by Little, Brown and Company
Published by Warner Books in 1999
Copyright © Peggy Eaton 1998

Daughter of the Downs first published in Great Britain in 1995 by Warner
Reprinted 1999
Copyright © Peggy Eaton 1995

A CIP catalogue record for this book is available from the British Library

ISBN 0 7515 3642 3

Printed and bound in Great Britain by
Mackays of Chatham Ltd, Chatham

Time Warner Paperbacks
An imprint of
Time Warner Books UK
Brettenham House
Lancaster Place
London WC2E 7EN

www.TimeWarnerBooks.co.uk

Silver Joey

CHAPTER ONE

Railway Cottages, 1930

'Are you awake, Lizzie? You'd better get up; your mum's real bad.'

Lizzie turned over and stretched. She'd been having such a lovely dream. Her favourite one about the day-trip Mum and Dad had taken her on when she was little. They'd gone to Brighton and Dad had bought her a bucket and spade. Although it was years ago Lizzie had never forgotten that golden day.

'Lizzie! Are you awake?'

'Yes, Dad.'

Lizzie sat up, jerked back into the present. She was lying on her bed and it wasn't even night-time. The room was full of sunshine. She was still wearing her faded mauve dress and the cotton stockings with the hole in the heel. Nothing had changed.

'I think she's taken a turn.'

Her father Ernie Sargent stood in the doorway. Although he was only forty-eight his hair was grizzled and his long moustache was drooping and stained yellow at the ends. The stub of a Woodbine was wedged in the corner of his mouth, a permanent comfort when he could afford the four-pence for a packet.

Lizzie jumped from the bed sliding her feet into her shoes.

'She's taken a turn, Dad? For the better, I hope.'

'I don't know,' Ernie admitted. 'She suddenly woke up and seemed to come to her senses like.'

'I'll go to her.'

Tossing her plait of brown hair over her shoulder, Lizzie headed for the door. She was a pretty girl of sixteen, tall and slim, with eyes as dark as her hair and a pale smooth complexion. Her hands were red and rough and there was the usual worried frown on her face, because her mother, Mary Sargent, was dying.

Sometimes, on good days, Lizzie couldn't believe it. Her mother had been ailing since the winter. First she'd complained of tiredness and pains, but she always managed to keep a cheerful smile on her face for Lizzie and her little brother Billy.

They thought she'd be better when the spring came and the weather warmed up, and for a while she did seem to improve. But now it was June, the trees were in full leaf, and Mary Sargent was confined to her bed.

Lizzie and Ernest took turns caring for her. Ernie was out of work, and his daughter had left school, so they could share the duties of the sickroom. But the few shillings they got from the dole wasn't enough to provide Mary with the comforts she needed. It was barely enough to feed the four of them; although Mary didn't seem to be able to keep anything down these days. But Billy at seven years old was growing fast, and Lizzie always looked hungry.

Forcing a smile on her face Lizzie entered her parents' bedroom. Her eyes went at once to the big iron-framed bed with the four shiny brass knobs, one at each corner.

The feather mattress was sagging in the middle so that Mary looked as if she was cradled in a nest. She was so thin and bird-like that the patchwork quilt lay flat and smooth over her emaciated body. Her eyes were open, huge and dark and sunk in their sockets, following Lizzie as she approached the bed. The day before, her gaze had roamed about the room, not recognising anyone, but today she looked aware of what was going on. Lizzie smiled, pleased at the improvement. She touched the bony hand that picked at the threads of the coverlet.

'You look better, Mum. Did you have a nice sleep?' Mary opened her mouth to answer but it was too much of an effort, so Lizzie said, 'Don't try and talk. It only tires you.'

'How do you think she is?'

Ernest had followed his daughter into the room. He stood the other side of the bed looking down at his wife – needing reassurance. The stub of cigarette made him cough and his face turned an unhealthy red. He'd been gassed at the Battle of the Somme and his lungs had never recovered properly. His hands still trembled with shell-shock making delicate work difficult, but he could still tend Mary gently.

'She's looking better,' Lizzie said. 'You go and put the kettle on while I see to her.'

Ernie left the room looking more optimistic. Lizzie kept up a flow of cheerful chatter, anything to keep her mother's attention.

The bedroom was small, but neat and spotlessly clean. The walls were papered with a design of tiny flowers on a blue background, and there were rag rugs, their colours faded to a mist, on the bare floor. The smell of furniture polish hid the odour of sickness. On the window-sill stood a jug containing a bunch of wild flowers. There was a chest for linen and a marble-topped wash-stand, but not much else.

'The sun felt really warm today, Mum,' Lizzie said. She sat down on the edge of the bed and took hold of her mother's hand. 'When you're feeling well enough you must sit outside. It will do you good.' She swung her long slender legs up in front of her and rested her head on the pillow beside her mother's. 'I've just had such a lovely dream; all about that day we spent beside the seaside.' A smile hovered around Mary's mouth showing that she remembered as well. 'Dad bought me a bucket with clowns painted on it. I filled it full of pebbles and shells to bring home. But you wouldn't let me because it was too heavy. We went on the pier and you gave me pennies to put in the slot-machines. I had my fortune told ...' Lizzie's voice faded as if her thoughts were far away. 'The sun was shining so brightly it looked just as if the streets were paved with gold. We walked back to the station singing "Oh, I do like to be beside the seaside".'

Lizzie hummed the tune, glancing sideways at her mother to see if she was listening. There was a smile on Mary's lips and her eyes were half closed. Lizzie closed her own eyes and held her mother's hand tighter. She was remembering the times when she'd crept into this bed for comfort; when she'd had a nightmare, been frightened by a storm, or just not been able to sleep. But now she was almost grown-up and too old for such things. It was her turn to do the comforting.

She must have dozed off because the next thing she heard was the rattle of teacups as her father climbed the stairs.

Lizzie sat up to rouse her mother, but there was something about the face on the pillow that made her pause. It was the same and yet different. The eyes half closed, the mouth slack, the frown of pain gone. For the first time in months Mary Sargent looked peaceful.

Ernie pushed open the door with his foot and came into the room carrying the tray. The tremor in his fingers made the cups dance on the saucers.

'I think she's asleep, Dad.'

He put down the tray and approached the bed; he stood there, staring, for such a long time that Lizzie said, 'What is it?'

'She's gone.'

Lizzie laughed. 'What do you mean – gone? She's just asleep. We'll keep the pot warm until she wakes up.'

'She's dead, Lizzie.'

'No, she's not. She can't be.'

But one glance at the still form convinced her that he was right. Death had wiped away the pain and the suffering, making Mary look almost young again. She looked like the young woman who Ernest Sargent had courted and married so many years ago.

'She looks like an angel,' he said softly.

And Lizzie said, 'She is an angel now.'

A blue-bottle had flown unnoticed in through the open window. As if sensing it wouldn't be disturbed it chose to settle on the dead woman's brow. Ernest leaned over to brush it away, and then, with a cry of anguish, gathered Mary in his arms. A sound, almost like an animal in pain, escaped him, and a tear fell upon the parchment-like cheek.

Lizzie crept out of the room. She couldn't help her parents any more, and she had her own grief to contend with.

She felt exhausted, as if she'd lived a life-time. It struck her that downstairs things were the same as usual. On the mantelpiece the marble clock ticked noisily, occasionally missing a beat and ticking when it should have tocked. The kettle sang on the hob, and in the rocking-chair the ginger cat purred on its cushion. A cacophony of sound that usually went unnoticed.

What to do? Billy would be home soon wanting his tea. Even with death upstairs people had to be fed.

Lizzie heard her brother coming from a long way off. She could tell he was happy by the tuneful whistle and the way his boots rattled on the gravel. Billy adored his mother and Lizzie knew that his happiness would be wiped away as soon as she broke the sad news.

He was in the open doorway, hands in pockets and

head thrown back to reach the high notes. As clear as a blackbird Billy's whistle was – lovely to hear. Seven years and three months old, four foot tall without his boots, and as fair as his sister was dark. A handsome boy.

When Billy saw Lizzie's face the whistle died on his lips. 'What is it?' he asked, standing in front of her and staring up into her face. 'What's happened?'

'It's Mum. She's dead.'

'No she's not. Don't be silly. I said goodbye to her before I went out. She was all right then.'

'She's dead now.'

Billy's bottom lip trembled, and then he threw himself at his sister and beat her with his fists as if it was her fault.

'She's not! She's not! I don't believe you.'

'Hush, Billy.' Lizzie tried to put her arms around him but he was like a wild thing; thrashing away with his arms and legs, his boots grazing her shins.

'I've learned "The March of the Gladiators" just for her. She told me to. I even know the difficult bits. She said I was to play it to her when I got home. I'm going to play it to her now.'

He was off, clomping into the parlour where the small upright piano had pride of place; for Mary Sargent had boosted the family income by giving music lessons. The two shillings an hour she charged made a difference to the thirty-three shillings a week Ernest picked up in assistance. The rent for the railway cottage they lived in was fourteen and sixpence, so there was never much over for food and clothes. But they were luckier than some who had no means of making extra money.

From the parlour the loud strains of the march by Theodore Bonheur made Lizzie run to the door.

'Stop that, Billy Sargent,' she hissed, banging down the lid and catching the tips of the child's fingers. 'You're making enough noise to wake the dead— Oh!' Suddenly realising what she'd just said Lizzie's face turned paper white. Billy's face was stricken with grief, and he was sucking the fingers of his right hand to ease the pain. 'I'm sorry.'

'What we gonna do, Lizzie?'

'I don't know. Dad'll tell us.'

'What's all that noise?' Ernest was halfway down the stairs, his eyes red but dry. In his hand he carried the leather belt from his trousers. They could see him through the open doorway.

'He's going to strap me,' Billy said in a low scared voice.

'No, he's not. He'd never do that.' Lizzie walked to the bottom of the stairs and looked up at her father. 'Sorry, Dad. I've just told Billy about Mum.'

'Well, you're to tell him he's never to play that piano again – do you hear?'

'I'll tell him.'

Lizzie knew her father didn't mean to be unkind. It was shock and grief, and quite understandable. Her mother had played the instrument to them on winter evenings, and at Christmas they'd sung carols around it. She'd taught Billy to play from the Ezra Read tutor, and said he showed signs of becoming a good musician. Although how she could tell at his age Lizzie couldn't imagine.

'Go out, the two of you,' Ernie said in an expressionless voice. 'I want to be by myself. I have things to do.'

'But, Dad, shouldn't I get somebody? The doctor perhaps.'

'We don't need no doctor. It's too late for quacks.'

Something in her father's face frightened Lizzie. She'd never seen him like this before. 'I could get Mr Bennet from next door.'

'We don't want nobody. Take your brother for a walk or something – come back in an hour.'

'Come on, Billy,' Lizzie said. The little boy got down from the piano stool and trotted to her side. 'We'll go down to the old railway line. You like going there.'

She gave him a gentle push and he hurried through the

door ahead of her. Now that they knew what they were
about they were both anxious to get away. Outside the
sun was shining; inside there was only a dead mother and
a father they hardly recognised.

'Lizzie!'

'Yes, Dad?' Lizzie turned in the doorway, silhouetted
against the light, one hand holding the frame.

'Look after Billy.'

'Of course I will.'

She didn't understand, but later she would. In her
innocence she followed Billy into the garden. He was
swinging on the broken fence that divided their patch of
garden from their neighbours. Mr Bennet was watering
his sweet-peas, which climbed the wire-netting and
sprawled along the path. He was proud of them and often
sent in a bunch for the invalid. He beamed at Lizzie.

'Glad to hear your mum's better,' he said cheerfully.

Lizzie looked at her brother, then pulled him behind
her out of the gate. 'Come on, Billy.' Outside there was a
grassy bank, the road, and then a field of corn. They
waited at the roadside while a horse and cart ambled past
and then, holding hands, hurried across the road. 'Now,
Billy,' Lizzie said when they were safely on the other side,
'what did you say to Mr Bennet then?'

'Nothing much.' Billy looked at the ground and shuffled
his feet guiltily.

'What did you say to him?' Lizzie grabbed Billy by the
shoulder and shook him as hard as she could. He pulled
away and flung himself down on the ground. Lizzie,
calmer now, sat down beside him, and said more gently,
'Tell me what you said, Billy.'

'He asked how Mum was. I couldn't say she was dead
just like that – so I said she was better. Sorry, Lizzie.'

'Don't worry. It's all right.'

She put her arm around her young brother's shoulders
and hugged him to her. They sat together in silence. Lizzie
could just see the roofs of the two railway cottages

nestling in a fold of the South Downs. It was the only home
she and Billy had ever known. Grandpa Sargent had
come south to work on the railway and been given a
rented cottage for his family. But the line had never been
finished. It should have been a tributary of the link with
the coast, but someone had changed their mind and it had
been abandoned. The remains of the track lay behind
them rusting and unused, most of it covered with nettles
and brambles. A place where the local children came to
play.

'What's going to happen now?' Billy asked after a
while.

'I don't know. I suppose there'll be a funeral.'

The boy looked up at his sister as if he'd just thought of
something fearful. 'Will Aunt Hannah come?'

'I suppose so. But don't worry, I'll look after you.'

Aunt Hannah Seymour was Ernest's sister, and came
to Railway Cottage only in times of trouble. She was a
wealthy widow who regarded her brother as a failure,
her sister-in-law as weak, and her niece a nuisance. But
she approved of Billy, much to his dismay. He was terrified
of his loud-voiced aunt, who always smelled of moth-balls
and wore black bombazine.

They lay back in the corn and tried not to think about
Aunt Hannah. In the clear blue sky overhead the sun
burned steadily, bathing everything in a quivering haze
of heat. All they could hear was the distant clip-clop of
horses' hooves, the drowsy hum of insects and the singing
of larks. Lizzie stretched out her hand and picked a
scarlet-headed poppy. She knew somehow that this was
the last day of her childhood.

'Do you want to go down to the line?'

Billy nodded. Usually they ran down the slope to the
deserted railway line, but today they picked their way as
if every step could bring a fresh disaster.

The blackberries weren't ripe, but there were the rosy
fruits of wild strawberries nestling under their flat green

leaves. Lizzie picked some and held them out on the palm of her hand, but Billy shook his head so she dropped them on to the ground and crushed them with her heel. Wild strawberries had been their mother's favourite. Every summer they'd picked the early ones to carry home as a treat. There was no one to gather them for now.

'Is it time to go home, Lizzie?'

'Dad said an hour.'

'It must be nearly time then.'

'All right. But we'll walk slowly.'

They wandered back, but the nearer they got to the cottage the more Lizzie dreaded going inside. Usually they raced home shouting and laughing; calling for Mum to come to see what they'd found in the hedgerow. The first primrose, the speckled egg, the spray of wild-briar. Never again.

Mr Bennet was still in his garden, but he was bent over his vegetable patch and didn't see them. Lizzie gave Billy a little push.

'Go in and tell Dad we're back. I'm just going to pick some mint for the potatoes.'

'But, Lizzie . . .' Billy's bottom lip trembled.

'It's all right. There's nothing to be afraid of.'

Lizzie was still bending over the bed of mint when she heard the scream. It sounded so unearthly that she thought at first that it was the cry of a wild animal in pain, not the sort of sound she'd associate with her brother.

'Billy!' Dropping the green sprigs on the path Lizzie raced for the house. Billy was standing in the doorway. She took him in her arms and he clung to her, stiff and shuddering. 'What is it? Where's Dad?'

Over her brother's shoulder Lizzie could see into the hall. It was bright with sunshine. Motes of dust danced around the boots swaying to and fro a few feet from the banister rail. She recognised the boots and the corduroy trousers, the rough grey shirt; but she didn't recognise the bloated purple face with the leather belt tightly knotted around the throat. She stared mesmerised at the swinging figure. Ernest Sargent had hanged himself.

The Reverend Michael Curren stood in the parlour of Railway Cottage, one arm resting on the mantelpiece with its border of bobbled fringe. Lizzie had offered him a drink; she'd even got the precious tin of Mazawattee tea down from the shelf, but he'd refused. He wouldn't even sit down.

'I prefer to stand, Miss Sargent,' he said in a deep gravelly voice, and continued to stare at Lizzie over the top of his horn-rimmed glasses. She felt her face flushing. She'd never been called Miss Sargent before.

'About the funeral,' Lizzie started to say. 'I've written to my aunt, Mrs Seymour, and she wants it to be held on Friday if that's convenient. How much will it cost?'

'The undertaker will tell you that. I think the cheapest interment is about two pounds ten shillings. And then of course there will be my fee.'

Lizzie was reckoning quickly in her head. Five pounds for two burials was a fortune, but the vicar's fee shouldn't be too high. She'd need at least six pounds to do things properly and all she had was the two pounds she'd found in the drawer of the dresser. If the worst came to the worst she'd have to ask Aunt Hannah for a loan.

'Now about the graves,' the vicar continued. 'There's a single spot right by the lynch-gate which is a very popular position. I suggest we reserve that for your mother. Your father's a different matter.'

'They must be buried together,' Lizzie said. 'That's what they would want.'

The Reverend Curren cleared his throat before saying, 'That, Miss Sargent, is quite impossible.'

'But why?' The title of Miss made Lizzie feel grown-up, and a grown-up would fight for the rights of her family. 'They were husband and wife. They'd been married for nearly twenty years. The first of November nineteen-eleven, Dad always said. They always made a special occasion of their anniversary. They were never separated except for the war; you can't separate them now.'

The vicar cleared his throat again. He didn't want to hurt this young girl standing so proudly before him. She'd been hurt enough already. He wondered what was going to happen to her, alone and unprotected. She couldn't be much more than fifteen, and there was a little brother as well, so he'd been told.

'It's the circumstances.'

'I don't understand.' Lizzie looked puzzled.

'Your father didn't die of natural causes.'

'I know.' Lizzie paled at the harrowing memory of the swinging figure with the bloated face and staring eyes. 'But that doesn't make any difference, does it?'

'I'm afraid it does, young lady. Your father took his own life, and because of that I can't bury him in consecrated ground.' He took off his glasses and inspected the lenses for dust before perching them back on his nose. 'There's a spot behind the church, before the wood begins; we could bury him there – without a headstone, of course.'

'You don't mean Hangman's Copse?'

Lizzie was horrified. Hangman's Copse was a notorious place, where in the old days the bodies of highway-men and cut-throats had been disposed of. It was said to be haunted.

'I think that is what the locals call it.'

'You're not going to bury my father in Hangman's Copse,' Lizzie said firmly. 'He wasn't a criminal.'

'He took his own life. In my view that is a criminal act. God gives us our lives, and only he has the right to take them away.'

Lizzie's head pounded. She burst out emotionally, 'I don't believe God can be so cruel. Father killed himself because he couldn't face life without my mother. God would understand, and forgive him.'

'I've no doubt, young lady,' the Reverend Curren continued, 'he is forgiven; but even so what he did was a sinful act and I can't bury him in consecrated ground.'

'Who says so?'

Neither of them had heard the sound of the car, or the crunching of feet on the gravel path, nor seen the large black shadow filling the doorway. Aunt Hannah Seymour had arrived.

The Reverend Curren was taken back by her imposing appearance. She reminded him of the nanny of his nursery days. The one who'd squashed all his childhood dreams, so that he'd grown up seeking power rather than affection. His yearning to control others was the reason he'd chosen to go into the church.

'Aunt Hannah,' Lizzie said weakly. 'This is our vicar, the Reverend Curren. He's come about the funeral.'

'So I heard.' Aunt Hannah strode into the room, her stiff black skirts almost sweeping the floor. The dead bird attached to the side of her straw hat bobbed up and down as if it had a life of its own. Under the brim her sharp black eyes took in the shabby room, her niece, the disagreeable presence of Michael Curren. He was the sort of man who was a challenge, and Hannah Seymour liked a dispute.

'So, Mr Curren,' Hannah Seymour began, taking away his title so that he felt his authority oozing away. 'I heard what you were telling my niece about my brother's resting place.'

'A suicide can't be buried in consecrated ground.'

'Why not?'

'Because ...' Michael Curren floundered for a moment, 'suicide is a sin.'

'And who knows that my brother took his own life?'

'Well. I do for one. And his children – and the doctor.'

'That's all right then.' Hannah Seymour sat down on the nearest chair and spread her skirts like an irate crow. 'Elizabeth and William won't say anything. The doctor can be bribed to keep his mouth shut, and as for you ...' She looked the priest up and down as if she didn't think much of what she saw. 'The bishop is a friend of mine, and he owes me a favour. As far as anybody else is concerned Ernest had a heart attack when he found Mary dead. He died instantly.'

'But—'

'No buts, Vicar. My brother and his wife are going to have a proper burial. Not that they deserve it, but I have my pride and no relation of mine is going into a pauper's grave. They will be buried together on the best site and I shall erect a suitable memorial. We will give them a funeral with plumes.'

A funeral with plumes was the height of extravagance, but Hannah was as good as her word.

The road to the church was lined with sightseers to watch the two hearses carry the brass-bound coffins, drawn by black horses with crests of waving plumes on their tossing heads. Behind walked the mourners. Hannah Seymour sailed regally in her black bombazine, with creaking stays, and smelling of Parma Violets and moth balls. On either side walked Lizzie and Billy in their mourning clothes. She'd brought her nephew's suit with her, packed in tissue paper in a Harrods box. It was ready-made because there hadn't been time to have Billy measured, and made of the finest quality black serge. It was a little on the large side, but that would allow for growth. With it he wore a matching black tie and shoes.

Lizzie was also in black. But her dress was an old afternoon frock of her mother's, dipped in dye and slightly streaked. Over it she wore a short black jacket and a velour hat that almost hid her face. Aunt Hannah had given her the money to buy new shoes and stockings with the warning that she was to make them last.

Neither Billy nor Lizzie had ever been to a funeral before. There was something dreamlike about the vicar's voice intoning prayers, the hole in the turf like an entry into another world, and the way the coffins were lowered and sprinkled with handfuls of soil. It didn't seem to have anything to do with their parents.

They remained dry-eyed during the whole proceeding, so that many thought them callous and unfeeling. Then it was over, they'd shaken hands with Michael Curren and returned to Railway Cottage.

At Aunt Hannah's request Lizzie made a pot of tea. There was just enough in the tin for two more pots, she noticed, and where she was going to get money for more she had no idea.

The hot day had made Hannah Seymour perspire. She pulled the long pins out of her hat and removed it, placing it carefully on the table-top. The dead bird stared at its owner out of one glass eye. Lizzie had never been able to decide whether it was artificial or real: stuffed by some taxidermist at her aunt's request.

Billy, still dressed in his uncomfortable suit, picked up his book of fairy-tales and turned to his favourite story: 'The Steadfast Tin Soldier'.

'Now, Elizabeth,' her aunt said when her tea was poured and she'd recovered her breath, 'I'm going home to Greenlock tomorrow.'

Lizzie tried not to look pleased. But it would be a relief when the tiresome woman had gone and she would be left on her own to think. There was so much to think about. How she and Billy were going to manage was the most important thing. She'd have to find a way of earning money, and at sixteen Lizzie had no idea how. Aunt Hannah had paid the funeral costs so she still had the two pound notes tucked away in the dresser drawer, but they wouldn't last long.

'We'll miss you,' Lizzie lied politely. 'I'm sorry the bed wasn't to your liking.'

When Hannah had first arrived she'd taken over the matrimonial bed, unconcerned that her sister-in-law had died there only a short while before. But she found the feather mattress lumpy, and the windows rattled and kept her awake. The following day she'd moved out and taken a room at the Bottle and Jug.

Billy had been greatly relieved. His aunt's commanding voice and bossy ways terrified him. He missed his parents acutely, particularly his mother, and had been having nightmares about his father's death, seeing again the swinging feet in his dreams. He tried to be brave for his sister's sake. Now, although his nose was buried in his book, he was listening to his aunt, relieved to hear that she was going home.

The harsh voice continued. 'I've ordered the village taxi to pick me up at ten in the morning, so I want you to have William's things packed.'

Billy's book dropped to his lap and his grey eyes turned appealingly to Lizzie. She saw his face, paper white, and her heart missed a beat. I must keep calm, she told herself, and picked up her cup with an almost steady hand and took a sip of tea.

'Billy's promised to help Mr Bennet clean out his hens tomorrow,' she said calmly. 'He always does on a Saturday.'

'Well, Mr Bennet must get someone else to help him. I've taken quite a fancy to William and I think he'll suit me very well.'

Lizzie tried to smile. 'A few days' holiday would be nice for Billy, but he mustn't miss his schooling.'

'You don't have to worry about his schooling, miss. I'll see to that. There are plenty of good schools at Greenlock. One of them will suit him. The fees average out at only just over a hundred a year.'

'But I like the village school,' Billy protested in a thin, scared voice.

'And I'm not talking about a holiday either,' Aunt Hannah continued. 'You're family, and I need someone to inherit Greenlock House when I die. I like boys; never had any of my own, so I think you'll do. You'll like living with me, young William. My house is a palace compared with what you're used to.' She looked around at the faded wallpaper and the wormy furniture. 'What do you say?'

The Hans Andersen book fell to the floor with a thud. Billy looked from his aunt to his sister with round frightened eyes.

'But I like it here, Aunt Hannah,' he whispered. 'We can stay here, can't we, Lizzie? We don't have to go to Greenlock?'

'We?' Hannah laughed her short sharp barking laugh. 'Who said anything about *we*? I don't want Elizabeth. Can't abide girls - never could. You're coming to live with me on your own, young man, and that's final.'

CHAPTER TWO

The Silver Joey

'What do you think I should do then?'
         'I don't know, Lizzie. It's up to you.'
Mr Bennet looked over the fence at the young girl
hanging a row of washing out in the next-door garden.
   'I can't make up my mind.' Lizzie sighed. 'One minute
I think I should go for Billy's sake, and the next I'm not
sure if I could stand it.'
   Bending down over his vegetable plot Mr Bennet
grasped the top of a carrot and with a pull yanked it out
of the earth. One twist removed the foliage which he
pushed between the bars of a nearby rabbit hutch. The
carrot he dropped into a waiting basket.
   'I've got a glut of carrots and onions,' he said. 'You'd be
doing me a favour if you'd take some off my hands.' He
saw how the girl's face lit up at the prospect of free food.
'Come through and help yourself.'
   Eagerly Lizzie climbed over the broken fence and let
her neighbour fill her apron with vegetables. He never
took away her pride by offering charity; he always made
out that the things he offered were surplus to his needs.
Over the last few weeks his wife seemed to have food in

plenty to give away, but it was always: 'You're doing us a favour' or 'It'll only go to the pigs' that made Lizzie accept the saucepans of stew or the home-baked loaves that saved her from starvation.

'What did your aunt say again?' Mr Bennet asked as he paused to rest his back.

Lizzie pulled out the tattered letter she'd read so many times over the last few days.

'Dear Elizabeth,
    My kitchen maid has given in her notice. She'll never get another post because I've refused to give her a reference. But I must have a replacement immediately. Have you found a position yet? If you haven't I'll give you a trial. The terms are as follows: free bed and board and ten shillings a week. I enclose five pounds for you to buy yourself a work dress and apron, and pay your fare. Be here by midday on Tuesday.'

Lizzie finished reading and looked at Mr Bennet for his advice.

'Have you heard from Billy yet?' he asked.

'No. He promised to write.'

'I expect it's that aunt of yours won't let him.'

'I expect so.'

Lizzie washed the dirt from a carrot in the water-butt and thoughtfully bit off the end. She knew Billy would have written if he'd been allowed to. The last sight of her brother had been when he was bundled into the back of a car, followed by his suitcase and Aunt Hannah. He'd looked so brave trying not to cry, but the sight of his white face pressed to the back window as the taxi carried him away had nearly broken Lizzie's heart. The last words her father had spoken to her before he died were 'Look after Billy'. But how could she when he was at Greenlock and she was still at Railway Cottage?

Even if she wanted to stay she didn't know how long she'd be able to. The two pounds hadn't lasted long, and she'd already sold some of the small household items to pay the rent.

'I suppose I'd better go to Greenlock,' she said sadly.

'Don't lose your spirit, Lizzie,' Mr Bennet said. 'That's something me and the missus have always admired about you. Even as a little girl you had spirit. No matter what happens, you'll survive.'

'Do you think so?' Lizzie looked so worried and weary that Mr Bennet thought she needed shaking up.

'Come on now,' he said. 'Haven't you any dreams?'

'I used to have,' Lizzie said. Her face lit up as she remembered. She was still pretty when she smiled although there were dark smudges under her eyes, and her dress was faded and torn at the hem. Even her shoes had given up: the heels turned over and the stitching was split. 'I used to dream that the streets were paved with gold.'

'What, here?' Mr Bennet burst out laughing at the very idea.

'No. In Brighton. Mum and Dad took me there once. It was a golden day. If I could choose between Greenlock and Brighton, I'd choose Brighton.'

'Greenlock's closer. And at least your aunt's offering you a home as well as a job. You could starve on the streets of Brighton.'

'So you think I ought to accept?'

'It sounds a sensible offer.'

The ginger cat stalked proudly out of the back door, paused a moment in the sun, his tail arched over his back, and then called hungrily to his mistress.

'What'll happen to Sandy?' Lizzie said. 'I can't take him with me.'

'The missus and I'll look after him. He's a fine creature; more like a lion than a cat.'

'Thank you, Mr Bennet.'

Impulsively Lizzie reached forward and kissed his stubbly cheek. He was so surprised he stood legs apart in the middle of his bed of carrots, his hand to his face and his mouth wide open. He watched the young girl scramble back into her own garden, pick up the ginger tom, and hurry indoors.

'Well I never!' Mr Bennet came to his senses and picked up his basket of pot vegetables. 'The missus'll never believe it.' Then he grinned as a thought occurred to him. 'P'raps I'd better not tell her.'

Now that Lizzie had made up her mind the time passed quickly. There was so much to do. More empty spaces appeared in the cottage as she sold the more portable items. China and kitchen utensils only raised a few pennies, but she got ten shillings for the mantel clock and a florin for a pair of candlesticks decorated with painted violets. They all held memories and she was sad to see them go, but as her pile of coins grew her spirits rose. At least when she left Railway Cottage she wouldn't be penniless.

As instructed by her aunt Lizzie purchased a grey cotton work frock, and a stiff white apron with a multitude of starched tucks around the bottom. It wasn't a particularly attractive outfit but it would wear well. The collar of the frock was so hard that it rubbed the tender skin of her neck.

Every evening Lizzie lit a bonfire and burned the rubbish. This included the worst of the worm-eaten furniture and anything else that wasn't saleable.

Her mother's piano was a problem and in the end she decided to leave it where it was. It stood in the empty parlour in solitary state, a sad reminder of the past.

On the last evening Lizzie took a walk around the garden. The remains of her final bonfire still glowed, spiralling smoke up into the night sky, scenting the air. She stirred the embers with a stick, remembering other bonfires. Dad burning garden rubbish and home-made guys on the fifth of November. Happy memories.

In the half-dark the humped shape of the cottage crouched before her. She'd left an oil lamp burning in the kitchen window, and the square uncurtained pane flickered golden, as if the room was occupied by dancing spirits. Lizzie's eyes filled with tears. She tried to control them, but it was a relief to feel her face wet in the darkness where nobody could see.

'Goodbye, dear home,' she whispered. Then she shook herself. At least she'd be seeing Billy again. It would be a new beginning for both of them.

Lizzie slept well that night, curled up in her clothes on the bare lumpy mattress. In the morning she rose early.

She'd packed only the bare necessities into two brown paper bags and disposed of everything else. Sandy, distressed by the upheaval, prowled about the stone flags looking for breakfast. She had nothing to give him.

'At least Mr Bennet's promised to feed you,' Lizzie said, ruffling his ginger mane. 'You're lucky. I don't know when I shall get another meal.'

She left it until last to take him next door. Mr Bennet and his wife were moved at the sight of the tall slender figure in the black coat and skirt clutching the ginger cat to her bosom.

'The bus goes at ten o'clock,' she said, choking back tears. 'I've brought Sandy round – he hasn't had any breakfast.'

Mrs Bennet was a small round woman who resembled a cottage loaf. She threw up her hands in welcome.

'He's come to the right place,' she said cheerfully. 'Bring him in and set him down on the hearth. We've just had kippers, and there was more than we could eat. There's one for the cat, and one for you, Lizzie. The bread and marg is on the table.'

So Lizzie's last breakfast at Railway Cottages was a

handsome one. Sandy decided, after he'd washed down his share with a saucer of creamy milk, that his new home was going to suit him very well.

'Wait a minute,' Mr Bennet said as Lizzie started to rise from the table. He crossed the room to a dresser against the far wall that held his wife's collection of blue and white china. Fishing awkwardly in a jug he turned to Lizzie carrying something small between his large clumsy hands. 'Just a little farewell present from the missus and me,' he said.

'What is it, Mr Bennet?'

'A lucky joey. I've made a hole in it, and the wife has threaded a cord so you can wear it round your neck.' Carefully he placed in Lizzie's palm a tiny silver three-penny piece on a thin string.

'Thank you.' Lizzie's eyes sparkled as she pulled the string over her head and felt the tiny cold coin lying against her skin. 'I'll keep it always.' She kissed them both on their old wrinkled faces, and they all cried unashamedly.

Then it was time for her to go to catch her bus. She locked the house door and slipped the key under the coconut matting rug for the landlord to find.

Mr Bennet and his wife watched Lizzie walk away with tears in their eyes, but she didn't look back. She walked tall and brave, with the brim of her straw hat hiding her face, and her heavy plait of brown hair swinging. Nobody passing or sitting next to her on the rocking bus could guess at the pain she was feeling, or the fears she had for the future.

Her father had told her to take care of her little brother and that's what she was going to do. Every so often Lizzie glanced at the rolled paper sticking out of her bag. It was Billy's favourite piece of music: 'The March of the Gladiators'. She'd discovered it when she was turning out the music stool. She didn't know if there was a piano at Greenlock House but she knew he'd be pleased to have it.

The bus took her to Penbury and put her down at the
Market Cross. Then she boarded a tram that rattled over
the points to her destination. The conductor seemed to
know the town well and gave her instructions that were
easy to follow. When the clock on the church tower struck
eleven Lizzie was walking along a wide tree-lined road
that led to Greenlock House.

It was the very last house in the road, and detached
from its neighbours as if it was too good for them. It was
the biggest house Lizzie had ever seen and she was
overawed. Mum and Dad had told her many times about
Aunt Hannah's home, but she'd never believed that one
elderly woman could need to live in a house this size.

It was built of red brick, and four rows of windows
stared disapprovingly down at Lizzie. The area window
peered slyly at her over an iron railing. The ground-floor
ones were square and curtained, the panes half covered
by creeper. And the upper ones were narrow and arched
like the windows of country churches, with useless little
balconies like babies' bibs. On the top of this edifice were
a scattering of protuberances with tiny windows like
blind eyes. They might have been perched there by a
child with its first set of building blocks: balancing shapes
haphazardly, imagination run riot. On the summit of this
precarious structure, a nightmare of architecture, was a
tall chimney with a more than lifesize stone griffin on
either side.

The griffins bore a remarkable resemblance to
Hannah Seymour and Lizzie wondered if this could be
deliberate. Had she perhaps been the model for some
mad sculptor, or had she slowly grown over the years to
resemble them?

Lizzie's thoughts turned to Billy. What sort of life was
he leading in a house like this, in the company of a
frightening old woman, even if she was a relation? She
would soon find out.

There were three steps leading up to a square porch

with a red-tiled floor and coloured glass set in the walls. The outer door was open and Lizzie stepped inside. There was a bell-rope hanging by the inner door so she pulled it.

She was facing a panelled door with alternate pieces of red and yellow glass set in the shape of the sun's rays, so her first impression of the approaching figure coming to welcome her was a rosy one. But then the door opened to reveal a tall thin woman of about thirty, dressed in a dark dress and apron. Her dark hair was pulled back tightly and the expression on her face wasn't encouraging.

'Yes? What do you want?'

Determined to be friendly, Lizzie smiled and held out her hand. 'I'm Lizzie Sargent,' she said. 'I think I'm expected.'

Her hand was ignored. 'Side door,' the thin woman said, and started to close the door in Lizzie's face.

'I'm Mrs Seymour's niece,' she protested.

As if that made no impression the woman repeated, 'Side door', and the door was firmly closed. Through the glass Lizzie watched the red and gold shape walk triumphantly away as if she'd scored some sort of point.

She hadn't expected a warm welcome, but she had hoped for more than this. Picking up her bags Lizzie had no option but to look for the side door. She found it set among a warren of dusty laurels, with an enamel plaque fixed to the green paint saying that beggars and trespassers weren't welcome.

There was no bell on this door, only a knocker. It was in the shape of an evil-looking imp: a descendant of the griffins? Lizzie wondered. She knocked loudly. She was tired, hungry and on the point of losing her temper – Aunt Hannah or no Aunt Hannah.

After a second knock Lizzie heard footsteps approaching and forced another smile on to her face. It was the same woman again, but this time she held the door open and beckoned.

'You'd better come in. And wipe your feet; I've just shaken that mat. I'm Ellen.'

Lizzie found herself in a long dark passage, and followed Ellen down a flight of uncarpeted stairs into the basement. The kitchen was a narrow room, with a stone-flagged floor that struck cold even on this warm July day. However, it was clean and tidy, and someone, probably Ellen, had been interrupted while preparing vegetables as there was a bowl of water on the table in which floated carrots and potatoes. A curling heap of peel was stacked nearby on an old newspaper.

Lizzie thought they were the only people in the room. She was just going to ask Ellen if she could see her aunt, and tell her she'd arrived safely, when a gruff voice spoke from a corner of the room. It belonged to a humped form crouched on hands and knees, wielding a scrubbing brush with more enthusiasm than expertise.

'Oo's that?' the gruff voice asked.

'This is Lizzie Sargent,' Ellen said. 'She's the new kitchen maid. Mrs Seymour said we were to expect her.'

The small dumpy figure stood up and waved the brush over its head in welcome. ''Ullo, Lizzie — I'm Daisy.'

'Hullo.'

Lizzie smiled, partly to be friendly and partly because Daisy was such a strange little person. Not much bigger than a child, she had tiny legs and feet and a squat figure, making her round face and head look top-heavy. Her face, brown and wrinkled, had eyes like twinkling boot buttons, and a thick-lipped mouth full of decaying yellow teeth. It was difficult to guess how old she was, but she certainly wasn't young. Malformed in body and also in mind, Lizzie guessed, by the grimaces that passed as smiles and the vague way her eyes wandered in an unfocused fashion.

'I've got to slice the meat,' Ellen said, bustling to a door in the corner of the room which led into a walk-in larder. 'Lizzie can finish peeling those vegetables.'

'But I've only just arrived,' Lizzie protested. 'Shouldn't I see my aunt first?'

'Look here, Lizzie Sargent,' Ellen said, backing out of the larder with a plate containing an unsavoury lump of cold beef in her hands. 'I hope you're not getting any fancy ideas about yourself, or expect favours, just because you're related to her upstairs? She said I was to be in charge of you – and as we're late you can finish the vegetables.' Daisy giggled as if she found the situation amusing, and wiped her nose on the end of her sacking apron. 'And you can get on with that floor, Daisy. You get slower by the minute.'

There was nothing for it but to do as she was told. Lizzie took off her coat, donned her new white apron, and commenced preparing the vegetables. Daisy giggled away to herself and passed curious glances in Lizzie's direction. Ellen sawed away at the meat with a vicious-looking knife.

They worked away in silence for a few minutes and then Ellen said, 'You'll have to work quicker than that, Lizzie. There's custard to make, and I've only got one pair of hands.'

Lizzie was just about to round on her, tell her she was working as fast as she could, but decided to hold her tongue, when she saw the disapproving way Ellen was staring at her. She dropped the last potato into a saucepan and wiped her hands on the front of her apron.

'I've finished, Ellen.'

'About time.'

Daisy giggled from somewhere on the floor.

'And it's about time you'd finished, Daisy. Get a move on, can't you, then you can show Lizzie where to put her things.'

Lizzie thought she'd be sleeping somewhere in the attics. In books that's where servants usually slept. She'd been quite looking forward to finding herself in one of the strange little rooms balanced so precariously on the roof, but that wasn't to be her lot. In Hannah Seymour's household the servants were kept in their place: below stairs. When Daisy led her into the little room behind the scullery she was disappointed, particularly when she realised that she had to share.

The room was dark; partly because it was half-underground and partly because it was at the back of the house, the window obscured by greenery. It was clean but bare, with two iron beds, a chest of drawers, and a washstand with a chipped chamber-pot underneath.

Lizzie sat down on the nearer bed and slipped off her shoes to ease her feet.

'Mine! Mine!' Daisy erupted into a ball of violent energy. She threw herself at Lizzie and tugged at her clothing. 'Off! Off!'

'Sorry.' Lizzie removed herself to the other bed and started to unpack the first of her carrier-bags.

The strange little woman soon recovered. She crept to Lizzie's side in order to investigate her belongings. She picked up a brightly coloured scarf that had belonged to Mary Sargent. Lizzie had kept it as a keepsake because it took up little room. Daisy placed the scarf against her brown cheek and beamed at its softness.

'Nice,' she cooed.

'Would you like it, Daisy?'

'For me?' It was obvious that for her to receive a present was a rare event and Daisy couldn't believe her good fortune. She stared at Lizzie, her eyes twinkling with disbelief.

'Yes,' Lizzie said. 'A present.'

'A present for Daisy.' The little woman suddenly became a dynamo of energy. She tugged the patchwork quilt from the bed and dived under the thin pillow like a burrowing mole. Lizzie watched in amazement as she hid the silky scarf among the other things stored there. There were crusts of bread blue with mould, a tangled hair-net, broken bone knitting needles, and other unidentifiable rubbish. It was like the nest of a magpie. Daisy replaced the pillow and faced Lizzie, beaming from ear to ear.

It was useless to try to keep up a conversation with Daisy because she didn't seem able to manage sentences of more than three or four words. But the scarf had done the trick. After that she became Lizzie's slave. Like a shadow she followed her about, grimacing happily, and saying that she was 'Lizzie's friend'.

Dinner in the kitchen of Greenlock House turned out to consist of the remains of the beef, plastered with mustard and squashed between hunks of bread sawed from a loaf Daisy produced from the bread-crock as proudly as a magician pulls a rabbit from a hat. Her hands were none too clean, even after the time she'd spent with the pail and scrubbing brush, but Lizzie was so hungry she didn't care. She wolfed the food as if she was starving, and washed it down with water from the tap.

It was Ellen's job to clear the dining room after Mrs Seymour had eaten, and she carried her mistress's loaded tray into the kitchen and thumped it down on the table. There was custard still left in the jug, and a triangle of apple pie that made Lizzie's mouth water. She thought the servants might be allowed to finish up the remains, but Ellen carried the custard and pie over to the larder and hid it away.

'Oh, well,' Lizzie thought. 'I expect Billy had some, wherever he is, and that's the important thing.'

Without being asked she started to unload the tray, but Ellen stopped her.

'Daisy can do that,' she said sharply. 'Mrs Seymour wants you upstairs at once,' and she gestured with her thumb.

'Naughty – naughty,' Daisy chanted, as if a summons upstairs could only mean one thing.

'Mrs Seymour is my aunt,' Lizzie tried to explain. 'I expect she wants to welcome me.'

'Slap!' Daisy placed her work-worn palm against her cheek. 'She slap.'

Lizzie turned to Ellen. 'Is she trying to tell me that my aunt hits her?'

'Only when she deserves it,' Ellen said calmly.

'Slap – slap,' Daisy chanted again. 'Slap boy.' She screwed up her face. 'Boy cry.'

Lizzie looked at the little maid in horror; then she turned to Ellen. 'What's she saying, Ellen?' she demanded. 'What boy does my aunt slap – not Billy?'

'I wouldn't know,' Ellen said. 'What goes on upstairs is none of my business. All I do know is that the boy is always crying. He's a real milk-sop.'

'If you're talking about my brother he's certainly not a milk-sop; and if my aunt treats him badly she has me to answer to.'

'Then you'd better hurry upstairs to the parlour or she'll be all ready to slap you,' Ellen said. 'I told you before that being related to Mrs Seymour isn't going to bring you any favours. The reverse if anything.'

By the time she found herself standing outside the parlour door Lizzie's anger had slightly cooled. Common-sense had taken its place. Losing her temper with Aunt Hannah wasn't going to achieve anything. She knocked and a voice inside bade her enter.

The parlour at Railway Cottage had been small, and although the furnishings had been old and worn it had always seemed to be full of light and colour. In contrast Aunt Hannah's parlour was a dark gloomy place. The windows were hung with heavy brocade curtains and every space was full of furniture. Even the walls were crammed with pictures in dark wood frames: portraits of men and women in old-fashioned clothes, horses and riders with dogs at their heels, and stags at bay on rocky cliffs.

On either side of the fireplace stood a high-backed chair. In one sat Aunt Hannah. She was wearing her usual black dress with a cameo brooch at its neck. Her dark hair was twisted into a knot on top of her head, and her black eyes glinted behind gold-rimmed spectacles. Billy sat in the other chair.

Lizzie hadn't seen her brother for at least a month and during that time he seemed to have grown smaller. He was still dressed in the black suit he'd worn at his parents' funeral; but where it had been comfortably loose it now looked ridiculously outsize. His thin neck rose out of the stiff collar like a stalk, and his legs dangled over the edge of the chair like match-sticks. His pale hair was cut shorter than Lizzie remembered and lay flat against his skull. In the past it had been wavy and fly-away, and Lizzie had loved to curl it around her finger.

At the sight of his sister Billy's face lit up. He started to climb down from his chair until his aunt stopped him.

'Stay where you are, William,' Aunt Hannah ordered in her sharp voice. Billy sat down again.

'But it's Lizzie ...'

'I know it's Elizabeth, but there is no need for a display of emotion.' She turned to Lizzie. 'I hope you've settled in?'

'Yes, thank you, Aunt.'

'And Ellen has told you your duties?'

'I've been helping her downstairs,' Lizzie said. Then bravely she burst out, 'But I was hoping you'd find me another position.'

'Oh?' Aunt Hannah removed her spectacles and let them dangle from a ribbon around her neck. 'Isn't kitchen work good enough for you?' Lizzie didn't answer. 'Perhaps you've not been brought up to getting your hands dirty?'

'I don't mind the work,' Lizzie said. 'It's not that. It's very kind of you to offer me a position in your house ...' Her voice trailed off.

'What is it then, girl?' Aunt Hannah asked impatiently. 'Out with it.'

Lizzie stood up straight and spoke bravely. 'I thought perhaps you would find me a place upstairs. I don't mind what I do - but then I could see Billy sometimes.'

There was a pause while Mrs Seymour digested this request. Billy's face lit up hopefully. The silence seemed to

go on for such a long time that he suddenly burst out:
'Please, Aunt Hannah.'

At last, coming to a decision, Hannah Seymour
replaced her spectacles and looked at her niece. 'When I
offered you a job, Elizabeth, it wasn't because you are a
relation.'

'I don't want charity, Aunt—'

'And you won't get it here, girl. I don't believe in
so-called good works. I think everyone should earn their
living – particularly girls, who are wayward if given half
a chance.' She looked Lizzie up and down, as if labelling
her particularly wayward. 'I didn't offer you a position in
my household because I felt sorry for you or because you
happen to be my brother's daughter – I needed a replacement for my last ungrateful domestic servant and I
thought you might suit.'

As if the matter was now closed she reached for a copy
of *Home Notes* and flicked through the pages. Billy looked
at his sister as if begging her to intervene.

'I will do the kitchen work willingly, Aunt,' Lizzie said,
'as long as I can see Billy sometimes. I know he misses me.
I could play with him in my spare time, or take him for
walks.'

Mrs Seymour laughed her hard harsh laugh. 'This is a
large house, Elizabeth. With a staff of three, or rather two
and one idiot if you count Daisy, you won't have much
spare time. I am training William to inherit Greenlock
House when I die, and for that reason I have to be strict
with him. Your father was a weak man – I won't have his
son growing up like him.'

This was too much. Lizzie didn't mind personal insults,
but she wasn't going to let anyone run down her father's
memory.

'My father was a brave man,' she said. 'He fought in the
war and won a medal. He had bad lungs and shell-shock,
but he never complained. He nursed my mother faithfully
and cared for Billy and me. He was a good father, a good

husband, and everyone loved him. Except you, Aunt Hannah – but then, I don't think you love anybody.'

Lizzie expected some sort of angry reaction, but her aunt just stared at her coldly. When she spoke her voice was carefully measured and cold as ice.

'There is no place in my life for love – only duty. I did my duty to your parents and for that you should be grateful. If it hadn't been for me they would be buried in a pauper's grave. Now you will do your duty and go about your work.'

With one agonised glance at Billy, Lizzie turned and walked out of the parlour. There were tears on her cheek as she ran down the back stairs but she brushed them away with her hand.

'You won't win, Aunt Hannah,' she muttered to herself. 'You won't separate Billy and me – I won't let you.'

CHAPTER THREE

Greenlock

'Ellen, do you know where my brother sleeps?'

"Course I do.' Ellen floured the rolling-pin liberally and began to roll out the pastry for a pie. 'I have to make his bed and empty his slops, and I don't know what else.'

Lizzie bent over the deep white sink and tried to speak casually. 'I suppose he's on the first floor then – or perhaps Aunt Hannah has given him one of those little rooms in the attic?' The hot soda water stung the cracks on her fingers but she didn't register the pain.

Ellen slapped the pastry lid over the pie-dish, and then with a knife fluted the edge into a frill before glazing the top with milk. 'What do you want to know for anyway, Miss Nosy?'

'No reason. Just curious.'

Ellen carried the pie over to the oven and nudged Daisy out of the way with the toe of her shoe. The little woman was humped over a row of boots with a blacking brush in her hand. She edged away to a safer distance and grimaced across at Lizzie.

'I knows,' she chanted. 'Daisy knows.'

'What do you know?' Lizzie picked up a dish from the draining board and began to dry it.

'Boy! Boy's room.'

'Be quiet, Daisy, and get on with your work,' Ellen snapped. 'You don't know anything.'

Daisy brushed harder and Lizzie continued to dry the plates thoughtfully. She'd been living at Greenlock House for five weeks and had seen Billy on only two occasions. Once when Ellen had been feeling poorly she'd had to carry dinner up to the dining room. Aunt Hannah had been sitting at one end of the long mahogany table and her brother at the other. He was perched on a hassock to make him taller, and when she placed the bowl of Mulligatawny soup in front of him he'd looked up at her with frightened eyes. She knew he hated Mulligatawny soup, and with a secret smile managed to whisk the bowl away while it was still half full. The steak and kidney pie that followed was his favourite so she made sure he had a good helping.

The other occasion was when Lizzie had been sent out to brush down the front steps. Billy had come out of the door with Aunt Hannah and had been driven away in a taxi. He'd been dressed in a miniature Harris Tweed suit and a checked cap. He handed his aunt into the car as if he'd learned his lessons well.

But the sight of him had made Lizzie sad. She'd preferred the little lad with the tuneful whistle and the scuffed boots. They'd managed a quick smile before Hannah Seymour had pulled Billy inside and ordered the driver to make haste.

Lizzie was getting used to life below stairs. The work was hard and the hours long, but there wasn't much time for brooding or feeling sorry for yourself. Lizzie was determined not to let life get her down because the situation wasn't going to last. One day, soon, she hoped, something would happen to change things. Hadn't she got a lucky silver joey hanging around her neck? When she was feeling particularly sad or despondent she'd put up her hand and touch the coldness of Mr Bennet's present and recall telling him about her dream.

A few days later they were ironing the week's linen at the kitchen table. The room was full of steam and the smell of scorching cloth. Ellen, red-faced and irritable, piled the neatly folded sheets and pillow-cases into Daisy's arms. The little maid, willing but clumsy, tripped over a rag rug on her way to the door. The pile of laundry fell in a heap on to the flagstones.

'Now look what you've done,' Ellen scolded. 'Lizzie, come and give a hand or I'll have to iron them all over again.'

Between them they rescued the linen, but there was too much for Daisy's short arms to cope with.

'I'll help,' Lizzie said, dividing the pile between them. 'Where does it go, Ellen?'

'In the big cupboard on the top landing. Use the back stairs. Mrs Seymour is fussy about kitchen maids being seen by visitors.'

Daisy led the way proudly, puffing up the first flight of uncarpeted stairs until they came out on ground-floor level. Lizzie followed close behind. She knew this part of the house: the hall, dining room and parlour, but she hadn't been allowed any farther.

Lizzie pointed to a door at the far end of the hall. 'What's through there?' she asked.

Daisy put her pile of linen down on a chair and pattered over to the door. She leaned her ear against the wooden panel as if she was listening intently and then beckoned to Lizzie.

'Is it safe, Daisy?' Lizzie knew they would get into trouble if Aunt Hannah was to find them. 'What if Mrs Seymour should come?'

But Daisy was clapping her hands and nodding encouragement, and when she turned the handle and pushed the door open Lizzie was right behind her.

She found herself in a beautiful drawing room. It was over-crowded with furniture like the parlour, but the ceilings were so high, and the windows so wide, that the chairs and table crowded with knickknacks had plenty of room to spread themselves over the thick Indian carpet. A chandelier hung from a central moulding, daylight catching the diamond-shaped crystals and dancing off the polished surfaces like glow-worms.

But the most important piece of furniture was the grand piano that stood in solitary state between the windows. It made her mother's little piano, with its tapestry inlay and brass candlesticks, look like a poor relation.

'Who plays the piano?' she asked, thinking of Billy and the way his gay tunes had vibrated around the parlour of Railway Cottage. 'Does my brother play?'

'No,' Daisy said, shaking her big head violently. She placed her hands together and looked heavenwards.

'Prayers?' Lizzie guessed and then when the little maid shook her head tried again. 'Hymns?'

'Hymns – yes. Sad hymns.' Daisy intoned mournfully. 'Her plays.'

'Mrs Seymour plays hymns?' Daisy clapped her hands together so Lizzie knew she'd guessed right. 'My brother can play the piano and he's only seven and a bit. He plays lovely cheerful pieces like "Festival of Roses". I've brought his favourite piece of music with me: it's called "The March of the Gladiators". He'll love playing that on this beautiful piano.'

Daisy seemed to be getting nervous and started pulling at Lizzie's apron, so they retraced their steps and climbed the next flight of stairs with their piles of linen.

The linen cupboard was so large it was like a small room. It took no time at all to sort the laundry into the correct piles.

'That's done,' Lizzie said.

She closed the door and looked about her with interest.

To right and left long passages stretched into the far distance. Dozens of doors, dozens of rooms, and somewhere in all this space little Billy was rattling around like a pea in a drum. But which door? Which room?

Ignoring Daisy's frantic tugs Lizzie opened the nearest door and peeped inside. It was a vast chamber full of the shadowy ghosts of furniture shrouded in dust-sheets. The next two rooms were the same, with the musty smell of unaired spaces. When she put her hand on the handle of the fourth door Daisy suddenly went frantic.

'No! No!' she muttered, and jumped from one foot to the other. 'Come, 'izzie.'

'Is this Mrs Seymour's room, Daisy? She can't be in there or she would have heard us. Does my aunt sleep in here?'

'Come – now,' Daisy pleaded. 'Smack! Smack!'

Lizzie thought quickly, trying to make sense of Daisy's words. 'Does Mrs Seymour smack you for going into her room? Or perhaps it's not her room – perhaps ...'

Daisy was wailing now, her ugly brown face screwed up tightly. Lizzie grabbed her arm and shook her.

'I know what you're trying to tell me. This is Billy's room, isn't it? My little brother – the room where he sleeps. And sometimes you hear him crying, don't you? Sometimes he cries because he's lonely, and sometimes because my aunt slaps him. Am I right?'

Daisy was silent now, exhausted by her effort at communication. She nodded her unwieldy head and wiped her sleeve across her face. 'Daisy don't like slaps,' she said at last. 'Boy cries at night and gets slaps. Daisy don't want slaps. Lizzie won't slap?'

It was the longest speech Lizzie had ever heard the little maid make. She smiled at her and held out her hand. 'I won't slap you, Daisy, and somehow I'm going to make sure that Billy is never ill treated again. Come on, let's go back downstairs before Ellen starts wondering what we're up to.'

The kitchen was in a worse state of upheaval, and so was Ellen. She grabbed Daisy and pushed her towards the scullery.

'You two've taken your time,' she said. 'I'm trying to make scones for tea and now the mistress has got a visitor. She wants a pot of tea sent up straight away, and the best silver. Daisy can polish the pot.'

'Is it anybody important?' Lizzie asked.

'Mr Bond, from up the road. I can guess what he's come for.'

'Is he my aunt's friend?'

'You'll have to take the tray up,' Ellen said. 'I'll finish the scones – the oven's almost hot enough. Use the cups with the gold rims; Mrs Seymour likes them when she has important visitors. Mr Bond is the headmaster of Greyhaven; that's a school for boys a few houses away. You can guess what that means, Lizzie?'

Lizzie stopped with a delicate cup in either hand. She wasn't sure if the news was good or bad. 'Do you think my aunt intends sending Billy to this school?'

'I can't think why else Mr Bond should be here – can you? Now if you're serving the tea you'd better wear my apron and cap. They're hanging behind the door over there. And wash your hands; and for God's sake don't break anything.'

'I'll be careful,' Lizzie promised.

She poured boiling water into the newly polished pot, and after a hasty glance at her reflection in the window pane picked up the tray. If Billy was being sent to his school she wanted to have a good look at this Mr Bond.

He was standing with his back to the fireplace: a big man dressed in a smart suit and double-breasted waistcoat. His head was almost bald, and his jowls hung over the edge of his stiff collar. Everything about Mr Bond was polished and stiff. In his hands he clasped a grey bowler hat as if he didn't know what to do with it.

Aunt Hannah was sitting in her high-backed chair with

an unusually pleasant smile on her face. Her eyes twinkled almost roguishly at her visitor.

'So kind of you to come promptly, Mr Bond,' she cooed. 'Elizabeth – take Mr Bond's hat. Do sit down, Mr Bond, and take some tea with me.'

Mr Bond lowered himself stiffly into the chair on the opposite side of the fireplace and accepted a cup and saucer. He placed it precariously on the padded arm-rest. Lizzie hovered over the tea-tray praying that her aunt would overlook her presence.

'I gather that you have a boy for me,' Mr Bond said, as if he was expecting Mrs Seymour to produce a boy from somewhere about her person.

'I have a nephew, Mr Bond. His education has been sadly neglected. He can hardly speak the King's English. In fact he hardly speaks at all.'

'How old?'

'Seven.'

'Seven, eh?' Mr Bond tapped his teeth with one carefully manicured finger-nail. 'Seven is a good age to start to discipline a boy. Eight is too late and six too early. But at seven a boy is pliable – like putty.' Mr Bond screwed his hands together as if he was wringing something – a boy's neck perhaps. 'What about parents?'

'Both dead.'

'That is satisfactory.' Mr Bond actually smiled. 'I don't like interference and parents are the worst offenders.'

'I shan't interfere, Mr Bond, you have my word upon that. His parents were weak and would have been the ruination of him. I intend to make him into a man.'

'I admire you, Mrs Seymour, I really do.' Mr Bond picked up his cup and sipped his tea, holding the delicate china between fat white fingers as if he would like to crush it. 'Between us we will mould this boy into something to be proud of.'

'What are your terms?'

Mr Bond knew the outcome of this interview depended

on how generous he was prepared to be. He thought carefully and then chose to hedge – it usually worked.

'Day or boarder?'

'Day. He has a good home here and your establishment is so close.'

'Dinner?'

'He can return home for meals; or if that is inconvenient my cook can prepare him something.'

'Excellent. Extras?'

'What extras are you referring to, Mr Bond?'

'I teach the basics, Mrs Seymour. Reading, writing, and arithmetic – taught by rote. But I have visiting masters in specialised subjects, like art, music, and exercises.'

'No extras,' Aunt Hannah said firmly.

'You're very wise. Any boy can rise to the top if he can read, write a fair hand, and do addition and subtraction.'

'And multiplication and division, I hope, Mr Bond?'

'Of course,' Mr Bond assured her, although he considered multiplication and division extras. Adding and subtraction were quite adequate for any boy. 'Shall we say fifty pounds a year, madam? And you supply paper and pencils.'

Hannah Seymour nodded. 'Fifty pounds sounds reasonable.'

'And I'll keep his nose to the grindstone.' Mr Bond licked his lips in anticipation. 'Do you believe in corporal punishment?'

'Oh, I do.' Hannah Seymour rubbed her hands together. She would be only too pleased to shoulder this responsibility should Mr Bond class it as an extra.

'You're very wise. I use the cane and the birch, or my hand for minor offences.'

'Then I think we can say it's settled, Mr Bond.' Mrs Seymour leaned back in her chair. 'More tea?'

The headmaster of Greyhaven held out his cup. Lizzie stepped forward to take it from him. She was trembling from head to foot with a combination of anger and fear.

They were talking about her brother as if he was of no consequence. Even his name hadn't been mentioned. Billy might be a number on a piece of paper for all Mr Bond or Aunt Hannah seemed to care. She filled the cup, wishing it were poison, and walked forward carrying it carefully so as not to slop the tea into the saucer.

The conversation between her aunt and Mr Bond carried on. Words washed over Lizzie's head: words like cleanliness, obedience, and duty. Her brain was spinning and she felt sick with the hopelessness of the situation. The worst thing was watching Aunt Hannah's obvious enjoyment, otherwise she would have sent Lizzie away earlier.

There was a large square rug in the centre of the floor, blue in colour and fringed with a knotted border, and because Lizzie's mind was in such a whirl she didn't look where she was going. Too late she felt her toe catch in the uneven surface, and before she could stop herself she stumbled forward towards the seated figures. The tea, thick as Brown Windsor soup, streamed down Mr Bond's jacket, trickling on to his shirt-front and waistcoat in a steaming river. The delicate china cup landed in the fireplace, shattering into a multitude of pieces on the coloured tiles.

Mrs Seymour uttered a shrill scream and jumped to her feet; but Mr Bond sat frozen to his chair, his mouth opened in an O of surprise.

'You stupid girl,' Aunt Hannah hissed. Her hand swung out and caught Lizzie's cheek a stinging blow. 'Look what you've done.'

'I'm sorry. I tripped.'

'My best china too ...'

'I'll get a cloth and a brush.'

'You'll do no such thing, girl. Get out of my sight – and send Ellen up. You'll pay for this out of your wages: the breakages and Mr Bond's laundry bill.'

Lizzie almost ran out of the room. Her cheek stung, but

the pain was nothing to the fury of emotions that consumed her. She must find Billy, comfort him, tell him to be brave. Somehow she was going to fulfil her promise to her father to take care of her brother. She didn't know how she was going to do it but somehow she'd find a way.

Ellen disappeared upstairs, and when she returned she was smiling unpleasantly. 'You've done it this time,' she said to Lizzie.

'It was an accident, Ellen. I tripped over the mat.'

'Don't make excuses. Mrs Seymour says you're to be punished so for a start you can take over from Daisy. She's scrubbing out the pots in the scullery.'

So Lizzie spent the rest of the day scouring pans black with grease and rust. The emery-paper took the skin from her fingers but she was hardly aware of the pain. At least she was alone in her misery so no one saw the tears that streamed down her cheeks as she worked.

It was nearly nine o'clock by the time she'd finished. She felt so exhausted she could hardly stand, but when she did finally crawl into her bed she couldn't sleep. In the other bed Daisy snored loudly, dead to the world, a humped figure under the bedclothes.

Lizzie's head ached and she tossed and turned, but there was a devil in her brain that had to be exorcised. She knew she wouldn't rest until she'd seen Billy. Now that she had a good idea where his bedroom was the way was clear. Trying not to disturb her companion she slid out of bed and groped amongst her belongings for Billy's piece of music. It might comfort him to have something from home.

A clock somewhere in the bowels of the house struck midnight. A streak of moonlight penetrated the area window and suddenly Lizzie could see and think clearly. Everyone was abed, even Aunt Hannah, so there was no one to stop her finding her way up to the upper floor.

'She'll catch you,' the voice of commonsense told her. 'Perhaps she sleeps in Billy's room on purpose to stop you. Or when you get there you'll find the door locked.'

But even these thoughts couldn't stop her. She had to find out the worst. Not possessing a dressing-gown she climbed the stairs in her cotton nightgown. It was patched, and worn so thin in places that the pattern of tiny daisies was almost erased. Her feet were bare and made no sound on the stairs, and her long brown hair, released from its usual braid, fell over her shoulders and reached almost to her waist. In her hands she carried a candle and Billy's sheet of music; but she didn't need the candle because the higher she climbed the brighter it became as the silvery beams of moonlight filled the corners and passages.

First Lizzie found the linen cupboard and tried the door to make sure that it wasn't locked. If someone came, Aunt Hannah on the prowl for instance, she would hide inside until the way was clear.

The passage stretched away in front of her, all the doors closed, but Lizzie remembered the one she suspected led to Billy's room. Taking a deep breath, her heart going pitter-patter in her chest, Lizzie turned the porcelain handle and pushed open the door.

She was dreaming – she must be. It wasn't a bedroom; in fact Lizzie had never been in a room like it in her life before. The floor was covered with black and white tiles, cold to the feet even on a warm August night. Strange-shaped objects reared their heads around her: unidentifiable and threatening. The largest object was white and squatted in the far corner on four clawed feet. It took Lizzie a few moments to realise that the room she'd stumbled into was not a bedroom but a bathroom.

She'd never seen a proper bathroom before. At Railway Cottage water had been heated once a week in a copper, and everyone had taken a turn in the tin hip bath in front of the fire. Since arriving at Greenlock Lizzie hadn't had a bath at all; instead she'd washed in cold water in the bedroom she shared with Daisy. She looked around in awe at the white porcelain sink with the shiny brass taps, and the bamboo towel-stand.

'Are you a ghost?'

The voice coming from behind her made Lizzie jump so that her heart missed a beat. She spun round. A little white figure was framed in the open doorway, and two huge eyes were staring at her. She wasn't a ghost, but the figure in the white cotton pyjamas could easily have been one if she hadn't recognised it as Billy.

'Billy,' she said. 'It's me – Lizzie.'

'Oh, Lizzie – is it really you?' He stretched out his hand and touched her arm as if he had to convince himself that he wasn't dreaming. Then he flung himself into her arms and buried his face on her chest.

'It's all right, Billy,' Lizzie crooned. 'It's all right. I'm here. Don't cry.'

'I'm not crying,' Billy said indignantly. He pulled away and rubbed his eyes with the sleeve of his jacket. 'Why didn't you come and find me before?'

'I couldn't. Aunt Hannah would have been cross.'

'I kept waiting and waiting and asking for you, but she wouldn't tell me anything sensible. She said you were a servant and had your work to do. Why do you have to be a servant, Lizzie?'

'Because it was the only way I could come here at all.' Lizzie looked over his shoulder at the empty passage. 'Which is your room?'

'That one.' Billy pointed to a door on the other side of the passage.

Tugging her by the hand Billy pulled Lizzie into his room and closed the door to give them privacy. It was a lovely room but more suitable for a grown-up. The walls were papered in brown and green plush, and the heavy curtains at the window were russet with a bobble fringe. The bed was high, with a carved headboard and a white crocheted cover. Facing the sleeper was a large gloomy picture of the crucifixion that was enough to give the bravest child nightmares.

'It's a nice room,' Lizzie said.

'Is it?' Billy was fiddling nervously with the buttons on his jacket. 'Can we go home now?'

Lizzie sat down on the edge of the bed and drew him down beside her. She put her arm around his shoulders. 'This is your home now,' she said.

'But I don't like it here; and I don't like Aunt Hannah. She says nasty things about Dad and Mum, and she smacks people.'

'I know. She smacked me today for breaking a cup.' Lizzie turned her face to show the red mark. 'Does she smack you?'

'Sometimes. She says I have to go to school, Lizzie. She says the master will beat me if I don't behave. I want to go to my old school – they didn't beat children there. Tell her we want to go home, Lizzie – please.'

'Oh, Billy, I wish I could.' Lizzie hugged her brother close. 'But Aunt Hannah won't listen to me. Look, I've got something for you.' She handed him the sheet of music. 'I brought it from home.'

'The Gladiators!' Billy's face lit up and he smiled for the first time; but the smile quickly faded. 'I can't play it here,' he said sadly.

'Why not? There's a beautiful grand piano downstairs.'

'Aunt Hannah wouldn't let me.'

'I'm sure she would if you asked her nicely. You can play "The March of the Gladiators" well. I'm sure she'd be impressed.'

'I learned the Gladiators for Mum,' Billy said firmly. 'I don't want to play it for anyone else.' Even so he slid the tatty page under his pillow as if it were a treasure. He leaned back and yawned widely, showing an even row of pearly white teeth.

'You're tired. Jump into bed and I'll tuck you in.'

'Don't go,' Billy said sleepily.

'I'll stay until you're asleep. I promise. Move over and I'll get in beside you like we used to do at home.' Lizzie slid under the covers. Billy's bed was more comfortable than her own: it had a soft feather mattress that she snuggled into. Beside her she could feel Billy trembling. 'Do you want a cuddle?'

'Yes please.'

Lizzie put her arms around the little boy and held him close. He felt so small and fragile, like a baby bird she'd once rescued from a cat – all brittle bones. He twined his arms around her neck and rested his head on her shoulder.

'What's this?' he asked, sleepily feeling the silver coin hanging around her neck.

'A lucky joey. Mr Bennet gave it to me.'

Billy played with the threepenny piece idly. 'I had one once. Mum put it in the Christmas pudding for me. I swapped it for a marble.'

'Would you like this one? You can have it if you like.'

'No. You keep it, Lizzie. I think you're going to need it more than me.'

'That's a funny thing to say, darling.' Even so Lizzie was pleased not to have to part with her lucky present. It was part of the past, a reminder of Railway Cottages where people cared about and loved you. She slipped it back inside the neck of her nightgown for safety. 'Go to sleep now.'

'Read me a story, Lizzie.'

There were some books on a shelf by the bed and Lizzie leaned over to study the titles. The room was darker now and she had to light her candle from the flame of the tiny night-light that glowed in a saucer. By the flickering flame she read the titles.

'Foxe's *Book of Martyrs* – *The Pilgrim's Progress* – *Who's Who* – Shakespeare.'

'I want the steadfast tin soldier.'

'But there aren't any children's books, Billy. Perhaps I can remember it.'

So she told him the story about the adventures of the brave little toy soldier, and what she couldn't remember she made up. He was asleep before she reached the end, his thumb contentedly in his mouth, and his pale lashes fanning his delicate cheek. She kissed his forehead.

'Sleep well, my steadfast soldier,' she said softly. 'I'm going to take care of you like Dad told me to.'

Lizzie yawned and closed her eyes. The bed was so warm and comfortable that she fell into a deep sleep. Usually her nights were restless with Daisy's snores, and cats prowling about the basement knocking dustbin lids off and crying at the moon. But Billy's room was quiet and she slept unaware of place or time.

Towards morning Lizzie started to dream. It was the happy dream again, about her childhood. The one where she was digging for pebbles on the beach and the sun had shone so everything was golden, even the pavements. The lovely day trip to Brighton. She turned on her back and stretched languidly. Someone was saying her name in a sharp voice. Not soft and gentle like Mum – or jolly and matey like Dad.

'Lizzie!'

Lizzie opened her eyes slowly and blinked in the bright daylight. She was in a strange room, and it was so full of sunlight that she had to shield her eyes with her hand. Where was she? This wasn't her bedroom at Railway Cottage, or the poky underground chamber at Greenlock. There was a movement at her side and Billy's face swam into focus. His head was on the pillow next to hers and then Lizzie remembered her lonely search for her brother through the empty passages. His sadness and need of comfort. Their arms around each other in the night. She must have dropped off to sleep out of sheer tiredness, and now it was morning.

'Lizzie!'

That sharp voice again; familiar and scolding. Lizzie, now wide awake, opened her eyes. Ellen was standing in the doorway, a ewer of water in her hands and a furious expression on her face. Lizzie sat up quickly, shaking the hair out of her face.

'Don't go, Lizzie.'

'It's all right, Billy,' she assured him.

'All right! You say it's all right!' Ellen strode across the floor and placed the ewer on the wash-stand before turning to the bed. 'Get out of there at once.'

Lizzie slid out from under the covers. She felt embarrassed and frightened at being caught at such a disadvantage. Even so her bare toes curled up in appreciation of the softness of the carpet. In her basement room there was only cold lino and a faded rag rug.

'I'm sorry, Ellen. I fell asleep.'

'So I see.'

'I'll go down to the kitchen at once and help Daisy with the breakfasts.' Lizzie took two steps towards the door and then stopped. 'Please don't tell Aunt Hannah.'

Ellen snorted, and it was an ugly sound. 'I didn't like you, Lizzie Sargent, from the moment you set foot in this house,' she said. 'All airs and graces: ringing at the front door and calling the mistress aunt.'

'She is my aunt.'

'That's beside the point. Mrs Seymour warned me you'd be a trouble-maker. She said you weren't to be given preferential treatment. You were to be treated just like any other kitchen maid.'

'I'm sorry. It won't happen again.'

'I don't think it will.' Ellen laughed then, but there was no humour in the sound. 'Not when Mrs Seymour hears about this. Now get downstairs and make yourself respectable. And you ...' she wagged a finger at Billy, 'can get out of there and be quick about it.'

'Lizzie ...' Billy put out his arms towards his sister but there was nothing she could do or say to comfort him.

'It's all right, Billy. Do what Ellen tells you.' Lizzie turned and ran out of the room.

CHAPTER FOUR

Gates Farm

'I'm not scared,' Lizzie told herself. 'She can't hurt me. I have to stand up to her for Billy's sake.'

It was the middle of the morning. Since Ellen had ordered her downstairs no one had spoken to her. She'd completed her duties diligently, trying to keep a cheerful expression on her face, but every smile, every bright remark, was received with stony coldness. Even Daisy seemed to have caught on and kept a wide berth.

Lizzie rolled the sleeves of her grey work dress up to the elbows and plunged her hands into a bowl of cold water; it was time to peel the potatoes for dinner. Ellen entered the kitchen with the day's menu.

'Are the potatoes to be baked or boiled?' Lizzie asked.

Ellen ignored the question. Instead she called to Daisy who was filling a bucket at the tap. 'Leave that, girl,' she commanded, 'and take over the potatoes. And you,' for the first time she turned to Lizzie and looked her full in the face. 'You're wanted upstairs. In the parlour. You'd better tidy yourself up first.'

There was no mirror so Lizzie had to make do with the shadowy window-pane. She smoothed back a lock of hair that had escaped from its plait and unrolled her sleeves. At least her apron was clean. She didn't think Aunt Hannah would be able to criticise her appearance.

Now she was standing outside the parlour door waiting for whatever was in store for her.

'I'm not afraid of you, Aunt Hannah,' she said softly. Then she knocked on the door – not timidly, but sharply, to give herself confidence.

There was no reply. Was this part of her punishment: to be summoned by the mistress of the house and then ignored?

'I'm not scared.' Lizzie turned the handle and walked into the room, her back straight and her lips curved into a smile.

Hannah Seymour was alone. She was sitting in her usual fire-side chair.

'Good morning, Aunt Hannah,' Lizzie said cheerfully.

Mrs Seymour was turning the pages of a magazine. It was her favourite journal, *John Bull*, and she liked to read it after the day's newspaper. A copy of the *Daily Express* was folded by her elbow. She didn't speak or look in her niece's direction.

Trying to control her nervousness Lizzie spoke first, the words tumbling out fast and furious.

'It's a lovely day, Aunt. You should go outside and enjoy it. Billy loves the sunshine. When we were at Railway Cottage he always wanted to be outside when the weather was fine.'

'Be silent, girl!'

The words were sharp and Lizzie stopped talking immediately. 'I'm not afraid,' the little voice said deep inside. 'She can't hurt me.'

'I've been hearing things about you which I find deeply disturbing.' Aunt Hannah closed her magazine, placed it carefully on top of the folded newspaper, and looked at Lizzie for the first time.

'Not about my work, I hope?' Lizzie said.

'No, not about your work, Elizabeth. It's your behaviour that leaves much to be desired.'

'I'm sorry. I'll try better in future.'

'You have no future.'

'I don't understand, Aunt Hannah.'

'And don't call me aunt.' Hannah Seymour's eyes were as black as coal and looked as hard as they studied Lizzie. 'I was your employer – call me Mrs Seymour like the rest of the servants.'

It was the final rejection. To be disowned by her only known relation, apart from Billy, was a blow to Lizzie's pride as well as to her heart. She had never liked her aunt but now she hated her. The hate took away the fear and she stood tall and proud. When she spoke her voice was clear and calm, as if she hadn't a worry in the world.

'You said was. Does that mean you're giving me notice?'

'I think you know what I mean, and why. Ellen has informed me of your disgusting behaviour.'

'And just what did Ellen tell you?'

Hannah Seymour paused and licked her lips. Lizzie could have sworn that she was relishing the situation, that she'd been waiting all these weeks for some complaint about Lizzie to reach her ears. Something she could twist to her own advantage. So that she could tell the world that she'd done her duty to her orphaned niece and been repaid badly.

'Ellen told me that she found you in an …' She paused, as if choosing her words carefully. 'Unnatural situation.'

For a moment Lizzie didn't understand what her aunt was implying. 'If you mean she found me in Billy's bed, why don't you say so?'

'Because, Elizabeth, the implications are too disgusting to contemplate.'

Lizzie started to laugh, she couldn't help herself. What Aunt Hannah was suggesting was too funny for words. 'Billy is seven years old, Aunt.'

'I'm no longer your aunt.'

'My brother is seven years old,' Lizzie continued ruthlessly. 'Before he came here he was a happy little boy who liked playing and having fun. You've driven all the fun out of him.'

'Don't speak to me like that.'

'I'll speak to you any way I want, because even if you don't sack me I wouldn't stay in this house for another night, not even if you paid me.'

'Leave the room this instant!' Mrs Seymour wasn't used to being answered back. She usually did all the talking.

Now that Lizzie had started she didn't seem able to stop. 'I'll leave the room when I'm ready and not before. I went to Billy's room last night because I was worried about him. I could see he was unhappy. I tried to comfort him – there's nothing unnatural about that unless you've got an evil mind.' Hannah put out her hand to ring the bell for Ellen but Lizzie carried on. 'That's what you've got: an evil mind. I hope wherever Mum and Dad are now they know what you're doing. I think they're in heaven – but when you die you'll go to hell.'

'Ellen!' Hannah shouted for her maid at the top of her lungs, at the same time ringing the bell by her chair. Ellen must have been close by because she was in the room almost immediately, a satisfied smirk on her face. How much she'd heard Lizzie could only guess. 'Ellen, this girl's to leave my house within the hour.'

'Yes, Mrs Seymour.'

'She is to take only the things she brought with her.'

'I'll see she does. Two carrier-bags was all she arrived with.'

Lizzie looked from one sour face to the other. 'Billy had a case. He'll need that for his things.'

'I put the boy's case up in the attic,' Ellen said doubtfully. 'It'll take a bit of finding.'

'It's all right, Ellen,' Aunt Hannah said. 'The case can stay where it is. William isn't going anywhere.'

'He's coming with me,' Lizzie said, and there was a bright spot of colour staining her cheeks. 'You can't keep him here.'

'I am his legal guardian. William stays at Greenlock with me. You are not of age and it was your father's wish that I should care for him until he reaches his majority.'

Lizzie knew Hannah Seymour had won. She held the trump card. How could she take Billy with her anyhow? She had no home to take him to and only a pound or two left from the money she'd made by selling the family possessions. It would be hard enough for herself, alone against the world, but it would be impossible with a little boy to care for. However much Billy hated it, here at Greenlock he would be fed, and clothed, and have a roof over his head. She would go away like the people in stories do and make her fortune, and then one day she'd come back for her brother. Billy would understand. He'd have to understand.

'Can I say goodbye to Billy?' she asked.

'No, you can't. You've done enough damage already.'

There was no use in arguing, so Lizzie turned away. Then she thought of something and faced her aunt again. 'You owe me two pounds and ten shillings,' she said.

'I owe you nothing.'

'We had an agreement. I still have the letter. Bed and board you offered me – and ten shillings a week. I've been here all of five weeks and you've paid me nothing, so I'll have my money before I go.'

Mrs Seymour knew she couldn't get out of it. 'Pass me my bag,' she snapped. She made quite a song and dance searching its interior for her purse, and then counting out notes and coins. 'There,' she said at last, and handed over two one-pound notes and some silver. Lizzie looked at the notes, the two florins and the sixpence, and then at her aunt.

'It's half a crown short,' she said at last.

'You broke one of my best cups. You're lucky I haven't

deducted more. And I paid for that dress and apron so don't take them with you.'

'I wouldn't want to. I wouldn't be seen dead in them once I've left here.'

On those brave words Lizzie marched out of the room. She might look as if she didn't care but she was trembling inside.

While she packed her things she had to control her fingers to stop them shaking. One of the bags was useless. It was only made of brown paper with a string handle and there was a big split in the bottom, so she had to make do with the other one. Still, it was better not to have too much luggage to carry.

She packed her black skirt and a blouse, a nightgown, and some clean underwear and stockings. Small things, like her thimble, pencils and comb, she kept in a cardboard box. This just fitted into the top of the bag.

Then she took off the hated grey frock and apron and folded them neatly on the foot of the bed. She dressed herself in her old mauve cotton dress and black jacket, and on her head pulled the straw hat that was by now the worse for wear.

Carrying her bag proudly and with her chin tilted, Lizzie marched into the kitchen to say goodbye to Ellen and Daisy. There was no one there, so she had to leave as she had arrived – alone.

Lizzie opened the back door and stepped into the sunshine. She'd considered leaving by the front door, just to confirm that she was more than just a servant even if she was homeless and out of a job, but she wasn't quite brave enough. When she'd made her fortune she'd come back for Billy and ring the front door bell. She'd be dressed in flowered chiffon, with elbow-length gloves and a fur coat. Ellen would stare at her in surprise and call her Miss Sargent. But today in her shabby clothes no one would give her a second look. No one knew how she felt – because no one cared.

'Hiss!'

Something was buzzing close by. Lizzie looked around to see if it was a bee or a blue-bottle. Then the sound came again and she saw a round brown face looking at her from among the dusty laurels. It was Daisy with her cap awry, trying to attract her attention.

'Oh, Daisy! I expect you've heard that Mrs Seymour's sending me away. I'm so glad I've seen you to say goodbye.'

'Friend.' Daisy stepped out of the shelter of the bushes. 'Daisy's friend.'

'Yes, I'm your friend. And you're my only friend.' Lizzie took the misshapen little woman in her arms and kissed her cheek. 'Goodbye.'

'Friend. Daisy's friend. Present.' From the pocket of her grubby apron Daisy produced a crumpled strip of brightly coloured material. It was the scarf Lizzie had given her on the day she'd arrived. The little woman was trying to give it back. Lizzie pushed her hand away.

'No,' she said firmly. 'I want you to keep it. I'd give you something else to remember me by but I haven't got anything.'

But Daisy insisted. She pushed the scarf into Lizzie's bag. Then she saw the coin hanging on its string and her hand reached out towards it.

'No.' Lizzie pushed her hand away. 'I'm sorry but you can't have that. It's my lucky silver joey: I mustn't give it away.' Daisy looked so disappointed she suddenly had an idea. 'Look, Daisy.' She held up a florin from her small hoard. 'This is bigger than a joey. I'll give it to you if you'll do something for me.' The little maid reached for it greedily but Lizzie held it just out of her grasp. 'If I write a note for my brother, will you make sure he gets it?'

'Boy?' Daisy jumped from one foot to the other. 'Boy – cry?'

'That's right. The boy who cries.' Lizzie tore a strip of cardboard from the box in her bag and wrote quickly on it with the stub of a pencil: 'Dear Billy, I have to go away for a while, but I'll come back for you when I've made my fortune. Do what Aunt Hannah tells you and you'll be all right.' She signed it 'Your loving sister Lizzie.' She held it out with the florin to Daisy. 'Now you'll make sure the boy gets it, won't you?' Daisy nodded like a marionette. 'Promise? And don't let Mrs Seymour know.'

'Daisy promise.'

The florin and the note changed hands and Daisy turned and shuffled towards the back door. Lizzie sighed. She didn't know how much Daisy was capable of understanding; she could only hope her note reached Billy before it fell into Aunt Hannah's hands. She squared her shoulders, picked up her bag, and walked away from Greenlock. She didn't dare look back in case she saw a pale face pressed to a window, or heard a child's voice calling her name.

At first Lizzie walked slowly without taking any notice of her surroundings. She followed one road to its end, and then another one, not knowing where it led. What did it matter anyway as long as every step took her further away from Aunt Hannah.

It was market day and she found herself pushing through crowds of bargain hunters. She stopped to buy a twopenny loaf and was suddenly dazzled by the colour and gaiety of her surroundings. She'd been living so long half-underground that she'd forgotten cabbages could be so green and lemons so yellow.

'Hey, put that down!' a rough stall-holder shouted when he saw her with a scarlet apple in her hand, looking at it with wonder in her eyes. Suddenly the world was a wonderful place. Lizzie grinned and bit into the crisp sweet flesh. 'Give us a half-penny or I'll call the bogies.'

Lizzie felt in her pocket; feeling generous she threw him a penny and went on her way with a light heart.

She had no home, it was true – no job either. But she

was young and strong and had money in her pocket. Her clothes might be shabby, but they were clean. The whole world stretched before her and she was eager to be part of it.

The walking made her hungry and she stopped to count her remaining money. With her wages she now had the princely sum of four pounds, one shilling and six pence. It seemed like a fortune but Lizzie knew she had to make it last so she passed by the attractive little coffee house with the marble-topped tables, where a cup of coffee could be bought for three pence.

She found a cheap café which was serving midday meals. According to the menu you could order a three-course lunch for one and sixpence. It consisted of soup, meat and two veg, and apple pie to follow – all home-made.

Lizzie was tempted. Instead she chose a small general store and bought a small loaf of bread, a sixpenny bar of Bournville chocolate and a bottle of ginger beer. She found a secluded corner in a churchyard and ate hungrily, tearing strips of bread from the loaf and cramming it into her mouth with her fingers. The chocolate was a treat, so she ate only one square, tucking the rest away in her bag for later.

She was now nearing the edge of the town. The houses were not only getting bigger, but farther apart. Soon she found herself in the countryside and had no idea where the road led.

But it didn't matter. Eventually she would reach another town, and then it would be time to look for somewhere cheap to spend the night.

After the first two hours of walking, there being no sign of a village let alone a town, Lizzie started to feel despondent. Occasionally traffic passed her on the road: a car travelling at a dangerous fifty miles an hour and a charabanc full of singing day-trippers; but no one that looked twice at the lonely walker or thought to offer her a lift. Her spirits rose when a horse-drawn carriage rolled past with a white-haired old lady as the only passenger, but although the old woman nodded and smiled in Lizzie's direction she didn't slow down.

The day was beginning to cool down and fire-flies danced lazily when Lizzie saw the first sign of habitation. It looked like a farm building set away from the road. By the green verge a coach was drawn up and a dozen or so young men and girls were climbing down on to the road. The men, who were not much more than boys, wore shorts or flannel trousers and open-necked shirts. The girls also wore cotton shorts with Aertex blouses. They all wore thick socks and shoes, and carried canvas haversacks.

The last to alight was a boy of about Lizzie's age, with rough red hair and a plump freckled face. Under his arm was a small black and white dog with a sharp nose and twitching ears. The dog was yapping frantically so the boy put it down on the grass where it headed for the nearest bush to relieve itself. Then it started to run around in circles still yapping with excitement.

'Come here, Spud,' the boy commanded. The dog ignored its master and ran faster. The boys and girls were now trooping through the gate so the red-haired boy was soon left on his own. 'Spud! Come here at once,' he shouted.

The little dog, intent on keeping his freedom, ran towards Lizzie. She bent down and grabbed its collar. Stopped in his headlong flight, Spud started to lick Lizzie's hands with his rough pink tongue. She picked him up in her free hand and carried him over to his master.

'You'd better put him on a lead before he gets away again,' she said. She liked the look of this boy. He wasn't good-looking but his eyes were gentle and kind.

'I left it at home,' the boy admitted. 'I'll have to beg for a length of string or use my belt.' He looked down at the narrow strip of leather holding up his khaki shorts. 'As long as my shorts don't fall down.' He laughed, showing a broken front tooth, and Lizzie found herself laughing as well.

'You hold him.' Lizzie passed Spud over. 'I'll see if I've got something you can use.'

The only thing suitable was the coloured scarf, but as it was now not much more than a rag after being in Daisy's possession, she held it out.

'I can't take that.'

'Why not? It's only a bit of material and you need it.' Lizzie fastened the scarf to the dog's collar, then tied a knot in the end for a handle. 'There.'

'Thanks.' Spud was put down on the ground again. He continued to yap intermittently at the end of his improvised lead. 'I didn't see you on the coach?'

'I wasn't on it,' Lizzie admitted. 'I'm just passing by.'

'Oh, I thought you were a fruit-picker. By the way, my name's Jack. Jack French – and this is Spud.'

'I'm Lizzie Sargent.' It was so nice to see a friendly face that Lizzie wanted the conversation to continue. She said the first thing that came into her head. 'Are you a fruit-picker?'

'Yes. We all are. It's the only way to take a holiday and earn extra money at the same time. They get you up at the crack of dawn, but the fresh air's good for you. I'd better be going or I'll lose my place.' Jack swung his haversack over his shoulder and whistled to his dog. 'Come on, Spud.'

'Just a minute.' Lizzie grabbed his arm to stop him going. 'Do you think they'd give me a job?'

'I don't know. Have you ever picked fruit before?'

'No, but it doesn't sound difficult.'

'It's not – but it's hard work. They only pay you two pence a bushel. It's the season for plums now. You have to know what you're doing because they have to be sorted properly. They let you eat the over-ripe fruit but after a while you get sick of it. And you have to watch out for wasps. Last year I got stung, and my arm was swollen to twice its size.'

'I'm not afraid of wasps,' Lizzie said. 'And I need a job.'

'Where do you live?' Jack's eyes were blue with spiky red lashes, but they were friendly. He looked at Lizzie and saw her inner confusion. 'Sorry, I'm not just being nosy. But if you live nearby you'll want to go home at night. Some of us sleep in tents, but there's a shed the farmer lets some of the girls use. The hardy ones sleep in the open air when the weather's fine.'

'I don't mind where I sleep.'

Jack asked no more questions. He was curious about the pretty dark-haired girl and guessed she was in some sort of trouble. Why else would she look so desperate and need a job so badly? To him it was just an adventure, a bit of fun, and a few extra bob at the end of the week to put towards the motor-bike he wanted to buy.

'Come on then,' he said, pulling Lizzie through the gate. 'Say you came in the coach with us. I'll say you're a friend of mine.'

The farmer's name was Gates, and he hadn't been told how many pickers to expect so an extra one was neither here nor there. He had a glut of plums this year. They needed picking before the wasps got at them, or before they dropped from the trees and rotted on the ground.

'Have you brought a tent?' he asked Lizzie.

'No. I don't mind sleeping out.'

'This is your first time, isn't it?' Mr Gates was curious but kindly. He had a daughter indoors about Lizzie's age. This girl wasn't dressed for picking fruit. Her shoes were thin, almost worn through, and how could she climb a ladder in a cotton dress?

Jack seemed to read his doubts. 'One of the girls will lend Lizzie some clothes,' he said. Spud yapped his approval and distracted the farmer.

'I see you've brought that animal with you again. Just

keep him away from my chickens.'

'I will.' They grinned at each other. Jack brought Spud with him every year and he'd become a fast favourite.

'Can I stay then?' Lizzie asked eagerly.

'I'll give you a trial. Start at seven in the morning. Two pence a bushel and no larking about. Tea first thing, bread and cheese for dinner, soup at night, and as many plums as you can eat. Don't make yourself ill though.'

'Thank you – you won't regret it.'

'I'd better not. What's your name, love?'

'Elizabeth Sargent – but everyone calls me Lizzie.'

'Take Lizzie round to the field, Jack.' Mr Gates had filled in his ledger and now snapped it shut. 'Some of the girls are sharing a tent, but there should be room for her in the shed. The wife'll be bringing the soup around later.'

'Follow me.' Jack led the way through a yard where chickens pecked on the cobbles and washing flapped in the breeze. Spud yapped at his heels, looking back every so often to make sure Lizzie was keeping up.

At the rear of the farmhouse was a small field where the tents were being pitched. There was much laughter and screaming as the canvas structures swayed and threatened to collapse. One young man in grey flannel trousers was trying to light a fire, while a group of girls with their arms around each others' shoulders cheered him on.

'Blow harder, Tom,' one of them shouted. 'You can do it.'

At the far end of the field, facing the orchard, stood a hut made of corrugated iron. In the doorway a fair girl wearing navy blue shorts was shaking a grey blanket. She smiled at Jack in a friendly fashion.

'Hullo, Jack – who's your friend?'

'This is Lizzie. She's never picked before, and she doesn't have any proper clothes. Is there room for her to sleep in here?'

'Of course. The more the merrier. I'm Jenny – and this

is Dorothy, Betty and Barbara.' Jenny introduced three other girls who were busy inside. 'This is Lizzie, everybody.'

Everyone seemed so friendly that Lizzie didn't mind when Jack and Spud left. She felt she was in capable hands.

'You can't climb a ladder and pick in a frock,' Jenny said. She was rummaging about in a corner. 'You can borrow these dungarees. They're hardly the latest Paris fashion but they'll stop the boys looking up your skirt.'

'Thank you, Jenny,' Lizzie said gratefully, taking the garment. 'Where do I sleep?'

'Grab a sack and stuff it full of straw for a mattress,' a little dark girl named Betty called out. She pulled her own home-made mattress away from the wall to give Lizzie more room. 'It gets perishing cold in the night, or it did last year, so you'll need a blanket. I've got a spare one I can lend you.'

'And sleep in your clothes,' the girl called Barbara added. 'They stink by the end of the week, but as we're all the same no one complains.'

'I've brought some scent.' Dorothy waved a small bottle. 'It's Californian Poppy. We can share it.'

'Who are you hoping to get off with?' Jenny asked jokingly. 'Jack or Tom?'

'I haven't decided yet.' Dorothy lay back on her straw mattress and stretched her long bare legs out in front so that she could admire her trim ankles. 'Jack makes me laugh, but Tom is the handsome one.'

Lizzie made her bed, and for two pins would have crawled under the blanket right away. All the walking had made her so tired she could hardly keep her eyes open. She had no idea of the time. But as the sun was slowly sinking over the distant hills she guessed it must be evening. Suddenly a bell started clanging close by. Her companions started getting to their feet.

'Supper time,' Jenny explained, digging a chipped bowl

out of the straw. 'Here, you can borrow this one.'

The farmer's wife was an enormous woman with short cropped grey hair. She was dressed in men's corduroy trousers. She stood in the middle of the clearing with a huge steaming pan in one hand and a ladle in the other. By her side was a small boy in cap and braces ringing a hand-bell to attract the campers.

'The soup's free,' Jenny whispered, 'but if you want bread you have to buy it.'

The soup was a greeny-brown colour, with pieces of unidentifiable matter floating on the greasy surface. Lizzie shuddered as she filled her spoon, but when she tasted it found it quite palatable as well as filling. The floating particles turned out to be chopped leeks and carrots, and the fat came from the pieces of meat that gave the soup a distinctive flavour. When Mrs Gates offered to refill her bowl Lizzie accepted hungrily.

'Here.' The farmer's wife thrust the crust of a loaf into Lizzie's hand. 'That bit's free because you're new; but don't let on or they'll all expect some.'

By the time supper was finished, and the bowls swilled clean under the pump in the yard, it was almost dark. Tom's campfire was going well and the smell of wood-smoke filled the air.

Everyone drifted towards the glowing embers, dragging their blankets behind them. When someone dropped a handful of kindling on top a reassuring crackle came from the heart of the fire and a flame licked upwards.

In groups of two or three the party arranged themselves around the fire, toasting themselves in the warmth. Someone produced a mouth-organ and started to play a popular tune and everyone swayed in time to the music. Lizzie sat apart, her blanket worn Indian fashion and her plait hanging over one shoulder. She was happy and didn't mind being alone. Jack was sitting cross-legged on the other side of the fire chatting amicably to Jenny and Barbara. He must have said something to amuse them because they were all laughing. At his feet Spud slept, nose on paws, ears twitching as he dreamed of the rabbits he was going to chase the next day.

'Make the most of it,' a voice said in Lizzie's ear. 'This time tomorrow you'll be exhausted.'

It was Tom, thin and wiry, with a lock of dark hair hanging over his forehead. He sank down on the grass by Lizzie's side.

'I don't mind hard work,' Lizzie said.

Someone started to sing 'Happy Days Are Here Again' and soon the whole party joined in. Those who didn't know the words hummed the tune or whistled. Then it was 'Beyond The Blue Horizon', followed by 'I Do Like To Be Beside The Seaside'. Suddenly Lizzie felt tearful because it reminded her of her parents. She brushed a hand across her cheek because she didn't have a handkerchief.

'Cheer up,' Tom said, and his arm crept around Lizzie's shoulders pulling her close. 'Give us a kiss.'

All around her couples were hugging and kissing, but Lizzie froze. She didn't want to be unfriendly but Tom was a stranger and she wasn't even sure that she liked him.

'No.' She tried to push him away. He was stronger than she was and more determined.

'Come on; what's the matter with you?'

'The lady said no – didn't you hear her?' It was Jack, with a white face under his freckles.

'What's it got to do with you?'

'It's got everything to do with me,' Jack replied. 'Lizzie's my girl.'

There was an unwritten code among pickers to respect boy- and girlfriends. Tom got to his feet and drifted away to try his luck elsewhere.

Jack took his place. When he took Lizzie's hand and pressed it reassuringly, a tide of warmth crept over her. She felt safe and drifted off to sleep with her head resting trustingly on his shoulder.

CHAPTER FIVE

The Red Barn

Lizzie couldn't sleep because it was so hot. Thunder rumbled in the distance, and she tossed and turned, feeling rivulets of perspiration trickling down her back and between her breasts. She was sleeping in her underwear and her chemise was so damp and uncomfortable that she would have liked to take it off if modesty hadn't stopped her.

Even with the door of the hut propped open, the air was still and oppressive. As the first light of a new dawn crept stealthily across the floor Lizzie knew that it foretold another burningly hot day.

There was a rustling of straw and Jenny stood up and stretched in the dim light. Wearing only a crumpled shift, and with her fair hair tousled, she looked very young and healthy. She tip-toed across the floor to the other make-shift beds and shook her companions awake. Lizzie watched curiously from under half-closed lids.

Carrying their blankets spiked with straw and giggling mysteriously the girls crept towards the doorway. Before they disappeared Lizzie called to them.

'Where are you going?'

'Did we wake you?' Jenny asked.

'No, I was already awake. It's too hot to sleep.'

'We're going to bathe.'

'Where?'

'There's a spring at the bottom of the orchard. Do you want to come?'

Lizzie hesitated for only a moment, then she jumped up, pushing her heavy curtain of brown hair away from her face. The thought of cool water on her hot sticky body was more than she could resist.

'Yes. Wait for me.'

'Hurry up then; we don't want the boys to hear us,' Jenny said. 'And bring your blanket to dry yourself on.'

Trailing their blankets behind them the five girls padded on bare feet through the grass. As they passed one of the tents a deep masculine snore set them giggling.

'Shhh!' Barbara put her finger over her lips, and they managed to restrain their laughter until they were safely past.

'Don't the boys ever bathe?' Lizzie asked.

'They never get up in time,' Jenny said. 'Anyway, we wouldn't want them with us. It wouldn't be decent because we haven't brought swimming costumes. That's why we creep out early before anybody's awake.'

At the end of the orchard the land fell away steeply and a small gushing stream cascaded out of the rocky wall to make a pool below. It was a quiet, secluded place, surrounded as it was by gnarled oaks and tall chestnuts. Even the early sun had difficulty penetrating the foliage, and the water was so clear and inviting, bubbling between smooth pebbles speckled with moss, that the girls started to strip off their clothes instantly.

Lizzie watched open-mouthed as her companions danced, proudly naked, into the water. They splashed each other like children, shrieking at the coldness.

She stood alone on the bank clutching her blanket,

embarrassed at the blatant nudity of her friends. Their arms and faces were brown as berries after exposure to the hot sun, but their bodies were pale in contrast, dimpled and hollowed, voluptuous in their newly awakened maturity.

'Come on, Lizzie,' Dorothy shouted. She was a tall slim girl with short bobbed hair and small, perfectly rounded buttocks. Betty was so tiny and flat-bosomed that she might have been mistaken for a young boy. Barbara and Jenny were the most feminine looking. Jenny had heavy swinging breasts and a tiny waist, and Barbara was broad hipped, with a bush of curly reddish hair sprouting between her muscular thighs.

Lizzie dropped her blanket and unlaced her chemise. She felt her face flush as her body was exposed for the first time to strangers. The air was cool on her skin and she crossed her arms over her breasts to hide them. The friction of the air on her nipples had hardened them and she felt embarrassed. But her companions found her blushes amusing and they scooped up water in their hands and splashed her with the icy droplets.

'It's freezing,' she gasped.

'No it's not,' Betty giggled. 'Jump in quickly and you won't notice it.'

Lizzie put one foot forward and shivered, but before she could change her mind Jenny grabbed her ankle so that she stumbled into the fair girl's arms. Laughing they clung to each other, breast to breast and belly to belly, until Jenny's bare foot slipped and they tumbled into the water. Betty was right: after the first icy splash, Lizzie was soon glowing. She joined her new-found friends laughing and splashing.

'It's lovely,' she admitted, letting the water stream down her body, and feeling the weight of her wet hair. After a while they tired and were content to lie in the shallow water, the patchy sunlight dappling their limbs.

'I've brought a cake of soap,' Barbara suddenly

announced. 'Let's wash our hair.'

The soap was yellow and smelled of disinfectant, but the water was soft so it lathered easily. Soon they were rinsing the rainbow-tinted bubbles from their hair, and shaking their heads in the increasing warmth of the sun's rays to dry their tresses.

Lizzie's hair was the longest and the thickest. She floated in the water, her hair streaming around her pale body while the others sat on the bank rubbing themselves dry on their blankets.

'We'd better get back,' Jenny said. 'We don't want Mr Gates to catch us before we're properly dressed.'

'I wouldn't mind Tom Grainger catching me,' Dorothy said dreamily. 'What about you, Betty?' Betty grinned but wouldn't commit herself, so she turned to Lizzie. 'What about you? I can see Jack fancies you.'

'He's just a friend,' Lizzie answered. She was busy trying to trap a minnow that was darting between the rocks. 'I don't think I want to be caught by anyone.'

'Well, Mr Gates will catch us if we don't hurry.' Betty started to scramble back over the rocks. 'Are you coming, Lizzie?'

'I think I'll stay for a few more minutes,' Lizzie said, lazily climbing out of the water and wringing the water out of her hair. 'I'll follow.'

'Don't be long then or you'll miss breakfast.'

Chattering and stumbling over the rough ground the girls disappeared into the ring of trees. Lizzie was glad to be alone. She didn't mind missing breakfast because the hot weather had dulled her appetite. It would only be Mrs Gates's stewed tea, and bread fried in bacon fat over a paraffin stove. Not exactly mouth-watering.

The sun was hotter now, dappling her limbs and drying her thick hair. She stood upright, glorying in the freedom of her young body, her face turned upwards to the blue sky. Taking deep breaths she filled her lungs with the sweet-scented air. Soon she would have to go back and face another exhausting day in the orchard, with the noisy tom-foolery of her companions and the unremitting work under the burning sun.

This quiet spot was like another world and Lizzie longed for a few more minutes' respite. She flung herself down on the grass and stretched like a cat, arching her back and closing her eyes, feeling the cushion of moss under her head.

In her innocence she had no idea how beautiful she was, or what passions she might arouse in anyone stumbling on her by accident. Her body was perfectly formed, slender and strong from hard work, her stomach flat and breasts small and rosy-tipped. Her waist was narrow as a boy's, but there was nothing boyish in the curve of her hips or the generous shadows that hid her secret places. Her skin was downy as a ripe peach, golden under the sun's rays, bursting with sweet promise. She wore her beauty carelessly, unaware of the watcher.

Thomas Grainger was nineteen years old, dedicated to the pursuit of pleasure and the company of attractive women. He was used to an easy life, waited on by a devoted mother, and a string of young housemaids on whom he practised his amorous exploits. The plain or ugly ones were ready for teasing, but the ones with a semblance of beauty were ripe for deflowering. Tom had his pick.

In two years' time, when he reached twenty-one, he was expected to go into the family business. His father, Victor Grainger, wanted to add 'and son' to the name over his gentleman's outfitters shop situated in a fashionable part of Brighton.

Tom had come fruit-picking thinking it would be a lark and not realising how hard the work was going to be. Jack French was a casual acquaintance he'd met in Sherrys Dance Hall only the week before. When Jack had told him there would be girls present he thought it sounded fun. At first he'd thought the week was going to turn out disappointing, and then he'd spotted Lizzie Sargent. At the sight of the beautiful girl with the long brown hair and innocent eyes, he'd warmed to the thrill of the chase.

Used to the comforts of a middle-class home Tom had soon found the camping life not suited to his tastes. The ground was hard and the night noises strange to someone used to the town. He couldn't sleep; so it was that he'd dressed early and decided on a solitary walk before breakfast. Hands in the pockets of his grey flannel trousers and his white shirt carelessly open at the neck, he'd prowled along the country lanes smoking Players Weights cigarettes and wondering where he'd be able to buy a fresh packet.

The girlish giggles had attracted his attention and he'd hidden himself in some bushes to eavesdrop. Now this was more like it, Tom thought – naked pubescent girls frolicking for his amusement. He settled down to enjoy the spectacle.

Jenny's flamboyant charms didn't appeal to him; nor did Betty's undeveloped body or Barbara's muscular frame. But Lizzie Sargent was everything he'd ever dreamed of. He'd thought her pretty enough in the dim glow of the camp fire, but then Jack French had come and claimed her. Lizzie's honey-coloured limbs charmed him, and the rippling fall of hair made him catch his breath with longing. Tom was smitten: he had to have her before the week was over.

He thought his chance had come when her friends left her and she was alone, and he could watch her grace and innocence paraded before him. When she flung herself down on the turf, like a sacrifice to his manhood, he longed to take her by force. He guessed she would cry and protest like a butterfly caught in a net; but he would master her. Tom licked his lips in anticipation as he planned his strategy.

'Slow down,' he told himself. 'She's like a wild animal – you mustn't frighten her.'

Lizzie looked as if she was asleep. Tom could see the gentle rise and fall of her breast, and the way the breeze caught the silky strands of hair and blew them around her shoulders. An insect alighted on her brow and she put up her hand, oh so gracefully, and brushed it away. The gesture was so delightful that Tom nearly fainted with longing. He couldn't wait any longer: he must have her - *now*

Before he could act Lizzie opened her eyes and sat up in alarm. Had he made a sound, or had some uncanny feminine instinct warned her of danger?

Tom took a step backwards and held his breath. The branches fell naturally into place in front of him. When he dared to look again Lizzie was on her feet with her blanket wound around her. She glanced just once over her shoulder and their eyes met, then she was running, leaping over stubbly bushes and dodging around trees like a gazelle.

Tom gave chase. Normally Lizzie could have out-stripped him, but the blanket and her bare feet were a disadvantage. He grabbed her arm, yanking it so that she gave a small cry of pain.

'You're hurting me.'

'Keep still then.'

Lizzie stopped struggling and Tom let her go. She leaned back against a tree trunk to get her breath back. There were red marks on her arm where his fingers had cruelly bruised the flesh. She rubbed at them with her hand. Her cheeks were flushed and her hair wild and tumbled and she looked more excited than distressed; almost as if she'd enjoyed the thrill of the chase.

'What do you want?'

'A kiss.'

'No.' Her voice was low. 'You were watching us.'

'It was you I was watching, Lizzie. You're the only one worth watching.'

'Why?' Lizzie asked curiously.

Tom laughed. 'Because you're beautiful. Has no one ever told you that before?'

'No.' Lizzie dropped her head so that her hair fell forward over her face. Her cheeks were rosier than ever. Tom leaned forward and pushed the hair away, revealing her blushes. 'Jenny's better looking than me,' she said defiantly. 'I'm too thin.'

'I wouldn't say so.' He was playing with a brown strand, winding it around his finger and then releasing it. The gentle tug to her scalp made Lizzie tingle; part of her wanted Tom to stop, but another part of her longed for him to continue. 'If you're thin, Lizzie, then I must prefer thin girls.'

'I must go,' she started to protest, seeing the determination in Tom's eyes. They were clear and grey, and a lock of dark hair fell forward over his forehead. But he was handsome in a wiry sort of way. His face was thin and his body slender, but the grip of his hand on her arm had been like steel. Lizzie didn't particularly like him, but those direct grey eyes seemed to see inside her head and read her thoughts. They mesmerised her and drained her of willpower. 'I'm going to miss breakfast anyway. I don't want to be late or it'll put me behind.'

'Do you like chocolate?'

The question made Lizzie smile. What had chocolate got to do with being late for work?

'Of course I like chocolate.'

'I've got some bars in my tent; I brought them with me. Meet me behind the barn when the dinner bell goes and I'll give you some. It'll make up for missing breakfast.'

Lizzie was tempted as Tom guessed she would be. 'Can I bring Jenny?' she asked innocently.

'If you come alone I'll give you enough to share with all your friends. What do you say?'

'All right.'

Lizzie was innocent but she wasn't stupid. She knew Tom was playing with her; that he wasn't going to give her presents for nothing. So if in exchange for chocolate he expected a kiss, it seemed fair enough. She'd seen her friends around the campfire in the evenings hugging and kissing and it all seemed harmless. Jack usually kept her company, but although he sometimes put his arm around her, it was all just friendly and light-hearted. Anyway Spud was always there to distract them.

By the time Lizzie got back to the hut the other girls were already dressed in their working clothes and just about to leave for the orchard.

'We thought you'd got lost,' Betty said. 'We were just thinking about sending out a search party.'

'I fell asleep,' Lizzie lied.

She folded her blanket and stepped into her dungarees. They were baggy and not at all becoming. She'd never minded what she looked like before, but now she'd been told she was beautiful, and felt the sun and air on her body, she didn't want to cover it up completely.

'Can anyone lend me a pair of shorts?' she asked. 'It's too hot for these things.'

Betty's clothes were too small, but Jenny had a spare pair of blue cotton shorts and Dorothy a blouse. Lizzie felt like a different person in her new outfit. She danced around in front of her friends.

'How do I look?'

'Fine,' Jenny said. 'You'll feel much cooler.'

'Why don't you cut off your hair?' Betty tossed her short dark tresses back. 'Long hair is so unfashionable now. A bob would suit you. I've never regretted cutting mine off.'

Lizzie lifted the weight of her hair up with her two hands and tried to imagine what it would feel like without it. She looked doubtful.

'I don't know.'

'I'll do it for you,' Dorothy said. 'I cut my sister's hair and everyone admired it. I'd like to be a hairdresser. Has anyone got any scissors?'

Betty had a pair but they were blunt. Lizzie was relieved when the bell rang to summon them to work and the haircut had to be postponed. They trooped out of the hut into the sunshine and joined the other pickers hurrying across the grass with their baskets.

It was usual to work in pairs and today Lizzie was pleased to discover that her partner was Jack French. He beamed at the sight of her and linked his arm through hers.

'What do you want to do, pick or pack?' he asked.

'Let's take it in turns. I'll pick first.'

Lizzie leaned the wooden ladder up against the trunk of the first tree and climbed up until her head was enveloped in green leaves. The purple fruit hung in heavy clusters and she picked the first plum and handed it down to Jack. He inspected it and then placed it carefully in the wide wicker basket. The day's work had begun.

Mid-morning they changed over. Lizzie's arms were beginning to ache from the constant stretching, but they were tanned golden brown, and even her legs were honey coloured now that they were uncovered. There were a lot of insects about but they were used to them. The flying kind were the worst: wasps and bees attracted by the sweet fruit.

Jack didn't notice the striped body of a wasp as he passed a large plum down to Lizzie. She took it in her hand and the angry insect stung her finger making her cry out in pain. Jack peered down in alarm.

'What's the matter?'

'A wasp. It's just stung me!' Lizzie jumped about nursing her injured finger, and by the time Jack joined her it looked red and angry.

'Keep still.'

'But it hurts.'

'Of course it hurts – but I came prepared.'

Jack grinned to reassure her that he knew what to do.

From his pocket he produced a screw of paper that contained some fine white crystals. He emptied them into the palm of his hand.

'What is it?' Lizzie asked.

'Only salt. Now spit.'

Lizzie did as she was told. Jack spread the damp salt on to her finger and covered it with a strip of material torn from the hem of his shirt. Almost at once the pain subsided.

'Better?'

'Yes. Thank you.'

Lizzie looked at Jack gratefully; he appeared so rough with his unruly red hair and freckled face. His hands were plump and stubby, with broken nails, and looked good enough only for manual work. And yet his touch had been so gentle, and his smile was tender now that he could see that she was feeling better.

'I got stung last year so Mum told me what to do. Of course a bee sting would have been more serious. You have to pull the sting out first; but with a wasp you treat the pain and stop it swelling. Are you all right now?'

'I'm grand. It hardly hurts at all.'

'Good. Come on then, let's get back to work.'

At midday Lizzie was first in the queue for her hunk of bread and cheese. Usually she sat with her friends in the shade, or joined Jack as he took Spud for a stroll. Today she had other plans.

Her stomach fluttered with excitement – partly at the thought of the promised mouth-watering chocolate, and partly at the idea of a rendezvous with Tom Grainger. She could still feel the steely pressure of his fingers and his voice telling her she was beautiful. She didn't believe him of course. She was no better looking than Jenny, or even the delicate little Betty. But it was nice to be told that she was attractive to the male sex.

Nobody noticed Lizzie slip away, and she didn't meet anyone on her walk to the barn. The doorframe and exposed rafters were stained a rusty red colour. It reminded her of an old tale she'd heard once about a young girl who was murdered by her sweetheart and her body buried in a red barn. But that was only a story, not true to life. Anyway, Tom wasn't her sweetheart and he didn't look like a murderer.

Even so, Lizzie wouldn't venture inside. She found a spot in the shade and sat down with her elbows propped on her bent knees and her chin in her cupped hands. She'd give Tom five minutes, then if he didn't turn up return to her friends.

'I knew you'd come.'

Lizzie jumped to her feet. Tom must have been waiting and watching for her all the time – as he'd watched down by the spring, his eyes clear and calculating. She backed against the wall of the barn, wishing she hadn't come.

'You said you'd bring me some . . .'

'Chocolate?' Tom laughed. 'So I did. But it would only melt in this heat. I was just testing you, Lizzie.'

'Why?' She was angry and confused; embarrassed that she could have been so easily tempted by sweets.

Tom didn't answer her question, he was too busy looking her up and down. He seemed to like what he saw: her flushed face and bare legs.

'Those overalls you used to wear were really ugly,' he said at last. 'Shorts are much better. I used to wonder what your legs were like – now I know.'

Lizzie's blush deepened. He knew more that that: he was the only man who'd seen her naked and his eyes were reminding her of that fact.

'I'd better get back. My friends will be looking for me.'

'Do you mean Jack?' He was barring her way; standing in front of her so that she felt trapped. Her back was pressed hard against the wall.

'We always take Spud for a walk. Jack'll be waiting.'

'I've been waiting, Lizzie, ever since I first saw you.' Tom's voice was low and urgent. He put his hands out and pressed them against the wall, trapping her between them. His face came closer and she could read the message in his eyes.

'No!'

But her protests came too late. His lips pressed greedily down on to hers, the hardness of his teeth forcing hers apart and supping her sweetness. Lizzie had never been kissed like this before. She'd exchanged gentle kisses with Billy, and affectionate ones with her parents, but she'd never guessed that kisses could be so cruel.

And yet they aroused something in her she couldn't identify. Her heart was beating faster and somewhere deep inside she felt a glow that was spreading through her whole body as Tom's mouth became more persistent. He let her go only when they were both out of breath and then laughed at the confused state she was in.

'You said no - but you liked it.'

'I didn't.' Lizzie wiped her hand across her face and trembled.

'Then you shouldn't be such a temptress. My God, Lizzie, you're beautiful. When you look at a fellow out of those big brown eyes I could swear you're as innocent as you look.'

Lizzie didn't understand. She didn't understand what Tom was saying or the feelings he had awakened in her. Until that moment life had seemed straightforward. One day she would meet a boy who said he loved her. They would get married and everyone would wish them well. Something would happen between them on their wedding night, something she could only guess at, and she would have a baby to love and protect, as her mum and dad had protected her and Billy. And then they'd grow comfortably old together. That was love.

But Tom hadn't said anything about love, and his kisses hadn't been tender. He looked as if he'd like to hurt, not nurture her, and she was afraid.

'I must get back,' Lizzie whispered through bruised lips. 'Let me go.'

'Only if you promise to meet me tonight while the others are round the campfire.'

'I don't want to. Anyway, they'll ask me where I'm going.'

'I'll bring the chocolate.'

'I don't want it.'

'All right then – go.' Tom dropped his hands and stepped back. His voice sounded angry, as if he wasn't used to not getting his own way. But he had a card up his sleeve; a trump card; and he was prepared to play it. Before Lizzie had taken two steps away from him he said casually, 'If you don't want my chocolate I've got something else you might be interested in.' Lizzie should have kept on walking, but she didn't. She looked at him with a question in her eyes. 'It's something that belongs to you. I thought you might want it back.'

'I don't know what you're talking about.'

Tom laughed. 'Jack will when I show it to him. He said you were his girl, but he won't want you when I show him what I've got.'

'You're lying. How could you have anything belonging to me?'

'Easily – when you leave your intimate things around for anyone to find. Only girls of easy virtue do that.'

'What have you got, Tom? Tell me.'

'Don't get so upset, Lizzie. After all, I'm sure Jack will understand when you explain. Although I'm not sure whether Mr Gates will when I tell him how I found your underwear down by the spring. He's very old fashioned is Farmer Gates, and he's bound to think the worst. You'll be turned out before the end of the week and he won't pay you if he can help it.'

Lizzie stared wide-eyed. She didn't know whether to believe Tom or not, or whether it was another one of his games. Of course he was talking about the chemise she'd carelessly left behind on the rocks after her early morning dip. If Tom had it in his possession it might very well make Jack look at her differently, and she didn't want him to think badly of her. Somehow it was important to her what Jack thought. And what Mr Gates would think about their early morning bathe she dreaded to think.

'I must have it back,' Lizzie said urgently.

'Meet me tonight then. I'll wait for you here.'

Tom turned away as if dismissing her, and at that moment Lizzie heard the bell ringing to summon them back to work. With a downcast heart she retraced her steps.

No one seemed to have missed her. No one asked any questions, so she took her turn up the ladder glad to hide her flushed cheeks in the greenery. She tried to forget what had taken place. But every so often she stopped picking and fell into a dream, remembering the tumult Tom had awakened in her body, and feeling again the pressure of his lips upon hers.

'Are you all right, Lizzie?' Jack's concerned voice broke into her reverie.

'I'm fine. Why?'

'You're miles away. Twice you've passed me down green fruit. You know what Mr Gates said.'

'Only to pick ripe plums. Sorry, Jack – I'll be more careful.'

Jack looked up at the slender figure perched on the top rung of the ladder and shaded his eyes. 'Are you sure there's nothing wrong? You've been awfully quiet all afternoon.'

'Just thinking. Jack!' Lizzie's face looked down appealingly from among the branches. 'Am I pretty?'

Jack laughed: he thought Lizzie was joking. But then he saw how serious she was and turned the question over in his mind before answering. 'I suppose so. I haven't really thought about it.'

'Well, think about it now. Am I pretty?'

'I guess you are; but it's not important.'

'It is to me.'

'All right, Lizzie – I think you're pretty. Now are you satisfied?'

Lizzie didn't answer but returned to the work in hand. She'd wanted to tell Jack about Tom's threat: to ask his advice; but somehow she couldn't. She hadn't intended going near the barn again, chemise or not, but now she knew she had to. It was the only way she could allay her fears, and get her tormentor to return her property.

For the first time the hours seemed to drag, but at last the day's work was finished and supper was over. Before Jack could link his arm through hers and pull her towards the campfire, Lizzie slipped into the shadows and headed for the barn. She would do whatever Tom wanted, retrieve her underwear, and rejoin her friends hopefully before she was missed.

If Tom wanted another kiss in payment she would give him one. But this was going to be the last time she would do anything to cloud her conscience or spoil her reputation.

He was waiting for her in the doorway of the barn, and she went forward to meet him bravely and innocently. He pulled her inside. It was so dark that all she could see was the pale oval of his face on a level with her own, and the dark lock of hair falling over his forehead.

'Did you bring it?' she asked.

'The chocolate?' Tom laughed harshly. 'Oh, yes, I remembered the chocolate.'

'And my chemise ...?'

'Why do you keep worrying about your damned underwear?' He was gripping her arms now, his fingers digging into her tender flesh. 'I prefer you without it – as you were this morning.' With a vicious movement he tore at the cotton blouse Lizzie was wearing, ripping it open at the front and exposing the pale swelling of her breast.

'Tom! Don't!' She struggled bravely and tried to push him away with all the strength she could muster. 'Please,

Tom. Stop!' But her pleading was in vain. He was stronger than she was, and his desire gave him added strength. He grasped her wrists cruelly in one hand and tore at her clothing like a wild animal, ignoring her protests and stifling her cries with the brutal pressure of his lips. Lizzie couldn't believe what was happening. It was a nightmare. Luckily she blacked out so she would be saved the memory of the worst of her ordeal.

When she regained consciousness she was alone, huddled like a wounded creature in the dark. Grasping the torn shreds of her clothing about her, Lizzie stumbled out of the barn. She met no one on her way back to the hut; her friends were still gathered around the glowing embers of the fire. She crept into her bed and was consumed by an exhausted, fitful sleep by the time they joined her.

CHAPTER SIX

A New Hat

'Ellen Smith: one pound, two shillings. Henry Burton: one pound, five shillings and four pence. Bertie Hamilton: nineteen shillings and eight pence.'

The Bookie consulted his ledger and called out each picker's weekly earnings, while Mr Gates stood behind his table where the piles of notes and coins were carefully arranged. As each name was called out the farmer checked the amount and then handed it over to the recipient with a beaming smile.

A good worker was capable of picking three bushels of fruit an hour. When the going rate was twopence a bushel a picker was capable of earning thirty shillings for a sixty-hour week, but most only managed to earn just over a pound. Anyone earning less than six shillings was considered a waste of time and blacklisted the following year. This seldom happened as most pickers needed the money and took their work seriously.

'Elizabeth Sargent: one pound, three shillings and sixpence.'

Lizzie hurried forward to collect her wages. Mr Gates handed her two ten-shilling notes, a half-crown, and two sixpences.

'You've done well, Lizzie,' he said. 'If you've enjoyed yourself I'll take you on next year. You're a good worker.'

'Thank you, Mr Gates.'

Lizzie slipped the money safely away. She now had almost five pounds with which to embark on her adventures. It sounded like a fortune, but she knew it wouldn't go far. The coach was already waiting outside the farm gate to take the fruit-pickers back to their homes, but Lizzie had no home to return to.

'What's the matter?' Jack was standing by her side, his haversack slung over one shoulder and Spud bounding excitedly around his feet. He'd noticed how sad and downcast Lizzie had been and thought she was worried about what the future held. He'd hoped she would trust him enough to confide in him but he wasn't the sort of lad to pry. Some people, he knew, preferred to keep their problems to themselves.

'Nothing's wrong,' Lizzie said with a watery smile.

'Thomas Grainger.' Lizzie shuddered as his name was called. Thankfully, her reaction went unnoticed by Jack. 'Eight shillings and four pence.'

Tom had done the least work and so earned the smallest amount; but as he strode forward to collect his money he tossed his head and grinned broadly at the other pickers as if he hadn't a care in the world.

Lizzie looked at the ground as he passed close by, but he didn't even glance in her direction. She was glad. Since the episode in the red barn she'd kept her distance, frightened that he might continue his pursuit. She'd told no one of the horrible experience he'd put her through, and hidden the bruises and soreness he'd inflicted. But her friends had noticed how quiet and reserved she'd become, and seen the dark shadows under her eyes caused by lack of sleep.

'Everybody aboard,' the driver called from the roadway. 'Hurry up or I'll leave you all behind.'

Lizzie stood aside and watched the girls and boys

climbing into the coach. The friends she'd shared her life with for the last seven days seemed to have forgotten her already; they were too busy gossiping about the lives they were going back to: their jobs and families.

'Coming, Lizzie?'

Jack was at her elbow, and the invitation in his eyes was easy to read.

'But, Jack …' she started to protest.

'Listen: you can't stay here, and there was plenty of room on the coach coming up. You're one of us now so no one will ask questions.'

'But where are you going?'

'Brighton. We all live thereabouts, so we'll be dropped off on the sea-front.'

Brighton! Lizzie's spirits lifted. The town she'd returned to in her dreams, where the streets were paved with gold. In Brighton she'd be able to get a job, and start making her fortune so that she could go back to Greenlock and rescue Billy.

'What do you say?'

'If you're going to Brighton, I'm coming too.'

She looked happier than she had for days, and Jack was glad. He insisted on holding her bag while she climbed aboard, and then steered her towards two empty seats at the back. They packed their luggage away on the overhead rack and flopped down into the comfortable seats. Spud leaped on to Lizzie's lap and she cuddled him in her arms; he squirmed with delight and tried to lick her face with his wet pink tongue.

Everyone was in high spirits and sang at the tops of their voices as the coach sped along the country lanes. Jack and Lizzie joined in, and Spud barked an accompaniment. They travelled through small towns and hamlets and every mile brought them nearer and nearer to the sea.

'Soon be there,' the driver shouted as the road became busier and they passed large villas set back from the road behind stone walls.

Lizzie looked out of the window dreamily. Her memories of Brighton took her back to her childhood: the busy railway station clouded with steam, and the roar of the monsters carrying day-trippers to their destination; the smell of fish and chips and the salty air; the beach crowded with holiday-makers, and the bucket and spade Dad had bought her; digging in the sand and collecting pebbles and shells; egg sandwiches and lemonade, followed by a cone of delicious ice-cream; the golden promenade and singing 'Oh, I do like to be beside the seaside'.

The sun was shining just as it had all those years before, but the world outside the coach window was green rather than golden. This was after all a different part of the town. The gardens around the houses had neatly mown lawns and beds of bright summer flowers, and there were bowling greens smooth as velvet.

And then they were in the town and driving along busy streets hemmed in by the traffic.

'Is that the palace?' Lizzie asked, as she spotted a large building on her left behind some trees. She remembered Dad telling her about a palace that some king or prince had built, but there hadn't been time to see it.

Jack laughed. 'You mean the Pavilion? No – that's only a manor house. The Stanford family live there. The Pavilion's much grander.'

Now they were bowling along a road lined with shops. The driver had to slow down because there was even more traffic about. There were taxi cabs, the occasional private car, horse-drawn drays from Tamplin's Brewery, a mounted policeman, and the burgundy and cream trams rattling along on their four wheels like monsters bent on destruction.

But Lizzie was more interested in the passers-by. Never had she seen such finery as the people wore. They passed a man wearing a check coat over a canary yellow waistcoat, with a grey bowler hat on his head. On his arm was a woman with brightly painted nails, wearing a high-crowned hat on her short bobbed hair, with a peacock blue feather on the side.

Lizzie looked down at her faded cotton frock in alarm. She'd forgotten how shabby and old her clothes were, and the week at Gates Farm hadn't improved them.

'There's the Pavilion,' Jack said, pointing out of the right-hand window. 'The Prince Regent built it.'

'It's like a fairy-tale castle,' Lizzie said dreamily, staring at the architectural monstrosity with its onion-shaped minarets.

'And here's the promenade.'

It was everything Lizzie remembered. The wide road with green railings overlooking the pebbly beach, the twin piers stretching out into the sparkling blue water, the ice-cream vendors, and the holiday-makers basking in their deck chairs under the glass shelters.

But there was nowhere for their coach to park. The road was lined with cars and charabancs, buses and cabs, and there was no space for the driver to let his passengers alight in safety.

In the end he drove around the Old Steine and turned left at Castle Square. He drew up on a corner outside the largest department store Lizzie had ever seen. She immediately hurried across the pavement to feast her eyes on the finery laid out in the window.

There was an evening dress made of stiff blue taffeta, with rows of gathers across the bodice, and yards of material in the skirt which was cut on the bias to make it hang gracefully. The epaulettes tapered to a point, and there was a bunch of artificial violets tucked into the bosom. The price of this wonderful dress was nearly three pounds. Lizzie couldn't imagine anybody being able to afford to pay such a large amount of money just for a dress.

In another window were evening shoes encrusted with variegated glitter for twelve and eleven, and a pair of elbow-length gloves in shocking pink suede that she couldn't imagine anybody wanting.

But it was the hats that attracted Lizzie most. Cloche hats trimmed with feathers and ribbons, plain velour hats, high-crowned felt hats with small brims and dents in their crowns and feathers tucked into their bands, and straw hats heavy with artificial fruit and flowers.

Lizzie's old straw hat had fallen to pieces long ago and she gazed at the array of headgear with longing. In the front of the window was a saucy little hat made of golden-brown velvet. It had a narrow brim and a yellow ribbon that hung from the back. It was priced at four and eleven-pence three farthings and was the smartest thing she'd ever seen.

'What are you staring at?' Jack was at her side with Spud tucked under his arm.

'The hats. Aren't they wonderful? I like that brown one at the front.'

'It would suit you. Are you going to buy it?'

'Oh, no! Look at the price: it's nearly five shillings.'

'I'll buy it for you.'

The offer surprised Lizzie, and it also surprised Jack. He'd made it spontaneously because he was feeling guilty. He knew Lizzie was homeless and he'd encouraged her to come to Brighton; but now she was here he didn't know what was going to happen to her. He couldn't take her home with him. His mother would have a fit if he walked in the front door with a young woman on his arm. The town was full of cheap lodging houses so she would soon find somewhere to stay, and she had her wages in her pocket to keep her going until she found a job, so she wouldn't starve. So why did the idea of abandoning her make him feel so uncomfortable? He realised he'd grown fond of this waif-like girl, and the thought of buying her a present pleased him − even if it did mean his dreams of owning a motor-bike would be pushed farther away.

'You'd buy me that hat?' Lizzie turned to Jack, her eyes glowing. 'You can't.'

'Yes I can – so there. Come on.'

He put his hand under Lizzie's elbow and started to propel her towards the glass door. At that moment Tom Grainger hailed him.

'Hey, Jack! Where are you going? I said we'd give you a lift home. Father will be waiting in Pool Valley with the Bentley. Hurry up.'

Jack saw Lizzie's downcast face. She was trying hard not to show her disappointment, but going with Tom and his father would save him a long trek home.

'It's all right,' Lizzie said bravely. 'You go with Tom – I don't need a hat anyway.'

'Yes you do.' Jack felt in his pocket and produced two half-crowns. He pressed them into Lizzie's hand. 'There's the money – go in and buy it.'

'Oh, Jack …'

'And don't thank me,' Jack said fiercely. He turned away and then stopped as an idea came to him. 'Listen, my auntie runs a boarding house near the railway station. Her name's Mrs Manville and she lives at number eighteen Terminus Road. Tell her I sent you.'

Tom called him again. He turned quickly and ran after his friend, leaving Lizzie standing in the shop doorway; her bag holding all her worldly possessions dangled from one hand and the money he'd just given her was clutched in the other. She felt terribly alone as they disappeared around the corner. Jenny and the other girls had also gone, waving cheerfully and shouting that they'd see her next year. But next year seemed a lifetime away: the next twenty-four hours were more important.

Lizzie looked at the coins in her palm and then at the wonderful hat. It was generous of Jack, but perhaps she shouldn't spend his money on luxuries. After all, five shillings might be enough to pay for a night's lodging.

'Out of my way, girl!'

A large figure loomed in front of Lizzie. It was a middle-aged woman wearing a tweed suit and a Postillion hat. Her face was red with impatience, and around her shoulders was draped a fox fur with staring glass eyes.

'I said – get out of my way.'

'I heard you,' Lizzie replied, stepping aside.

'And you needn't be cheeky.' The red-faced woman charged through the glass doors of the store, letting them swing back in Lizzie's face.

'How dare she talk to me like that,' Lizzie said to herself. 'Just because I'm poor and she's rich.' The woman had reminded her of Aunt Hannah, and awakened all her deep-seated feelings of anger and resentment. 'I'm as good as she is any day. I'll show her. I'll go in and buy myself that hat right now.'

Before she could change her mind, Lizzie pushed through the door into the shop. It was even grander inside than she'd expected. Bright lights sparkled on shiny wooden surfaces and glass-topped counters. Dresses fashioned in all the latest styles were draped on models or hanging from rails, made from chiffon, crêpe de Chine, wool, artificial silk and shantung. There were coats and costumes, and beautiful shoes made from real leather. It was a paradise for a sixteen-year-old girl who'd never known the joy of buying anything ready-made.

Even the shop-assistants were better dressed than Lizzie. They were wearing identical dresses made of black silk, and their shoes were also black with high heels. All the assistants, young and old, had short bobbed hair, making Lizzie realise how old fashioned her long plait was. Perhaps Betty had been sensible when she'd suggested cutting it off.

'Did you want something?'

One of the senior staff, a tall thin woman with greying hair, had come forward. She looked at Lizzie as if she'd just found her under a stone.

'I want a hat.'

'We only sell model hats. I suggest you try the market – or Vokins has an end of season sale.'

'I want to buy one of your hats,' Lizzie said firmly. She wasn't going to be browbeaten by this unfriendly woman. She had just as much right to good service as the rude woman with the fox fur. 'I have the money.' She opened her palm to reveal the two silvery coins.

The senior assistant beckoned to a girl who was not much older than Lizzie. She was busy arranging a coat with a fur collar on a model; around her neck dangled a tape-measure and there were rows of pins stuck in the bodice of her black dress.

'Miss Smith, show this person the way to the millinery department.'

'Yes, Mrs Parsons,' Miss Smith whispered nervously. 'Follow me.'

They walked through the haberdashery and lingerie departments until they came to a long narrow room overlooking the busy main road. Down one side were polished wooden counters holding the hat stands. Each stand was covered by a piece of veiling with the head-piece arranged on top, in front of a backdrop of grey satin and an arrangement of flowers and feathers. On the other side were a number of dressing-tables, with stools padded with striped silk for the customers to sit on while they tried on the merchandise. In the window was a large settee capable of seating at least four waiting customers.

A handsome woman of about thirty was putting the final touches to a frivolous affair made of white straw and decorated with one big red rose.

'That's Miss Turner – the milliner,' Miss Smith whispered, and disappeared quickly as if she was afraid of being reprimanded.

Miss Turner glanced over her shoulder at Lizzie, taking in her shabby appearance. 'Sorry, dear,' she said. 'I don't need any more assistants. I have a new girl starting on Monday.'

'I haven't come about a job. I want to buy a hat.'

Miss Turner put down the piece of white ribbon she'd been thinking of pinning to the side of the white straw and stared at Lizzie. Then she laughed. 'But we don't stock the sort of hats working girls want. Our hats are unique.'

'That's why I want one of them,' Lizzie said firmly. 'The brown velvet one in the front of the window, with the yellow ribbon.'

'I can't disarrange a window display.' Miss Turner turned back to the straw hat and adjusted the stand slightly to get a better angle.

'Why not?'

'Because …' The milliner was temporarily lost for words. She couldn't tell this girl the truth: that it was too much bother or that Lizzie wasn't a valued customer. She starred at Lizzie and Lizzie stared back. Lizzie intended to have the hat now more than ever.

'It's four and eleven pence, three farthings,' she said. 'Here are five shillings. Please get the hat out of the window for me.'

Miss Turner knew when she was beaten. After all, she'd been trained to believe that the customer was always right, even when they were a child in an old cotton dress. She snorted her disapproval but complied with the command.

Left alone Lizzie hugged herself with glee. She'd won: she'd asserted herself and she was going to be the proud owner of a beautiful hat. In the meantime she had the run of the millinery department, and Lizzie was never one to waste time.

She sat herself down on a stool in front of one of the mirrors and surveyed herself, laughing out loud at what she saw reflected there. No wonder Miss Turner hadn't wanted to serve her. She looked like a gypsy. Her hair and eyes were so dark, and her skin quite weatherbeaten by its recent exposure to the sun. The mauve dress was not only faded, it was also grubby, and her nails were broken and stained purple with fruit juice. Even so, Lizzie held herself proudly, and when she lifted the straw hat with the nodding rose and balanced it on her head she had the poise of a queen.

After the straw she tried on a round pill-box with a tall feather and made a face at her reflection; but when the milliner returned carrying the velvet hat she was sitting demurely with a sweet smile on her face.

It was even lovelier than she'd expected: the smooth surface of the velvet and the silky sheen of the ribbon felt so good under her workworn fingers. Miss Turner placed it firmly on the top of Lizzie's head and their eyes met in the looking-glass. Lizzie smiled, put up her hands and rearranged it so that it sat jauntily with the brim tipped over one eye. She shook her head and the yellow ribbon danced cheekily. When she looked again at Miss Turner she saw that her grim face had softened slightly. She was smiling as if she was remembering what it was like to be sixteen and buying a new hat for the first time.

'Thank you,' Lizzie said, and they exchanged glances as if they shared a secret. 'I'll take it.'

'I'll pack it for you.'

'No.' Lizzie put up a protective hand to her head. 'I'll wear it.'

She handed over the money and headed for the door. The hat made her feel quite different; her spirits rose and she was full of confidence. After all, she'd not done so badly. She was in her dream town of Brighton; she had money in her pocket and a new hat; now all she had to do was find somewhere to live. After that she would be able to start making her fortune so that she could rescue Billy from Aunt Hannah's clutches. Her fingers touched the silver coin hanging round her neck: her silver joey, her lucky charm would protect her and see her through.

Outside in the busy street Lizzie paused. Everything

seemed to be going at such a speed: people hurrying about their business and cars honking impatiently. Suddenly she was scared. She was in a strange town and didn't know her way about.

It was a long time since she'd eaten so she bought herself a pie and a bottle of lemonade and sat down on a park bench in some public gardens to eat. Through the trees she could just see the greenish domes of the Pavilion silhouetted against the sky. Then she wandered through the town, following the flow of sightseers until she found herself in a mysterious warren of alleyways with cobbled walls and poky shops. Lizzie didn't know it but she was in the oldest part of the town, where in days gone by fishermen and smugglers had followed their trades – the ancient Lanes.

A second-hand bookshop attracted her attention. She stopped to look through the worn covered volumes stacked on a folding table outside. She picked up a green and black book priced at two-pence and glanced through it. At Railway Cottage they'd only had a few books and Lizzie had read them all. She loved reading, but had no way of comparing whether a story was good or bad. Excitement attracted her: a tale that would take her on a journey to a new life where the heroine would find romance in the arms of a handsome stranger.

The book she'd chanced on sounded just what she liked. It was called *Love goes Travelling* by Sylvia Sark, and was all about a girl called Opal who becomes a sort of companion to a rich widow who takes her on a romantic holiday to the South of France.

Lizzie read the first two pages. She was just going to turn the page over when she saw a man's face peering at her over a pile of encyclopaedias in the dusty window. If she wanted to find out what happened to Opal she'd have to buy the book.

A bell jangled as she pushed the shop door open. The musty smell of old leather and rotting paper made her screw up her face. The shopkeeper was old and bent, but he looked friendlier now that Lizzie had become a customer. He rubbed the book on his shiny sleeve and peered shortsightedly at the title.

'If you like love stories,' he leered, 'I've got better ones downstairs in the basement.' He cackled evilly. 'Would you like to see them, my dear?'

'No, thank you,' Lizzie said firmly. She passed over two pennies and hurried out of the shop. She'd planned to ask the bookseller to give her directions to the address in Terminus Road where Jack's aunt lived, but she thought a policeman or even a passer-by would be better than the horrible old shopkeeper.

In the end a paper boy told her the way. He was standing on the corner of Duke Street with a pile of *Evening Arguses* under his arm. He couldn't have been much more than ten years old, with a smooth round face and curly black hair tucked away under a greasy man's cap, but he looked friendly. The way he called out 'Argis – evening piper – only a penny', reminded Lizzie of her brother Billy.

She bought a paper to be polite and then made her enquiry. 'Can you tell me the way to Terminus Road please?'

"Course I can.' The boy dropped Lizzie's penny into his pocket and then wiped his nose on his sleeve cheerfully. 'See that tall thing in the middle of the road? That's called the Clock Tower. Go past there, and then keep on going until you come to the railway station. Terminus Road is up the side – you can't miss it.'

'Thanks.' Lizzie started walking, her spirits rising now that she knew where she was going.

This must have been the way she'd walked with Mum and Dad when she was little. She'd carried a bucket with clowns painted on the side, and they'd sung 'Oh, I do like to be beside the seaside'. Today she was carrying all her worldly belongings in one hand: a change of clothes, a cardboard box, and a cheap novel about a girl who'd dreamed of the good life.

When she was small the road had seemed to be a wide bright highway, but today it was disappointing. It was dirty, with discarded fish and chip papers and other rubbish blowing about, and there was a man without legs, who looked like an old soldier, sitting in a shop doorway begging. Lizzie dropped a half-penny into his cap and he shouted abuse instead of thanks. Even the frontage of the station was different: the glass and iron structure was dull with grime and the droppings of a thousand birds.

But if Lizzie was disappointed there were some who weren't. As she passed, a hundred or so children burst out of the main entrance shrieking with excitement.

'Mum, I've won a coconut,' one small boy shouted.

'And I've got a jam-dish.'

'Bertie, come here.' A young woman standing near Lizzie grabbed the two boys by the scruff of their necks and proceeded to cuff them in a friendly fashion.

'Give over, Jimmy,' she said, grinning at Lizzie. 'They've been to Hassocks for a day's outing. The Corporation Tramways gives them a treat every year. They put on special trains just for our kids, and they give 'em a real good time. Come on now do – there's kippers for your tea.'

'I were sick,' the child with the jam-dish announced as he followed his mother, but he looked cheerful enough. 'It was a right big blow out they gave us.'

Lizzie had to wait until the crowd of excited children had passed, and then she walked across the forecourt and looked about her. As the news-boy had said, there was a road running up the side, a narrow road that climbed the steep hill and curved away round a bend. On the wall over a working man's café was a plate saying that it was Terminus Road.

The fronts of the houses Lizzie passed were dirty with years of grime, and every time a train steamed into the station a cloud of vapour enveloped the chimneys. It must be a noisy place to live, was Lizzie's first thought.

Number eighteen was easy to find and it was reassuringly smart compared to its neighbours. The front door opened directly on to the pavement, but it was freshly painted in a dark shade of green. The step looked as if it was whitened regularly and the brass shone with elbow-grease. There were starched nets draped across the small front window, and an aspidistra in a china pot on the sill. A printed card in the window said 'Bed & Breakfast' and underneath 'Vacancies'.

With rising spirits Lizzie rapped on the door using the brass knocker in the shape of a grinning gnome. It was opened by a smiling woman in her forties, her brown hair trapped in a net, and her ample shape enveloped in a large white pinafore. The sleeves of her frock were rolled to the elbows, and her hands and forearms were covered with flour. She clapped them together and laughed as a white cloud rose about her.

'You caught me in the middle of baking,' she said. 'Just rolling out the pastry for an apple pie. What can I do for you, my dear?'

'Are you Mrs Manville?' Lizzie asked, immediately liking the homely woman.

'Julia Manville? Yes, I am.'

'Jack French gave me your address. I met him when we were picking plums.'

'Grace's boy Jack. He picks every year, on top of his job at Staggs.'

'Staggs?'

'Didn't he tell you? He works for George Stagg the greengrocer, t'other side of the Dials. He's saving up to buy a motor-bike so he told me the last time I seen him. But he keeps wasting his money on other things.'

'I know.' Lizzie tapped her head to make sure the brown velvet arrangement was still there. 'He paid for this hat.'

'Well now, that's just the sort of thing Jack would do. It

suits you, my dear. Now what exactly can I do for you?'

'I need a room for a couple of nights; just till I find somewhere permanent. I can pay.'

'I'm sure you can. Come inside and join me in a cup of tea while I think about it.'

In the cosy kitchen, where a white cat was curled on a settee and a tabby cat slept on the mat, Mrs Manville cleared a place at the deal table and poured tea into two thick white cups.

'Get that inside you while I have a word with Sam,' she said, and left the room.

Left alone Lizzie looked around her. Her lucky joey must be working. This would be a lovely place to live while she looked around for a job of work. She liked Julia Manville: the friendly woman reminded her of her mother before she was taken ill. All in all Lizzie felt she'd fallen on her feet, thanks to Jack French. But when Mrs Manville re-entered the room she could see by her face that there was a problem.

'It's like this,' the landlady explained, clearing away the tea-things before Lizzie had finished, and picking up her rolling pin as if she was anxious to get back to her baking. 'I thought Sam in the top back was leaving: he said as much only yesterday. Told me he'd been called back to Manchester by his firm. But it seems he's changed his mind.'

'But you must have other rooms,' Lizzie protested. 'I don't mind how small – and I don't mind sharing.'

'The thing is, the boys from the Salvation Army have all the other rooms. There's some sort of convention at the Congress Hall and they're three to a room. So you see I couldn't squeeze you in even if I wanted to.' She saw Lizzie's disappointed face and her voice softened. 'You know I'd help you if I could, dear: you being a friend of Jack's, but I'm sure you'll find somewhere else if you put your mind to it. Would you like a slice of my home-made cake to take with you …?'

But Lizzie had picked up her bag and was already walking back down the narrow passage towards the front door. She was so disappointed that she could feel tears pricking her eyes. She wasn't going to cry in front of Jack's auntie – not if she could help it.

CHAPTER SEVEN

Hell House

Terminus Street was one of the turnings off Terminus Road and it ended in an alleyway known as Clifton Street Passage. There was a public house on one corner and about ten houses on either side of the road. They were dingy dwelling places housing the poorer occupants of the town, who made their livings by letting rooms for a few shillings a night.

Number ten was the last house on the left-hand side. The front door was splintered at the bottom by the toe-caps of many drunks trying to gain entrance; and the bay windows had sixteen small panes of glass in them, most of them cracked.

Lizzie had tried every other house in the street and been turned away. Although it was nearing the end of the season there were still plenty of visitors looking for cheap lodgings. Trains from Victoria steamed into the terminus every quarter of an hour or so, and on Bank Holidays there was one every five minutes.

After a day's heavy drinking and carousing around the town many were in no condition to board a train back to London and needed somewhere to sleep it off. Railway

Street and its neighbour Terminus Street were only a stone's throw away.

Lizzie was nearly at the end of her tether when she knocked on the door of number ten. It was dirty but it had a name-plate on the wall. 'Hill House' it said, which sounded rather smart, but Lizzie didn't know that the local residents had another name for it. 'Hell House' was its nickname, because of its reputation.

Her heart sank when she was admitted by an untidy skivvy wearing a dress even dirtier than her own. It had once, a long time ago, been pink, but there were dark stains under the arms, and the bottom of the skirt looked as if it had been used in place of a dish-cloth. The apron tied around the skivvy's waist was the dirtiest Lizzie had ever seen. The girl was probably not much older than herself, but the eyes staring at her from under a dingy cap looked old and tired.

'You'd better come in and see Mrs 'ill,' the apparition said in answer to Lizzie's request for a bed.

'Who is it, Aggie?' a booming voice called from somewhere close by.

'Someone after a room,' Aggie yelled back. 'A girl.'

'Let's have a look at her then.'

Lizzie was ushered into the presence of Mrs Hill, who turned out to be as alarming as her house. To start with she was the largest woman Lizzie had ever seen. She was propped up on a sofa in the living room as if she was part of the fixtures and fittings.

Later Lizzie discovered that Mrs Hill was a widow who had turned to food in compensation for losing her husband. The amount she managed to consume in one day would have fed an entire family, and because she never took any exercise it all turned to fat. Great mounts of flesh wobbled bonelessly as Mrs Hill tried to shift her position to look at her visitor.

'Come closer, girl, so I can see you,' she commanded in the same loud voice. Stepping over a heap of rags on the floor that looked like dirty washing, Lizzie moved forward. It was the filthiest room she'd ever been in. There was thick dust on all the surfaces and cobwebs hung like lace from the pictures and gas-mantle. The smell of unwashed flesh, boiled cabbage and other undescribable odours made her stomach turn over. 'Have you run away from home, girl?'

'No,' Lizzie said indignantly. 'I just need a bed for a night or two while I look for work.'

'You look very young. How old are you?'

'Seventeen,' Lizzie lied, thinking an added year might make all the difference. Not that she was all that keen on becoming one of Mrs Hill's lodgers: after seeing the living room she dreaded to think what the bedrooms would be like. But she had to find somewhere to spend the night and tomorrow she could look for something better.

'There's room with the factory girls at the back. Two single beds and a double. But I've squeezed three into the double bed before now.'

'There's Dora's room . . .' Aggie reminded her mistress.

'Shut up, Aggie, and cut me some bread and jam. You're dreaming again.' Mrs Hill shifted her huge bulk into a more comfortable position and regarded her potential tenant. 'There's the upstairs back. The police took Dora away this morning and she owes me a week's rent.'

'How much?' Lizzie didn't like to enquire what Dora had done.

Mrs Hill pondered, wondering how much she dare ask. The girl looked poor, but she must have money in her pocket or she wouldn't be asking the price.

'The factory girls pay one and a tanner a night; but you can call it a shilling to share the double. That's just the bed of course.'

'What about the room?'

Lizzie was watching in alarm as Aggie picked up a half loaf from the sideboard, and holding it against her belly began to carve it into thick doorsteps. She laid these out on the soiled oil-cloth covering the table in front of her mistress, and started to spoon on dollops of jam from a crusted jar. By the time she'd finished there were black fingerprints edging the slices, and Lizzie had spotted her licking her fingers in the process.

Mrs Hill crammed a slice into her mouth before replying. 'Three and six for Dora's room and one and six for breakfast – that's five bob a night. Cheap at the price.'

'I'll take the room,' Lizzie said quickly. 'But I shan't be needing breakfast.'

'Please yourself. Show her up, Aggie, and then I'd like a cup of tea, and some toast if there's any bread left.'

The room was even worse than Lizzie had imagined it would be. The only furniture was an iron bed with a thin flock mattress, a chair with a broken leg, and a cupboard made from an empty orange crate. The wallpaper was peeling in places, and there were water-stains as if the roof leaked every time it rained. Lizzie wouldn't have minded a Spartan existence, but the sight of soiled sheets and a half-full chamber-pot sticking out from under the bed was too much for her.

'Aggie,' she said sternly to the skivvy, who was trying to creep away. 'Who's supposed to keep this room clean?'

'I does – when I got the time,' came the hesitant reply.

'Well, it doesn't look as if it's been touched for ages,' Lizzie scolded. 'Look at the dust.' She ran her finger along the mantelpiece; it came away black. She could have written her name in the dirt if she'd wanted to.

'Dora never complained,' Aggie said sulkily.

'Well, Dora's not here and it's my room now. I want clean sheets, and a pillow-case.' Lizzie pointed to the striped ticking. 'And please would you empty that.' She indicated the offensive article under the bed.

Aggie went away grumbling and Lizzie thought it would be the last she'd see of her. Much to her surprise the skivvy returned promptly with a slop pail and some clean sheets. They were rough in texture, unironed and not very white, but at least they were clean.

Between them they stripped the bed and remade it; and while Aggie emptied the slops and swept the floor, Lizzie borrowed a ragged duster and did her bit. By the time they'd finished the room looked much better and Aggie had become quite vocal. She told Lizzie the story of her employer's dead husband, and how the poor woman hadn't been outside the house for years.

'All she does is eat and give me orders,' Aggie complained. 'She's so fat now I don't think she'd be able to get through the door if she tried.'

'Can she walk?'

'Walk!' Aggie let out a shriek of laughter. 'Waddles more like it. Round the room's as far as she goes. She kips on that sofa: couldn't get up the stairs to bed even if she wanted to. I does everything for 'er. She'd be lorst without me,' she added proudly.

While the girl was talking Lizzie thought she heard an unusual noise. It seemed to be coming through the wall from the next room. It sounded like a cry, or it might have been a moan, she couldn't decide which.

'Did you hear that, Aggie?'

'What?'

'It sounded like someone crying next door. Is there a baby in there?'

'Mrs 'ill don't allow no babies in the house,' Aggie said. 'That's Willy.'

'Willy?'

''E belongs to Rose. She'll be in presently no doubt. I expect you'll hear 'er.' Without further explanation Aggie departed.

Left to herself Lizzie chose to go to bed: she was tired out with the day's traumas. She didn't unpack her things because she didn't intend staying in this awful place, but before getting into bed she placed the brown velvet hat where she could see it. Just looking at it cheered her up, and she dropped off to sleep with a smile on her face.

It was the noise that woke Lizzie a few hours later. Shouts, laughter, and that moaning sound again. She sat up in alarm. For a minute she thought that she was back in the hut at Gates Farm and the noise was the fruit-pickers getting ready for work. Then a door slammed somewhere close by and memory came flooding back: she was in Brighton, at number ten Terminus Street.

Now wide awake, Lizzie leaned back against the hard pillow and took stock of things. It must be the middle of the night because the room was still dark although there were no curtains at the window.

Her skin itched and felt lumpy. For a dreadful moment Lizzie wondered whether the house was infested with bugs; she'd heard that they came out at night. After investigating she decided they were only heat-bumps and relaxed. Perhaps if she opened the window and let in some air she'd cool down. That was easier said than done. The window hadn't been opened for years and the sash-cords were broken; she couldn't budge it an inch.

Determined to make the best of things Lizzie returned to her bed – and then the noises started through the wall.

First the moaning started again, only this time it was more like a wail, and then a man's voice shouted, 'Shut up, you!'

'Don't talk to him like that,' a woman's voice said in lower tones. 'He can't help it.'

'I'll give 'im "can't 'elp it". He can shut up, or else.'

'Or else what?'

'I goes.'

'Go then. It's all the same to me.'

'Don't say that, Rosie.' Now the man's voice was wheedling. 'Come 'ere.'

'Why?'

'You knows why. Oh god, Rosie!'

The woman called Rosie started laughing and Lizzie could only guess what was going on on the other side of the thin wall. She closed her eyes tightly and willed herself to sleep, but then she heard clearly the creak of bedsprings and throaty protestations of passion. Her eyes flew open again.

'Oh – Rosie!'

'Get off – you're hurting me.'

'You like being hurt.'

'No I don't, you brute.' But the tone of the woman's voice sounded as if she didn't mind all that much, and the way she said 'brute' was teasing rather than angry.

The passionate exchanges seemed to go on for hours, but eventually even the lovers tired and the house became quiet again. At last Lizzie managed to drift back to sleep.

When she woke it was morning and someone was banging on the door of her room.

She sat up in bed, rubbing the sleep out of her eyes. 'Come in,' she called.

The door opened and Lizzie stared wide-eyed at the apparition standing in the doorway. It was a woman, not particularly old or young, neither beautiful nor ugly, but to Lizzie the most strikingly handsome person she'd ever set eyes on. She was tall with a shapely figure, wearing a silky white nightgown that clung revealingly to her body like a second skin, and with a fringed shawl decorated with multi-coloured embroidery thrown carelessly around her bare shoulders. Her face was long, with a generously broad mouth and wide blue eyes, and to top it all a head of wild red curly hair. The hair was so brilliant that it couldn't have been as nature intended.

'Hullo,' the woman said cheerfully, adjusting the trailing end of her shawl and smiling at Lizzie's obvious alarm. 'I live in the room next door. My name's Rose Harrison.'

'I'm Lizzie Sargent. I only arrived yesterday.'

'I know. Aggie told me. Would you like some breakfast?'

Lizzie thought of the dirty room downstairs and the bread bordered with black fingerprints. She shuddered and said quickly, 'No, thank you. I'm not hungry.'

Rose threw back her head so that her red curls danced, and laughed the deep throaty laugh Lizzie had heard through the wall. 'Not Mother Hill's breakfast – mine. I cook it in my room. Come next door when you're dressed. Don't knock – Willy makes such a noise in the mornings I wouldn't hear you.'

She left as abruptly as she'd appeared, leaving Lizzie to get up and dress. There was nowhere to wash so she had no alternative but to put her old cotton frock back on and replait her hair. She was reassured by the fact that her neighbour was clean and her hands looked well cared for, although her nails were painted bright orange. Any food Rose prepared would at least be safe to eat, and Lizzie suddenly realised that she was hungry. The last time she'd eaten was the previous afternoon when she'd stopped to buy a pie and a bottle of lemonade.

The groans and cries started again as she turned the handle of her neighbour's door; and added to it came bangs and rattlings that reminded Lizzie of the noise a wild animal would make if it tried to escape from a trap. If the noises were being made by the person called Willy, Lizzie wasn't at all sure that she wanted to meet him. But Rose had seemed friendly enough so she turned the handle and stepped inside before she could change her mind.

Lizzie didn't know what she expected to see, but even so she was agreeably surprised. Rose's room was larger than her own, but that wasn't the only difference. It was also like a palace compared to the other rooms she'd seen in Mrs Hill's lodging house.

To start with there were curtains at the window and a carpet in the middle of the floor. There was a horse-hair sofa covered in gold brocade and two armchairs, a bamboo plant stand, a fumed oak table covered with a white cloth, and a large brass bedstead, still unmade, but with spotless bed-linen. Lizzie noticed that the twin pillows had dents in them, but there was no sign of the other occupant of the bed.

Rose was standing by the bed clad only in peach coloured cami-knickers and a silk brassiere. She was pulling over her head a dress of flowered chiffon. She wriggled her bottom and smoothed the thin material down over her hips, slipped her narrow feet into high-heeled shoes, and turned to smile at Lizzie.

'There's porridge in the saucepan,' she said, indicating a steaming pan standing on a small paraffin stove in the corner. 'And tea in the pot. Help yourself. But first you'd better say hullo to Willy. Willy, this is Lizzie – she's a new friend.'

For the first time Lizzie noticed the cot in the corner of the room. It was shaped like the sort of crib a baby would sleep in but it was much larger, with metal bars down the side and a rubber covered mattress in the bottom.

But the occupant wasn't a baby; in fact Lizzie backed away fearfully because she wasn't even sure it was human. Willy, for that was the creature's name, was sitting crouched on the mattress hugging a rag doll. He was the size of a small adult, with twisted limbs and a humped misshapen back. His head was almost bald, and his features were twisted and malevolent. Small eyes sunk into veined flesh stared at Lizzie. He had almost non-existent lips that barely covered his uneven teeth, and his nose was flat and running with mucus. Naked apart from a nappy, he was tethered to the bars by a sort of harness made from strips of coarse linen. This primitive contraption prevented Willy from moving more than a few inches in any direction. At the sight of Lizzie he moaned and began to rattle the bars of his prison.

'That's enough, Willy,' Rose said calmly. 'What will Lizzie think of you?'

Lizzie didn't know what to think. Rose was surprise enough: the way she'd introduced the horror in the corner so casually, and the smartness of herself and her surroundings.

As Lizzie watched, Rose filled a bowl with porridge and began to spoonfeed Willy tenderly; then she wiped his face clean with a flannel. During her ministrations he continued to dribble and grimace like a wild thing. Only when Willy had been fed did Rose fill her own bowl, so Lizzie waited and they ate together.

Sprinkled with sugar the porridge tasted good and was filling, and the tea was strong, just the way Lizzie liked it. When they'd finished she looked around curiously: there were so many questions she wanted to ask but didn't know where to start.

'Your room's lovely,' she said at last. 'Does Mrs Hill charge you a lot?'

Rose smiled lazily, fished out a packet of cigarettes and lit one before answering. 'I pay the same as everyone else. Oh, when I moved in two years ago it was as bad as all the other rooms, but I wasn't going to have Willy living in a slum. So I bought furniture bit by bit, second-hand of course; but the bed-linen was new. I keep the room clean myself, but I pay Aggie to take the washing to the laundry. She's a good soul, but not very bright.'

'You must be rich,' Lizzie said enviously. How else could Rose afford such luxuries, but why then did she choose to live in Hill House?

'I started with nothing,' Rose admitted. 'But I had to earn money to care for Willy. He's my son, my darling, aren't you, Willy?' She bent over the cot and planted a kiss on the monster's puffy cheek. Willy stretched out a crooked hand and grabbed a handful of his mother's hair, yanking it cruelly. 'Let go – you're hurting me.' Rose smiled and pulled his fingers open, freeing herself. 'I'm so lucky,' she said softly.

'Lucky!'

Lizzie couldn't imagine how anybody could consider themselves lucky to have someone like Willy for a son. And yet Rose looked as if she meant it. How old was Willy? Lizzie wondered: fifteen – perhaps twenty. And yet

Rose had to care for him as if he was a baby, and her eyes were full of maternal pride.

'Yes – lucky. I'd been alone all my life, and down on my luck; and then I met Willy's father and fell in love. He was a grand man: so handsome. I thought the baby I was carrying would be like him. I dreamed of a wedding, and a little house for the three of us, but it was all dreams.' Rose's voice was soft with memories.

'What happened?'

'When I told him I was pregnant he went away; I never saw him again. So I sat down and thought things through. I wasn't going to get the husband or the house, but he'd given me the next best thing: a baby to remind me of him. Of course I didn't know then that Willy was going to be different.'

'Go on.'

'Some people said it was a judgment. That God had made Willy like he is because his father and I weren't married; a warning to other girls. But I didn't see it like that.' Rose drew on her cigarette and blew a smoke-ring in Willy's direction. He put out a hand to snatch it but it floated past. He gibbered angrily. 'If he'd been like other children he'd have grown up and left me by now – he's eighteen you see. His father left me, but Willy can never leave. We're together for life and I'm never lonely now. Would you like some more tea?'

Lizzie held out her empty cup. 'You must have a good job,' she said, 'to be able to afford all this.'

Rose laughed. 'I work hard, if that's what you mean.'

'I need a job. I've earned some money picking fruit, but that isn't going to last me long.' Lizzie looked down at her shabby frock and compared it to Rose's pretty chiffon. 'I suppose you don't know of any work I could do?'

Rose looked her up and down and shook her head. 'How old are you?'

'Sixteen.'

'Just a kid,' Rose said softly. 'Are you trained for anything?'

'Not really. I worked in someone's kitchen for a while before I picked fruit. That's all ...' she ended lamely.

Rose frowned. 'You're never going to get anywhere looking like that,' she said.

'I know. I've got a skirt and a jacket packed away, but they're too hot to wear.'

'Perhaps I could spare you something.' Rose stubbed out her cigarette and crossed to a tall cupboard set in an alcove. When she swung the door open Lizzie saw that it was full of the most beautiful clothes: dresses in bright colours, coats with fur collars and silk linings, costumes, skirts and blouses in all manner of designs and fabrics. She rifled through them and selected a dress which she held out to Lizzie. It was made of cream linen, with a square cut yoke fastened by two big brown buttons, and a fashionable tie belt. 'Try this on. You're thinner than me, but it should fit you.'

Lizzie took the dress in her hands and stroked the smooth material. It would look perfect with her new brown velvet hat. 'I might soil it,' she said. 'I haven't washed yet.'

Rose laughed. 'What did you expect – a chambermaid? You have to carry your own water up from the scullery. Aggie should have told you. I always keep a full jug on the washstand. Help yourself. There's soap and a towel as well.'

Lizzie hesitated only for a minute and then she slipped off her dress and washed herself. The water was cold, but the soap was pink and smelled of flowers. She saw Willy's piggy eyes staring at her as she dried herself. She had no idea how much he was capable of taking in; but his mother had stood before him clad only in her underwear so he must be used to it.

Even so she felt embarrassed, and was pleased to step into the cream frock and feel its softness against her clean skin. It fitted quite well although her bust and hips were smaller than Rose's. The skirt reached to her calf and was slightly flared at the bottom. She spun around on her heel, pleased with herself and the dress.

'How do I look?'

'Lovely,' Rose said approvingly. 'I've never liked it: it's not colourful enough for me.'

'I think it's grand. I feel ever so smart and grown-up. You wait until Jack sees me.'

'Jack?'

'Jack French. He's my friend. He bought me a hat that'll match this frock a treat.' Lizzie's face fell. 'But I don't know if I shall ever see him again.'

'Cheer up, kid,' Rose said gaily. 'Your Jack'll come looking for you, I'll be bound; and if he doesn't there are plenty of other blokes. Brighton is full of them.'

'I suppose so,' Lizzie said, but she felt sad at the thought of never seeing the red-haired youth again. Then she cheered up. 'Anyway, I feel quite different now. Last night I thought nothing nice was ever going to happen to me again – and this morning I've met you, and now I've got a new frock.'

Rose looked her up and down shrewdly. 'There's one thing that needs changing,' she said at last.

'What's that?'

'Your hair.'

Lizzie felt the heavy plait with her hand. 'What's the matter with it?'

'Only little girls wear their hair long nowadays, Lizzie.'

'I could put it up.' Lizzie coiled the plait around her hand and balanced it on the top of her head.

'Why don't you cut it off?'

Lizzie stared at Rose in horror. 'I couldn't do that.'

'Why not? I'll do it for you if you like.'

'I couldn't. I've always had long hair, but thanks for the offer – and for the dress. It's beautiful. I don't know how I can repay you.'

'Easily.' Rose was powdering her nose while she studied her face in the tiny mirror of her compact. 'I've arranged to meet someone this morning and Willy likes company. Aggie usually keeps an eye on him for me, but she's not here today. He won't be any trouble.'

'But ...' Lizzie glanced at the mound of flesh rocking backwards and forwards in the cot. Her skin crawled at the idea of being left alone with him. 'I wouldn't know what to do,' she said lamely.

'You won't have to do anything. He's quite contented as long as you don't take his dolly away from him, and there's soup if he seems hungry. You could read a book or do some knitting; he's not demanding, are you, Willy?'

'How long will you be?'

'A couple of hours, I should think. What do you say?'

What could Lizzie say but yes. She watched in trepidation as Rose painted her lips bright orange to match her nails, and balanced a straw hat coquettishly over one eye. 'Be a good boy now,' she said to Willy, and leaned over the cot to kiss his cheek. He grunted and moaned and rattled the bars in protest but his mother hurried out of the room without looking back. Lizzie heard the tapping of her heels on the stairs. Then the house was silent – she was alone with Willy.

Lizzie's first instinct was to run away; particularly when her charge began to rock his cot so violently that she thought he would wreck it or tip it over.

'Stop that!' she said bravely, in the sort of voice she used to use to her little brother when he was being naughty. 'If you stay quiet I'll read to you.'

There didn't seem to be any books in the room, so Lizzie fetched her copy of *Love goes Travelling* and settled in a chair as near to the door as she could. She turned the pages until she found the place where the bookseller had interrupted her the day before, and then continued Opal's story.

Opal, it appeared, worked in a beauty parlour in Bond

Street, earning a meagre living by pandering to the
whims of the wealthy. Her boyfriend Jimmy doesn't
approve of the new life she discovers when she's whisked
away to France by a wealthy widow and starts to mix
with princes and countesses. Breathlessly Lizzie turned
the pages, forgetting Willy in the excitement of the tale.
Does Opal marry the prince, or does she return to her old
love? Feverishly Lizzie turned to the last page. She was
quite disappointed to find that Opal didn't marry the
prince.

'I would have done,' she muttered to herself. 'All
Jimmy could give her was love in a cottage, when she
wanted jewels and a fine life-style.'

Disappointed, Lizzie flung down the book. Willy started up his wailing again now that her voice had ceased.

'What's the matter?' she asked. 'Don't tell me you were
listening to the story?' Crossly Willy dropped his doll over
the side of the cot, and then he began to cry real tears. 'I
do believe you were listening,' Lizzie said as she handed
the toy back. 'I know: I'll tell you Billy's favourite story.
Billy's my little brother. He likes the Hans Christian
Andersen story about the steadfast tin soldier.'

She couldn't remember it all so she just told him the
bits she could recall. When she got to the bit where the
two little boys make a boat out of old newspaper and
send the tin-soldier sailing down the flooded gutter she
realised that Willy was sitting motionless. When she
stopped mid-sentence he clapped his hands together, and
his misshapen mouth stretched into the semblance of a
smile.

'You do understand, don't you, Willy?' Lizzie marvelled
as she lost her fear of Rose's son, and stood by the cot
looking down at the tragic figure.

After that the time passed quickly and she found she
could understand some of Willy's gestures. When he was
pleased he clapped his hands together, and when he was
sad or wanted something he started the endless moaning

and wailing noises Lizzie had first heard through the wall. When he was angry he took it out on the rag doll, tearing at it with his hands or throwing it on to the floor. But when she returned it to him he hugged it to his chest and crooned. When he began to suck his fists Lizzie made a guess at what he wanted.

'You're hungry, aren't you?' she said. 'Your mother left you some soup. Be good while I heat it up for you.'

Spooning the soup into Willy's lopsided mouth was easier than Lizzie had imagined it would be. When the bowl was empty she leaned over to wipe his face. Her close proximity seemed to excite him. He put out his hand and grabbed at the plait of hair hanging over her shoulder, pulling it cruelly.

'Let go, Willy,' she begged. 'You're hurting me.'

But he was stronger than she'd imagined. When Rose returned she found the two of them locked together by the braid of hair. Lizzie was laughing, and Willy was babbling contentedly.

'You see,' Rose said, taking off her hat and shaking out her red curls. 'He likes you – I knew you'd get on.'

'I like him too,' Lizzie admitted. 'But I've made up my mind about one thing – I want you to cut my hair off after all.'

CHAPTER EIGHT

Seventeen

The weather gradually broke down and the glorious summer slowly turned to a bleak autumn. The worst weather that Brighton remembered came on the second day of November. Luckily it was a Sunday. so not too many people were abroad. Mid-morning a violent storm raged along the coast, bringing with it torrential rain and strong winds. Gutters overflowed, roads were flooded, shop windows blew in and slates were toppled from roof tops.

Terminus Street wasn't too badly hit. A gate was blown from its hinges and landed up in the middle of the main road and one house lost a chimney stack. Lizzie watched helplessly as the water trickled down the wall of her room from the leaking roof.

By the evening the storm was over and everything was still. The mopping-up operations would start tomorrow, but tonight Lizzie slept soundly. She'd forgotten that the following day was important.

'Happy birthday to you. Happy birthday, dear Lizzie. Happy birthday to you.'

The singing coming from the landing outside her door

woke Lizzie and she sat up with a start. She smiled as she recognised Rose's voice. Pulling on a cardigan over her nightgown she slipped out of bed. Now she remembered: it was November the third, her seventeenth birthday.

'Come in,' she called.

Rose didn't need asking twice. She flung open the door and stood there draped in her colourful shawl, her bright hair tumbling down over her shoulders. In her hands she carried a large parcel wrapped in brown paper. She held it out to Lizzie with a beaming smile.

'Happy birthday.'

'For me?'

'Of course. From Willy and me.'

'What is it?'

Rose laughed. 'Why don't you open it and see.'

Excitedly Lizzie loosened the string and pulled off the wrappings. Inside was a full-length coat made of brown cloth, and a pair of matching shoes with small heels. 'I hope they fit. I didn't know your size so I had to guess.'

'They're perfect.' Lizzie slipped her bare feet into the shoes and looked down admiringly. 'Oh, Rose, you are kind. They're just what I needed; and the coat too. You must have spent a fortune.'

'I thought you deserved something smart for your interview. What time do you have to be there?'

'Three o'clock.' Lizzie put on the coat and fastened the buttons. 'It's a perfect fit.'

'You've filled out a bit since I've been keeping an eye on you,' Rose said, looking Lizzie up and down with a contemplative eye. 'But you're a bit pale – are you feeling all right?'

'I'm fine,' Lizzie said brightly. 'How do I look?'

'You need a hat.'

'My brown velvet.'

'Perfect. And stockings.'

Lizzie's face fell. 'I haven't any without holes.'

'I'll lend you a pair.'

'What about my hair?'

Lizzie put a hand up to her shorn head. She still couldn't get used to losing her long plait. Rose had cut it off for her at her request, and although she wasn't a proper hairdresser she'd made quite a good job of it. It now fell to just above Lizzie's shoulders, and the ends had a natural curl so that it framed her face. But she would never forget the feeling that overcame her when the scissors snipped and she saw the first lock of hair fall to the ground.

'Your hair's another present,' Rose said gaily. 'My hairdresser's going to shape it for you, and give you a shampoo and set. It's all arranged.'

'You are kind.'

Lizzie had never been inside a hairdressing salon and the idea was quite frightening.

'Don't look so scared,' Rose laughed. 'They won't eat you. Remember that you're the customer and they have to do as you say. Now get dressed and come next door. I'm going to give you breakfast.'

'I'm not really hungry,' Lizzie admitted.

'You will be when you see what I've got for you. Bacon and eggs because it's your birthday. Don't be long or it'll spoil.' And Rose was gone as quickly as she'd come.

Lizzie made her bed, and then laid out the new coat and shoes where she could admire them. The shoes had felt a bit tight but she hoped that they'd stretch with wear. She washed quickly in the cold water she carried up every night from the tap in the scullery, and then put on the cream linen frock with the big buttons. She touched the silver joey hanging around her neck on its thin string and closed her eyes as if she was praying.

'I need some extra luck today,' she said softly. 'It would be wonderful if I got that job at Burroughs in the cosmetics department. I'd be like that girl Opal in the love story. I'd be selling lipsticks and powder, and who knows if some rich widow might take a liking to me and whisk me away to somewhere romantic.'

Lizzie laughed at her imaginings and opened her eyes. At least her new clothes would give her a chance, thanks to Rose's generosity. She tied the belt on the dress. Rose was right, she had put on weight. The dress had been quite loose when she'd been given it two months before, but now it fitted perfectly.

And how things had changed in those eight weeks, and it was all due to Rose and Willy. It had been a shocking revelation when she'd discovered how her friend managed to support herself and her son so well. But Rose had explained that it was the only way she knew of making money.

'I'm not any good at anything else,' she'd explained light-heartedly. 'But I like men, I like my body, and I like making love. If it earns me a living at the same time I can't see the harm in it.'

'But don't you want to get married and have …?' Lizzie had stopped, not wanting to upset her friend, but Rose had only laughed.

'Have babies? I've got one already, why should I need others? Willy will be my baby for ever and ever.'

'But a husband would support you.'

'Not as well as I can support myself. No, thank you. I've got the best of both worlds.'

And she did seem to have. Most nights, and sometimes in the daytime, Rose would bring home her menfriends, and Lizzie would have to listen to the things that went on on the other side of the wall. But the men were always gone by daylight, leaving Rose with twinkling eyes and money in her hand. And she was generous. It wasn't long before Lizzie was helping to care for Willy, and keep him company when his mother was out and Aggie wasn't available. In return Rose brought her treats and slipped her money when she was short with the rent. Lizzie was grateful, but she didn't want to stay in Terminus Street for ever. The vacancy for a shop assistant at Burroughs would be a step in the right direction.

When she was ready Lizzie knocked on Rose's door. The smell of bacon frying hit her as she entered the room. Usually she would have found it delicious but today her stomach turned over.

Rose looked up from her cooking and smiled. 'Nearly ready.'

'I'm really not very hungry.'

'Nonsense.' Rose thought Lizzie was being polite. 'It's your birthday and I bought it specially. Would you give Willy his bread and milk while I fry some bread.'

Lizzie picked up the bowl and spoon and crossed to the cot. Willy was playing happily with his doll. Now that the weather was cooler he was wearing one of the garments his mother had made him. It wasn't easy to find clothes to fit because of his grotesque shape, so she'd compromised by adapting a blue chenille table-cloth. His bald head poked through the hole cut in the material, and the rest covered his deformed limbs adequately and kept him warm.

'Hullo, Willy.' Lizzie sat down on a chair and began to spoon food into his mouth. He ate well and the bowl was empty in no time at all.

'Ready,' Rose called.

She handed Lizzie a plate holding two slices of juicy bacon, an egg, and a thick piece of fried bread dripping with grease. Lizzie took it and began to eat although her stomach rebelled at every mouthful. She managed a small piece of bacon and a mouthful of bread and then felt so sick that she put down the plate and scrambled hastily to her feet. Rose, seeing her white face, rushed for a chamber-pot and held it for her while she retched.

'Sorry,' she said when she was feeling better. 'I must have eaten something yesterday that upset me.'

'Never mind. Drink some tea – it'll help.'

And it did. When it was time to leave for the hairdresser's she was feeling fine. The House of Hyman was in West Street, and offered permanent waving for as little as two guineas a time. From their elegant shop window you could see the sea. Their advertising slogan was 'Hyman's Rules the Waves'.

Rose left Lizzie outside the glass frontage and gave her a little push. 'I'm going down to Alig's in East Street,' she said. 'They serve the most delicious pastries and Swiss chocolate; and the place is always full of exciting foreigners smoking those long thin cigars. I'll be back in time to pay the bill, and then we'll have lunch.'

When Lizzie finally emerged from Hyman's she felt like a different person. To start with she'd been addressed as Madame for the first time, which made her feel very grown-up and important.

The new hairstyle was becoming. A junior had been allowed to shampoo her hair before the leading stylist had cut it into a neat bob. Then it had been set into light waves. While it was drying the manicurist had shaped her nails with an emery board and then buffed them until they shone.

Rose was delighted with Lizzie's transformation. 'That hairstyle really suits you,' she said, linking arms. 'The waves make your face fuller.'

'Do I look older?' Lizzie asked, trying not to look too pleased with her new image.

'I don't know about older – more beautiful certainly.'

Lizzie had the grace to blush. 'Do you think I'll impress them at Burroughs? I do want that job.'

'I know,' Rose laughed, and pulled Lizzie along the road. 'You want to be a beautician like that girl Opal in the book you were telling me about, don't you? Even if you do get the job you'll only be a shop assistant.'

'Well, it's a start.'

'If you're hungry we could have something to eat in Staffords,' Rose said when they reached Western Road. 'They do a three-course lunch for one and six.'

'You mustn't spend any more money on me,' Lizzie

protested. 'Let's buy some doughnuts at Ogdens and eat them as we go along.'

The doughnuts were still warm and Lizzie was scared that she'd drop jam down her new coat, so they sat on a wall to eat. Lizzie took off her velvet hat so that her new hairstyle wouldn't spoil. Then to pass the time they wandered around the big stores admiring the new season's fashions.

They wandered around Boots the Chemists, and admired the Art Deco façade of Wades, but unfortunately the windows were boarded over because the storm of the day before had blown some of the plate glass in. There were plenty of other shops to browse around though. But at five minutes to three Rose left her outside one of the grandest shops in the road: Burroughs of Brighton. She had to walk in and find the manager's office all by herself.

'Good luck,' Rose said, and gave her a hug. 'I'll wait for you outside the Scala cinema.' Then she walked away, her high heels tapping on the pavement – she was soon lost to sight among the crowd.

Lizzie was impressed by the interior of Burroughs. It was so clean, brightly lit and spacious. The young ladies serving behind the counters were so smartly dressed in their white overalls, with B.B. embroidered in blue on their pockets. She would have liked to wander among the customers in their fashionably expensive clothes and inspect the merchandise, but there wasn't time.

She asked one of the assistants for directions to the manager's office and was pointed towards the rear of the shop floor. The office was against the back wall: a long narrow room with a glass window. From this vantage point, Mr Davies, the store manager, could keep an eye on everything that was going on. He was a tall thin man wearing a black suit. Lizzie could see his balding head and pale face bobbing about behind the glass window, while she hesitated, trying to decide whether to knock or wait to be noticed.

She'd been aware of the clatter of typewriter keys, and when they suddenly ceased she heard footsteps approaching from another small office behind the manager's. A middle-aged woman appeared. Her hair was pulled tightly back into a bun and her body was encased in an unattractive tweed costume. She carried a pile of papers in one hand and a note book in the other. She stared curiously at Lizzie.

'Did you want something?'

'I was told to be here at three – for an interview.'

'I'll tell Mr Davies you're here. What's your name?'

'Elizabeth Sargent.'

'Sit down on that chair and wait.'

Lizzie perched herself uncomfortably on the edge of the chair. The woman rapped on the glass window and then entered the manager's office. She could see them talking through the window and guessed that they were discussing her. She smoothed down her coat, and inspected her shoes nervously. Everyone looked so much smarter than she was, and she felt out of place. It was time to take herself in hand.

'You're as good as anyone who works here, Lizzie Sargent,' she told herself sternly. 'And don't forget you've got a lucky joey.' She put up her hand and touched the coin to reassure herself.

When Lizzie was finally admitted into Mr Davies's presence she was calm again.

'Good afternoon, Miss Sargent,' Mr Davies said, rubbing his nose thoughtfully and looking Lizzie up and down. She couldn't read anything into his expression. 'You can stay, Miss Norman.' The woman smiled for the first time and sat down with an open note-pad on her knee. 'Is your mother outside?'

For one crazy moment Lizzie thought the question was directed at Miss Norman. She wanted to laugh when she realised her mistake. 'My mother?'

'Yes. We always like young girls to bring their mothers

with them because we have to ask personal questions.'

'I didn't know.'

'Never mind.' Mr Davies cleared his throat noisily. 'Miss Norman can chaperone you. Now, I hope you live at home because we only employ girls who come from good backgrounds. They have to be honest, reliable, and clean-living.'

Lizzie didn't like the way the interview was progressing. If she admitted that she was an orphan and lived in one squalid room next door to a prostitute they probably wouldn't employ her. Much as she hated doing so she would have to lie.

'I live with my parents,' she said in a low voice. She looked down at her hands, knowing that her face would give her away. 'My mum couldn't come with me because she wasn't feeling well.'

'I'm sorry,' Mr Davies said kindly. 'And what exactly is the matter with her? Nothing serious I hope.'

'No. She just has a headache – a bad one.' Lizzie didn't dare look up, she knew they'd read the falsehood in her eyes.

'You must give her my regards.'

'Oh, I will.'

'Now – your address?'

'Pardon?' Lizzie was playing for time.

'Where do you live?'

'The number of the house, and the street name,' Miss Norman snapped. Her pencil was poised over the pad ready to write.

Lizzie was just about to say number ten Terminus Street but then she thought quickly. What if they knew what a terrible street it was? What if Mrs Hill had a police record as well as her late lodger, Dora? They'd be able to find out all about her. A false address would be better by far. And then she remembered Jack French's auntie and the spotless kitchen in Mrs Manville's house.

Lizzie raised her eyes and looked at her questioners

boldly. 'I live at number eighteen Terminus Road,' she said.

Miss Norman scribbled quickly, and Mr Davies rubbed his nose with a long bony finger. He was trying to frame his next question: the one he had to ask but preferred to voice in front of a young girl's mother.

'And what about your menses, Miss Sargent?' he asked at last; and then cleared his throat noisily.

'Pardon?'

'Your menses – are they regular?'

Puzzled, Lizzie looked from one face to the other. She had no idea what Mr Davies was talking about. He might have been talking to her in a foreign language for all the sense his question made.

Miss Norman had the grace to look embarrassed. She glanced at the manager and then said, 'Mr Davies is asking about your menstruation cycle, the time of the month when you are unwell. Do you have much pain?'

Sick of beating around the bush, Mr Davies added, 'All we need to know, Miss Sargent, is if you would be taking days off every month? We only employ girls with healthy bodies.'

Now Lizzie understood the personal nature of their questioning and her cheeks flushed scarlet. Even her mum had only spoken in a hushed voice about such things. To have her bodily functions discussed by strangers, and one of them a man, was almost more than she could bear.

'I am very well,' she said in a clear voice. 'I won't need to take time off every month.'

The embarrassing question out of the way they all relaxed, and while Mr Davies discussed possible vacancies with Miss Norman, Lizzie had time to think. She couldn't remember the last time she'd been bothered by the monthly bleeding – certainly not since she'd been living in Terminus Street. Life had been so eventful over the last couple of months that she hadn't had time to think about it.

But she'd had an upset stomach, hadn't she? She'd felt sick a couple of times, and only this morning she'd vomited after eating the fried breakfast. She would buy some Beechams Pills, or ask Rose to recommend something, and then she'd be fine again. There was nothing to worry about. Mr Davies was talking, and she pulled her attention back to the matter in hand.

'There is a vacancy on the cosmetic counter, Miss Sargent,' he said. 'Would that suit you?'

'Yes, please. I'd like to be a beautician,' Lizzie said, thinking of Opal.

'You'll only be selling make-up – not applying it. How old are you?'

'Seventeen. It's my birthday today.'

'Then let me be the first to wish you a happy birthday and welcome you to the firm.' He held out his hand and smiled. 'Congratulations.'

'Thank you.' His hand was cold and bony and he held Lizzie's far too long. 'When do I start?'

'Next Monday – nine o'clock sharp. Three months trial. Eighteen and six a week, rising to a pound when you're made a permanent member of staff. Overalls provided; but you're responsible for your own laundry. One shilling in the pound discount on purchases ...'

'Mr Davies,' Miss Norman interrupted. 'What about Miss Leggins?'

'Who?' The manager let go of Lizzie's hand at last. She massaged her fingers.

'Elsie Leggins. You interviewed her earlier. I thought you offered her the job as junior on cosmetics.'

'Did I?' Mr Davies rubbed his nose thoughtfully. 'What else is there, Miss Norman?'

They bent their heads together in consultation, and spoke in such low voices that Lizzie couldn't make out what they were saying. Perhaps they weren't going to offer her a job after all.

She touched her silver joey and whispered, 'Come on,

don't let me down now. I must have a job.'

At last they seemed to come to a decision. Miss Norman closed her note-book with a snap, and Mr Davies smiled. 'How would you like a job in the Fancy Goods department?'

'Where's that?' Lizzie asked, looking puzzled.

'In the basement. It's a department specialising in luxury goods for the home. China, glass, pictures – that sort of thing. It needs a special sort of young lady to work there, because we don't want too many breakages. I hope you're not clumsy, Miss Sargent?'

'I don't think so,' Lizzie said doubtfully. She hoped they didn't stock valuable items of glass and china, because when she was nervous she was inclined to drop things however careful she tried to be.

'How is your mental arithmetic?'

'My what?'

'Can you do sums in your head?' Miss Norman prompted impatiently.

'I think so – why?'

'Because we sell greeting cards in the Fancy Goods department,' Mr Davies explained. 'Many include farthings and half-pennies – so you have to have a quick brain. Miss Norman, set Miss Sargent some sums.'

Miss Norman scribbled rapidly on a sheet of paper and then handed it to Lizzie. She found it quite easy and quickly handed it back. She'd only made one mistake.

'Very good, Miss Sargent,' Mr Davies said. 'I think we can offer you a job. What do you say?'

'Thank you very much,' Lizzie said.

She was pleased although it wasn't the position she'd wanted. But if she hated it she could always leave. They wouldn't be able to trace her because she'd given a false address, so there was no harm done.

The manager shook Lizzie by the hand. 'Welcome to Burroughs of Brighton,' he said heartily. 'You are now a Burroughs' young lady.'

Burroughs' young lady or not, Lizzie was glad to get out of the store and into the fresh air. She could see Rose standing among the crowd of people outside the Scala cinema. She started to run towards her friend, and when Rose saw her face she knew that the news was good.

'You got the job,' Rose shouted and flung her arms around Lizzie, kissing her warmly.

Lizzie nodded. 'Not the one I wanted. Not the one selling make-up to rich ladies.' She struck a pose. 'I'm going to work in the Fancy Goods department.'

'Whatever's that?' Rose looked as puzzled as Lizzie had been.

'China and glass – and greetings cards.'

'How boring. Good luck anyway. When do you start?'

'Next week. Monday.'

'We'd better celebrate.' Rose looked up at the façade of the Scala. 'Let's go to the flicks.'

'What's on?'

'John Barrymore in *General Crack*.'

'All right, but only if you let me pay,' Lizzie insisted. 'I've still got some money left. I might as well spend it because next week I shall be earning a regular wage.'

Lizzie paid for two cheap seats, and treated Rose to a packet of her favourite cigarettes. They entered the dark cinema and groped their way to their seats as there was no sign of an usherette. The film showing was the second feature. It was a comedy called *Hold that Monkey* but Lizzie didn't think it was very funny.

The main picture was more to her taste: the leading man was so handsome. He portrayed a foreign prince called Christian. Made up to look dark and swarthy, John Barrymore was perfect as an aristocrat disguised as a gypsy who swept maidens off their feet. There were battles that Prince Christian always managed to win, stormy relationships, and tearful declarations of eternal love.

Lizzie was bewitched. She wiped her eyes secretly on

her handkerchief when Rose wasn't looking.

And then the film was over, and they filed out of the cinema still in a world of dreams and fantasies.

'That was John Barrymore's first talking picture,' Rose said, taking Lizzie's arm. 'I wonder if his accent was real.'

'I don't know,' Lizzie replied dreamily. 'But I'm not surprised all those beautiful girls fell in love with him.' She suddenly stopped in the middle of the pavement, pulling her companion to a halt. 'I wonder if it was a mistake to take that job?'

'Why?'

'Because I think I'd rather be a film star.'

'You're pretty enough anyway,' Rose said, and they both burst out laughing.

They were still laughing when they found a cheap café and ordered cod and chips and tea. The greasy meal didn't make Lizzie feel queasy at all. She decided that her upset stomach of the morning had recovered, so she didn't bother to mention it to Rose or ask her advice.

When they'd finished Lizzie sat back with a sigh of contentment. 'This is the best birthday I've ever had,' she said.

She was trying not to remember the simpler ones she'd enjoyed at Railway Cottage: when Mum had baked and iced a cake, and they'd blown out the candles and sung around the piano. Last year her parents had given her some ribbons for her hair and Billy had drawn her a picture. She wiped away a tear at the memory.

'It's not over yet.' Rose took her hand and pulled her to her feet. 'Let's go for a walk by the sea. Then I'm taking you dancing.'

'But I can't dance,' Lizzie protested. 'I'll only make a fool of myself.'

'No, you won't. You're graceful and light on your feet. You'll soon pick it up.'

It was dark now and the public houses had just opened. There seemed to be one every few yards, with their doors wide open and light streaming out into the street. The promenade was packed with strolling couples with their arms entwined. Their way was lit by the tall cast-iron lamp-standards with their ornamental mouldings, set over twenty feet apart and lit by electricity. The twin piers stretched out into the dark water, lit by strings of fairy-lights that looked like coloured lace.

Rose wanted to go on the Palace Pier, so they paid their three-pence admission and pushed their way through the turnstile. There was new silver paint coating the rails and central windscreen, and the deck-chairs were folded and heaped in piles along the walkway. They passed the bandstand and the concert hall, and watched people queuing for tickets at the theatre box-office.

'Come on,' Rose said. 'Let's have a go on the slot machines.'

They raced miniature cars, watched ghosts pop up from behind gravestones, and made a fat sailor in a glass case laugh; then Lizzie used her last penny to have her fortune told.

'What does it say?' she asked, as Rose snatched the piece of stiff card from her hand.

'This is your lucky day,' Rose pretended to read. 'Look out for a tall dark stranger.'

Outside the Palace of Pleasure a group of youths were pushing and shoving their way. They were seedy-looking individuals wearing string ties and striped shirts, their hair oiled and the toes of their shoes sharply pointed. Their voices loud with drink, they barred the path and jeered at passers-by.

'Give us a smacker, love,' a boy dressed in a hideous purple suit called to Rose.

She grinned, knowing it would be dangerous to upset the rough louts. Better to humour them. 'You're off your chump,' she called back. 'I'm old enough to be your ma.'

'What about your friend?'

'You must be mad if you think she'd be interested in the

likes of you. Get out of our way. Come on, Lizzie.'

'Come on, Lizzie,' a couple of the lads started to chant. 'Come with us, Lizzie. We'll give you a good time.'

Rose tossed her head and pushed past. Lizzie was close behind but one of the boys made a playful lunge in her direction. She tried to dodge, tripped, and fell against another of the lads. They hooted with laughter, and began to push her from one to another. Panic-stricken, she shouted to attract Rose's attention.

'Rose! Help me!'

Rose turned and took in the situation immediately. She rounded on the troublemakers shouting, 'Leave her alone, you louts. You shouldn't manhandle a pregnant woman. If she loses her baby you'll end up in prison.'

The boys froze as if they'd been struck; and then, one by one, they slunk away into the shadows.

'That was clever of you,' Lizzie said. 'Telling them I'm pregnant certainly worked. What made you think of that?'

'But you are – aren't you?'

'Don't be silly,' Lizzie laughed. 'I'm only seventeen.'

'What's that got to do with it? I was younger than you when I fell with Willy.'

They walked side by side towards the exit. Neither spoke until they were on the promenade walking in the direction of West Street. Lizzie was deep in thought.

'Penny for them,' Rose said.

'I was just wondering why you said that about my being pregnant,' Lizzie said at last.

'I thought you were, kid.'

'Why?'

'You've been showing all the signs. Sickness in the mornings, you've put on weight, and there's something about your eyes. Don't forget I've been through it – a woman knows these things.'

'But I can't be – *can I?*'

'Have you had a fellow? You told me once about someone called Jack.'

'Jack French. He's just a friend.'

'So was Willy's dad.' Rose laughed. 'That's how it all began.'

'We've only kissed,' Lizzie said, remembering Jack's friendly kisses and bear-hugs. 'There's never been anyone else.'

'Well then, I've made a mistake. Silly me.' Rose laughed again. 'Sorry, kid – I won't mention it again.' But Lizzie could see that her friend wasn't convinced.

'Really, Rose,' she insisted. 'I'd tell you if there was.'

'Of course you would.' Rose patted her arm. 'Come on, let's go dancing.'

They went to Sherrys. It was noisy and packed with revellers, quickstepping and foxtrotting around the floor under the spot-lights and chinese lanterns.

Rose settled Lizzie at a side table where she could watch the orchestra and went to buy drinks. She seemed to know everyone by name, and called to the Jewish violinist as she passed, 'Hey, Alfie – play "Jealousy", would you?'

'Just for you, Rose,' he replied, and his bow began to dance across the strings.

The crooner, wearing a black dinner-jacket and bow tie, picked up his microphone and began to sing in a low haunting voice. Rose pulled a man who seemed to be on his own to his feet. They began to tango slowly in time to the music.

But the music and the gaiety passed over Lizzie's head. She was deep in thought. Pregnant? No, she couldn't be. But memories kept returning. The dark interior of a barn: a man with a thin face and dark hair. Hard lips bruising hers, cruel hands tearing at her clothes. Tears and pain – and then, nothing. Her brain had tried to erase the event, so terrible had it been; but now Rose's questioning was awakening the memories – the memory of what Tom Grainger had done to her at Gates Farm.

CHAPTER NINE

The Cruel World

Lizzie sat on a hard chair outside Miss Norman's office. Through the door she could hear the rhythmic tapping of a typewriter. She'd been summoned from the basement half an hour before, and guessed that she was in some sort of trouble.

She'd been working for Burroughs now for five months and had upset Miss Norman on numerous occasions. It had all started during the first few weeks.

Mr Davies, the manager, insisted on punctuality, and Miss Norman was there to enforce it. At first she'd felt shocked and confused but had finally accepted the inescapable fact that she was going to have a baby, and that Tom Grainger was the father. It was, of course, the result of what he had done to her in the barn, but she had been too young and ignorant to recognise the symptoms until Rose had pointed them out to her.

At that time it was still early days and she had to earn her living. So she went ahead with the job in the Fancy Goods department at Burroughs without confiding in anybody, although she was frightened of what the future held for her and her baby. Rose didn't bring her suspicions up again, although Lizzie sometimes caught her looking at her thoughtfully. As a result their friendship was strained. Sometimes they went out together, and Lizzie still took her turn at caring for Willy, but the laughter and gossiping was a thing of the past.

Lizzie now knew that the occasional queasiness she felt when she got out of bed was not the result of a stomach upset, but morning sickness. It made being punctual for work difficult. Several times she'd arrived a few minutes late, with a white face and a churning stomach, and been reprimanded by Miss Norman. She'd tried excuses to no avail. She could hardly tell the truth because that would have meant instant dismissal. Burroughs of Brighton only employed single girls with impeccable backgrounds; so employing an unmarried girl who was expecting a baby would have been unthinkable.

But Lizzie needed to keep her job for as long as possible, otherwise she would be penniless again. But she hated it. The long hours spent underground, the strict discipline and the rudeness of the customers, took their toll on her nerves and health.

Her dreams of following in the fictitious Opal's footsteps and becoming a beautician were fast fading; as was the idea of being befriended by a wealthy widow and swept off to the South of France. During her lonely evenings Lizzie reread *Love goes Travelling* and almost changed her mind about Opal's decision to settle for love in a cottage – almost.

'Miss Sargent – you may come in now.'

Lizzie had been so deep in thought that she hadn't noticed that the tapping of the typewriter had ceased. Miss Norman was standing in the doorway of her office. She didn't look at all friendly; in fact the expression on her face was downright disagreeable.

'You asked to see me.'

'Sit down, Miss Sargent.'

Lizzie sat down on the edge of a chair and waited. Miss

Norman resumed her seat behind her desk and started searching through some piles of what looked like letters. She ignored Lizzie completely.

Lizzie was just about to remind her of her presence when she looked up and said, 'Mr Davies asked me to see you. He is too shocked to handle the matter himself.'

'Why? What have I done?'

'You should know that, Miss Sargent.'

'But I don't.'

Lizzie racked her brains but couldn't think of anything. She hadn't been late for ages, she hadn't broken anything, she hadn't been rude to anybody.

'When we employed you it was explained that Burroughs' young ladies must have impeccable backgrounds. That's why we expect their mothers to be present at the initial interview.'

'My mother was ill.'

'So you informed us.' Miss Norman looked at Lizzie distastefully. 'But because of other matters that have come to our notice, Mr Davies instructed me to write to her.' There was a silence while Lizzie recalled the interview and the reason why she'd given a fictitious address. 'The letter has been returned. The occupant of number eighteen Terminus Road doesn't appear to know either you or your mother.'

'We did stay there,' Lizzie said desperately. 'We had to move.'

Knowing that she was lying, Miss Norman carried on relentlessly. 'Also you've been seen in the town; in questionable places like Sherrys dance hall ...'

'There's no law against that, is there?' Lizzie said quickly. She knew she shouldn't answer back but couldn't help herself.

'Not so much the place as the company you were keeping. You were with a well-known lady of the town – a common prostitute.'

'Rose isn't common,' Lizzie burst out angrily.

'So you're not denying it?'

'Of course not. Rose is my friend. I can have friends, can't I?'

'And there is another matter – a more serious one.' Miss Norman paused, as if she was summoning up her strength to mention something unsavoury. 'Why aren't you wearing your belt?'

Lizzie looked down at her white overall. She could just manage to fasten the buttons still, but her pregnancy had made the tight belt impossible. She'd hoped that by leaving it loose no one would notice her swollen belly. Was Miss Norman aware of it, or was she just being fastidious about dress rules?

'I lost it,' she said hopefully.

'I don't think so,' Miss Norman said softly. Lizzie could tell by her face that she knew her secret, and in her sour spinsterhood was enjoying Lizzie's discomfort. 'Not only have you lied to Mr Davies and me, but you have also been living the sort of life that no decent girl would even know about.' The older woman paused as if she was relishing what she had to say next. 'And now you're pregnant, aren't you? There's no point in trying to deny it.'

'I'm not denying anything,' Lizzie said bitterly. It was almost a relief to find that her closely guarded secret was out in the open. Miss Norman was shocked, of course, but she was a woman herself, surely there would be some compassion behind the stern mask of her face. She would try to explain, and if necessary beg for Miss Norman's mercy. 'I am having a baby,' she said in a low voice. 'But I was taken advantage of. Believe me, I didn't know what was happening and didn't have the strength to resist.'

'You expect me to believe that?'

'Yes. Because it's the truth.'

'So you took this job under false pretences?'

'Only because I was desperate for work. That's also why I gave a false address, and said my mum was ill. She died last summer – and so did my dad.'

'Well, at least we're getting to the truth at last,' Miss Norman said.

'What will happen to me now?'

'What will happen now, Miss Sargent, is up to Mr Davies. Wait there.' She was gone only a matter of minutes, and when she returned her face was expressionless. Lizzie looked up hopefully. 'Mr Davies agrees with me: that we must terminate your employment at once. You will not return to your department but spend the rest of the day in the staffroom. I'll find some work for you to do there. At the end of the day I'll pay you any wages due to you.'

'But, Miss Norman,' Lizzie pulled herself to her feet. 'I need this job. I can still work for a few more weeks.'

'You may go, Miss Sargent.'

Miss Norman sat down at her typewriter and began to insert a clean sheet of paper. Lizzie stood her ground; she wasn't going to be dismissed so easily.

'I'd like to speak to Mr Davies.'

'Well, he doesn't want to speak to you.'

'Please, Miss Norman.'

But the clattering of the keys drowned Lizzie's voice. There was nothing she could do but obey orders. She stood outside the office and leaned against the wall. She'd lost her job, and no one else was going to employ her in her condition. The child in her womb moved in sympathy; she put her hands over her stomach as if to protect it.

In the staffroom Lizzie sank down on a chair and cried for the first time. The tears were healing, and when she felt better she had time to think. She wasn't beaten even if she was alone in the world. She had to be strong, not only for herself but for her unborn child. She'd find a way, and show them all – Mr Davies, Miss Norman, Aunt Hannah, and Tom Grainger.

As she'd been given the sack Lizzie didn't know why she was sitting there feeling sorry for herself. She didn't have to wait for the end of the day; there was nothing to stop her leaving that very minute. But while she was still deciding what to do, the door opened and Miss Norman came into the room. She was carrying a pile of printed leaflets, a bottle of red ink, and a pen.

'We can't have you wasting time,' she said curtly. 'You'll be paid up until half past five, so you must work up to then.' She placed the leaflets on the table and gestured Lizzie to pull up her chair. 'These prices have to be altered for the sale next week. You cross out the old price and insert the new one boldly in red. The alterations are listed on this separate sheet. Do you understand?'

'Yes, Miss Norman.'

Lizzie picked up the pen with its broad nib, dipped it in the ink, and started work. Miss Norman watched her for a few minutes and then went away.

Lizzie worked steadily, but after a while her fingers felt stiff and she stopped to rub them. Her back ached. She stretched and caught the ink bottle with her elbow, sending a scarlet stream over the papers and down the front of her white overall.

'Bother!' she muttered.

There was nothing to mop up the mess and the ink was soaking relentlessly into the leaflets. Her overall was ruined anyway, so she took it off and used it to soak up the spilt ink on the table. When she'd finished the overall looked as if some butcher had worn it to carry out a particularly barbaric dissection.

What was the use? She wouldn't get paid for her afternoon's work now, and Miss Norman would probably deduct the cost of the ruined overall. So she might as well leave right away and not wait for another reprimand.

Lizzie unhooked her coat from its peg, and rammed her brown velvet hat down over her ears. It was limp and shabby now, but she loved it because Jack French had bought it for her.

The overall with its crimson stains she left in a heap on

the floor. Lizzie grinned wickedly. It would give Miss Norman a start when she saw it: she might think it was blood, and wonder if Lizzie had lost her baby or perhaps killed herself. She didn't care what deductions Miss Norman made, as long as they made her feel guilty. Lizzie was determined to put Burroughs behind her and make a fresh start.

Lizzie's last act of defiance was to stop at the cosmetic counter and buy herself a new lipstick in the brightest shade of red they had.

'I suppose you want discount,' the assistant said, recognising Lizzie's face.

'No, thank you,' Lizzie said proudly. 'I don't work here. You're mistaking me for somebody else.'

She pocketed her purchase and marched out of the impressive front door. It was an unheard of thing for a member of the staff to use the front entrance, but Lizzie wasn't employed by Burroughs any more so she felt she could do what she liked.

With her head held high and a swing in her step, her pride carried Lizzie away from the shopping centre towards home. It was only when she stood at the bottom of Terminus Street and saw the row of gloomy dwellings that her spirits wilted. She was suddenly aware that her back ached, and her ankles were swollen with the extra weight they had to carry. The last few yards towards number ten were almost too much for her.

She leaned against a wall to get her breath back, and undid the buttons on her coat. It was a relief to feel that she needn't hide her condition any longer. There was no point. It would only have been a matter of time before everyone would have known anyway.

Slowly Lizzie plodded the last few yards. All she wanted to do was climb into her bed and close her eyes. Blot out the cruel world and all its problems until she felt able to cope with them. But even that brief respite wasn't to be.

Mrs Hill never locked her front door because her tenants came and went at all hours of the day and night. Also, from her vantage point on the living-room sofa, her sharp ears didn't miss a thing. What was the point of locking up anyway? She'd only have to give her lodgers keys. They'd only lose them, and then she'd have to go to the added expense of having new ones cut.

So Lizzie knew that the door would be on the latch; but it might not be so easy to make it up the stairs without her landlady hearing her.

But she didn't get as far as disturbing Mrs Hill. As Lizzie stepped into the hall, screwing up her nose at the familiar smells, Aggie, the skivvy, was descending the stairs carrying the inevitable slop-pail.

'You're early,' Aggie said. Then she added gloomily, 'I only jist finished upstairs. That there Willy's bin making a fuss all day.'

'Is he all right?'

'As right as 'e'll ever be.' Aggie stopped on the bottom step as if she was ready for a chat. She was standing directly in Lizzie's way.

'I was going up to my room to have a lie down,' Lizzie said pointedly. 'I'm a bit tired.'

'Aggie! What are you doing out there?' The whole house seemed to shake as Mrs Hill shouted from the end of the passage.

'Jist coming, Mrs 'ill.'

'Who's just come in? I heard the front door open. Who are you talking to?'

'It's only Lizzie.'

'Is it now. Just the person I want to see. Tell her to come in here.'

'You'd better go,' Aggie whispered. 'You know what she's like.'

Lizzie sighed, but she knew it was best to obey. Her landlady looked fatter than ever: like some enormous pale whale, beached on the soiled coverings of the sofa.

The twin cushions of her bust were covered by a sprinkling of crumbs, and in her hand was a wedge of fruit cake. Her sharp eyes darted about as if afraid they were going to miss something important, and her mouth champed furiously up and down like an angry cow chewing the cud.

'You wanted me, Mrs Hill?'

'Yes.' Mrs Hill's free hand stretched out and picked up a piece of paper covered with her bold black writing. She wouldn't give her tenants rent-books: just jotted down what was paid her on scraps of paper. 'You owe me five bob.'

'I don't think so,' Lizzie said carefully. It was dangerous to argue, even if she was in the right. 'I paid you last Saturday when I got my wages.'

'But you already owed me for the week before. It's all written down here.' Mrs Hill pointed with a dirty finger at a row of figures that Lizzie couldn't make head or tail of.

'I expect you're right,' she said doubtfully.

'Of course I'm right. I've heard you creeping in and out, hoping I'll forget no doubt. I'm a bit fussy who I take in. This is a respectable house.'

'I know – and I'm grateful.'

'I'll have the five bob now then.'

Lizzie opened her purse. She would have had five shillings if she hadn't bought the lipstick. But as she'd walked out of Burroughs without waiting for her wages all she had left was half a crown. She held it out to Mrs Hill.

'I'm sorry – this is all I've got.'

Mrs Hill stretched out her hand greedily. She hadn't expected to get the whole five shillings, but half a crown was better than nothing. A crumb of cake stuck in her throat and she coughed. The coin shot out of her plump hand on to the floor and rolled away across the cracked linoleum.

'Don't stand there, girl. Get it for me.'

It had landed in the dust under a gate-legged table and Lizzie had to bend over awkwardly to reach it. It still evaded her fingers so she had to go down on her hands and knees. That was difficult enough, but to get back on her feet she had to use the table-top to pull herself erect. In the struggle her coat had fallen open, and as she turned with the half-crown in her hand she felt Mrs Hill's eyes upon her.

'Here it is,' she said, placing it within reach.

'You're pregnant, aren't you.'

It wasn't so much a question as a statement of fact. Mrs Hill was staring at the exposed swelling between the lapels of Lizzie's coat. She tried unsuccessfully to pull it together.

'Yes.' There was no use in denying it: the evidence was clear.

'I don't allow babies in my house. They're noisy and dirty and I can't abide them.'

'I promise not to let it disturb you.'

'That's not the point. My rules are – no babies.'

'You let Rose stay with Willy.'

'Willy isn't a baby.'

'He was once – and he hasn't changed much.'

'Don't answer me back, girl.' Mrs Hill rubbed the coin on her sleeve as if she wasn't sure if it was genuine. Satisfied of its authenticity she dropped it into her capacious handbag that was propped against the leg of the sofa. 'My rules are "no babies" so you'll have to leave.'

'When?'

'Today. I can't have you going into labour in my house. It'll upset me.'

'I'm not due for a few weeks yet.'

'I said I want you gone today.' Mrs Hill stared at Lizzie unblinkingly. 'A woman came knocking only this afternoon. She wants a room, and she has the money to pay for it – in advance. She was a respectable woman,' she ended pointedly.

'But I have nowhere to go.'

'I expect there are places for girls like you. You'll manage. Now, call Aggie: it's tea-time.'

Lizzie knew when she was beaten. When Mrs Hill started talking about food there was no more to be said. She walked to the door with her head held high, not wanting the landlady to see how desperate she felt inside. In the doorway she turned, holding on to the frame for support.

'I'll go and pack my things now,' she said proudly. 'I want my baby to have a decent start in life.' She hoped Mrs Hill understood her inference: that any baby born under this roof would be damned from the start. In the passage she nearly collided with Aggie who'd been lurking within earshot.

'I 'erd,' the skivvy said in a low voice. 'Wot you going to do, Lizzie?'

'Don't worry, Aggie. I'll be all right. Go to your mistress now, there's a good girl.'

In the safety of her room Lizzie closed the door and leaned against it. She wanted to be brave but it was difficult. When she'd recovered slightly she crossed to the bed and sank down with her head in her hands.

'Lizzie, can I come in?' It was Aggie who'd followed her up the stairs.

'What do you want?'

'Is you crying, Lizzie?'

Lizzie pushed back the hair from her throbbing forehead and tried to smile. Nobody had ever been kind to Aggie, but she could still show concern for a fellow sufferer at Mrs Hill's cruel hands.

'No, Aggie, I'm not crying. It's all right.'

'But I 'erd Mrs Hill telling you you got ter go.'

'I was going anyway,' Lizzie lied.

The door was open just wide enough for Aggie to see into the room and assure herself that its occupant was indeed all right.

'Is you getting married, Lizzie?'

'No.'

'But you're 'aving a babe, ain't yer?'

'Yes.' Up to that day nobody had even seemed to notice her condition, and now it was public knowledge everyone was interested. 'But you don't have to worry about me.'

'Aggie!' Mrs Hill bellowed from downstairs. 'Where are you, Aggie?'

'I gotta go,' the little skivvy mumbled. Before leaving she pattered across the room, wiped her mouth on her sleeve, and then planted a wet kiss on Lizzie's cheek. 'Good luck, Lizzie,' she said, and was gone, closing the door quietly behind her.

The gesture of affection was more than Lizzie could bear. She lay across the bed and abandoned herself to the tears she'd been holding back for far too long. Once started she feared she'd never be able to stop. Like a tidal-wave the feelings of grief overwhelmed her and her body shook with sobs. At last, out of sheer exhaustion she lay still. Her head ached and her face felt tight and swollen – but then a miracle happened.

When she was at her lowest ebb the baby in her womb moved as if in sympathy. Lizzie sat up slowly and stroked her belly, feeling the pulse of new life under her sensitive fingers. Whatever life had in store for her she had to bear it for the sake of this baby.

She rose then, and washed her face in cold water. Slowly she started to pack her things; but every few minutes she had to pause and rest because of the lively child within. It seemed intent on making itself known. As if it was saying: 'Don't be afraid – I'm here. We'll be all right. You're not alone any more: you have me.'

There wasn't much to pack, so it didn't take very long. The bag she'd arrived with had long since fallen to pieces, so she parcelled her belongings inside an old sheet and tied it with a belt.

At last Lizzie was ready, the coat hanging open at the

front now that she had nothing to hide, and the brown velvet hat sitting comfortably on her shorn head, its yellow ribbon still fluttering gaily.

She felt in her pocket, hopeful of finding an overlooked penny, but there was nothing there. She'd given Mrs Hill the last of her money. But her fingers felt something narrow and round, and when she pulled it out she saw that it was the lipstick she'd bought as she'd left Burroughs. Smiling, Lizzie coloured her lips. But it was a sad smile, because she knew now that her dreams of becoming a beautician, like Opal, were only fantasy.

But no one could take away Lizzie's pride. She took a last look around the shabby room, tucked her bundle under her arm, and walked down the stairs and out of the front door with her head held high.

The feeling of well-being stayed with her until she reached the bottom of the road; but then she faltered, not knowing whether to turn to the left or right. The public house on the corner was just opening its doors, and the rough men who frequented it might try to accost a lone female. Lizzie chose quickly. To turn right would bring her to the centre of the town and the railway station, but left was unknown territory. She decided to go left and see what was waiting for her around the bend in the road. Who knows: perhaps she'd find the street of her dreams – paved with gold.

She had to pass number eighteen, the house where Jack French's auntie lived, and where she'd knocked last year with such high hopes. The grinning brass gnome on the green door seemed to mock her. She wondered if Jack had visited Mrs Manville since and she'd told him about Lizzie's visit. But why should she? Lizzie hadn't even given her name, so why should she remember?

The road led uphill and got steeper at every step. As Lizzie trudged along she remembered that she'd left without saying goodbye to Rose and Willy. Not that she'd had much to do with them lately. They'd never spoken of

Lizzie's pregnancy since Rose had first mentioned it and it had spoiled their friendship. And yet Rose had been so kind. And when Lizzie had got used to Willy, and overcome her fear, she'd become quite fond of him.

Once Rose had been in Lizzie's position: pregnant and alone. What must she have felt when she first saw the creature she'd given birth to? Lizzie shuddered, and then she remembered Rose's words.

'Some people said it was a judgment. That God had made Willy the way he is because his dad and I weren't married. A warning to other girls.'

'I'm not married either,' Lizzie thought. 'Is my baby going to be a judgment?'

The child in her womb seemed aware of her thoughts and stirred as if to reassure her. She pushed the terrible thoughts away and pressed bravely onward to the brow of the hill. She mustn't think about Willy – that way led to madness.

Now the way led downhill. The road was wider, with larger houses protected by walls and gardens, villas where rich people lived. Church spires pointed into the sky and in the distance she could see the sea.

Lizzie crossed roads and passed shops; wandering aimlessly with her thoughts far away. She had no idea where she was going or what life had in store for her. It was enough to feel the fresh air on her face and the hard pavement under her feet.

In the middle of a built-up area she found a park. There were trees and benches, and around the sweep of green grass were tall houses with many windows, like eyes watching the passers-by.

Lizzie sank gratefully on to the nearest bench to rest, and put her bundle down on the ground beside her. It was getting dark and lights were coming on behind the lace curtains. People who led normal lives were cooking their suppers and exchanging news of the day, oblivious to the weary girl outside.

'Wake up, lass. Haven't you got a home to go to?'

Lizzie jumped up with a start. A policeman was looking down at her: a broad figure in a dark uniform, with a kindly face.

'I was just resting.'

'It's turning a bit nippy. I should get on home if I were you.'

'I shall.'

'Sure you're all right?'

'Yes, thank you.'

Reassured, the policeman continued on his beat. At least he hadn't mistaken her for a tramp. But he was right: it was turning cold. Lizzie pulled up the collar of her coat for warmth. Across the road she heard a door opening; someone was whistling and there was dance music blaring from somebody's wireless. Then the door closed with a bang and all was quiet again.

A curious cat approached, but Lizzie was dozing and didn't see him. He sniffed at the hem of her coat and then jumped up beside her with a wild cry. Lizzie jumped, and then relaxed when she saw it was only a cat. It was a ginger tom, scarred with battle wounds, and blind in one eye. Lizzie welcomed him as only truly lonely people can welcome any sort of company.

'Hullo, puss,' she whispered so as not to frighten him away. 'Are you homeless too?'

The cat answered her mournfully but seemed unafraid. She stroked its rough coat and it purred throatily. As the night deepened they huddled together, sharing their warmth, each glad of the other's closeness.

In the early hours it started to rain. Not heavily, but a fine mist that settled on Lizzie's coat, its coldness penetrating the fabric and chilling her to the bone. The cat stirred restlessly and when she opened her eyes she thought for a minute that it was Sandy: the pet she'd left behind at Railway Cottage in the care of Mr Bennet.

'We're soaked,' she said, and shivered.

If she stayed here, in the open, she'd be ill. She felt faint and feverish already; but perhaps it was just tiredness and lack of food. She would seek shelter near one of the houses. She got slowly to her feet and picked up her bundle, calling to the cat. But he, not caring about the weather, stalked away, his ragged tail waving in the air like a tattered flag.

Lizzie spent the remainder of the night in the basement area of one of the houses. She found a cubby-hole built to house coal and bins, but it was empty apart from a scattering of rubbish. She huddled in a corner using her bundle for a seat and waited for daylight.

When Lizzie emerged into the grey light of a March morning it had at least stopped raining. Her clothes still felt damp, and she had to pull herself up the steps by the handrail. She didn't feel hungry although she couldn't remember when she'd last eaten. Her body wasn't cold either: it burned with fever, and she coughed harshly.

Every step was a nightmare but Lizzie forced herself along. She wasn't beaten yet. She must keep walking; she must look as if she was going somewhere or she would be arrested as a vagrant.

But the weakness increased. Her head spun and she knew that she was nearly at the end of her tether. Food would help even though she wasn't hungry. Food would give her strength and stop her head spinning.

Around her people were starting the day. She passed bank-clerks in dark suits with rolled umbrellas and bowler hats, shopkeepers rolling up blinds and unlocking doors. Everyone except Lizzie seemed to have somewhere to go and a purpose in life.

In front of her was a greengrocer's shop; it had the name 'George Stagg' painted over the lintel. Two men in working clothes were busy opening up. The younger was stacking boxes, and the older arranging fruit on a wooden trestle outside. He balanced one rosy apple too many, and it toppled to the ground and rolled across the pavement directly into Lizzie's path.

She saw the fruit as a gift from heaven. The juice would moisten her cracked lips and the flesh line her empty stomach and take away the threatened faintness. She bent down awkwardly and picked up the apple.

'Hey!' the man shouted angrily. 'Give that back.'

Lizzie tried to run but her damp coat clung to her legs. She staggered for a few steps, the apple clutched tightly in her hand. She heard the man's voice again: 'Get after that girl, Jack. She's pinched one of our apples,' and then everything went black.

CHAPTER TEN

Sanctuary

Grace French sat in a low chair crooning to the baby in her arms. Grace was as round and comfortable as a dumpling, with curly ginger hair, and eyes as large as saucers and as blue as cornflowers. She was forty-one years old, the mother of four children, and had long ago decided to let her figure fend for itself.

She lived for her big blond husband Albert – and Jack, Johnnie, Marjorie and Eileen. In that order. At the moment Eileen had priority because she was so new. Mother and child were still discovering wonderful things about each other.

Eileen was round, dimpled and pink. Everyone said she was adorable, from her chubby toes right up to her ginger top-knot that looked just like a question mark on the top of her head.

'Aren't you a clever little thing then?' Grace said as Eileen burped happily, and blew a milky bubble. 'Now I'm going to make you dry and comfortable, and then you must have a little nap.'

Grace fastened the buttons of her blouse over her blue-veined breasts, still heavy with milk. She always had enough and to spare. Bert had once laughingly suggested that she could make her fortune as a wet nurse. But Grace was content. As long as she could feed and clothe her family she didn't want anything more.

With the hands of an expert she undressed the baby and changed her wet napkin for a warm fluffy dry one. Eileen was alert and energetic for two months old, and when her mother placed her gently in her crib she kicked off the blankets and waved her feet and fists defiantly.

'Go to sleep, my darling,' Grace ordered, pretending to be stern. 'I'll play with you later.'

Eileen's eyes were soon closing, and Grace put the kettle on the hob to make herself a cup of tea. She would take a five-minute rest before starting the morning's chores.

This was the favourite time of her day. When Bert had left for his caretaking duties, Jack was at the green-grocer's shop just around the corner, Johnnie and Marjorie were safely at school, and Eileen was asleep. It was the only time when the house was quiet. Later she would hang the washing out on the line; she loved to see it blowing in the fresh air. It came in smelling sweet and fresh. Not like the garments she sometimes had to dry around the fire on wet days. Then she planned to bake a batch of fruit buns and fill the house with spicy smells. Grace smiled with the sheer pleasure of the day's work as she poured the boiling water onto the damp tea-leaves that had been used only once before.

She just had the cup poised halfway to her lips when there was an almighty racket in the front passage. Grace jumped, and the tea splashed into the saucer. The front door was flung open so violently that it hit the wall with a resounding thud, and then she heard the clatter of boots in the hall.

It was one of the men of the house – but what were they doing home at this hour? Grace poked her head round the door to satisfy her curiosity.

It was Jack, his rough red hair standing on end and his freckled face red with exertion. He was carrying in his arms something that looked like a dirty old brown sack.

'What have you brought home now, boy?' Grace asked suspiciously. She was used to her family trying to smuggle things into the house, rubbish that she wouldn't give room to. Only last week it had been some rusty old bits of metal that Jack insisted would come in useful when he got his bike.

'Help me, Mum,' Jack panted as he struggled with his burden into the living room. 'Put something over the settee – she's wet through.'

'She? What have you got there, Jack?' Grace followed her eldest son through the door. 'Is it a dog?'

'No – it's Lizzie.'

'Lizzie?'

'Don't stand there staring, Mum. Help me.'

Grace peered at the bundle and saw a pale face with closed eyes and bloodless lips. Damp brown hair was plastered to the scalp, and one thin hand hung lifelessly from what she saw now was a coat.

'It's a girl!'

'I know, Mum. Is she going to die?'

By the look of her Grace thought that the girl, whoever she was, was dead already. She pulled a shawl over the settee and gestured to her son.

'Put her down there and I'll have a look at her.'

Gently Jack lowered Lizzie down on to the settee and then stepped back. He trusted his mother; if anyone would know what to do, she would.

He hadn't recognised her when she collapsed on the pavement outside the greengrocer's shop where he worked; but he'd never forgotten her. He remembered Lizzie as a pretty girl with a bounce in her step and long shining hair. But this creature looked more like a tramp. The way she'd snatched at the apple showed that she was starving. His boss, George Stagg, was a soft-hearted man, and probably would have given it to her if only she'd asked. It was only when he bent over the still form and saw the silver joey hanging around her neck that he realised it was Lizzie.

He'd left her standing outside a big department store. He'd pressed two half-crowns into her hand to ease his conscience. She was going to buy a hat, a brown velvet hat with a fluttering yellow ribbon. Tom Grainger had called to him and he'd left her – but he'd thought about her many times. Had she found a job? Where was she living? Was she happy?

The answer was before him and he wanted to weep. Ignoring George's suggestion to call a policeman, Jack had gathered the still form into his arms and headed for home. Mum would know what to do – his mother would save her.

Grace made a brief inspection and turned to her son. 'Get some hot water and towels, a blanket, and the bottle of smelling-salts from my handbag – and hurry.'

Jack returned quickly with the bottle and blanket. 'I've put the kettle on,' he said. 'How is she?'

In his absence Grace had removed Lizzie's coat and her eyes had saddened at what was revealed. 'She's going to have a baby, Jack. Did you know?'

'A baby!'

'Yes – and quite soon by the look of her. Who is she, son?'

'Her name's Elizabeth Sargent. I met her last year when I went fruit-picking. She came back to Brighton with us and I haven't seen her since.'

'Has she no folks?'

'Not that I know of. She wouldn't talk about things like that.'

'That's better. Come along now.' Grace had covered Lizzie with the blanket and was holding the smelling-salts under her nose. 'Breathe deeply, girl.' She spoke in the sort of voice she used for Eileen. It reached into Lizzie's unconsciousness and pulled her back from the deep pit in which she'd been drowning.

Slowly her eyes fluttered open and she looked around as if she was in a dream. Such a kind face was looking down at her reassuringly: a woman's. There was another face frowning with worry: a face that looked familiar with its freckled nose and broken tooth. Where had she seen it before?

'Lizzie,' Jack said. 'Don't you know me? Jack French.'

'Jack? I thought I was dreaming. Is it really you?'

'It certainly is. Are you feeling better?'

'I think so. But where am I?' Lizzie tried to sit up and look around but the effort made her dizzy.

'Don't try to move,' Grace instructed. 'You need something warm inside you and some clean, dry clothes. Jack will brew you some tea, and I'll help you wash and find you something to wear. There'll be plenty of time to talk afterwards.'

She was strong but gentle, and by the time Jack carried in a tray Lizzie was propped up in the corner of the sofa. She was wearing one of Grace's gingham dresses and a warm shawl was draped around her shoulders. It was a transformation, but even so her brown eyes were too bright for her thin face and every so often she coughed harshly.

'Put plenty of sugar in the cup,' Grace said. 'It'll give her strength.'

Jack held the cup while Lizzie drank. She was so thirsty that she tried to take it too fast and almost choked. He made her take little sips until her thirst was quenched. He'd brought a plate of Barmouth biscuits but her lips were too dry and cracked to take anything solid; so he broke them into small pieces, soaked them in tea, and fed her with a spoon.

Grace stood back watching her son's ministrations with wonder. She knew he was a caring lad but she'd never seen him so gentle before, and with such a tender expression on his rough, round face. 'He loves her,' she thought, 'but he doesn't know it yet,' and she turned to go as if her presence was an intrusion.

But Jack joined her outside the door and spoke in a low voice. 'She's almost asleep, Mum,' he said. 'I'll carry her upstairs. She can have my bed.'

'That would never do,' Grace protested. 'Marjorie can come in with your dad and me, and Lizzie can have her room. It'll be more seemly.'

'Thanks,' Jack said gratefully.

The house in Coventry Street was small and already packed to overflowing. There were three bedrooms. His mother and father slept in the largest, with the baby's cot in the corner. Jack shared a room with his twelve-year-old brother, Johnnie; and Marjorie, who was only eight, had a tiny room to herself. She was a kindly little girl and Grace knew she wouldn't object to the move when it was explained to her.

The sheets were changed, and in no time at all Lizzie was installed. She hardly had time to take in her new surroundings before she fell asleep. All she knew was that the bed was soft, the linen smelled sweet, and the hands that tended her were gentle.

Such a feeling of peace surrounded her that as Lizzie slept she dreamed she was in heaven, and thought it was her mother bending over her bed with love in her eyes. She was a child again, digging on the beach for shells and collecting pretty pebbles to fill her bucket. Dad, with his braces dangling and his trouser legs rolled up, was helping her.

'Come on,' Dad said. 'It's time to go home. We don't want to miss the train,' and she was walking between her parents up the hill towards the station, and the pavements were made of gold.

Lizzie was so happy she wanted the road to go on for ever, but suddenly her mother and father disappeared and her way was barred by a monstrous barrel of fat. It was her landlady, Mrs Hill, wobbling along like a life-size rubber toy. She beckoned to Lizzie with a fat finger.

'You have to come with me,' Mrs Hill said. 'You owe me half a crown. You can't leave until you've paid me.'

Lizzie tried to dodge past. She didn't want to miss the train that was waiting to carry her home to the safety of Railway Cottage. But Mrs Hill was getting bigger and bigger, filling the road with her enormous girth. When Lizzie tried to dodge under her arm she was trapped against the bulging flesh so tightly that she couldn't breathe. She tried to scream, but woke up choking and crying instead.

'It's all right, girl, you're safe. We've sent for the doctor. He'll be here any minute.' It was Jack's mother, sitting by her bed and talking in a soothing voice and cooling her feverish brow with cold flannels.

And then Dr Waite hurried in. He was an elderly man dressed in sombre black, with half-glasses that reflected the light and a gold watch-chain with a dangling seal.

His examination was brief. He muttered to himself as he peered at the patient and asked questions that no one could answer. At last he packed his black bag and beckoned to Grace French who'd been hovering in the background. Dr Waite might be a family doctor, but a young girl like Lizzie needed a woman present at a time like this.

'When is the baby due, Mrs French?'

'I don't know, doctor. I thought you could tell us that.'

'By its position I shouldn't think she'll carry for more than four or five more weeks. That is if she's lucky enough to go that long. The fever might bring about premature labour.'

'Will she be all right?'

Dr Waite buttoned his coat and picked up his bag before answering. 'Who can say, Mrs French? But she must be a healthy lass, I've never treated her before. In fact I thought Eileen and Marjorie were your only daughters.'

Grace looked uncomfortable, but she was an honest woman. 'Lizzie isn't my daughter, doctor.'

'Perhaps she's a cousin or sister – or some other relation?'

'No. In fact I never saw her before today.' The doctor looked puzzled so she continued. 'My Jack found her in the street and carried her home. We didn't know what else to do, so we put the poor soul to bed and called you.'

Dr Waite looked as if he was about to have an apoplectic fit. He gestured to the bed. 'I can't believe my ears, Mrs French. She might be anybody – a carrier of some dreadful disease, or a burglar's accomplice for instance. Come to see if you have any valuables.'

Grace drew herself up haughtily. 'If we have, I wish she'd show us where they're hidden. No – she's some poor soul turned out by her family, no doubt.'

'And that is what you should do,' Dr Waite said sternly. 'Let her go back to where she came from. I would suggest the work-house, but now that it's been renamed the Elm Grove Home they only take the aged and infirm.'

'I couldn't send a girl like that to the work-house,' Grace said indignantly.

'There are other places.'

'No, Dr Waite,' she said firmly. 'She stays here. I'll do what I can for her.'

'She won't thank you for it. Girls like that are never grateful.' The doctor made a hasty exit. He had other calls to make to wealthier patients: young women who had wedding rings on their fingers and husbands who worked in the city.

The fever broke the next day. When he hurried in from work Jack could see that the news was good by the expression on his mother's face.

'She's going to be all right,' Grace assured him.

'Thank God for that.' Jack looked near to tears. If Lizzie had died he'd have felt responsible.

'She's been asking for you. You'd better go up.'

Jack didn't need telling twice. He bounded up the stairs two at a time and almost fell into the room. Then he pulled himself up with a start. Lizzie certainly looked better, but she was still pale and thin, her big brown eyes too large for her face. But her smile of welcome was beautiful to behold. Jack fell to his knees beside the bed and took her small hands between his big strong ones.

'Mum says you're feeling better.'

'Yes. She's been so kind – you all have.'

'No more than you deserve.'

'I don't want to be a nuisance. I shall be well enough to move on in a few days.'

'Never!' The violence in Jack's voice shook them both. 'You're staying right here. I want to look after you.'

'But, Jack ...' Lizzie's voice was low with embarrassment. 'Didn't your mum tell you? I'm going to have a baby.'

'All the more reason.'

He didn't ask who the father was: he didn't want to know. Enough that Lizzie was under his parents' roof, and safe.

Lizzie's progress was slow but everyone took a part. Grace French had the biggest burden to shoulder, with Eileen still a baby and a growing family to tend. But she fetched and carried, washed and cleaned, and tended her patient as if her life depended on it. Her hands were never still, and there was always a smile on her face.

Her husband Albert backed her to the hilt. He was too big and clumsy to be any good in the sick room, but he brought home extra treats for the invalid, and inquired about her progress before he'd even pulled his boots off.

The children did their part as well. Young Johnnie drew pictures and made up puzzles and funny poems to amuse Lizzie, and his younger sister Marjorie brought in bunches of wild flowers to decorate the sick room. Even two-month-old Eileen did her bit. Grace would deposit the tiny infant on Lizzie's bed, where she would kick her chubby feet and wave her tiny fists in the air. Lizzie found the baby so entertaining that she often smiled even when she was feeling low.

'Eileen is as good as any tonic the doctor could prescribe,' Grace confided to her husband.

Even Spud was allowed into the house to keep her company. With his furry nose tucked between his paws he'd doze for hours cuddled by Lizzie's side, to wake and lick her hand as if to reassure her of the family's commitment.

The weather improved. The damp cold March changed to a gloriously warm April; and one day Grace entered the sick room to find Lizzie on her feet. She was still weak and pale, and her body was unwieldy with the increased weight of her pregnancy, but she turned a radiant face to Grace.

'I feel so much better,' she said. 'I can't stay in bed any longer.'

'You must still take things easily, my girl,' Grace told her. 'We don't want you having a relapse for the baby's sake. You'll have plenty to do when it's born.'

On sunny days a chair was put outside in the yard. Lizzie sat there warmly wrapped in shawls, with Spud at her feet, and some knitting or mending in her hands. She could hear the clatter of pots in the kitchen and Grace singing to herself, and would smile and fall into a daydream. The daydreams would always be happy ones: her baby safely delivered, and she free from her burden doing a woman's work in a home of her own.

'Penny for them?' It was Jack lounging in the doorway. He always sought Lizzie out when he came home from work.

'I dreamed I'd had the baby,' Lizzie said with a dreamy smile.

'Was it a boy or a girl?'

'A boy – and so beautiful. I called him Joey because he

was going to bring me luck.' Lizzie laughed and fingered
the silver coin hanging around her neck. It had become
more than a lucky charm to her: it held memories of her
past life and the key to a happy future. Jack had heard
the story of the silver joey many times and knew how
important it was to Lizzie.

'Tell me about it again,' he said, knowing that it was
good for her to talk about the past.

So Lizzie told him about her childhood at Railway
Cottage; and about her mum and dad and her little
brother. Many a time during the telling she shed a tear,
and then Jack would put his arm around her shoulders
and hold her fast. She also told him about Greenlock and
Aunt Hannah Seymour.

'So I came to Brighton to make my fortune so that I can
go back for Billy. I promised Dad that I'd look after him
and he'll be waiting for me.'

But there were two things Lizzie didn't tell Jack. She
didn't tell him about Tom Grainger and what he'd done to
her in the barn, and she didn't tell him about Willy and
Rose.

Even if she did find a way of putting what had
happened into words she didn't think Jack would believe
her because Tom was his friend. And Willy's birth had
been a judgment on Rose, and Lizzie was afraid that the
same thing might happen to her. In her daydreams her
Joey was perfect but in her nightmares he became a
creature of horror: a judgment on an unmarried girl. And
yet Rose loved her son. So if the worst should happen,
Lizzie knew she would have to learn to love the flesh of
her flesh. In the meantime she hid the bad thoughts and
smiled at Jack.

'It won't be long now,' he said, and held her hand
tightly.

May dawned gloriously. The sun shone down out of a
cloudless sky and the winds from the west were gentle

and warm. The children stripped off their winter woollens and donned cotton shirts and gay print dresses.

Eileen, now three months old, soaked up the fresh air from the depths of her big black perambulator, wearing a tiny dress of white linen, and a cotton sun-bonnet on her ginger curls.

Eileen and Jack had both inherited their mother's colouring; but Marjorie and Johnnie were blond and fair-skinned like their father.

Marjorie ran in from school one day, her face radiant with excitement. 'There's going to be a fair at the school tomorrow,' she announced. 'There'll be games and things to buy and eat. Can we go?'

Grace smiled at her daughter. 'I don't see why not,' she said.

'And Lizzie - can Lizzie come?'

Lizzie looked up from her seat in the doorway where she was busy peeling potatoes. 'Can I go, Mrs French? I'd like to.'

'If you feel well enough.'

Lizzie hadn't been outside the door since her arrival, so an outing of any kind would be a novelty. The school was very close and if she got tired she could easily return to the house. Anyway, Grace French would be with her so she couldn't come to any harm.

The school-yard was decorated with coloured bunting, and a group of lads in military uniforms were playing brass instruments with more enthusiasm than expertise. There were stalls of all kinds; some were selling home-made cakes and sweets, others embroidered handker-chiefs and knitted garments. There were games for the children including shove-halfpenny and apple-bobbing.

Marjorie ran off to join her school-friends - she had three new pennies to spend. Lizzie followed Grace around the stalls, enjoying the freedom and fresh air. But the unexpected exercise soon tired her and when Grace noticed her pale face she drew her to one side.

'There's a seat over there in the shade,' she said. 'Take the pram and go and rest a while.'

Lizzie soon felt better. She rocked the pram gently and enjoyed watching everything going on around her. From her seat she spotted Marjorie tagging along behind two little girls who were strolling across the playground with their arms linked. They seemed to be deep in conversation and every time Marjorie tried to join them they pushed her away. At last they stopped and seemed to be arguing about something, and when they looked in Lizzie's direction she guessed she was the subject of their discussion. She couldn't hear what they were saying but suddenly there were raised voices. Marjorie broke away and came running towards her and flopped down on the ground at her feet. Her face looked tragic.

'What's the matter?' Lizzie asked. 'Have you had an argument with your friends?'

The little girl shuffled her shoes in the dust. 'They wouldn't let me join their game,' she said, tearfully.

'Why not?' Lizzie asked, suspecting some childish disagreement.

'Their mothers say they mustn't play with me any more. They say we're not a nice family.'

Lizzie laughed. 'What are you supposed to have done?'

'It's because of you,' Marjorie said in a small sad voice. 'They said we're not respectable because you and our Jack are living in sin – whatever that means. They said your baby will be a bastard because Jack won't marry you. They said Mum and Dad are bad people for letting you live with us, so they mustn't play with me any more.'

'Oh, Marjorie, I'm so sorry,' Lizzie said.

'I don't mind,' Marjorie said bravely. 'I stood up for you. I told them you're my friend, and when the baby comes I'm going to help you look after it. I think they're just jealous.'

'I expect that's it,' Lizzie said sadly.

'I think I'll take Eileen for a walk now.' Marjorie got up

and started to wheel the pram away.

Lizzie sat helplessly watching the child disappear into the crowd. Wherever she went she seemed to cause trouble. She felt that everybody's eyes were upon her: watching – criticising. Was no one on her side? Would Jack and his family be labelled for befriending her? If so, it was best that she left now before things got worse. Her whole life seemed to consist of moving on – but this move was going to be the most painful.

Her head felt light. Was it her imagination or was everybody watching her with cruel eyes, and talking about her with cruel voices? Nearby someone spoke and Lizzie thought she heard the words *bastard* and *slut*. They were talking about her and her baby. Then someone laughed.

She couldn't bear it any longer. Pulling herself to her feet Lizzie looked around for Grace French, but there was no sign of her. Perhaps it was just as well. She would collect her belongings and be gone without the added pain of farewells.

Lizzie pushed her way through the bustling crowd towards the gate. She felt enormous: bigger than Mrs Hill. She felt as if she was swelling up like a balloon. She mustn't explode here in front of everyone.

At least when she reached Coventry Street it was deserted. Everybody was at the fair. She must have sat too long on the bench because she had a stitch in her side. She stretched and the pain went away, leaving a dull ache.

The house was deserted, apart from Spud who rushed to meet her barking a welcome. Lizzie spoke softly to him and he seemed to understand that it wasn't the time for games. With sad drooping ears he returned to his basket and from soulful eyes watched Lizzie climb the stairs.

In the safety of her room Lizzie looked around. She must tidy herself, collect her belongings, and leave everything as she'd found it. She would compose a note to the kind family who'd taken her to their hearts; a note of thanks so they would know she was grateful. She would reassure them that she would be safe. She must write to Jack...

But it was all too much effort. The stitch in her side returned, doubling her up in pain. She lay down on the bed to ease it.

'Are you all right, Lizzie?'

It was Grace calling from downstairs. She'd parked the pram in the hall and lifted out the baby who was demanding her attention. Trying to keep her voice normal Lizzie called back: 'I'm just resting, Mrs French. I'll be down in a minute.'

'You shouldn't have gone to the fair. You've tired yourself out.' Grace's voice faded as she pushed a door closed and began to nurse Eileen.

Soon afterwards the pains began in earnest. The baby was on its way and Lizzie knew she wouldn't be able to go anywhere. The powerful contractions consumed her, driving everything else aside. Her strongest wish was not to be a nuisance to the Frenches. Hadn't she brought enough shame to the family? At least she could spare them this.

Time passed and Lizzie suffered in silent agony, stuffing the corner of the sheet into her mouth to stifle her cries. Downstairs, Grace began to prepare supper. Bert came home from work, kicked off his boots and reached for his newspaper. Jack followed, whistling cheerfully as he sluiced his head under the scullery tap.

'Where's Lizzie?' he asked as he rubbed his hair dry. It stood up in rough red spikes like the spines on a hedgehog.

Spud whined as if he had a message for his master, but Jack didn't understand.

'She's resting,' his mother said. 'She'll be down for supper.'

When Lizzie didn't appear Marjorie was sent up to

fetch her. Her cry of alarm sent Grace running. She found Lizzie in the last stages of labour.

'I'm sorry,' Lizzie sobbed, and gripped the older woman's hand as if her life depended on it.

'Sorry for what?' Grace asked herself afterwards, not understanding. But there was no time for questions. She yelled over the banisters for hot water, towels and newspapers, and then went back to Lizzie to urge her on.

Jack paced about on the landing, his face creased and ashen with worry. He looked like a husband waiting for news of the birth of his first child. And that's just what he felt like.

There was a period of silence while the whole house seemed to hold its breath. Then Jack heard a tiny cry and his heart leaped. When his mother opened the door he didn't wait to be invited – he almost fell into the room.

Lizzie lay exhausted on the bed; but her face was radiant and in her arms nestled the tiniest bundle. Jack walked forward as if he was approaching royalty. He saw a tiny wrinkled face, a tuft of brown hair, and a pink fist waving rebelliously in the air.

Lizzie looked up at him and smiled. All fear was in the past, all terrors gone. Her baby was perfect in every way and Lizzie was at peace.

'Jack,' she said in a tender voice, 'meet Silver Joey – my lucky charm.'

CHAPTER ELEVEN

The Steadfast Tin Soldier

'Are you awake, Master William?'

'Yes, Ellen.' Billy stretched and turned over in his comfortable bed, shading his eyes against the light. 'Where's Gladys?'

'She's helping Daisy with the breakfast. I had to come up and tend your aunt; she's not very well.'

'What's the matter with her?' Billy asked in an interested voice. He'd never known Aunt Hannah be anything but strong and healthy. 'Has she got spots?'

'Indeed she hasn't.' Ellen strode purposefully across the room to fill the bowl on the dresser with hot water from the can she carried. 'Now don't dawdle. There's a clean shirt and combinations and your shoes are downstairs. I hope Daisy remembered to black them. Now get yourself washed and dressed. Can you manage?'

'I want Gladys.'

Billy swung his spindly legs over the edge of the bed and wriggled his toes. Gladys Buttery had replaced Lizzie in the Greenlock household. Her first duty of the day was to see Billy up, dressed, and ready for school. Billy missed his sister, but Gladys had turned out to be the next best thing. She was middle-aged, plump and kindly, and she made Billy laugh. There wasn't much to laugh about at Greenlock House.

'You can't have Gladys this morning,' Ellen said firmly, pulling back the counterpane to air the bed. 'You'll have to make do with me.'

While Ellen busied herself, Billy padded across the floor on his bare feet. He began to wash his face in the warm water.

'Don't forget your neck.'

'I won't, Ellen. I'm doing it now.'

'What's this?'

Billy turned with the wet soapy flannel clutched in his hand. He looked younger than his eight years: his thin neck sprouted from the collar of his pyjama jacket like a bean stalk, and his hair was still ruffled. Ellen had been plumping up the pillows and found the papers that were hidden underneath.

'They're mine, Ellen,' Billy said, and his bottom lip trembled slightly.

'What do you want hoarding these ragged old pieces of paper for?' Ellen smoothed out one sheet and peered at it short-sightedly. 'What are all these squiggles? It looks like a foreign language to me.'

'It's music,' Billy said. 'It's called "The March of the Gladiators". Can I have it back, please, Ellen?'

But Ellen had already screwed it up and thrust it into her apron pocket. 'Rubbish!' she said scathingly. 'What's this other one? It looks like a letter.'

'It is a letter – it's from Lizzie. Please don't throw it away, Ellen.'

Ellen was reading Lizzie's last missive thoughtfully. 'How did you come by this?' she asked at last.

'Lizzie left it in my room,' Billy said, not wanting to get Daisy into trouble.

'Did she now. Does your aunt know?'

'I don't think so. It's none of her business,' Billy said bravely.

'What a thing to say, you ungrateful little boy,' Ellen said crossly. 'So your sister's gone to seek her fortune, has she, and she's coming back to get you, is she?'

'Yes. That's what she says, and Lizzie never tells a lie.'

'Well, she's taking a long time about it,' and Ellen laughed harshly. 'It can't be soon enough for me; none of us are used to children. I think Mrs Seymour already regrets her generosity in taking you in. All heart, she is – and look how you betray her.'

'I haven't done anything, Ellen.'

'Laziness, secrets, all the extra work. You wait until I show her this rubbish you've been hoarding,' and Ellen started for the door as if she was going to her mistress that instant.

'Please, Ellen ...'

But Ellen was gone, carrying away Billy's precious reminders of home and Lizzie. He scrubbed his face dry on a towel. He wasn't going to cry. He knew every word of the letter by heart anyway, he'd read it so many times. And he could play 'The March of the Gladiators' blindfolded. Like the tin soldier in his favourite story he would be steadfast and brave and everything would come out all right in the end. The only thing was, it seemed to be taking an awfully long time.

A distant bell reminded Billy not to be late for breakfast, so he dressed hurriedly, smoothed his hair, and ran down the wide staircase in his socks to the dining-room. He could smell toast so that meant boiled eggs. The toast would probably be burnt around the edges and the white of the egg raw and runny, but he'd have to finish every mouthful or Aunt Hannah would be cross and give him a lecture about ungrateful children and the starving multitudes.

Billy pushed open the door and opened his mouth to say 'Good morning, Aunt Hannah' but stopped in surprise with his mouth hanging wide open. There was only one place set at the long table and his aunt's high-backed chair was empty.

'Sit down, love. I've saved you the cream off the milk for your porridge, and the eggs have had a good five minutes.'

It was Gladys Buttery, all smiles, presiding over the breakfast tray. Billy smiled in return; suddenly his spirits lifted and he felt hungry.

'Where's my aunt?' he asked, slipping into his seat and unfolding his stiff damask napkin.

'She's staying in bed. Ellen's with her, so I'm to look after you.'

'I am glad,' Billy said, spooning sugar over his porridge and stirring it in. 'Not about Aunt Hannah, but that you've cooked the breakfast. Can I have two eggs?'

'Have as many as you like. You could do with a bit of flesh on your bones – you look just like a plucked chicken.'

'Do I, Gladys?'

Billy grinned and flapped his arms and clucked. They laughed together at his antics. He finished the porridge and started on the first egg. It was just the way he liked it: a firm white, and a yolk just runny enough to dip his strips of buttered toast in. He ate with relish which was unusual, because meals at Greenlock House were usually scenes of misery under the watchful eye of Hannah Seymour. She demanded perfect table manners and empty plates, even if you weren't feeling hungry.

'You enjoyed that, didn't you, love?' Gladys said as she poured him a second glass of foaming milk.

'It was lovely. I wish you could make my breakfast every day.'

'If I did you'd soon be the size of a suet pudding,' Gladys joked.

Billy finished his milk and wiped away the white moustache with the back of his hand. Suddenly he looked serious and the worried look Gladys hated to see was back.

'Gladys,' he said, 'if Aunt Hannah isn't well perhaps I won't have to go to school today.'

'I don't know, love,' Gladys replied. 'But she wants you to go up and see her so you'll soon find out.'

Billy sighed and looked sad. He climbed down from his chair and followed Gladys to the door. It didn't really matter whether he went to school or stayed at home – in neither place was he happy or relaxed. At home in the company of Hannah Seymour he was either bored or frightened, and Mr Bond's academy for boys did nothing to stimulate a child's love of learning. It was almost as boring as being at home, and although no one had actually ill treated him, he was always aware of the possibilities if he misbehaved.

Ellen was waiting for him on the landing outside Mrs Seymour's bedroom door. 'Now don't you go upsetting her,' she said in a low, threatening voice. She tweaked his shirt collar into place, and brushed some imaginary dust from the shoulder of his grey jacket. Then she opened the door and pushed Billy roughly into the room.

'You can go, Ellen.'

The maid seemed to be surprised at the order. After hovering in the doorway for a few seconds she did as she was bid, closing the bedroom door quietly behind her.

'Come here, William. Come into the light where I can see you.'

Billy walked forward, his newly polished shoes making no sound on the thick, heavily patterned carpet. He'd never been inside his aunt's bed-chamber before and he found it a trifle overwhelming. First there was the stuffy odour of a room that was rarely, if ever, aired, mingled with Mrs Seymour's usual scent of moth-balls and Parma Violets. The mixture of smells made the air sweet and clammy; the breakfast he'd enjoyed only a few minutes before turned over in his stomach.

Like all the other rooms in Greenlock House there was
too much furniture. Huge wardrobes large enough to
house a whole regiment of family skeletons stood either
side of the black and white marble fireplace. The
dressing-table was adorned with pots and jars, brushes
and candle-sticks, and a strange china contraption with a
hole in its lid from which protruded a tuft of black hair-
combings, as thick and coarse as the hair on a mongrel
dog. A triptych of mirrors reflected the horrible necessities of Hannah Seymour's toilet.

Luckily Billy didn't have time to dwell on the room's
contents because as he stepped forward all he could see
was the huge brass bed in the centre of the floor.

His aunt was propped up against a mound of pillows,
with a shiny eiderdown covered in magenta silk pulled up
to her waist. She was wearing a flannel nightgown with a
crocheted edging around both the neck and the cuffs of
the long sleeves. Around her shoulders was draped a
multi-coloured shawl with a knotted fringe. Her hair,
which she usually wore in a bun on the top of her head,
hung in a bristly plait over one shoulder, and her gold-
rimmed spectacles were perched on the bridge of her
bony nose.

She looked up from the magazine she had open on her
lap and beckoned her nephew in the way the wolf might
have beckoned Red Riding Hood when she entered her
grandmother's cottage so innocently.

'Good morning, Aunt Hannah.' This was Billy's usual
form of greeting and was expected.

'You may kiss me, William.'

Billy leaned over and kissed the proffered cheek. His
aunt's skin had the texture of crepe paper and was
unpleasantly moist.

'I hope you're feeling better.'

'If I were feeling better I wouldn't be confined to bed,
William. But I haven't called you here to discuss my
health. I want to know why you aren't working harder at

Greyhaven? Mr Bond seems disappointed in you. If I didn't pay your fees regularly you'd probably have had the strap by now.'

Billy looked down at the shiny toes of his newly polished shoes and shuffled his feet miserably. 'I'm sorry, Aunt Hannah.'

'Sorry! What kind of answer's that?'

'I do try – but the lessons are too easy and I get bored.'

'What do you mean by "too easy"?'

'Well, in arithmetic we only do adding up and taking away sums. At my old school we'd started to do fractions.'

'And when, may I ask, are you likely to use fractions?' Hannah Seymour asked, although she only had a vague idea herself what they were. 'I asked Mr Bond to make sure that you had a good grounding in numbers; there's nothing wrong in that. If you can add up and subtract you can do anything.'

'I know, Aunt,' Billy said meekly. 'But the sums Mr Bond sets are too easy. Couldn't you ask him to give me more difficult ones?'

'I suppose you think you know best?' his aunt snapped.

'No,' Billy said meekly. 'But last week in English we had to write a story. Most of the boys wrote about animals and things. I wrote about a little boy who became a famous pianist and travelled the world. I wrote six pages and Mr Gross, the English teacher, said I was showing off. He tore my story up in front of the class.' Billy's lip trembled at the memory of his humiliation.

'He was quite right to do so,' Hannah Seymour snapped. 'But I will have a word with Mr Bond. I sent you to Greyhaven to learn to write a fair hand, not compose rubbishy stories out of your imagination.'

'My story wasn't rubbish.' His aunt's words had put Billy on the defensive. He'd enjoyed writing his story, and had planned on keeping it to show Lizzie when she came for him. He wasn't going to have anyone, even Aunt

Hannah, calling his hard work rubbish. 'I came top in the spelling test,' he ended.

'I'm glad to hear it. Spelling is important.'

'But it was too easy. The hardest word was BOAT, and everybody should be able to spell that. I can spell much longer words beginning with B. I can spell BOISTEROUS. Shall I spell it for you now?'

'I don't think so,' Mrs Seymour said weakly. Her nephew's enthusiasm was making her head ache again.

But now Billy had started he couldn't stop. 'And the reading books are silly. At Railway Cottage I was reading Hans Christian Andersen and *Alice in Wonderland.* They're really good books. Why can't we read books like that at Greyhaven?'

'Because Mr Bond doesn't consider them educational, I expect. Children need books with moral values. You must understand, William, that your teacher knows best.'

'I suppose so,' Billy said, although he didn't understand at all. 'Do I have to go to school today, Aunt Hannah?'

'Of course you have to go to school,' Hannah Seymour snapped. 'I don't pay fees for you to waste your time here getting under Ellen's feet. That's why I wanted to see you. You are not to come home for dinner today as Ellen will be too busy. I am unwell, and the doctor is coming to see me. It will be more convenient for you to have your dinner at school. Gladys Buttery is packing something up for you, so you can collect it from the kitchen. You may go now – I'm feeling very tired.'

Billy tiptoed out of the sick room. His aunt certainly looked ill; her face was pale compared to its usual florid complexion, and her bony nose stood out like a beak, making her look more wolf-like than ever.

He could hear the rattling of pots and pans as he crept down the stairs to the basement. He'd never been allowed in the kitchen before, but he was curious because it was where Lizzie had spent most of her time.

Gladys was busy at the sink, her plump dimpled arms

making light work of the washing-up. When she saw Billy she smiled a welcome and wiped her hands on the rough apron tied around her waist. She picked up a package wrapped in grease-proof paper from the table and thrust it into his hands.

'There's a meat and potato pasty, an apple, and a piece of plum cake for afters,' she said with a wink.

'Thank you, Gladys.'

'And Ellen says there's to be steak and kidney pie and treacle pudding for tonight.'

'Lovely.'

'Now get along and don't you worry about your old auntie. She's tough as old boots that one is. Be a good boy now and I'll see you after school. How about a goodbye kiss?' She bent over and proffered her cheek.

Billy kissed her. Her skin was soft and smelled faintly of onions; it was a warm honest smell and reminded him of home. He suddenly flung his arms around her waist and buried his face in the folds of her apron.

'Hey, my love, what's all this then?' she said, laughing at the unusual show of affection. She thought for a moment that he was crying, but when he surfaced he was grinning cheekily.

'I like you, Gladys,' he said. 'You smell nice.'

'Get along with you, you little varmint,' she said fondly, and she patted his small bottom with her large hand and pushed him towards the stairs.

Billy was feeling more cheerful and he wasn't looking where he was going, so he almost tripped over the hunched figure of Daisy who was lurking in the shadows pretending to brush the stairs with a balding broom.

'Sorry, Daisy,' he said, as he edged around her squat figure. 'I didn't see you there.'

He was almost past when she put out a dirty hand and grabbed his arm.

'Boy!'

They stood facing each other and they were the same

height. Billy looked into the scullery maid's wrinkled face and saw that the boot-button eyes were trying to convey something to him.

'What is it, Daisy?'

'For you, boy.' With a swift movement she pushed something into Billy's hand. 'Boy's letter. Mustn't burn.'

He looked down at the torn and screwed-up papers: it was the remains of his sister's letter and his precious music. He guessed that, instead of giving them to his aunt, Ellen had taken it upon herself to burn them. Good, kind Daisy had rescued them for him. He beamed with delight and pushed them into his pocket. He'd have to find a safer hiding-place for them in future.

Leaving Daisy to her sweeping, Billy let himself out of the front door. It swung to behind him, freckling the hall with sunlight as the rays shone through the coloured glass.

He was almost happy. His satchel containing his school books and dinner was slung over his shoulder, and the letter from Lizzie and the remains of his music were safely hidden. The first few bars of the gladiators tune played through his head so that he marched down the path in time to the music. One-two, one-two – just like a real soldier.

At the gate he turned left towards Greyhaven: Mr Bond's academy for boys. It was only a few yards down the road but even so his feet slowed the nearer he got to the house that masqueraded as a school.

It was well named: a tall grey house with a slate roof and square secretive windows hiding the bare cheerless classrooms within. Only the top floor had curtains, but that was because the headmaster lived his solitary existence in the upper part of the house with just a housekeeper to see to his needs.

Greyhaven was not the only school in the area. The houses were large and not crowded together, so no nuisance could be caused to other residents by the coming and going of children.

It was an easy way to make money: set up a private establishment, and employ a couple of retired or out-of-work teachers to impart a rudimentary education to a group of local children who were not particularly bright or even had the desire to learn. These schools were rarely inspected as they opened and closed their doors too frequently for the proper authorities to bother.

On the gate of Greyhaven hung a large board that announced in big black letters that within boys were taught arithmetic and English to a high standard. All ages were accepted between six and sixteen, and private instruction could be given in French, Latin, and Algebra. Music lessons could also be arranged. In smaller print at the bottom it stated: Headmaster – Mr C. Bond, B.A. Hons. Prospectus by request.

Billy's steps slowed down. Another lad was approaching, a disenchanting lad with no front teeth and big ears. Wordlessly they acknowledged each other by a physical scuffle for supremacy. The boy with big ears won and strode through the gate with Billy trailing in his wake. He had no friends at Greyhaven, only fellow sufferers. Older and bigger boys sneered at him and called him names. 'Pretty Boy' was one because of his delicate looks, and 'Creep' was another because of the speed with which he accomplished his allotted tasks.

The few younger boys huddled together for protection, too terrified to invite him to join their ranks. They were frequently caned to bring them into line; particularly if their parents were late paying the fees of five guineas a term. At least Aunt Hannah paid promptly so Billy was spared this humiliation.

The gravel crunched under the soles of his feet and he stopped and crouched down to tie a dangling lace. When he stood up a movement from the top floor of the house caught his eye. Was Mr Bond, or his housekeeper, keeping a watchful eye open for offenders? No. Billy caught a flash of blue and gold; the headmaster and his staff always wore black clothing, and neither of them had fair hair. The blue was a dress with puffed sleeves, and the gold a mass of dancing curls that could only belong to a little girl.

Billy stood with his legs apart staring upwards, hoping to catch another glimpse of the apparition. But the curtain was back in place. Perhaps he'd seen a ghost, or the little girl had been just a figment of his imagination.

'What are you dawdling for, William Sargent?'

The harsh voice made Billy jump. It was Mr Bond, in his mortar-board and gown, standing in the open doorway, a stop-watch in his hand.

'Sorry, sir.'

'You have two minutes before I put your name down for the strap.'

Billy knew the threat was an idle one but he hurried nevertheless. Into the gloomy interior he scurried, and down the bare passage past Mr Bond's office to the one big classroom.

There were nineteen boys at Greyhaven and they were taught simultaneously, with no consideration for age or ability. Mr Bond would no doubt have crammed in double the number if there had been enough applicants.

Most of them were sons of local tradesmen who believed the school's prospectus and were impressed by the letters after the headmaster's name. Nobody had bothered to check up whether he'd ever been inside a university, let alone earned a degree with honours. The public have always been very trusting about these things.

There were two rows of small double desks in the classroom, with a gangway between just wide enough to prevent the pupils from cheating or throwing paper darts. The lids of these desks were mottled with ink blots and riddled with initials carved with broken pocket-knives. Apart from the larger teacher's desk, a collapsible black-board and a rusty stove with a chimney, the room was

bare. No books, pictures or maps; just bare brown walls
and an off-white ceiling from which dangled a central
gas-jet.

Billy slipped into his seat in the second row. He was
lucky because it was just the right size for him. Some of
the smaller and younger pupils had to perch on hassocks
to see over the desk lids, while bigger boys sat uncomfortably with their knees almost up to their chins.

Mr Gross, the English teacher, stood in the doorway
and rang a handbell to summon latecomers. There was a
thump of boots as the last boy hurtled through the door
and sank down behind his desk, sweaty and panting. Billy
screwed up his nose as the smell of chalk and unwashed
bodies assailed his nostrils. His mother had taught him to
be particular about cleanliness, and Lizzie had kept up
the good work for as long as she was able; reminding him
to wash behind his ears and making sure he had clean
socks and underwear.

At Mr Bond's entrance the boys staggered to their feet,
rattling their desk lids and clearing their throats in
readiness for the daily act of worship.

First came prayers: lengthy and composed on the spur
of the moment by the headmaster. They prayed for their
families and each other, for their teachers, especially the
kindness and generosity of their benefactor, and ended
by praying for the blessings of cleanliness, diligence, and
punctuality. Then Mr Bond announced the hymn.

'You will now raise your voices and sing hymn number
one hundred and twenty-nine – "Onward Christian Soldiers".'

This was Billy's favourite hymn. It had a marching
rhythm and reminded him of his favourite story. He stood
tall and sang loudly in his clear childish treble so that
some of the other boys turned to look at him. At the end
of the second verse Mr Bond raised his hand for silence.

'Somebody,' he said in a steely voice, 'seems to be
showing off.'

'It's Billy Sargent,' a boy in the front row said. 'He always thinks he can sing better than the rest of us.'

'Is that so.' Mr Bond leaned forward so that he could get a good look at the culprit. 'Why is that, William?'

'I'm not showing off, sir,' Billy said, his ears burning red with embarrassment. 'I just like that hymn.'

'That doesn't mean you have to shout.'

'I wasn't shouting.'

'And don't answer me back.'

'I only want to explain.'

'There is nothing to explain, boy. You were shouting and disrupting the class; you will remain silent while we show you how to sing reverently. You will also stay indoors at playtime.'

There was no point in arguing, it would only bring a worse punishment down on him. He wouldn't be caned or beaten like a poorer boy, but a complaint to Aunt Hannah would be trouble enough. He didn't mind missing the outside playtime because he was excluded from his companions' rough pastimes. Usually he spent the time standing by himself and waiting for the bell to ring and summon him back inside for the next lesson.

But first he had to endure history. This morning they were being taught about Henry VIII and his wives. Billy was interested in the Kings of England but instead of hearing about battles and wars, all they had to do was learn the names of Henry's wives by rote – in the correct order, of course. He didn't find this at all interesting.

After that came arithmetic. The boys recited in unison the times-tables, and did the usual adding and subtraction sums. It was with relief that Billy heard the bell ring for the mid-morning break.

There was an immediate stampede in the direction of freedom and soon he found himself alone. He'd had enough of the stuffy classroom so he wandered into the corridor to eat the apple Gladys Buttery had packed for his dinner. It was crisp and juicy and his spirits rose slightly.

There was no one about and as he explored he found a door marked 'Library'. He wanted to look inside but guessed the books would be boring like everything else at Greyhaven. Sermons and volumes of essays probably – not tales of adventure or fairy stories. Billy grinned to himself as he tried to imagine Mr Bond reading Hans Christian Andersen.

Somewhere close by he could hear the tinkling notes of a piano. He knew that music was taught at Greyhaven, but it was always by private arrangement, and not many pupils had parents who could afford the extra fees even if they'd wanted to.

Billy hadn't touched a piano since leaving Railway Cottage, and although he'd asked Aunt Hannah if he could have lessons he hadn't been surprised at her refusal. The piano at Greenlock was kept firmly locked, its polished surface protected by a chenille cloth. Aunt Hannah insisted that it was a valuable instrument and too much thumping would spoil its tone.

'I don't thump,' Billy had insisted, but his aunt had still refused.

He pressed his ear to the panel of the door in order to hear the music more clearly. He didn't quite know what to expect: someone practising scales perhaps with clumsy boyish fingers.

It wasn't a scale. Whoever was inside was playing a tune, and it was a tune that Billy recognised. It was called 'Wonderland' and it was one of the first little pieces his mother had taught him to play from the Ezra Read Pianoforte Tutor. Billy's eyes filled with tears as he listened to the one-two-three of the waltz. Then the pianist hit a wrong note and there was a pause before the melody continued hesitantly.

Billy's curiosity got the better of him. Without thinking twice he put out his hand and grasped the door-knob, turning it gently. Unfortunately the hinges creaked a warning. Before the door was open wide enough for him to see inside the music stopped in the middle of a bar; there was the scuffling of feet and then silence. The room seemed to be empty.

Billy stood in the doorway and stared at the piano. It looked like a jewel in the middle of the room: a full-size grand in a rich deeply polished wooden case. The lid was open showing even white pearly keys that were begging to be played.

As if in a dream Billy walked across the floor towards the instrument. It was the most beautiful piano he'd ever seen. He put out his hand and stroked the wood: it felt like satin. There was a padded stool which looked just the right height. He had to try it for size. And then of course he had to press a key to hear the sound. His index finger struck middle C and the sound was so mellow that he played a scale; and then it seemed natural to play his favourite piece of music: 'The March of the Gladiators'.

Billy played it for his mother. Every note was a prayer of longing, and tears of emotion ran down his cheeks as the music filled his soul. He remembered the piece perfectly, and when he reached the last chord he sat there with his head bent and his hands still on the keys.

'Why are you crying, boy?'

Billy looked up. A vision of blue and gold swam before his eyes. A little girl was standing by the piano – a child of about his own age, with bouncing yellow curls and a dress of sky-blue. She was so pretty, and her smile was so friendly, that Billy fell in love with her at once.

CHAPTER TWELVE

Caroline

'I'm not crying,' Billy said, and sniffed.

'Yes, you are – your face is all wet.'

'That's because I've got a cold.' Billy wiped his face on his sleeve and looked at the little girl from under his lashes. She was still smiling; Billy found himself smiling back.

'You play ever so nicely, boy. You haven't even got any music.'

'It's in my pocket.' Billy pulled out the crumpled sheet and smoothed it out for the little girl to see.

'"The March of the Gladi ..." What's that long word, boy?'

'Gladiators.' Seeing that the child was puzzled Billy tried to explain. 'That was the name the Romans called a man who was paid to fight in the amphitheatre.'

'A soldier?'

'I suppose he was a sort of soldier. That's why it's called a march.'

'I like it. It makes my toes tingle.'

'Shall I play it again?'

'Yes please, boy.'

'All right – but don't call me boy. My name's Billy.' Daisy called him boy, and so sometimes did Mr Bond. It made him feel invisible, as if he hadn't got a proper identity of his own.

'I'm Caroline.'

The small girl perched herself on the edge of a chair. Her tiny feet in their strap shoes swung backwards and forwards, and the skirt of her sky-blue frock hung in folds like the petals of a flower. She was so pretty and clean that Billy should have been overawed, but there was something in her eye that indicated mischief, and when she spoke the corner of her rose-pink mouth twitched as if she was a born tease.

Billy played the piece of music again and Caroline swung her feet in time to the rhythm. He finished with a loud dramatic chord and she clapped her hands with pleasure.

'I wish I could play it, Billy,' she said. 'Is it hard?'

'It's harder than "Wonderland", and your hands are small. You may not be able to stretch. But come here and I'll show you.'

There was plenty of room on the stool for two small people. Caroline tried hard to follow Billy's instructions but she soon displayed her ignorance. The Theodore Bonheur piece was much too difficult for her, even with her teacher's patient tuition. She brought her small hands down on the keys with a discordant thump and burst into noisy sobs. The din she made, and the way she screwed up her face, was so dramatic that Billy wanted to laugh.

'You don't have to make such a fuss,' he said, when he could make himself heard.

'Yes I do,' Caroline said between sobs. 'If you can play it, I should be able to.'

'But I've been playing it for ages. My mummy taught me before she died. And I thought you played "Wonderland" beautifully.'

'Did you?' She peered at Billy through her splayed

fingers to see if he was teasing. 'Even the wrong notes?'

'I didn't notice any wrong notes.'

'Didn't you?' She was all dimples and smiles again. 'How old are you, Billy?'

'I'm eight.'

'Well, I'm not eight until June, so I expect that's the reason. Do you think I'll be able to play your march when I'm eight?'

'I'm sure you will.' Billy grinned. 'You'll probably play it better than me. Why don't we play "Wonderland" again?'

'We?'

'As a duet. You can play it at the top of the piano and I'll play it at the bottom – then we'll change over.'

'All right.'

So they played 'Wonderland' through several times, and it became a sort of game to see who could finish first and race to a new position. It didn't matter how many wrong notes Caroline played; and Billy was having such fun with his new friend that he didn't even hear them.

'What's going on in here?'

The children had been so occupied that neither of them had heard the door open. The harsh voice made Billy stop abruptly and swing around on the stool, while Caroline waited until she'd reached the last bar before taking her hands from the ivory keys.

'I asked what was going on in here?'

It was Mr Bond, his gown trailing behind him like the ragged wings of a crow, and his purple jowls wobbling indignantly. He looked in a bad mood. Billy trembled.

'I'm sorry, sir—' he started to say.

But Caroline took the matter into her own hands. She swung her legs over the padded seat, showing Billy an enchanting glimpse of lacy undergarments, and ran across the room to the headmaster as if she was really pleased to see him.

'Oh, Uncle Charles, why are you looking so cross?' she asked, taking his hand and stroking it fondly. 'Billy's been so kind: he's been teaching me to play the piano. He plays wonderfully, but I expect you know that.'

'Does he now?'

Mr Bond looked down at the tiny creature hanging on to his hand and, to Billy's amazement, a smile creased his shiny face. With his free hand he patted Caroline's golden head.

'Yes, he does. He's eight years old and he's my new friend.'

Mr Bond cleared his throat noisily before saying, 'I'm sure it's very nice for you to have found a playmate, Caroline, but William should be at his lessons. I rang the bell myself five minutes ago.'

'I'm sorry, sir. I'll go straight away.'

Snatching his ragged music from the piano lid and thrusting it into his pocket, Billy started for the door. Mr Bond and Caroline were in his way so he slowed to a halt. If he tried to push past, the headmaster might help him on his way with a crafty push. Caroline's lip quivered as if she was getting ready to cry again.

'What's the matter now, you little minx?' Mr Bond demanded. He put his finger under her chin and tipped her head back so that he could see into her eyes.

'I don't want Billy to go back to his lessons,' she admitted. There was just the suspicion of a whine in her voice. 'I want him to stay and play with me, Uncle Charles.'

Mr Bond considered his niece's request; then he asked, 'And what do I get if I let William play truant?'

'I'll give you a kiss.'

Caroline simpered so that Billy felt quite sick. But Charles Bond seemed besotted with the pretty child. He bent down so that she could reach to put her arms around his neck, and then she kissed his cheek as if she really wanted to.

'Very well, Caroline,' he said at last. 'But you must take him upstairs and find something quiet to do. And get

Martha to make you both some dinner. Don't get under
her feet or I'll strap you both.'

'No, Uncle Charles. Thank you, Uncle Charles. Come
on, Billy – follow me.'

Before Billy knew what was happening he found
himself following Caroline through a green baize door
and up a flight of carpeted stairs to Mr Bond's private
living quarters.

He looked around him with interest. It was a palace
compared to the dreary bare rooms below, but even so it
was not as opulent as Aunt Hannah's house. The passages
had slip rugs on polished wooden boards, that threatened
to trip you up so you had to walk with care. There were
lots of pictures and an old oak chest pushed against one
wall. The living room was sparsely furnished with chairs
and sofas padded with hard horse-hair and covered with
rough green moquette. There were also a lot of little
tables with bamboo legs. The tables were neatly stacked
with books and newspapers, as if the occupier were a
great reader. Billy could imagine the big bald-headed
man sitting in front of the gas-fire with a heavy tome in
his hands, studying something really deep.

'Come on,' Caroline said impatiently, as if there was no
time to waste. 'What do you want to play?'

'I don't mind,' Billy said, thinking his companion meant
something sedate like dominoes or snakes and ladders.

'How about hide-and-seek?'

Billy looked around doubtfully. There didn't seem to be
many places to hide, even for two small children. But he'd
overlooked his companion's powers of imagination.
Where Billy was content to crouch down behind a chair
or try to seek shelter in a shadowy corner, Caroline
squeezed herself into the most unexpected places. He
discovered her in the depths of a sideboard cupboard
amongst a tangle of table-linen; stretched out flat along
the top of a tall bookcase; and under one of the rag rugs
that he almost stepped on. If he discovered her her lip

quivered in disappointment, and if he 'gave up' she would jump out of her hiding place with a triumphant smile all over her pretty face.

Billy was beginning to tire of the game. His companion had hidden herself away so securely that he had no idea of her whereabouts, and when he called repeatedly for her to appear she didn't answer. At last he sat down wearily on the old chest in the passage and called out for the last time.

'I give up, Caroline. Where are you? Come out or I'm going downstairs.'

That did the trick. The threat of losing her playmate was too much for the naughty child. There was a rap on the lid of the chest, making Billy jump. When he lifted it, there was his companion curled up in the bottom, with her knees up to her chin and an angelic smile on her face.

'I beat you! You didn't find me. I beat you!'

'Yes, you beat me,' Billy admitted. 'But that's a silly place to hide.'

'You're only saying that because you couldn't find me,' Caroline sulked. 'Give me a hand out now.'

Billy leaned over and took Caroline's outstretched hand and helped her climb out of the chest. 'Don't you know the story of the mistletoe bough?'

'What's that then?' Caroline was busy dusting herself down and shaking out her skirt.

Billy was glad the game was over; it was more to his taste to watch Caroline's eyes grow wide with fright as he related the story of the bride who hid in a trunk during a game of hide-and-seek. Her pitiful skeleton was discovered years later still wearing the remains of her musty bridal dress.

'That's awful,' Caroline said with a shudder. 'But it's only a story.'

'No, it's not,' Billy said. 'It's true – so don't go hiding in that chest again.'

'I'm not scared,' Caroline said defiantly, tossing her

head. Even so, she looked warily in the direction of the heavy chest as if it had given her something to think about.

After that they played eye-spy. When Martha, Mr Bond's housekeeper, rustled in in her black dress to call them in to dinner, she found them sitting side by side on the window-seat as if they'd known each other all their lives.

'Well now,' she said cheerily. 'You look just like two little angels; but if you come to the table there's hot sausage-rolls and a pot of vegetables.'

Billy couldn't believe his good fortune. Downstairs in the school-room the other pupils of Greyhaven would be eating watery stew, or munching on squashed sandwiches, while up above their heads he was being fed like a king, in the company of a princess.

After the sausage-rolls, parsnips and potatoes, there was treacle tart covered in hot yellow custard. Caroline even let him have the wrinkled skin – not because she was especially generous, but because she didn't care for it.

'Is Mr Bond really your uncle?' Billy asked in disbelief as he sat back contentedly in his chair, his tummy stretched to the limits, and the buttons on his trousers in danger of bursting.

'Of course.' Caroline daintily licked sticky crumbs from the tips of her fingers. 'He's my mummy's brother.'

'My mummy's dead,' Billy said sadly.

'Is she?' Caroline glanced at him curiously. 'What did she die of?'

'I don't know. She was ill for a long time and Daddy and Lizzie looked after her. Then she just died.'

'Who's Lizzie?'

'My sister. She's older than me; almost grown-up. When Daddy died she was supposed to take care of me – but Aunt Hannah stepped in and made me come and live with her here at Greenlock.'

'Where's your sister now?'

'I don't know.' Billy's eyes filled with tears. Thinking about Lizzie always made him sad. 'She went away to make her fortune.'

Caroline's eyes grew round as saucers on hearing the story. It sounded, to her, a bit like a fairy-tale. 'Perhaps she got herself kidnapped, or stolen away by gypsies.'

'Not Lizzie!' Billy said stoutly. 'Lizzie's brave and fearless. She always wanted to go to Brighton, because she said the pavements there are paved with gold. I bet that's where she's gone, to Brighton. One day she'll be coming back for me – one day soon, when she's made her fortune. The thing is – I don't even know where Brighton is.'

'Don't you?' Caroline spoke scornfully, as if Billy was an ignoramus. 'I thought everybody knew that.'

'Well, I don't,' Billy said crossly. 'If you're so clever – tell me.'

'It's near where I live, so there,' Caroline said, preening herself at her knowledge. 'It's a big town by the seaside, with two piers, and a palace where a king used to live. So you have to be rich to live there. We go there on the bus sometimes as a treat. I live in a little village called Rottingdean.'

'Never heard of it,' Billy admitted.

'I'll ask Mummy and Daddy if you can come and stay. Of course you'll have to wait until Mummy's better. That's why I'm staying here with Uncle Charles, because Mummy's not well.'

'What's the matter with her?'

'She's in a decline I think; whatever that is. I asked, but they wouldn't tell me.'

'I expect it's something like measles.'

'I expect so. Anyway, they said she'd never get better with me in the house because I'm so noisy.' Caroline grinned wickedly as if they'd paid her a compliment. 'So Uncle Charles said I could come here because my noise wouldn't be noticed among all you boys.'

'How long are you staying?'

'I don't know. Another week at least. You will keep me company, won't you, Billy? It's ever so lonely by myself.'

'I will if I can,' Billy answered stoutly. 'But only if Mr Bond lets me.'

'Uncle Charles!' Caroline laughed. 'He'll let you if I ask him. You sound as if you're afraid of him.'

'I am rather,' Billy admitted. 'It's all right for you, you're a girl, and a relation.'

When it was put to Mr Bond he made no objection; in fact he seemed pleased at the idea of one of his pupils keeping his niece occupied. Of course he had to get Mrs Seymour's approval, but she was in favour as well. She was still confined to her bed and feeling so poorly that she was prepared to agree to anything. As it was, she saw it as a way of saving money as she didn't intend paying fees when William wasn't receiving tuition.

So began days of glorious freedom for Billy, such as he hadn't known since leaving Railway Cottage. Ellen would call him early, and then after a good breakfast served by Gladys Buttery, off he would fly to Greyhaven. Caroline would be waiting for him, full of exciting plans for the day.

Luckily the weather was fine, so first they explored the garden which was large and overgrown. Although Caroline was always daintily dressed, she was as adventurous as any boy, and didn't seem to care if she tore her dress or lost her hair-ribbon. She could run quicker than Billy, and climb trees faster and higher, shouting at him to 'Keep up, can't you?'

After a few days they knew every inch of the garden and Caroline set her sights farther afield. Perched among the swaying branches of a tree she surveyed the surrounding gardens like an explorer looking for new territories to conquer.

'I can see a pond,' she said. 'With a waterfall, I think. I

bet there are gold-fish in it, Billy.'

'Where?' Billy strained his eyes.

'There, stupid! Where I'm pointing.'

Between the branches Billy could just catch the sparkle of water. 'It'll be private. They won't let us in.'

'We won't ask. We'll go over the walls, like burglars. We can paddle in the water and try to catch the fish. It'll be fun.'

Billy wasn't so sure. But when Caroline got an idea in her head she was difficult to sway. Of course he eventually gave in.

The first wall was easy to scale as there were sturdy bushes each side to give them plenty to hold on to. On the other side they found an overgrown lawn and flower-beds full of late spring and early summer flowers – but they were hidden from the house by some stout trees. Caroline dropped to her knees and began to search among the long grasses.

'What are you looking for?' Billy asked. He was impatient to get on in case someone came from the house and discovered them.

'There are daisies – look.' Caroline held up a starry flower on its thick green stem. 'I want to make a necklace – you can help me.'

Billy picked the flowers and Caroline punctured the stems with her fingernail and threaded them into a chain. She was wearing a dress the colour of buttercups, and with the necklace of daisies hanging around her throat Billy thought she looked like a fairy princess. But Caroline wasn't satisfied until she had a crown of flowers on her golden curls, and bracelets of blossoms adorning her delicate wrists. Only then was she ready to venture farther afield. Shedding bruised daisies in her wake she suddenly raced across the grass to the next wall.

'Come on,' she shouted. 'I'll beat you.'

This wall was more difficult. It was higher and there were pieces of broken glass embedded in the top. Billy cut his finger and Caroline ripped her skirt, but they were both laughing when they landed on the ground on the other side.

'Your face is all dirty,' Caroline said, unaware that there was a grubby patch on her own cheek.

'I don't care,' Billy said brazenly. He wiped his forehead with his sleeve, spreading the dirt further.

This garden was more workmanlike. There was a vegetable patch, with the bushy heads of carrots and radishes pushing their way out of the rich brown earth. Peas and beans twined their way up bamboo canes, and fruit trees had left a carpet of blossom on the ground.

Billy picked his way carefully, remembering their neighbour at Railway Cottage, Mr Bennet, and the pride he took in his cultivated garden. But Caroline had no such feelings and walked carelessly through a bed of lettuces, crushing the delicate leaves under her feet.

'Mind where you're going,' Billy warned her. 'You'll get us into trouble.'

'But I want to see the rabbits.' Caroline had spotted a row of wooden hutches tucked away in the shelter of the house wall, and had taken the short cut in order to inspect them. There were three hutches each housing two long-eared rabbits. Most of them were grey with short fur, but one hutch contained a pair of white animals with long fur, flapping ears, and red eyes. 'Aren't they pretty.' Caroline poked her finger through the wire-netting, but the rabbits backed away nervously.

'You're frightening them,' Billy said. 'Leave them alone.'

'But I want to stroke them.'

Caroline, to Billy's horror, opened the hutch door and stretched her arms inside. The furry white creatures scrabbled in the straw and trembled with fear.

'Leave them alone, can't you. I thought you wanted to see the pond. I think it's in the next garden. Come on.'

But Caroline was fascinated by the rabbits. She managed to stroke one on its nose and then succeeded in picking it up. She stood triumphantly, clutching the furry bundle to her narrow chest. Even Billy couldn't resist putting out his hand to feel the silkiness of its coat.

But the added attention terrified the rabbit and it suddenly kicked out with its powerful back legs. Caroline was unprepared. She tried to hold on to the wriggling body but it managed to free itself and leaped to the ground.

'Catch it!' she screamed. 'It's running away.'

The two children chased around the garden but the rabbit was too fast for them. It dodged and delved, leaving the chasers hot and breathless.

'We'll never catch it,' Billy said in despair. 'Perhaps they won't notice one is missing.'

'Two,' Caroline said.

Billy looked back at the hutch in horror: it was empty with the door swinging open. The white scut of the other rabbit was just disappearing behind a thick hedge.

He was all for continuing the chase, but changed his mind when a big black dog appeared and began to bark loudly at the intruders. Caroline was already halfway over the next wall, her torn yellow skirt blowing in the wind and her feet scrabbling for footholds.

Distance dulled the dog's noise, and it was with relief that Billy found himself in the peace and quiet of the next garden.

It was a pretty place with neat beds of herbaceous plants, rockeries covered with alpines, and bushes of sweet-smelling lavender and rosemary. In the centre was an ornamental lake with a waterfall that splashed its way over rocks, making ever-growing circles on the clear surface. A green frog was sunning itself on the flat leaf of a water-lily, its throat pulsating as it croaked its message to the newcomers.

'Let's see if there are any fish.' Forgetful of their earlier adventures Caroline flung herself down on the grass, and flat on her stomach was dabbling her hand in the water.

'You'll frighten them away if you do that,' Billy said.

'No, I won't. They'll think I've got something for them to eat.'

Billy wandered away. He couldn't swim and the lake looked deep and dangerous. After a few minutes Caroline followed him, wiping her wet fingers on the hem of her dress.

'Look,' she said. 'There are apples over there. I'm hungry.'

Someone had discarded a sack of apples outside a wooden shed. They were tumbled on the grass, bruised and maggoty, waiting to be emptied on to the compost heap. Caroline picked up one that looked undamaged and took a bite.

'It tastes fine,' she said, holding it out towards Billy. 'Try it.'

But Billy had already found one for himself. One side was riddled with wormy holes, but most of it was edible. Between them the children managed to consume several apples, although they tasted somewhat bitter. Then Caroline wandered back to the lake, seating herself on a rock and looking down into the water avidly. She still had a half-eaten apple in her hand.

'There are fish,' she suddenly called over her shoulder. 'Golden fish with spotted backs. Do come and see, Billy.'

Billy joined his friend doubtfully. She was leaning forward with her golden curls hanging over her face. The rock she was perched on was swaying dangerously.

'Be careful,' Billy warned. 'You'll fall into the water.'

'No, I won't. Look, Billy, there's a big one – it's blowing bubbles at me. Oh! I've dropped my apple.' In her excitement the apple had slipped out of Caroline's grasp. With a splash it fell into the water and quickly disappeared.

'Get back,' Billy shouted. 'I'll get it for you. My arm's longer than yours.'

They changed places. The rock wobbled precariously,

but Billy felt just like a knight in shining armour coming to the aid of a damsel in distress. He could just see a round shape bobbing about among the weeds, so pushing up the sleeve of his shirt he plunged his arm into the water. It was deeper than he'd thought and his small body proved to be top-heavy on the swaying rock.

'Just a bit farther,' Caroline shouted excitedly. 'Down there – I can see it. Just a few inches to your right.'

But the added inches were Billy's undoing. Just as his fingers touched the round outline, the rock tipped sideways, and as there was nothing to hold on to Billy slid headfirst into the water.

Caroline stood on the bank laughing as he surfaced with water streaming from his hair, and a trail of duckweed wound around his neck. She didn't seem aware that he was out of his depth and frightened.

'Help me,' he sobbed, splashing frantically with his arms. 'I can't swim.'

At last Caroline recognised her friend's plight. She waded into the lake until the water reached her waist before she could reach him.

'Hold on to me,' she instructed the terrified boy. 'I'll tow you out.'

They were soon on dry land, but looked a sorry sight with their limbs caked with wet mud. Caroline was almost as wet as Billy, but where he stood with a pale face shivering wretchedly, she jumped up and down and waved her arms in the air.

'I saved your life, Billy. If it hadn't been for me you would have drowned. You'd be dead if I hadn't saved you. Now you'll have to do everything I tell you to.'

Billy couldn't see the logic behind this statement but he wasn't going to argue. As it was, two figures were approaching the children from the house. One was a large woman wearing a green tweed skirt that almost reached her ankles and a baggy brown cardigan. Her hair was coiled into braided bands, called ear-phones, and there were heavy horn-rimmed spectacles bouncing against her ample chest on the end of a black ribbon. Behind her scurried a thin figure in a black and white uniform carrying a folding canvas chair.

'Oh, Lord!' Caroline muttered. 'It's Miss Madjewick. She came to call on Uncle Charles last night. She said I needed taking in hand just because I spilt milk all down her skirt.'

Miss Madjewick raised her spectacles and positioned them on the bridge of her nose in order to inspect the intruders. Billy shivered, partly from cold, but mostly from fear.

Caroline, for her part, rallied bravely. 'Hullo, Miss Madjewick,' she said, as if it was the normal thing to be found uninvited in a private garden looking like a drowned rat.

'Caroline!' Miss Madjewick surveyed the children in horror. 'What on earth have you been up to?'

'It was an accident,' Caroline said gaily. 'I can explain—'

'You'd better. And who is this?' and she turned her gaze on Caroline's companion.

'This is Billy.'

'Well, you'd better go into the kitchen with Edith and get out of those wet clothes before you catch cold. And don't look so pleased with yourself, young lady, because I'm going to telephone your uncle.'

Edith was the maid, and although she seemed to have lost her tongue, she was very competent. She stripped the children of their wet clothes, wrapped them in blankets, and set them in front of the range while their things were drying. Billy felt ill at ease until she plied them with cups of hot cocoa and Barmouth biscuits. It was surprising how quickly their spirits rose when they were dry, warm, and fed.

But all good things had to come to an end, and when at last they were respectable they were ushered into Miss Madjewick's presence. She was standing by the drawing-room windows, staring out at the garden and the ornamental lake that had been the cause of all their troubles.

'I'm sorry, Miss Madjewick,' Caroline began boldly. 'We shouldn't have come into your garden I know, but Billy wanted to see if there were any goldfish in your pond. Didn't you, Billy?'

'But …' Billy opened his mouth to protest, but before he could get any words out Miss Madjewick held up her hand for silence.

'You'll have to explain and apologise some other time. I've been speaking to your uncle on the telephone, and it appears he's been quite worried about your whereabouts.'

'We only went out to play…'

'Let me finish, Caroline. While you have been breaking into people's private gardens, your father has paid him a visit. You are to return home immediately. Edith will take you, just in case you lose your way.'

Caroline's father was the most dashing figure Billy had ever seen. He was tall and military-looking, with broad shoulders and a bristling moustache. Caroline ran towards him letting out little squeals of pleasure. He lifted her from the floor and swung her round so that she was all flying skirts and curls.

'How's my precious?' he asked as he put the dizzy child back on her feet.

'I've been naughty,' Caroline announced proudly.

'Well, I'm sure Uncle Charles will forgive you. You're coming home with me tomorrow; Mummy's much better and longing to see you. What do you say to that? Are you pleased?'

'Yes, of course,' Caroline said. 'But what about Billy?' and she pushed him forward. 'He's my new friend.'

Before Billy could be introduced, Mr Bond entered the room. There was a grim smile around his mouth. He stretched out his hand and grabbed Billy's shoulder.

'William is staying with us tonight – as our guest. I've just had a message from Greenlock House. His aunt, Mrs Seymour, has just taken a turn for the worse.'

CHAPTER THIRTEEN

Park Cottage

Billy tried to feel sorry that his aunt had taken a turn for the worse; but it was difficult when he was so excited at the prospect of spending the rest of the day and the night near Caroline. When Caroline's father, Sydney Hayler, said he was taking her home to Rottingdean the following day, Billy's heart had sunk. So Hannah Seymour's relapse couldn't have come at a better moment. Billy didn't even mind when Caroline put the blame for their escapade on him by telling Miss Madjewick that it was his idea to look for goldfish.

Billy, like Caroline's father and uncle, was mesmerised by the pretty child. Her gaiety and beauty touched everyone's heart. She was continually naughty, but she only had to turn her big blue eyes upon her victim and squeeze out a tear, and she was forgiven everything.

But now she was all smiles as she followed Martha from room to room supervising the preparations for the two new visitors. There was a room empty for her father, but Billy had to be squeezed into a tiny dressing-room opening from Caroline's own room. His bed turned out to be a folding chair.

'Now, you must promise not to chatter,' Martha said, trying not to smile.

'We'll be quiet,' Caroline assured her, but she gave Billy a wink behind the housekeeper's back.

'Ellen's sent you over some night things,' Martha continued, laying out a pair of striped pyjamas on the make-shift bed. 'Now, wash your hands like good children while I serve up supper. You're to join the grown-ups so you'd better behave yourselves.'

'What is it?' Caroline enquired.

'Steamed fish and mashed potatoes – and a milk pudding to follow.'

They remembered to be on their best behaviour, but neither of them had much appetite because of the amount of apples they'd consumed in Miss Madjewick's garden.

'It's the excitement,' Sydney Hayler said, smiling at his daughter across the white cloth. 'She's so pleased to see me, and the thought of seeing her mother again. That's it, isn't it, precious?'

'Yes, Daddy,' Caroline said quietly. 'Can I get down, please?'

'Don't you want to see what I've bought you?' Mr Hayler pulled a small packet out of his jacket pocket and held it out towards his daughter. 'It's a card game called Happy Families. I thought we could play it before you go to bed.'

'I don't think I want to,' Caroline said, suddenly bending over as if she had a pain in her tummy. 'I don't feel well.'

One look at her white face confirmed this statement to the grown-ups. While Mr Hayler gathered his daughter on to his knee, Mr Bond called for Martha, who luckily wasn't far away.

'Bring a bowl quickly,' he called. 'I think Caroline's going to be sick.'

She recovered slightly after the first attack and then it was Billy's turn. Soon both children were propped up in chairs, with bowls on their laps and cold flannels on their foreheads.

'It was those apples,' Billy whispered. 'I said they were bad. We shouldn't have eaten them.'

'I know,' Caroline whispered back. 'But don't tell or we'll get into more trouble. They'll think the fish was off.'

Billy wanted to say that it wasn't fair on Martha in case she got the blame but he was overcome by another fit of vomiting. They never did play Happy Families because, by the time they'd finished being sick, they both felt so weak and ill that bed was the only place for them.

'Mr Bond's called the doctor,' Martha told them as she tucked in the covers. 'He wanted to wait for the morning, but your father insisted, Caroline.'

'If they wait until the morning I shall be dead,' Caroline moaned.

'Don't exaggerate, young lady. Look at Billy now; he's being brave.'

'He wasn't as sick as me,' Caroline said, determined to get in the last word.

The doctor was kind but in a hurry. He'd been called away from a really sick patient and guessed, correctly, that the children's ailments were self-induced. However, he had kiddies of his own and decided that confinement and nasty-tasting medicine would teach them a lesson. He also said that in his opinion Caroline wouldn't be fit to travel for a few days; that both children must be starved for at least forty-eight hours; and the medicine he prescribed administered regularly.

'It's horrible,' Caroline sobbed, trying to push away the proffered spoon. 'I'd rather be sick.'

'Now don't be so silly,' Martha begged. 'Hold your nose and you won't taste it.'

Nature took its course and by the next morning they were feeling much better. Soon they were sitting up in bed calling out to each other; and by the time they were allowed to get up and dressed they both looked so bonny that you would hardly have believed that there had ever been anything wrong with either of them.

'Well, that's a sight for sore eyes,' Sydney Hayler said, lowering his newspaper and looking at the children as they trooped into the room. 'Come over here and let me have a look at you. And you, Billy...' He held out his hand to the little boy who'd remained in the background.

Caroline perched herself on her father's knee and wound her arms around his neck. Billy pulled forward a footstool, and sat himself down as near as seemed polite.

It was a warm June day and the window was wide open. He could hear the schoolboys playing down below and his heart sank. Now that Caroline was better Mr Hayler would be taking her home, and it would be back to the schoolroom for him.

'I had a word with Dr Grant this morning,' Sydney Hayler said. 'He thinks you're well enough to travel now; so I've sent a telegram to Mummy saying we'll be coming home tomorrow.'

Caroline's face lit up. 'Is Mummy really better?'

'Yes,' her father assured her. 'She especially wants you to be home for your birthday.'

Caroline seemed to have forgotten that she was soon to be eight years old. She let out a shriek of excitement. 'My birthday. I'd almost forgotten. Are you going to get me a present?'

'Of course. In fact there's already one at home waiting for you.'

'What is it?'

'You must wait and see. But I know you're going to like it. It's the best present any little girl could want.'

'What do you think it can be?' Caroline turned to Billy for help in guessing.

'I don't know.' Billy tried to think what a little girl could want. 'A doll?'

'Is it a doll?' Caroline begged. 'Do tell, Daddy.'

'Better than a doll. Much better.'

'It's no good,' Caroline pouted. 'I can't wait.'

'You must be patient, darling. I'll tell you what – if there's something you really want, tell me now and I'll get it for you.'

'Promise?'

'I promise.'

'What shall I ask for, Billy?'

Billy looked at the floor. He wished Caroline wouldn't involve him. Whatever she had for her birthday, he wouldn't be there to share it.

'Come on,' Mr Hayler prompted. 'There must be something that you want. Put your thinking cap on.'

Caroline thought deeply. Her eyes were on Billy when she seemed to come to a decision. 'I know, Daddy. I know what I want. And it won't cost you anything.' Sydney Hayler and Billy both waited to be enlightened. By the look on Caroline's face she was going to ask for something unusual. 'I want Billy to come home with us and share my birthday.'

'But ...' Mr Hayler started to protest.

'You promised, Daddy – you promised.'

'So I did.' Sydney sighed and raised his hands in despair. 'I suppose it could be arranged. Would you like to come to Rottingdean with us, Billy?'

Would he indeed? Billy couldn't believe that Caroline's father could grant her wish even if he wanted to. There was Mr Bond to consider and Aunt Hannah, as well as Caroline's mother.

But all difficulties were swept away. Mrs Seymour was still very ill and Greenlock House was no place for a little boy. Charles Bond seemed to have no say in the matter, and Caroline's mother, Margaret Hayler, wasn't consulted. Before Billy knew what was happening Gladys Buttery had packed him a suitcase, and he was sitting beside Caroline in a first-class carriage as the train rattled over the tracks towards the south coast.

'We get out at Brighton,' Sydney Hayler told them.

'That's the end of the line. Then we'll take a taxi and be home in time for tea.'

Caroline smiled and pressed Billy's hand reassuringly. 'Don't look so frightened, Billy. You'll like Mummy.'

'I'm not frightened,' Billy said.

He wasn't frightened: just excited. Lizzie had talked a lot about Brighton. Perhaps she was there now; perhaps if he looked out of the car window and kept his eyes skinned he'd see her walking along the street. She would be wearing a silk dress and a hat with poppies on it, because she'd had plenty of time to make her fortune.

By now the train was steaming into the station. Such a noise, such a clatter, such a banging of doors. Billy had to run to keep up with Mr Hayler and Caroline, but soon they were seated in a big black cab. It reminded him of the hearse that had carried his parents' coffins to their last resting place. Then they were bowling down a wide road edged with tall buildings towards the sea.

Billy had never seen the sea before and he was a bit scared. He'd never imagined it would be so big or so blue. The sun shining on the water dazzled his eyes so that he had to shade them with his hand. Because the day was so warm, the window was partly open, and he was almost deafened by the crashing of the waves on the shingle. Their foaming heads looked just like wild sea-horses.

'What's that smell?' Billy wrinkled his nose.

Sydney Hayler heard the question and laughed. 'A mixture of salt, tar, and fish,' he said. 'You'll get used to it.'

Soon they left the town far behind and were driving along a wide road. The sea was on the right and the Downs on the left.

'Watch for a windmill,' Caroline said, bouncing up and down on the slippery leather seat. 'Then we'll be nearly home.'

Windmills were no novelty for Billy. There had been one where he'd grown up that ground the corn into flour for the residents of Railway Cottages. But the one they passed as they entered the village of Rottingdean soared like a lonely ghost stretching its thin arms heavenwards.

'Park Cottage,' Mr Hayler directed the driver, and Billy's spirits rose.

He'd thought that Caroline would be bound to live in a fine big house, but Park Cottage sounded cosy. Perhaps it would be like Railway Cottage, and Caroline's mother would be waiting for them at the door like his mother used to do.

They passed the old sixteenth-century coaching inn called the White Horse. It stood with its back to the sea by a stretch of roadway called locally The Gap.

Then they turned into the High Street, which was bordered with narrow pavements and pretty little houses. The driver must have been a stranger to the village because he missed Park Road and took them to a row of pebble-walled cottages with overgrown gardens and dusty windows. Even so they were picturesque buildings, and the children playing on the cobblestones looked healthy and well fed.

'You should have taken the first turning,' Mr Hayler said. 'This is Bunkers Row – we want Park Road.'

In the end it was easier to walk the last few yards carrying their luggage. Billy got quite a surprise when he saw where Caroline lived: it wasn't his idea of a cottage at all.

Just off the High Street stood two newly built houses with their backs to the sea. They were both large and modern compared to the other dwellings they'd passed, and Park Cottage was the larger of the two. Square and compact and faced with red tiles, it was built as a family villa on a new design. There were two chimneys, and four windows facing the road. The panes were diamond shaped and leaded, standing open so that the muslin curtains blew a welcome to the homecomers. Under a deep pillared porch the front door was also ajar. Billy could see a vase of roses standing on the hall table, and the glitter of brass.

He expected that Caroline would rush inside to greet her mother, but to his surprise she turned to her father and grabbed his arm.

'My present, Daddy. You said there's a present waiting for me.'

'So there is, pickle.' Mr Hayler laughed.

'Where is it? Is it inside?'

'You'd better come in and see.'

'I hope it's a puppy,' Caroline whispered to Billy. 'I'd like a puppy of my own.'

They trooped inside. Caroline forgot her present for a moment when a woman's voice called from a room on the right of the hall. 'Is that you, Sydney? Have you brought my little girl home?'

'Mummy!'

With a yell of excitement Caroline ran forward into a large airy drawing room. It was the prettiest room Billy had ever seen, with white painted furniture and lots of delicate pictures hanging on the cream-washed walls. There were china ornaments everywhere: little animals in quaint positions, and shepherds and shepherdesses. Billy vowed to move carefully so as not to knock anything over.

Caroline, however, wasn't so thoughtful. China tinkled against china as she hurtled across the room towards a frilly couch set in front of the fireplace. On it reclined a beautiful woman.

Margaret Hayler made a charming picture of femininity. She was a pale slender woman with a mass of golden red hair piled loosely on the top of her head. Her eyes were as blue as her daughter's, and her dress of pearly grey voile hung in loose misty folds. There was the glint of gold in the lobes of her ears and around her neck, and the hand she put out towards Caroline was heavy with rings.

They exchanged kisses; and the mother didn't seem to mind the child creasing her dress and pawing her with sticky fingers. They hugged each other so warmly that

Billy felt a lump in his throat. Once he'd had a mother to hug and kiss – but it seemed a long time ago.

'This is my friend Billy,' Caroline announced.

Suddenly he found himself drawn into the Hayler family circle. Explanations and introductions were soon made and Billy relaxed happily. He thought he was going to enjoy his stay at Park Cottage.

'Have you missed me?' Margaret Hayler was asking Caroline. 'Are you glad to be home?'

'Yes.' The fair-haired child nodded and began to play with the rings on her mother's fingers. 'But it's my birthday soon. Daddy says you've bought me a present.'

'It's not that sort of a present.' Margaret smiled indulgently, and then exchanged secret glances with her husband. 'It's a surprise – it's special.'

'Billy and I think it's a puppy, don't we, Billy? Is it a puppy?'

'No.' Mrs Hayler laughed as her daughter's face fell with disappointment.

'A rabbit?'

'Better than either. It's not a puppy or a rabbit, but you'll be able to pet it and love it – and later on play with it as well.'

'But where is it?' Caroline looked around the room as if she expected to find a small furry creature hiding in a corner.

'It's asleep upstairs. If you promise to be quiet we'll all go up and you can see it. And you, Billy – you can come as well.'

Billy felt very honoured, and he climbed the stairs keeping close to Caroline. He couldn't imagine what it could be, but as they crossed the landing she whispered, 'It must be a kitten.'

With his arm about his wife's waist Sydney opened a door and they entered the loveliest bedroom. There were frilled curtains at the windows and a high four-poster bed with lace hangings.

'Over there,' Margaret whispered, and she pushed the children towards a deep basket on a stand in one corner. Like the bed it was dripping with white lace, but it was threaded with pink ribbon nosegays and embroidered edgings. It wasn't at all the sort of basket where an animal would be kept.

When they looked inside they saw a tiny pink face with tightly closed eyes and a rosebud mouth: a tiny baby cuddled down in a nest of shawls.

'It's a baby,' Billy said in surprise.

'It's a little sister for you, Caroline,' Mrs Hayler said. 'Her name is Ann.'

'Isn't that a lovely surprise?' Sydney Hayler added. 'Aren't you pleased?'

Mrs Hayler bent over and picked the sleeping baby out of the basket. She held it in her arms where it fitted perfectly. Her face was full of love as she looked down at the sleeping infant. 'Would you like to hold your little sister, Caroline?'

Caroline didn't answer. Her face had turned quite pale and had no expression. When her mother held out the baby she didn't say a word, just turned on her heel and ran out of the room. Billy didn't know whether to follow or stay where he was. The grown-ups gave him no guide – they were too concerned with their own affairs.

'I told you we should have warned her,' Mrs Hayler said.

'I thought it would be best this way.' Sydney patted his wife's arm.

'But you know how wilful she is.'

'She'll get over it. All little girls love babies. She'll learn to love Ann in time.'

'I hope so.'

'And she's got a little friend to take her mind off things. Don't worry, darling, she'll get used to the idea.'

'You know how stubborn she can be.'

'She's so funny. She kept asking about the surprise, and then she runs away.'

'She was hoping you'd bought her a puppy,' Billy burst out. 'That's what Caroline wanted – a puppy,' and he ran out of the room after his friend.

The house was strange and suddenly seemed unfriendly. All the doors were closed against him and he felt very much alone.

'Caroline!' he called softly. There was no answer.

Billy crept down the stairs silently. The front door was still standing ajar and his first impulse was to run away. But where could he go? Brighton wasn't far – if he went there perhaps he would find Lizzie. But even passing through, it had seemed a big place, and the likelihood of bumping into his sister would be small. It was too far to walk and he hadn't any money for the bus.

One of the downstairs doors was standing open and he could hear sounds of activity coming from within. So, thinking it might be Caroline, Billy went to explore.

There was no sign of his playmate. He found himself in a kitchen, and a grey-haired woman was sitting at a scrubbed pine table chopping vegetables for the pot. She didn't look very friendly.

On seeing Billy she pushed back her hair from her forehead and said, 'Look what the cat's brought in. I told them not to leave the front door open: it attracts all sorts. What do you want then?'

'I don't want anything.'

'Then you'd better get out of my kitchen. I can't abide strangers nosing around when I'm working. Are you a thief?'

'No!' Billy said indignantly. 'My name's Billy Sargent and I'm visiting.'

'Oh, are you then?' and the woman raised her hands in despair. 'Nobody said nothing to me.'

'I'm a friend of Caroline's.'

'That little miss! The new baby'll take her down a peg or two. Spoiled rotten she is.'

Billy wasn't going to have his playmate spoken about

in these terms, even if the woman was right. 'You mustn't say such things,' he said.

'I speak as I find.'

'Well, Caroline is my best friend and I can't find her.'

'She went through here only five minutes ago and out into the garden.' The unfriendly woman waved her vegetable knife in the direction of the back door. 'Didn't even stop to say "Hullo, Dora, how are you?" But that's Miss Caroline all over.'

'Thank you, Dora,' Billy said, trying to correct Caroline's oversight.

As he passed out of earshot he heard Dora mutter, 'Come to no good that one will. See if I'm not right.'

The garden Billy found himself in wasn't large, but it was well maintained and colourful. There were neatly trimmed hedges of box and privet, a strip of carefully mown lawn, and beds of bright summer flowers. At the far end was an ancient apple tree sheltering a small wooden shed painted white.

As there was no sign of Caroline's yellow head or pink dress Billy thought she might have taken her sulks inside the shed. It was just the sort of thing she would do, in the hope that someone would come and find her. Her ill humour would be worse if no one bothered.

There was a wheelbarrow leaning against the side so the shed was obviously used to store garden equipment. He pushed the door open and was immediately entangled in a web that a busy spider had just completed. Billy wasn't scared of spiders but the web was horrible: all sticky and clinging. He brushed it away. Caroline wasn't there, she hated crawling things, and all the shed seemed to contain was neatly stacked flowerpots arranged on open shelves.

He went back outside into the sunlight, and stood under the apple tree pulling the last fragment of web from his hair and clothes.

Billy was just contemplating his next move when something hit him sharply on the head. It was a small green apple, hard and shiny, about the size of a marble. While he was still rubbing the spot another apple hit him behind the ear, and then a third on his bare arm. He looked up to see the reason for the sudden avalanche of unripe fruit, and saw a small foot in a white sock and a brown sandal dangling over a branch. The rest of the body was hidden among the green foliage, but the foot certainly belonged to Caroline.

Even so, he called, 'Caroline, is that you?'

'Of course it is,' came the cross reply.

'Why are you hiding?'

'Because I hate everybody, that's why.'

'Do you hate me?'

'Especially you, Billy Sargent.'

Billy was dumbfounded. He stood open-mouthed, and just managed to field the next green apple that Caroline aimed at him. 'But what have I done?'

His only answer was a storm of uncontrolled weeping.

'I'm coming up,' he called.

Caroline didn't attempt to stop him so he hauled himself into the lower branches. The tree was old and gnarled with plenty of footholds, and soon Billy was sitting across the branch next to Caroline. Her cheeks were wet with genuine tears.

'What's the matter?' Billy asked as she didn't say anything.

'You know what's the matter, you stupid boy. They sent me away so that they could get a horrible baby.'

'I don't think it's a horrible baby,' Billy said. 'I think it's a sweet little thing.'

'You don't know anything then – you haven't got a sister.'

'Yes I have – so there.'

'Not a baby sister. I thought it was going to be a dear little puppy.' Caroline started to cry again.

'It won't be so bad,' Billy tried to console her. 'It won't be a baby for ever; and when it gets bigger you'll be able to play with it.'

'I won't, so there.' Caroline wiped her face on her arm and sat deep in thought. Suddenly she brightened up. 'I know what I'm going to do.'

'What?'

'I'm going to get my own back – and you're going to help me.'

'Me?'

'You have to: I saved your life, remember. If it hadn't been for me you'd have drowned in old Miss Madjewick's pond. You have to do what I say.'

Billy wanted to argue, but he knew it would do no good when she was in this frame of mind. She had saved his life, and he was grateful, but helping her now depended on what she was planning.

'What are you going to do?'

'I'm going to think of a way of making them get rid of it. Perhaps if I pretended that I was very ill they'd feel sorry for me and send it away.'

'If they thought you were very ill it's you they'd send away – to a hospital.'

'That's true.'

Caroline sat deep in thought, then she said, 'I know. We'll ask if we can take it out in its pram, I suppose it has got a pram, and then we'll leave it somewhere.'

Billy was horrified. 'We can't do that. It'll die if nobody feeds it. And stop saying IT. Her name is Ann.'

Caroline glowered. 'All right, we'll wait until the gypsies come. They usually camp under Beacon Hill. Gypsies like babies; they'll look after it.'

Billy wasn't sure if this was a good idea. Gypsies were rough people, and Ann looked a delicate little thing.

Caroline's ideas got more and more fantastic. They ranged from smothering the baby with a pillow, to setting fire to the house while she was in it. Billy hoped she wouldn't do anything quite so dreadful; although with Caroline you could never be sure.

At last she sighed, as if she'd run out of ideas. 'Don't

worry,' she said, seeing Billy's frightened face. 'I wouldn't really hurt Ann. I'll get my own back on Mummy and Daddy instead.'

'What are you going to do?'

'I don't know – but I'll think of something.'

Billy had been looking forward to his visit. Meeting Caroline had changed his life after the dreary routine at Greenlock House and the boring austerity of Greyhaven. Margaret and Sydney Hayler were kindness itself, but couldn't understand what their lively daughter saw in the quiet little boy who looked so nervous all the time. They didn't know that Billy lived every day as if he was perched on the edge of a volcano that was about to erupt any minute.

On the third morning of his stay, Caroline came down to breakfast looking unusually cheerful. She kissed her parents warmly, and even inspected the baby who was being nursed by its mother.

'What are you going to do today, darling?' Margaret asked as she rocked Ann in her arms.

'Billy wants to go out,' Caroline said without consulting him. 'He wants me to show him the village.'

'There's not much to see.' Mr Hayler laughed over the top of his *Daily Express*. He was wearing pin-striped trousers and a starched shirt with a stiff collar. 'Only a few old cottages, a pond, and a windmill.'

'Perhaps you could take them in to Brighton,' Margaret suggested brightly. 'You could take them on the pier or to the cinema.'

'Yes – yes,' Caroline shouted excitedly. 'Can we go to Brighton, Daddy?'

'Sorry.' Sydney raised his hand for silence. 'Not today. I have an appointment: too important to miss.'

'But, Daddy—'

'Another day, Caroline. I'm sure you can think of some way to amuse your friend.'

'It's not fair—'

'Perhaps tomorrow – if it's fine.'

Caroline knew that she was beaten. She left her breakfast half eaten, and closed the door a little too noisily when she left the room.

Billy finished his boiled egg, wiped his mouth on his napkin and asked if he could leave the table. Mrs Hayler smiled vaguely and waved him away. He joined Caroline, who was waiting for him on the front path. She was wearing Clarks sandals on her bare feet, and a short printed smock with patch pockets. Billy was relieved to see that she'd brightened up considerably.

'Come on,' she said, and led the way towards the High Street.

'Where are we going?'

'Brighton.'

'Brighton! But your daddy said—'

'We're not going with Daddy. Look, there's a bus waiting outside the White Horse Hotel. I'll beat you to it.'

Her enthusiasm was catching, and when Billy reached the bus Caroline was already clutching two stiff cardboard tickets. She climbed the stairs to the top deck and Billy followed.

'Behave yourselves up there,' the conductor called after them.

He thought they were rather young to be travelling by themselves, but the little girl had paid for the tickets and he didn't want to ask questions and spoil their happiness.

It was a perfect morning for a ride along the cliff top. The bus lurched drunkenly, eating up the miles, while down below the sun sparked on the blue water. Little fluffy clouds drifted overhead like powder-puffs. Billy sank back on his seat with a sigh of contentment.

'We're nearly there. I can see the pier.'

Billy looked in the direction of Caroline's pointing finger. The coastline reached as far as the eye could see, with miles and miles of pebbly beach peopled with brightly clothed holiday-makers. The pier was a glorious sight, stretching into the sea like a glittering necklace, the sun reflecting on glass and steel.

'First we'll have ice-creams,' Caroline said excitedly. 'And then we'll go on the pier: it only costs threepence. We'll go on the Ghost Train, and put pennies in the slot machines. We'll have doughnuts and fish and chips; and I want you to win me a prize on the coconut-shy.'

Billy laughed. 'And who's going to pay for all that? I haven't got any money.'

'But I have.' Caroline fished in her pocket and pulled out a folded piece of white paper. 'There.'

'What's that?'

'It's a five-pound note,' Caroline said, unfolding it before Billy's startled eyes. 'I stole it out of Mummy's bag to get my own back. We'll spend it all and have a lovely time. And if you give me away I'll say it was your idea. Don't forget, Billy, I saved your life.'

CHAPTER FOURTEEN

Trouble

The streets of Brighton weren't paved with gold as Lizzie had told him. Billy wasn't really disappointed: he hadn't expected them to be.

The bus put them down outside the Palace Pier. Caroline immediately grabbed his hand and started to pull him towards an open stall with a striped awning.

'I'm going to buy some rock,' she said, and waving the money at the startled stall-holder demanded, 'Two big sticks of Brighton Rock.'

The man looked at the two small figures, and the five-pound note, and frowned. 'That'll cost you a bob, lass,' he said. 'I can't change that. Haven't you anything smaller?' Caroline shook her head. 'Where's your mum and dad?'

'I don't want any rock,' Billy whispered, pulling on Caroline's arm. 'Look, there's a puppet show down by the beach. Let's go and watch that.'

The Punch and Judy was fun, particularly when the dog ran away with the string of sausages. But Billy didn't like the way Judy beat the baby's head on the floor, and when the policeman popped up he looked over his shoulder in alarm.

Everything cost money, and everyone questioned the two small children when they produced the five-pound note.

'Perhaps it's not a real one,' Billy said, after Caroline failed to change it in a sweet shop. He'd never seen paper money before.

In the end a man in a chip shop gave them change. He cheated them of course; but Caroline was quite content to pocket two pound notes and a handful of sixpences and shillings in exchange for a newspaper parcel of greasy chips. They bought a bottle of fizzy lemonade as well, and sat down in a hollow on the beach to eat their dinner.

'What do you want to do next?' Caroline asked. She was trying to tempt a seagull with a piece of chip. It flapped its wings in a frightening way and turned its back on them.

'We could paddle.' Billy felt hot and uncomfortable and the water looked inviting.

'We can paddle anytime,' Caroline replied scathingly. Her eye was caught by a speed-boat ploughing its way between the piers. 'I wonder how much it costs?' she said longingly.

'I don't know. Anyway, they wouldn't let us on without a grown-up.'

'You're scared.'

'No, I'm not.' Billy didn't like the way the boat tossed up and down on the waves but he wasn't going to admit it.

'We'll go on the pier first and then see if we've got enough left for a ride.'

'All right.'

Caroline scrambled to her feet, her shoes sliding over the pebbles. Some of the money dropped out of her pocket and she had to search for it. 'Help me,' she ordered.

Billy found some pennies and a florin, and then he found a tiny silver coin hiding away under a stone. He rubbed the sand off with his finger and saw the outline of

Queen Victoria's head. He held it out.

'Is this ours?'

'No. It's too small. Somebody's lost it – throw it away.' Caroline didn't think such a small coin could be worth anything compared to the heavy pennies that made her pocket bulge.

Billy was still peering at it with interest. 'It's a three-penny bit,' he said. 'And it's got a hole in it. Lizzie had one just like it; she wore it round her neck. She said it was a joey and would bring her luck. I'm going to keep it.'

He found a piece of tarry twine caught on a rock and threaded the lucky joey on to it; then he pulled it over his head and tucked it into his shirt. He wondered if Lizzie was still wearing hers.

Caroline was already halfway up the beach, scrambling over the stones so that Billy had difficulty catching up with her. She paid their three-pence admission and they pushed their way through the turnstile on to the pier.

It was a glorious, if slightly frightening, place. They walked over slatted boards under which the waves foamed and sucked at the shingle, and the only thing that prevented them from being pushed over the side were the green-painted iron railings. There were little shops selling shell-fish and all manner of sweet-meats, traders selling balloons and paper hats, and anglers watching their lines and hoping for a catch.

They slid down a helter-skelter on prickly mats, tumbling off at the bottom in a laughing heap and then leaping to their feet to escape being landed on by the next merrymaker. They spent an hour in the Palace of Pleasure putting pennies in slot-machines until they'd run out of loose coins. Then there was the Hall of Mirrors that Billy was sure was magic; and the Ghost Train that frightened Caroline more than Billy.

At last, exhausted by their adventures, they climbed a ladder up to the sun-terrace and pressed their noses against the glass window of the tea-room.

A tightly corseted lady with long brightly painted fingernails and permed hair was pouring tea for a young man dressed in grey flannels and a blue blazer with a badge on the breast pocket. The lady suddenly spotted the children through the glass. Caroline crossed her blue eyes and waggled her tongue so rudely that the woman gave a little shriek of alarm and almost dropped the teapot.

They ran away before they were caught: down the ladder two steps at a time, and flung themselves into a corner. Caroline commenced dropping pieces of paper and stones through the cracks in the boards, and watching them fall into the water.

'What shall we do now?' Billy asked.

'I want one of those golliwogs they were selling in the shop we passed,' Caroline said. 'They only cost two and sixpence.'

'Is there enough money left?'

'Of course.' Caroline's hand dipped into her pocket. She frowned and dipped deeper. The corners of her mouth drooped and she turned mournful eyes upon Billy. 'It's all gone.'

'What do you mean, all gone? We can't have spent a whole five pounds.'

'I must have lost it.'

'Perhaps it dropped out when you went down the slide.'

'I expect so.' A tear trickled out of Caroline's eye and ran down her cheek. When it reached the corner of her mouth she licked it away with the tip of her pink tongue. 'Oh dear! And I did want one of those golliwogs.'

'If the money dropped out of your pocket we may be able to find it. Let's search.'

They retraced their footsteps, but all they found was a copper halfpenny under a deck chair.

'That won't even pay for our bus-fares home,' Caroline complained.

'I don't mind,' Billy said, although he was tired. Rotting-dean seemed an awfully long way to walk.

The excitement had gone out of the day. They wandered along the pier, past the booths and glass-fronted shops that had once seemed so attractive. The toyshop had bears and dolls wearing sailor-hats, as well as golli-wogs in striped trousers and scarlet jackets with black woolly hair and cheerful faces.

The man behind the counter was small and dark, with gold earrings and a tattooed spider on his forearm. He was unpacking a cardboard box and kept disappearing from view. The children were hidden from his sight by the edge of the counter. Caroline picked up the nearest golliwog and hugged it to her chest.

'Put it back,' Billy whispered. 'He'll see you.'

'But I want it.' The whine Caroline used to get her own way was back in her voice.

'Well, you can't have it. Put it back!'

But she ignored his advice and started to walk towards the turnstile still carrying the black toy. Billy was horri-fied. He was an honest little boy and even at eight years old knew the consequences of Caroline's action. They'd be arrested and sent to prison. Aunt Hannah would be angry, and Lizzie would be disappointed in him. He trotted after his companion, determined to make her return it.

'Please, Caroline,' he begged. 'We'll get into awful trouble. Take it back.'

'But I want to keep it,' Caroline said, tossing her head. She was used to getting what she wanted. 'I'm tired and I want to go home. And you have to do as I say because I saved your life – remember?'

'But, Caroline ...'

'Come on.' She started to walk away from him.

It would have been all too easy to give in and follow her – but that would have made him feel as much a thief as Caroline was. He couldn't do it. He ran forward and grabbed the striped leg dangling from under Caroline's arm and pulled. At first nothing happened, but his second tug was successful. He stood there with the toy in his hand while Caroline turned a furious face on him.

'Give it to me – it's mine.'

'No it's not. I'm going to take it back.'

But they might as well have held their words because the dark man's head suddenly appeared over the counter. He took in the situation at once. 'Hey!' he yelled; his voice was loud for such a small man. 'Bring that golliwog back, you little varmints.'

Billy wanted to. Surely if they explained, the store-holder would understand. But Caroline panicked. She started to run towards the turnstile, and Billy, fearful of being left on his own, followed.

If there hadn't been a queue of people filing past the pay-desk they might have made it. One loudly dressed fellow in Harris Tweed suit and checked cap, alerted by the man's cries, stepped forward and grabbed Billy by the arm. Caroline dodged, but tripped over the leg of a deck chair and fell sprawling. As she struggled to her feet she was grabbed by his free hand.

'What's the hurry?' the man asked, shaking them until their teeth rattled.

'Let me go!'

Caroline tried to kick her captor on the shins but he held her at arm's length. Billy stood meekly, his face ashen, with the tell-tale golliwog still clutched in his hand. The man with the gold earrings came hurrying up and snatched it away.

'Look at him, the little villain,' he yelled. 'Pinched it from under my nose, he did. I'd give him a larruping if he was mine.'

'I didn't steal it …'

'Shut your clapper or I'll shut it for you.' He turned to the watching crowd. 'Don't stand there staring as if you're all off your chumps. One of you fetch a bogey.'

A policeman appeared as if by magic and the crowd started to disappear. Caroline immediately burst into tears. Someone called out, 'Leave the poor little beggar alone.' But the uniformed man wasn't so easily moved. When Billy admitted they were on their own he escorted them through the turnstile and pointed to a sign. It said clearly 'Children must be accompanied by an adult'.

There was a police car parked a few yards along the promenade and they were pushed firmly into the back. 'Now sit quietly, kids,' the policeman said over his shoulder. 'We'll sort this out at the station.'

'I don't want to go to the police station,' Caroline sobbed. 'I want you to take me home. My daddy will pay you.'

'This isn't a taxi service. Sit quiet now, both of you.'

At the station they were ushered into an interview room, and told to sit down on two hard chairs and wait. After a few minutes a kindly looking man dressed in a dark uniform with shiny buttons entered with a woman. They introduced themselves as Inspector Brill and WPC Meadows.

'Now,' the inspector prompted. 'Who's going to tell me what happened?'

Before Billy could open his mouth Caroline said, 'Billy did it. Billy took the golly. I want to go home. I want my daddy.'

'If you tell us your name and where you live we'll try to contact him.'

Constable Meadows produced a note-pad and fountain pen from her uniform pocket, unscrewed the top, and sat waiting. She even smiled encouragingly.

'I'm Caroline Hayler, and I live at Rottingdean in Park Cottage.'

'And you?' She smiled at Billy.

'Billy Sargent,' he said in a small voice.

'And do you live at Park Cottage?'

Billy shook his head, so Caroline tried to explain. 'Billy

hasn't got a proper home because his mummy and daddy are dead. He's only got an old aunt, and a sister who's gone away to make her fortune.'

'Well, that sorts one thing out,' Inspector Brill said. 'Your father's in the other office this very minute, young lady. He's in quite a state, I can tell you. Thought he'd lost you for good.'

'Daddy's here?'

'Come and see.'

He took Caroline's hand and led the way. Constable Meadows smiled at Billy reassuringly as they followed close behind.

Sydney Hayler was sitting with his head in his hands. His tie was crooked, and his usually neat hair was standing on end as if he'd been running his fingers through it. He took one look at his little daughter and leaped to his feet.

'Caroline!'

'Daddy!' Caroline burst into tears and ran into her father's outstretched arms.

'You see, sir,' Inspector Brill said. 'I said we'd find them. As good as new, and no harm done.'

'Thank God for that!' Mr Hayler hugged his daughter as if he was never going to let her go. 'My wife is distraught, and I had to mess up an important engagement to search for her.'

'Well, I'm glad to say she's come to no harm – or the boy.'

Sydney Hayler was so pleased to find Caroline safe that he'd forgotten Billy. He stared at the little boy over his daughter's golden head and his face was stern. 'That boy,' he said, 'is the cause of all the trouble.'

'In what way, sir?'

'I took him into my house, Inspector, as a favour. And what does he do in return but steal money out of my wife's purse.'

'Did he now?' Inspector Brill looked down at Billy, and his mouth tightened.

'Five pounds he took. He repays our generosity by thieving.'

'What do you say about that, Billy my lad?' the inspector asked.

'Please, sir, I didn't take anything.'

'Who did then?'

'It was ...' Billy looked at Caroline. Her face was still wet with tears, but as she turned to bury her face in her father's coat he saw her eyes. They were daring him not to give her away. He remembered her words: *I saved your life, remember.* 'I don't know who took it,' he finished lamely. 'But it wasn't me.'

'And the golliwog – I suppose it wasn't you who stole it from the stall on the pier?'

'No, sir.'

'It was too!' Caroline burst out. 'It was Billy's idea to come to Brighton. He had a five-pound note he said his auntie had given him. He made me come. And I saw him steal the golly. I told him not to. Daddy, I want to go home.'

'So you shall, my pet.' Sydney set her down on her feet and patted her head.

'And Billy Sargent?' Inspector Brill asked as father and daughter turned to the door. 'What shall we do with the boy?'

'I won't bring charges if that's what you mean; but I can't take him back into my house after this. I wouldn't have a moment's peace. And my wife is delicate; we have a new baby.'

'Well, sir, what do you suggest?'

'His nearest relative is an aunt, I believe,' Sydney Hayler said impatiently. Billy's welfare was suddenly no concern of his. 'My brother-in-law can give you the details. I'll give you his address.' Constable Meadows handed him her pad and he scribbled busily. 'There. Now I must get my daughter safely back home and put my wife's mind at rest,' and leading Caroline by the hand he strode out of the room. The last Billy saw of Caroline was a curly head and an expressionless face before the door closed behind them.

Inspector Brill studied the address on the constable's pad and tapped his teeth thoughtfully with a pencil. 'Well, Billy my lad,' he said to the frightened child, 'what are we going to do with you?' Billy didn't answer.

'Shall I get on to this Charles Bond? It's a school, so I expect it's on the telephone,' Constable Meadows suggested. 'I can get the aunt's address from him.'

'I'll do it,' Inspector Brill said briskly. 'You can look after this poor little mite. He looks as though he needs a woman's touch,' and he left them alone.

Sally Meadows was a policewoman and a spinster, but underneath her stiff exterior she had a kind heart. She'd quickly summed up Caroline Hayler as a spoiled brat, and probably a liar as well as a thief. Billy Sargent, she thought, had made a bad choice of friend. She sat down on the chair next to the boy and spoke gently.

'Are you all right, love?'

Billy nodded, but his eyes were bright with unshed tears. 'I didn't do it,' he said at last. 'I didn't take the money or the toy. I'm not a thief.'

'I believe you,' Sally said. 'Even if no one else does.' The kind words were almost too much for him, so she quickly changed the subject. 'Are you hungry?' Billy shook his head. 'Well, I guess a glass of milk would be welcome.'

It was; he even managed a chocolate biscuit. When Inspector Brill returned after making his telephone call Billy looked, and felt, a lot better. He called the constable aside to tell her the bad news.

'I spoke to that Bond fellow. The aunt's a neighbour of his, a Mrs Seymour. Only living relative as far as he knows. Anyway, she's been rushed in to hospital; heart attack or something equally nasty. The house is shut up. There was a couple of maids but they've been sent away.'

'So we can't send him home,' Sally Meadows said sadly.

'Doesn't look like it.'

'So what do we do with him?'

'You're a woman, constable. What do you suggest?'

'I don't see that my being a woman has anything to do with it. Harden your heart, you told me, when we had to bring those parents in to identify that little Pargeter boy. You're a policewoman, remember. That's what you told me.'

They were both silent, thinking back to that awful day, only a few weeks before, when nine-year-old Jimmy Pargeter had gone fishing from the West Pier. In the excitement of feeling a pull on his line he'd leaned too far over the railings and fallen headfirst into the water. The current had swept him out to sea. By the time the coast-guards had been alerted, and he'd been spotted a mile or more off the coast, he was dead.

It had fallen to Sally Meadows to break the news to Jimmy's parents, and bring them in to identify their only son's body. Sally had until that day regretted her single, motherless state, but when she saw the emptiness in Mr and Mrs Pargeter's eyes she was almost glad that it could never happen to her.

The inspector pushed the memory away and got back to business. 'I suppose it'll have to be the orphanage.'

Sally was silent. Kempe House on the outskirts of the town was renowned for its strictness. The unfortunate children who found themselves within its grey walls knew that they would be hungry, cold and miserable. But they would have a roof over their heads, and this was preferable to a life on the streets.

'Shall I see to it?'

Sally nodded, and glanced at Billy. He'd helped himself to another biscuit and was dunking it in his milk. He was so small, so innocent, she longed to carry him away and protect him. But there was nothing she could do.

'I'll take him,' she said suddenly. 'He'll be better with me. You ring Kempe House and tell them to expect us.'

Inspector Brill left the room. He was a family man himself and not unmoved by Billy's plight. But he was also a policeman and had learned to push his emotions into the background.

Sally crossed to Billy. He looked up at her trustingly, a smear of chocolate on his cheek. 'I suppose you're sending me back to Aunt Hannah,' he said. 'She's going to be awfully cross.'

'You can't go home, Billy,' Sally said. 'Your aunt is ill in hospital and there's nobody there to look after you.'

'I can look after myself. Or Gladys and Ellen will. They're Aunt Hannah's maids – but Gladys's the nicer one.'

'They've gone as well. The inspector's making arrangements for you to go to Kempe House.'

'What's that?'

'An orphanage.' Billy's face fell and Sally felt the urge to gather him into her arms. She managed to restrain herself. 'It's quite a nice place really. You'll make lots of new friends, and if you're good they'll be kind to you. When your auntie's better she'll probably send for you.'

'I expect so.' Billy got down from his chair and his voice was resigned for the worst. He held out his hand. 'Shall we go, then?'

Kempe House was in the north of the town. It was a large grey building overlooking the sea, but that was the only thing in its favour. Set in flat featureless grounds, it looked more like a prison than a home for over six hundred parentless children. It was surrounded by a wall with an iron gate in the middle. A big iron ring hung at the side.

Sally put out her hand to pull the ring and announce their arrival when half a dozen boys of assorted sizes and ages filed out of the main door and marched across the grass. They wore identical shapeless shorts and rough grey shirts, and their hair was cropped, showing thin vulnerable necks. They looked listless and uninterested in each other, and didn't even have the energy to mess about in the way of most small boys.

'Aren't you going to ring the bell, miss?' Billy asked, looking up into Sally's face.

The constable stood there without moving, with her hand still reaching for the bell. Her eyes were on the forlorn figures as they marched away and disappeared from view. She looked down at the small boy by her side, still clinging trustingly to her hand. Suddenly she came to a decision.

'No, Billy,' she said. 'I'm not going to ring the bell. I've got an idea. Come with me.'

As she was still holding his hand Billy had to comply, and he found himself almost dragged along the pavement behind Sally's uniformed figure. People stared and stepped out of the way, but she was oblivious to them. She'd just had an idea. A daring idea that would solve everything if it worked – and if it didn't would probably cost her her job.

She remembered the address; she'd had to visit there several times. It was within walking distance. She gave no explanations and Billy asked no questions, even when they stood side by side outside a neat little terraced house in a back street off Elm Grove.

The door opened before Sally had a chance to lift the knocker. A short woman dressed in a grey frock, an apron and comfortable slippers, stood in the doorway with a milk-bottle in her hand. She was plump but pale, with watery blue eyes and limp brown hair. Everything about her looked washed-out; and yet you could tell that if she smiled she would be quite nice-looking in a homely sort of way.

'Mrs Pargeter,' Constable Meadows said. 'Do you remember me?'

'You're the police lady, aren't you?'

Mrs Pargeter bent down to put the bottle in its place, and when she stood up she seemed to notice Billy for the first time. Firstly a look of delight and recognition passed across her pale features, and then it was wiped away and replaced by a look of pain.

'Yes. I'm Constable Meadows,' Sally said. 'How are you keeping?'

'Not so badly, in the circumstances. It's Mr Pargeter I'm worried about: can't seem to pull himself out of it. But I suppose it'll take time for both of us.'

'They say that time heals all things,' Constable Meadows said gently. 'I hope you and your husband won't think I'm interfering but I've come to ask a favour.'

'What's that then?' Mrs Pargeter's eyes kept straying back to Billy. He was tired and leaned against the garden wall, his face white and pinched, with mauve shadows under his eyes. 'You were ever so kind to us in our time of sorrow, so we'll help if we can.'

'I'm sure you will, Mrs Pargeter. What I'm going to ask may be hard for you, so don't be afraid to say no.'

'That child's worn out,' Mrs Pargeter interrupted before Sally could state her request. 'Look at him – he can hardly stand upright. What's your name, child?'

'Billy,' Billy said, and wiped his face on his grubby sleeve.

'Well, Constable Meadows, you'd better get Billy home to his mother while he can still walk.'

'I would if I could,' Sally said softly. 'The thing is Billy has no mother, or father for that matter, and at the moment he has no home.'

'No home!' Mrs Pargeter looked aghast. 'And there's me with an empty chair at my table and an empty bed upstairs.'

'That's what I wanted to ask you,' Sally continued. 'I know how you miss your Jimmy – but this little chap's about the same age, and I wondered if you and your husband could find it in your Christian souls to look after him for a few days?'

For a moment Sally Meadows thought she'd gone too

far. How could she expect Mrs Pargeter to welcome into her home a little boy whose presence would only re-open raw wounds, and remind her of her drowned son?

But Mrs Pargeter turned out to be made of sterner stuff. 'You'd better come in,' she said, and led the way down a narrow passage towards a door at the far end. 'He's in there.'

The door opened into a cosy living room. Everything was cheap and well worn; but the geraniums on the windowsill, the shabby armchairs heaped with cushions and the threadbare carpet reminded Billy of Railway Cottage. There was even a pair of Staffordshire dogs on the mantel, and a big marble clock with a loud brassy tick.

Mr Pargeter was sitting in one of the chairs. The handkerchief draped over his head and face puffed in and out as he breathed deeply in his sleep. He was plump and comfortable like his wife; but his braces dangled, and he wasn't wearing a collar or tie.

'Wake up, Father, we've got company,' Mrs Pargeter said.

'What! Who!' With a splutter and a sigh that blew the handkerchief right off his face and into the fireplace, Mr Pargeter came to his senses.

'This is Billy,' Mrs Pargeter said matter-of-factly. 'He's got no parents and no home to go to. We're parents, but we've got an empty bed upstairs, so it seems only sensible that he should stay.' Mr Pargeter opened his mouth, but before he could utter an opinion his wife continued, 'And I don't care what you say, Father, I want him to stay, so that's settled. Now, I'll see Constable Meadows out while you two get acquainted.'

Sally smiled encouragingly at Billy before following Mrs Pargeter out of the room. Billy shuffled his feet and looked at the floor.

'Come here, boy, and let's have a look at you. Now, what did she say your name is?'

'Billy, sir.' Billy looked up and saw kind eyes staring at him. Sad eyes – but not frightening.

'I think my wife's taken a fancy to you. We had a little boy: his name was Jimmy.'

'Where is he?' Billy looked around; he didn't understand.

'He's in heaven – with Jesus.'

'That's where my mummy and daddy are.'

'Well, perhaps your mum and dad will meet up with our Jimmy and look after him for us.'

'I hope so.' Billy's eyes were round with wonder at the idea.

'In which case Ma and me had better look after you. Would you like that?' Billy nodded: it was what he wanted more than anything else. 'Our Jimmy liked football and fishing. What do you like?'

Billy thought carefully before replying. 'I like reading – playing the piano,' he said at last.

'Do you now?' Mr Pargeter chuckled. 'You'd better see what you can get out of that then.' He gestured with his thumb towards a corner of the room.

It was a little harmonium in a wooden case. The keys were cracked and yellow and there were only five octaves, but Billy sat down on a stool and soon learned to pump air into the pedals while his fingers played a scale. He glanced over his shoulder, but Mr Pargeter was leaning back in his chair with a smile on his face, as if he was waiting. So, falteringly, Billy started to play 'The March of the Gladiators'. He made a few mistakes but Mr Pargeter didn't seem to mind; in fact he got up from his chair and stood by the harmonium so that he could hear properly.

'That was fine,' he said when Billy had finished. 'I suppose you want to be a famous pianist when you grow up?'

'No, sir,' Billy said firmly. 'All I want to do when I grow up is find my sister Lizzie. I don't know how I'm going to do it, but I've got a silver joey to help me.' He put his hand inside the neck of his shirt and pulled out the threepenny piece he'd found on the beach and held it out for his new friend to admire.

CHAPTER FIFTEEN

September 1936

'Now hold tightly to Marjorie's hand and be a good boy.'
'Yes, Mum.'

Lizzie gave five-year-old Joey a little push towards the waiting couple. Marjorie French, now thirteen, had grown into a pretty teenager; her fair hair hung in a neat plait and her cotton frock was crisp and clean. By her side and clinging to her hand was Eileen, the same age as Joey, with a head of unruly ginger curls tied back with a blue ribbon bow. Joey trotted down the path and took Marjorie's free hand.

'Will I like school?' he asked, staring up into her face.

'Of course you will. There's lots of things to do and games to play; and Mrs Canton, she's the headmistress, is really kind.'

It was September, and the first day at Stanford Road Mixed Infants School for Eileen and Joey. The small boy looked even smaller beside the plump figure of Eileen, but he was a wiry child who was hardly ever ill and usually cheerful. Even the thought of the new experience he was about to undertake couldn't wipe the smile completely from his face.

He was a charmer without a doubt, with his mother's big brown eyes and dark hair that fell in a quiff over his forehead. His skin was brown after long days spent in the sun, and the collar of his new shirt felt uncomfortably stiff. It was the first time he'd had to wear a tie and he was proud of it – and his grey shorts and knee-length socks held up by garters made from knicker elastic.

'Come on then,' Marjorie said gaily. 'You mustn't be late on your first day. Wave goodbye to your mum, Joey.'

Joey waved obediently and Lizzie sighed. She'd looked forward to taking her son to school herself on his first day, but Mrs Marshall wanted a bed-bath because the doctor was coming, so Marjorie had offered to stand in for her.

Suddenly Joey ran back and flung his arms around his mother. 'Give me a kiss for luck, Mum,' he demanded.

Lizzie laughed. 'I've got something better than a kiss,' she said, and putting up her hands pulled a thin black ribbon over her head. On the end was a small silver coin. She held it out to her son.

'But, Mum – that's your silver joey.'

'I don't need it any more,' Lizzie assured him. 'Haven't I got you – a real live lucky Joey? I want you to have the luck.'

Joey took the tiny coin in his hand and smiled before looping the ribbon over his head and tucking it into his collar. 'Thanks, Mum,' and he was off, confident now to join Marjorie and Eileen.

Lizzie smiled with pride, and leaned against the wall to watch the trio until they were out of sight. She'd changed from the thin shabby girl who'd arrived in Brighton five years before. Maternity had filled out her figure attractively, and although her dress of blue cotton wasn't expensive, it was well cut and the fitted bodice and flared skirt suited her. She'd grown her hair again, and although it would never be as long as it was when she'd left Railway Cottage, the sleek shoulder-length style was most becoming.

She smoothed her skirt over her hips and turned up her face to the sun. What wouldn't she give for a brisk walk across the Downs or a bus ride to the Devil's Dyke; but that would have to wait until Jack called for her this afternoon. Now she had work to do.

'Lizzie!' Granny Marshall called from the downstairs back room where she suffered her old-age and invalidism with humour and cheerfulness. 'Lizzie! If you don't come now I'll get off myself and then you'll have to clean up after me.'

Lizzie grinned. 'Coming, Gran,' she called, and hurried back into the house. She'd left the old woman seated on her commode, and if she didn't go to her aid at once Gran was perfectly capable of carrying out her threat.

She soon had her back in bed and then with hot water, towels and blankets, saw to her toilet. When Mrs Marshall was propped up for the day against the soft pillows, with a multi-coloured shawl draped around her shoulders and her thin white hair neatly brushed, they exchanged smiles.

'Did he get off all right?'

Lizzie knew the old woman was referring to Joey. 'Yes. Marjorie took him with Eileen, so he won't be alone.'

'You'll have time on your hands now. What will you do with yourself?'

'Jack's coming this afternoon. I expect we'll go for a walk.'

'It's time you and Jack French did more than walk.' Gran grinned wickedly. 'I wish I was young enough – I'd soon have that young man up to the altar.'

'I'm sure you would, Gran.' Lizzie laughed and gathered up the towels and enamel bowl. 'Jack says you're young in spirit so you'd better watch out. I sometimes think he has designs on you.'

Granny Marshall grinned delightedly. She'd already buried two husbands and only missed a third because the prospective bridegroom dropped dead two days before the ceremony.

'It was the excitement,' Gran said proudly when she related the event. 'I over-excited him and his heart gave out. But he died happy.'

'Now, I'll get your pills, and a cup of tea to wash them down,' Lizzie said.

'I'd rather have a Guinness.'

'I'm sure you would, but Dr Thwaites would never forgive me if I gave you one.'

'He doesn't have to know,' Gran said wistfully.

'No, Gran. I'll get you your library book. Which would you like? J. B. Priestly or Warwick Deeping?'

Mrs Marshall settled for *The Good Companions*, leaving Lizzie to start her daily chores.

There was plenty to keep her occupied: washing Gran's clothes and bed-linen because she was sometimes incontinent, her own underclothing, which she liked to change daily, and of course Joey's things. Then there was the house to sweep and dust, the cat to feed and dinner to prepare.

Today she was going to make a rolled-bacon pudding with cabbage and potatoes, followed by stewed apples and custard. A cheap meal because she'd managed to get some streaky bacon from the International Stores for fivepence a pound. The apples were from a tree in the back garden. It wasn't that Lizzie had to be particularly frugal, but she still couldn't get out of the habit of economising even after five years.

She smiled as she worked; her mind going back to that day when Joey had been born in Grace French's house next door. How young and innocent she'd been then – and how frightened. Life had held no promise for her in those days, but as soon as she'd held her lucky Joey in her arms she knew she had someone to fight for – someone who would make her life worthwhile.

Jack French and his family had continued to stand by her, even though she was the cause of gossip in the neighbourhood. She, an unmarried girl, and dear Jack, who, the tale-tellers insisted, must be Joey's father.

He'd even asked her to marry him, but of course she'd had to turn him down. To start with she was too young to marry without permission; and who was there to ask? No parents, and an aunt who had turned her out of the house. If she went back to Greenlock to ask Aunt Hannah a favour, with a baby in her arms and no ring on her finger, she knew she would be met with scorn. Even for Billy's sake she couldn't go back – not yet.

Lizzie tried not to think about her brother. He'd been only a few years older than Joey when she'd left him, with the promise to return when she'd made her fortune. Apart from that they were not very alike. Billy with his gentle ways and fair complexion, and the swarthy Joey, sparky and full of life. Her brother would be thirteen now. Was he still waiting? Would he even recognise his sister again after all this long time? Lizzie could only hope so.

It was Mrs Marshall, or Granny as everyone called her, who had come to Lizzie's rescue. The Frenches would never have turned her out, but the little house in Coventry Street was full even before she came along. But then, with Marjorie giving up her room to the newcomer, it was bursting at the seams.

Lizzie insisted that she would move on as soon as she was strong enough but they begged her to stay. But every time Joey cried and kept the household awake, or Johnnie or Marjorie searched the house for a quiet corner, Lizzie felt guilty.

She'd thought about getting a job, but who would employ her when she still had a baby to feed? Her dreams of being a beautician and travelling the world to find love in the arms of a handsome prince, like Opal in the romantic novel, were not for the likes of her. She gave the book away. Lizzie had no time for dreams – reality took up all of her spare time.

And then Granny Marshall had a fall. She was a game old lady of nearly eighty who lived in the house next door.

Grace French tried to keep an eye on her, but she was sprightly and independent and didn't accept help gracefully. The accident wouldn't have been serious for a younger person, but Gran's age was against her, and when she came home after a short spell in hospital it was obvious that she needed help.

Lizzie was soon roped in to giving a hand, and the young mother and the old woman soon grew fond of each other. Gran adored Joey as well, saying that a baby in the house took her mind off her ailments and made her feel young again. When she offered them a home and a small wage in return for nursing-care and help around the house, Lizzie jumped at the chance. She had a bedroom to herself, and a smaller one opening from it for the baby, and the rest of the house they shared.

It was a good arrangement as Granny Marshall slowly got worse. A bedroom was made up for her on the ground floor and soon she rarely left it. But she had a strong willpower and was always cheerful, which made Lizzie's task easier, and there was always Grace on hand in case of difficulty. She had only to knock on the wall and someone would come running: either Jack or his mother or father, determined to make Lizzie's life as easy as possible.

Lizzie was pulled back to the present by the sound of the front door opening and the doctor's heavy footsteps marching down the hall. He called a greeting to Lizzie and she smiled: Dr Thwaites was such an improvement on the doctor who called on her when she was pregnant. He'd talked to Grace French as if she, Lizzie, wasn't there, and then had the audacity to suggest the workhouse or the street. Luckily Grace had been horrified and changed doctors immediately.

'I hope she's been behaving herself?' the doctor asked in a voice loud enough for even the old lady to hear.

'Well, she wanted a Guinness instead of tea,' Lizzie said.

'I hope you didn't give her one?'

'No. I said you'd be shocked. I've just given her a blanket bath and she's looking pretty.'

'All dressed up to see me?' Dr Thwaites poked his head around the door and winked at Granny Marshall. 'My, my, I am flattered.'

'Stop your nonsense,' Gran commanded. 'My heart's going pitter-patter. I'm sure it's going to stop any minute. Give me something quickly – or take my pulse to see if it's still beating.'

'Well, if it wasn't, you wouldn't be looking so perky.' There was a silence and in the kitchen Lizzie started rolling out the pastry. 'Why, you're as strong as an ox, woman. You'll outlive all of us,' and the doctor came out of the sick room pocketing his stethoscope.

'How is she?' Lizzie asked.

'As fit as a woman her age can be, by all accounts,' Dr Thwaites reported. 'I've left a prescription on the mantel-piece, and …' he lowered his voice for Lizzie's ears alone, 'an occasional glass of Guinness won't do her any harm. But don't tell her I said so: she likes to think she knows best.'

After the doctor had gone about his business, the morning passed quickly. Grace French was collecting Joey and Eileen and taking them next door for their dinner. She was sharing this duty with Lizzie on a rota system.

Of course Joey had to run in for a quick kiss, and to report that school was lovely. He'd drawn a picture, learned a new song, and could he go now please because Eileen was waiting?

Lizzie smiled as she sliced the bacon pudding and piled vegetables on to two plates. At least Mrs Marshall still had a healthy appetite. She decorated the tray with a lacy cloth and a pink rosebud in an egg-cup before carrying it in to the invalid.

'Vinegar!' Gran demanded. 'You know that I have vinegar on bacon pud.'

Lizzie ate her meal at the kitchen table with the wireless switched on for company. A female vocalist was singing 'September Song' and Lizzie hummed an accompaniment as she washed the dishes.

When Gran Marshall was settled for her afternoon nap Lizzie was free. The old lady would sleep until tea-time, and Grace was next door keeping an eye on things.

Jack would arrive about two o'clock so she had plenty of time to make herself look nice. She changed into a brown tweed costume and a cream blouse that she'd made herself; and then from the top of the wardrobe took down the brown velvet hat with its yellow ribbon. It was old now, and past its best, but she brushed it regularly and pressed the brim under a damp cloth. Lizzie was fond of the old hat because Jack had bought it for her. She placed it carefully on her newly brushed hair and viewed herself in the mirror.

Her nose powdered, a touch of pink lipstick, and Lizzie was ready. She knew she looked nice, and hoped Jack would notice how much trouble she'd gone to.

When she heard Spud barking she knew he was on his way. That meant they were going walking. Lizzie opened the front door and the little black and white dog leaped up at her. He was middle-aged now, but still as frisky as a puppy. She gathered him into her arms and he licked the powder from her nose with his long pink tongue.

'He's moulting, Jack,' she said. 'Look at my jacket; it's all over hairs.'

'Put him down then,' Jack said, lounging in the doorway, his freckled face screwed up because of the smoke from his cigarette.

'I don't mind,' Lizzie laughed. But she put the friendly animal down on the path where he commenced running up and down excitedly, anxious to be off.

'You look nice,' Jack said, knowing how to please her. 'I like the hat. Is it a new one?'

Lizzie blushed. 'It's all of five years old, Jack French,

and well you should know it. You bought it for me – don't you remember?'

'Of course I do.' Jack's face misted over with memories. Lizzie realised he'd been teasing her when he thrust a paper-bag into her hands, saying, 'I thought it was time it had a fresh trimming.' Inside the bag was a new length of ribbon – blue this time. Lizzie laughed with delight.

'Thank you. I'll sew it on tonight. The old yellow will have its last airing.'

Snapping Spud's lead on to his collar, they set out. 'Where are we off to?' Lizzie asked as Jack slipped his arm through hers and marched her off along Coventry Street.

'Spud wants a run in the park, and I'm going to buy you tea in the café. We'll go the long way round.'

The long way round took them past the school, where they peered through the gates at the children playing rounders on the tarmac. They were older than Joey, serious and athletic in their Aertex shirts and black gym-shoes. One day Joey would graduate from the infants class to compete against other children and grow strong and robust. Sometimes Lizzie longed to keep him a baby for ever, but knew that it wasn't possible.

'Come on,' Jack said, pulling her away.

There was a shop on either side of the school's gate. On the left was a grocer's, and on the right a sweet shop that was frequented by the schoolchildren. They spent their pocket-money on liquorice allsorts and fruit gums, or twists of fizzy lemonade powder that stained their fingers and tongues bright yellow.

In the next road they passed Staggs: the greengrocer's shop where Jack still worked. George Stagg, the proprietor, was arranging fruit on an open display. He waved as they passed and threw Lizzie an orange. He still remembered the day when she'd tried to steal an apple because she was starving, and had then collapsed in a heap almost on his doorstep.

George thought Lizzie had turned into a fine-looking woman. And Jack was still fond of her; you could see it in his eyes, and hear it in his voice when he talked about her. They made a lovely couple: she in her costume and perky hat, and he in his flannels and sports jacket.

They reached the iron railings that overlooked the railway line with its row of horse-chestnut trees and trailing brambles heavy with ripe blackberries. Down below, steam-engines shunted noisily up and down, carrying coal, coke and sometimes cattle. Then over the bridge and down the flight of steps called Lover's Walk towards the park.

'I hate this place,' Lizzie said, clinging to Jack's arm. 'Gran Marshall told me that a woman was murdered here.'

'So she was,' Jack said. 'But it was a long time ago so don't look so scared.'

'I'm not scared when you're with me,' Lizzie admitted. 'But I wouldn't like to be here alone when it's dark.'

Spud loved Preston Park. He chased across the grass after everything that moved: a flying stick, other dogs, feathers and leaves that were just turning brown and beginning to fall. When he got bored Jack found an old tennis ball and the game began all over again. However far the little dog had to run to retrieve the ball he soon found them again. He dropped it at their feet and looked up at them out of liquid eyes begging for another throw. They tried to outwit him by hiding, but although he had to search around he always found them eventually.

'Come with me,' Jack said, and taking Lizzie by the hand he pulled her into some thick bushes. The branches fell together behind them and they stood there close together, his arm around her waist.

'We've beaten him this time,' Lizzie said.

'Don't talk,' Jack whispered into her ear, and then, 'I can feel your heart beating.'

'Can you?' Lizzie slid her hand inside his jacket. 'I can feel yours.'

They stood there close together, friends of many years standing, comfortable in each other's presence. He'd asked her to marry him several times; for her sake, for Joey's, but she'd always refused. Perhaps she would have accepted right at the very beginning, but she thought he was trying to be kind. Perhaps he was only sorry for her; she couldn't bear that. She still had her pride.

Love should be a wonderful thing, like it had been for Opal in the story, sweeping a girl off her feet and into another world. Lizzie only wanted to marry for love.

But as they stood there amongst the cool greenery something happened. Their hands trembled at the other's touch; and when Lizzie's brown eyes met Jack's blue ones she saw love, not sympathy.

And then Jack kissed her. Of course he'd kissed her before, many times, brotherly kisses that showed how fond he was of her. But this time he kissed her on the lips. There were no fireworks, no tidal-waves, just a pleasant glow that started in the pit of Lizzie's stomach and spread through her body. Her nerve ends tingled as if a small electric charge had taken place. When he kissed her a second time his mouth was hard and demanding, so that her limbs turned to water and she thought she was drowning in pleasure. She was trembling, and it was only Jack's strong arm that stopped her from falling.

'I love you,' he said softly.

'And I love you,' and suddenly Lizzie knew that she did.

Since Tom Grainger's cruel attack, her body had been frozen against intimate physical contact. Her unconscious mind had warned her that men were dangerous, sex brought pain not pleasure, and it was safer to deny the urges of her young healthy body. But Jack's patience, his tenderness, had melted the ice in her heart and now she was all softness and light.

Spud's yapping brought them to their senses. He'd found their hiding-place, wriggled under the bushes, and placed the ball like a trophy at their feet. Gently Jack released her.

'Damn dog,' he said, with a lopsided grin.

They emerged into the sunshine, blinking their eyes against the light. Jack's collar was askew, and Lizzie had to retrieve her precious hat which had dropped off during their embrace. The rough turf beneath their feet felt soft as velvet and they walked as if on air.

In the rose-garden Jack picked a late bud and threaded it through Lizzie's button-hole. There was a sign saying 'Dogs must be kept on a lead' but they didn't notice it, and they looked so happy that no one had the heart to point it out.

'Let's go into the café and have some tea.' Jack guided Lizzie towards the terraced tea-rooms overlooking a pond with stepping-stones and waterlilies. 'I've got something for you.'

'It's not my birthday until November,' Lizzie protested as she sat down at one of the little white-painted tables and watched Jack give the order.

He waited until the waitress had brought the tray and Lizzie had poured the tea from the plated pot, adding milk and sugar just as he liked it. Then he said shyly, 'I've sold my bike.'

Lizzie was so surprised she put down her cup and stared at him. He'd been saving up for as long as she could remember for a motor-bike, and only last Christmas had acquired the longed-for machine. How proudly he'd shown it off to her, and insisted on giving her a ride although she hadn't liked it very much. What had happened to make him part with his most treasured possession?

'You've sold your bike, Jack. But why?'

'Because I needed the money.'

'I could have lent you some. I've managed to save quite a bit since I've been living at Gran's.'

Jack smiled. 'I couldn't take your money, Lizzie, not for

what I wanted to buy.' Before she could ask any more questions he put his hand in his pocket and pulled out a small square box made of black leather. 'Open it,' he said, pushing it across the table. 'It's for you.'

Inside the box, nestling on a bed of white silk, was an engagement ring – a garnet with a small diamond on either side – the prettiest ring Lizzie had ever seen.

'Oh, Jack!' was all she could say. 'You sold your bike for me.'

'Yes. Because I want you to marry me, Lizzie, and I'm not going to take no for an answer. I want you to wear this ring so that everyone will know we're promised to each other. I want to be a father to Joey.'

Lizzie didn't know what to say. Spud, lying at their feet, looked up, staring first at Jack then at Lizzie, as if he was trying to understand.

'You'd do that for me – and Joey?'

'And myself. I love you, Lizzie, I think I always have. But things were never right. If I don't speak out now I never will. Joey's starting school today made me think. All the other boys will have fathers to care about them, to play football with and take their troubles to. Joey mustn't grow up feeling different. Will you, Lizzie? Will you marry me?'

Lizzie looked from the ring to Jack and her eyes filled with tears. 'Of course I will,' she said softly. 'I shall be proud to be your wife.'

'You'd better try it on then.' Jack took her hand and tried to slip the ring over the correct finger. It slid easily as far as the knuckle and then refused to go any further. Even when Lizzie tried it wouldn't budge.

'It's too small,' she said, trying not to show her disappointment.

'I should have taken you with me to choose it. Don't worry, I'll take it back to the shop and have it made larger.'

'In the meantime I can wear it around my neck on a ribbon.'

Lizzie couldn't explain, even to herself, why she felt so disappointed. After all, the wearing of a ring shouldn't be so important. But her spirits had plummeted when the ring had refused to slide over her knuckle. She wasn't particularly superstitious so why did she have the feeling that it was an omen?

'What about your silver coin,' Jack laughed. 'You always wear that around your neck.'

Lizzie put up her hand to feel for the lucky coin but her throat was bare. Then she remembered. 'I haven't got it any more. I gave it to Joey this morning to bring him luck on his first day at school.'

'Let's hope he didn't need it.'

They finished their tea and left the café. Lizzie brightened up. She did love Jack, and she was going to make him a good wife. Nothing was going to spoil things; certainly not the fact that the ring he'd chosen didn't fit.

When they reached Coventry Street they were both anxious to impart the good news. First Jack's mother had to be told. She'd collected the children from school, and was now spreading margarine on to slices of bread to make sandwiches for their tea.

Lizzie expected that Joey would come hurtling towards her to tell her about his day. But he didn't. He just looked up from the toy soldier he was playing with, and said, 'Hullo, Mum.'

'Did you have a nice time?' Lizzie asked.

'Yes.'

'Aren't you going to give me a kiss?'

'I'm a big boy now,' and carrying his soldier Joey marched out of the room to find Eileen. Lizzie and Grace looked at each other.

'Don't worry,' Grace said. 'Boys like to think they're independent. I've been through it twice, remember. He's waiting until he's got you alone.'

'Mum,' Jack said, standing by Lizzie and taking her

hand. 'Put that bread-knife down. We've got something to tell you.'

Grace looked from one shining face to the other and smiled. 'I don't think you need tell me,' she said. 'I can read it in your faces.'

'Is it so obvious?' Lizzie asked, laughing.

'It is to me. When are you planning on getting married then?'

'The sooner the better. We've waited too long.'

'Better that, than rush into things and regret it later,' Grace said. 'Oh dear, I've got nothing to celebrate with – only tea.'

'Tea'll be fine.'

'I want to take Lizzie out for a drink this evening,' Jack said. 'Just to make things special. Do you mind?'

'Of course not. I'll see to Gran, and Joey can stay here tonight. You two run along.'

They decided to go to the Marquis of Exeter, a local public house that was always busy. Lizzie had never been there before because she wasn't used to drinking and her mother had always said that women should never go into pubs on their own. But tonight was an occasion and she wanted to enjoy it.

She changed into her best dress: a silky green frock that clung to her figure and showed it off to its best advantage. Her hair shone with brushing, and she reddened her lips and dabbed perfume behind her ears. She wanted Jack to be proud of her.

They entered the saloon bar arm in arm. Jack guided her to a table in a quiet corner.

'What will you have?'

'I don't know. Something with lemonade in it.'

'I'll get you a shandy.'

He pushed his way towards the bar and Lizzie looked around nervously. The ring was hanging inside her dress on a thin cord; she could feel it cold between her breasts. She prayed that Jack wouldn't be long.

'Here we are.' Jack was back, carrying two glasses which he placed carefully on the table. 'Guess who's here? An old friend of ours – someone we haven't seen for years. Over here!' he called to a thin upright figure who was approaching with a cigarette in one hand and a glass in the other. 'It's Tom Grainger. You remember Tom, don't you, Lizzie?'

CHAPTER SIXTEEN

Tom

'Would you like eggs or kedgeree?' Frances Grainger asked as she hovered over the silver dishes on the sideboard.

Her husband, Victor, plumped himself down at the table, and unrolled his linen napkin before spreading it over his knees. His newly shaven face was pink and dimpled, and his white moustache neatly trimmed. He looked what he was: well fed, well groomed and well heeled. After all, wasn't he the owner of Grainger's, the finest gentleman's outfitters along the south coast, and he liked to look the part.

'Is there any bacon?'

'Yes. Some nice back rashers.'

'I'll have egg and bacon then.'

Frances filled a plate and carried it to the table. She was a tall, thin, nervous woman, who made a drama of everything. Now it was some spilt tea on the cloth. She made her husband lift his plate so that she could spread a clean one. Then she sat down on the opposite chair with her own breakfast – a finger of toast.

'Now that autumn's near perhaps we should be having

porridge for a change, Victor.'

'Or kippers,' Victor said with his mouth full. He liked his food, and masticated carefully with his new set of false teeth. He took them out every night to rest his gums and they took a while to get going in the mornings. 'Is Tom down yet?'

'I don't think so. I haven't heard him.' Frances was pouring coffee, and the mention of her only son's name made her hand tremble. 'I think he was late in last night.'

'He's always late in.'

'He's only a boy.'

'A boy!' Victor swallowed too quickly and a piece of bacon caught in his throat. He coughed and then took a mouthful of tea. 'He's twenty-five, Frances, although you still insist on treating him as if he was still a child. He drinks too much and smokes too many cigarettes, and we hardly ever see him at the shop.'

'That's not Tom's fault ...'

'And when he does appear he spends his time lazing about and chasing every pretty girl in sight.'

'That's because he's bored, Victor.' Frances defended her son tearfully, although she knew her husband was right. 'He says you never give him any interesting jobs to do. How can he learn the business when you leave him in the stockroom doing menial jobs?'

'He has to start from the bottom like I did. You can't walk into a shop as a floor manager without knowing the ropes. If I wasn't his father he'd have been sacked years ago.'

His plate empty, Victor wiped his fingers and left his napkin in a crumpled heap. He insisted on a clean one at every meal: neatly pressed and rolled into its silver ring.

'You're cruel.' Frances dabbed her eye, which looked ominously moist.

'Don't cry, woman!' Victor exploded. 'I can't stand tears at breakfast. Has the post arrived yet?'

'Yes. It's on the drawing-room table.'

'Then I'll take my coffee in there as well. And you can send Tom in to me. I want a word with him.'

'He's still asleep.'

'Then he can wake up.' Victor pushed back his chair so sharply that it almost toppled over. 'I'll give him ten minutes.'

All of a fluster Frances jumped to her feet. 'I'll go and tell him at once.'

'Send the girl,' Victor bellowed over his shoulder as he marched out of the room. 'That's what I pay her for.'

But where Tom was concerned Frances Grainger was prepared to defy her husband, and although the girl, whose name was Mabel, was only wandering around the hall flicking the tops of the pictures with a feather duster, she pattered past her up the stairs. Outside her son's bedroom she stopped, took a deep breath to stop her heart pounding, and tapped on the door.

'Tommy – are you awake?'

A faint groan reached her ears through the panels. It assured her that if Tom wasn't fully conscious he was at least alive.

'Tommy!' she said in a louder voice. 'It's Mummy.'

'Go away!'

'I can't, darling boy. I'm coming in.' Frances turned the handle and entered the room.

The air smelled stale, laced with a distinct odour of alcohol. Clothes littered the carpet. She had to pick her way through discarded shoes and underwear to reach the window and open the curtains. The additional light disclosed even more disorder. Trousers that she'd pressed only the day before lay in an untidy heap, a shirt ripped at the front where its wearer had struggled to remove it without bothering to unfasten the buttons, and dried vomit in the hand wash-basin.

In the bed Frances could just see her son's head on the pillow, pale and bleary eyed, with an unshaven chin and dark hair ruffled from sleep. When he'd left the house the previous evening, calling a cheery goodbye, she'd congratulated herself on having such a handsome son, but in the first light of day there was nothing to be proud of.

'Close the curtains, Ma, I've got a splitting headache.'

'Daddy wants to see you, Tommy, in the drawing room. He's in one of his moods, I'm afraid.'

'Oh, Lord!' Tom turned over in the bed and pulled the sheet up over his head to protect his eyes from the bright light.

'You won't have time to dress. He said ten minutes.'

'Tell him I'm ill.'

Frances dithered; she knew her husband wouldn't be palmed off with lies. 'You must come, Tommy,' she begged. 'Put your dressing-gown on and brush your hair.' She unhooked a silk paisley robe from behind the door and held it out.

Grudgingly Tom pushed aside the bedclothes and allowed himself to be dressed. Even so, he looked in sorry shape when he opened the drawing-room door. He needed a black coffee, or a cigarette, before facing his father. He had neither, so he squared his shoulders and tried to look nonchalant.

'Morning, Pa,' he said cheerfully.

Victor Grainger was standing in the bow window with a bone letter-opener in one hand and an envelope in the other. He looked at his son and frowned, obviously displeased with what he saw.

'Don't call me Pa,' he snapped.

'Sorry, Father.' Tom slouched across the room. 'Is there any coffee left?'

'No.'

'All right, I'll get Ma to make me some more.'

'You'll stay where you are; and don't call your mother Ma. Sit down where I can see you.'

'Sorry, Father.' Tom pulled out a chair and sat down uneasily.

'And where were you last night, may I ask?'

'I went to Sherry's with a few friends. Had a dance and a few drinks and then came home.'

'What time?'

'I don't know. Eleven, twelve – does it matter?'

'It does when you're employed to start work at nine in the morning and you're in no condition.'

'Oh, come off it, Pa – I mean, Father.' Tom leaned back in his chair and grinned. 'You were young once.'

'When I was young we knew our responsibilities. You have a duty to me and to the business.'

'OK, I'm sorry. It won't happen again. Can I go now?' Tom got up, staggered slightly, and steadied himself on the back of the chair. 'I'll be fine when I've had some coffee. Then I'll get along to the shop.'

'I haven't finished.'

'Oh!'

As if overcome by weariness Tom sank back into the chair. Did he dare ask his father for a cigarette? He could see a packet of Woodbines on the sideboard. No, perhaps he'd better wait; wouldn't do to rile the old boy further.

Victor folded his letter and slowly placed it back in its envelope before pocketing it. Then he faced his son with his thumbs neatly tucked into the revers of his coat.

'You remember the terms of your grandfather's will, I suppose?'

'Of course. I get the dosh when I'm twenty-five. So, I'm twenty-five and a few weeks – when do I get it?'

'That's up to me, Tom.'

Tom stared at his father blankly; then he relaxed and grinned. 'What are you trying to do – frighten me?'

'Not at all.' Victor looked at his son and didn't care for what he saw. Tom never failed to be a disappointment to him. Of course he blamed Frances; she'd spoiled him all his life. But perhaps it wasn't too late if he put his foot down now. 'It's ten years since your grandfather died. You were only fifteen, and too young to appreciate the terms of his will.'

'He left me half of his estate,' Tom said, licking his lips in anticipation. 'In trust until I reach twenty-five.'

'There was also a clause, Tom, that may have meant little to you at the time.'

'Oh, that!' Tom shrugged his shoulders. 'Something to do with me getting married.'

'Your grandfather was anxious for the business to continue, and the family line. So, if you'd married and had a son before your twenty-fifth birthday you would have got your legacy then.'

'Well, I didn't.' Tom grinned. 'I've been a good boy and waited.'

'And now you're going to have to wait a bit longer.'

The smile slipped from Tom's face. 'What are you talking about?'

'The trust fund is in my control,' Victor Grainger said. 'That is also in the will. You only get your inheritance when I think fit; and from the sort of life you've been leading I can only see you frittering away your grandfather's money by extravagant living. I want you to settle down, start taking responsibilities, do a good day's work at the shop. It's not too late.'

Tom glowered. 'I hate the shop.'

'You just hate work.' Victor strode across the room and put his hand on his son's shoulder, not unkindly. 'I've thought this over carefully and it's for your own good. I want to see you make something of yourself, so your mother and I can be proud of you. The same terms will apply.'

'What terms?'

'You'll have to wait another five years for your inheritance unless you can prove to me that you're settling down.'

'Five years!' Tom looked aghast. 'I'll be thirty.'

Victor carried on as if he hadn't spoken. 'I'll expect you to turn up regularly for work and take an interest; so you'll be ready to take over when I retire. Five years will soon pass, and reaching thirty isn't the end of the world. Of course, if in the meantime you get married and your wife produces a son, you'll get your inheritance at once.'

'It's not fair!'

'It's about time you realised that life isn't always fair,' his father said, who many times had complained about the unfairness of life at being landed with such a son. And on these words he marched out of the room.

The first thing Tom did was help himself to a cigarette. He lit it with shaking fingers, and stood there frowning as he watched the grey smoke spiral upwards.

Suddenly he seemed to come to a decision and an unpleasant smile curved his lips. So that was the way it was to be, was it? He didn't intend waiting five more years for what was his by right. He'd go to work and put his father's mind at rest, and then, when the shop was closed, he'd go and see Milly. She'd know what he should do. She might even marry him – and even if she refused it would be fun finding out.

By now Tom was wide awake. He was feeling so much better that he even gave Mabel a crafty peck on the cheek as he passed her on the stairs.

'Give over, Mister Tom,' she said, pushing him away. His only answer was to give her bottom a sharp pinch.

When it suited him Tom could work fast. Within half an hour he was washed, shaved and dressed in clean clothes. While he'd been occupied with his father, his mother had tidied his room and laid out freshly pressed and laundered apparel. She wouldn't let the girl, Mabel, do such intimate things for her son. It might give them both ideas.

By the time Tom was ready to leave the house his father had already gone. The Bentley wasn't in the garage so he'd have to walk to work. But it was a fine day, he'd got over his hangover and made his plans.

When he reached Grainger's he paused to admire the new frontage. The shop was in a good position, occupying a busy corner of Western Road, and the windows were brightly lit and full of the new season's fashions for men.

Motoring coats made of camel-hair, corduroy trousers and pin-striped suits, plus-fours and blazers. Grainger's was proud to sell ready-made clothes, or alternatively make them to measure. They supplied all tastes, from the man about town to the fresh-faced young fellow with his first pay-packet. No matter how small or large the income, Grainger's aimed to please. A ready-made suit could be purchased for as little as thirty bob, while a tailor-made would cost ten times as much. A side-window was full of head-gear: bowlers and opera-hats were arranged among caps and trilbys.

Tom adjusted his own trilby. He liked to wear it at an angle like Ronald Colman. Then he swaggered towards the main entrance whose double doors were flanked by marble pillars. As he pushed them open he almost fell over the store's stock-room attendant, who combined his job with the duties of caretaker, and any other jobs that needed doing. At that moment he was cutting a strip of grey drugget to fit around the angle of the doorway.

'Mind out of my way, Pargeter,' Tom snapped impatiently.

'Sorry, Mr Grainger.'

Slowly the middle-aged man rose to his feet and stepped aside in his own good time. None of the staff had much time for the boss's lazy son.

But Tom didn't care what the staff thought about him: they were beneath his notice. But he did like being called Mr Grainger so he was in a good humour as he hung his hat and jacket in the staff room and looked to see what jobs had been allotted to him. There was a list pinned to a notice-board. It seemed that his morning was to be spent unpacking and marking up prices in the basement, and in the afternoon he was expected to fit out a display unit in the shirt department. Not too bad, he thought. With luck he'd be able to slip away early without his father noticing, to visit Milly.

Victor Grainger had forgotten all about his son until he made his afternoon check around the shop floor and found Tom, his mouth full of pins, struggling to dress a dummy in an evening shirt.

'Good boy,' he said, patting Tom on the shoulder as he passed. It was a good thing he didn't see the expression on his son's face as he walked away.

The store closed its doors at five thirty, but Tom had had more than enough by five o'clock. Without waiting for permission he donned his jacket and trilby and marched out of the main door calling an airy "Night, Pargeter' to the caretaker, who was ushering out the last of the day's customers.

Tom walked confidently, pausing only to light a cigarette, before dodging away from the opulence of the main road into the warren of mean streets that were sandwiched between Western Road and the sea-front, with their big hotels like the Grand and the Metropole. He strode down Grenville Place, through Russell Street, until he reached Artillery Street where Milly lived and plied her trade.

Milly was thirty-eight years old, but claimed to be thirty and got away with it. She was a high-class prostitute, and was respected by her rougher sisters who stood on street corners and took their clients back to seedy boarding houses, or sometimes just dirty shop doorways.

She lived at number five, which was not only the cleanest, but also the most colourful house in the street. The door and window-frames were painted bright green, and the step brick red. The sills were laden with window-boxes full of trailing ivy, marigolds with heads the size of saucers, and geraniums. Milly loved colour and excitement, and enjoyed life to the full.

Tom stood still on the opposite side of the street. He was looking for the tell-tale signs that denoted whether Milly was alone.

A bird-cage stood in the upstairs window. Tom knew it

contained a canary with a loud vocal range; but there was a fringed shawl flung over the top, which was the only known way Milly had found to silence the noisy bird. As Tom watched a hand suddenly pulled the shawl away, and the canary started hopping from perch to perch, its throat vibrating with ecstasy. Then the front door opened and a small man dressed in a dark overcoat and bowler hat emerged. He looked craftily from left to right, and then marched away briskly towards the sea-front. Tom knew Milly would now be on her own.

He boldly crossed the street and opened the green door, which was never locked. Whistling 'Happy days are here again' he strolled along the hall and up the stairs. A bead curtain hung over the doorway of Milly's bedroom, the wooden beads clinking like castanets in the draught.

'Come in, Tom,' a voice trilled from within.

Tom pulled aside the curtain and stepped into the room. Milly's bedroom was as colourful as the outside of the house, with silk and velvet drapes in rich hues. The bed was heaped with cushions of purple silk, and the heavy curtains were tied back with gold cords with tassels on the ends.

Milly Taylor was sitting at the dressing-table painting her lips. She was a beautiful woman with black hair curling on to her shoulders and a clear white complexion. She was wearing a long wrapper of orange silk, with loose sleeves and a border of ruffles around the neck and down the front. Tom crossed the floor and stood behind her. They smiled at each other in the glass.

'You're looking delicious,' Tom said softly. 'Just like a cat who's been given the cream. Was that fellow in the bowler hat good?'

'I don't care what they wear.' Milly laughed, and her voice tinkled with good humour. 'One bloke is much the same as the next.'

'Except me, Milly. Tell me I'm special.'

Tom's hands were caressing Milly's shoulders. He liked

the feel of the silk, but the smoothness of her flesh was even better. Still watching her face in the mirror he slid the material off her shoulder and leaned over to kiss the bare skin. Milly half closed her eyes with pleasure and that galled Tom: he preferred to give pain. When he bit her shoulder he expected her to tell him to stop, but instead she whimpered with delight.

'Did I hurt you?' he asked.

Now he was kneeling by her, pulling aside the gown and revealing her nakedness. She had a magnificent body, plump and flawless, with heavy rose-tipped breasts and a curved dimpled belly. He caressed her roughly, teasing her with his fingers and tongue until she was moist and pleading, and only then did he lead her to the bed. She opened her legs too willingly, and when he mounted her began to moan even before he was ready to enter. He knelt over her, waiting for her to beg.

'Please, Tom,' she whispered at last. 'Please!'

'Silly bitch,' he said, and thrust deeply into her so that her moan turned to a scream of ecstasy.

When he'd taken his pleasure Milly lay back against the pillows. Her black hair was tossed about her like a curly fan and there were teeth marks upon the whiteness of her breast. Tom liked to leave his mark; proof that he was better than the bowler-hatted gent who'd preceded him.

He lay beside her with his hands behind his head and his clothes still unbuttoned. As usual he was filled with a feeling of disappointment. It was always the same: the initial excitement, the swift climax, and then the feeling of being let down. It was Milly's fault, not his. She was too eager – too greedy for it. Tom liked a woman to fight and cry, so that he could master her and show her who was in charge. He wanted to inflict pain and see fear in a woman's eyes. Yes, fear was the thing Tom liked best of all. Women should be afraid of him – that's what gave him the keenest pleasure.

Once there had been a girl who he'd especially enjoyed. A girl with long brown hair and a slender but feminine body. What had been her name now? Lisa – no, Lizzie. That was it – Lizzie Sargent. He recalled how a fellow he'd palled up with, Jack French, had persuaded him to join a party of fruit-pickers, years ago it was, and a mistake for a town boy like he'd been.

The dark-haired beauty had been innocent, and a virgin, and he'd taken her on the rough floor of a barn, leaving her bleeding and broken. Afterwards he'd felt all-powerful – like a god. He'd give anything to meet up with that girl again; but by now she was probably married to some country oaf and living miles away.

'You asleep, Tom?' Milly turned to him, her hand slipping inside his shirt. He shook her off roughly. She laughed.

'No. I was thinking.'

'What about?'

'My father. He wants me to get married.'

Milly laughed again. She found the idea of Tom Grainger with a wife vastly amusing. 'I suppose he's got someone in mind.'

'Not that I know of. How about it, Milly?'

'What?'

'How would you like to marry me and be Mrs Grainger?'

'You're joking.' Milly sat up and pulled on her robe, and then with one graceful movement swung her feet down to the floor.

'I'm not joking, Milly.' Tom reached over and grabbed her arm, pulling her back on to the bed. 'My grandfather left me a legacy, but my father had to put his spoke in. Seems I've got to wait until I'm thirty unless I can produce a wife and a son.'

Milly burst out laughing. 'And you think I might suit?'

'We get on all right. You'd have a comfortable home – money to buy pretty things. What more can a girl like you want?'

'What do you mean by "a girl like me"?'

'Surely a husband is better than this?' Tom looked around, and his lip curled with scorn.

'This is my home, Tom. I like it. And my way of life happens to suit me.'

'You mean you're turning me down?' Tom couldn't believe it. He'd expected Milly to fall at his feet, to leap at the chance of a comfortable future. Of course the old man wouldn't have been keen, he'd expect him to choose some silly little domestic woman like his mother, but he'd have to stick by the terms of the will. 'You're turning me down?' he asked again.

'Yes, Tom.' Milly moved away. 'You're good in bed – but I wouldn't marry you if you were the last man on earth.'

That was when Tom snapped. The rage that was always there, deep inside him, erupted into sudden fury. With one hand he grabbed Milly by the hair, forcing her head back until she thought her neck would snap, and with his free hand he slapped her around the face – once, twice, three times. She swayed drunkenly. Then he flung her down on the bed like a broken toy and strode out of the room, buttoning his clothes as he went.

Tom didn't pause for breath until he reached the Clock Tower. He stopped and felt in his pocket for a cigarette to calm his nerves. The crumpled packet he pulled out was empty, so he entered the nearest tobacconists and exchanged a shilling for twenty Gold Flake.

The evening stretched ahead, and although his mother would have a meal prepared for him he didn't want to go home. The public houses were open but he didn't feel like drinking so early in the evening. He decided to pass a couple of hours at a picture palace. The nearest was the Regent Theatre on the corner of Queen's Road and North Street, or the Princes Cinema. He had the choice of two films: Greta Garbo in *Camille*, or *Don Quixote*, with George Robey playing the part of Sancho Panza.

Paying the princely sum of three shillings and sixpence

he was shown to his seat, and soon found he'd made a bad choice. Garbo was nice enough to look at, but the film wasn't at all erotic, and Tom was soon dozing with boredom.

He left the picture house before the end of the film and headed for home. His head ached, he'd wasted his day, and he was in a particularly bad temper by the time he reached the front door. The Bentley was in the drive so his father was home. This only increased his anger: he didn't want any more confrontations. He opened the front door quietly and tiptoed across the hall towards the stairs.

'Is that you, Tommy?' Frances Grainger called from the dining-room. 'We're still eating and I've saved you some supper.'

Tom sighed, but he knew he had to comply or his mother would get upset. He couldn't bear hysterical women. He tossed his trilby on to the hallstand, squared his shoulders and, forcing a smile on to his face, entered the room.

His father was seated in his usual place at the end of the long table. He was eating cheese and biscuits and the *Evening Argus* was open before him. His mother was nibbling her way through a lettuce leaf. She immediately left her place to fetch Tom's plate from the sideboard.

'It's a good thing it's a cold supper or it would have been spoiled,' she said. 'Tinned salmon and salad, and there's bread on the table. Did you have a good day?'

'It was all right,' Tom replied grudgingly. Anger always took his appetite away and he had to force himself to eat.

'At least he showed up at the shop,' Victor said over his paper. 'Made quite a good job of a display unit too.'

'Oh, darling, I'm so pleased.' Frances beamed as if the news was the best she'd ever had. 'I knew you'd like it once you'd made the effort.'

'Who said anything about liking it, Ma?' Tom snapped.

'But—'

'And don't call your mother Ma. You didn't do badly, but you've still got a lot to learn.' Victor folded his paper and slapped it down on the table. 'You've wasted enough time with your gadding about; so I've had a word with Pargeter and he's going to start you off at the very beginning.'

'But what does Mr Pargeter know about Grainger's?' Frances asked. 'Isn't he a sort of glorified caretaker?'

'Who better than a caretaker to show Tom the ropes,' Victor said. 'He works in the stock-room as well, and it needs a thorough going over to get ready for the new winter lines. You can help him clean the place out tomorrow. Bit mucky down there so you'd better get yourself some overalls.'

Tom looked at his father in horror. At least on the shop floor he felt important as the boss's son in a smart suit; but down in the basement with old Pargeter – and wearing overalls!

'I'm not sure about tomorrow—'

'If you want to continue drawing a wage, Tom, you'd better be there – and I meant what I said about your grandfather's money.'

Tom slammed down his knife and fork; if he ate another mouthful he'd be sick. Ignoring the pleading in his mother's eyes he pushed back his chair and strode out of the room, slamming the door behind him. A drink – that was what he needed. A stiff drink and some cheerful company. He grabbed his hat from the hall-stand, cocked it at an angle, and left the house.

It was almost dark but Tom didn't make for the nearest public house. First he strode through the streets trying to walk off his anger. He wasn't going to be under his father's thumb for ever; or at the beck and call of old Pargeter. He'd get himself a wife, any woman would do as long as she was capable of bearing him a son, and then he'd get his legacy and Grainger's could go to hell.

Tom felt calmer by the time he pushed open the door

of the Marquis of Exeter and strode towards the bar calling, 'A double whisky, girl, and be quick about it.'

Glass in hand he turned to survey the saloon bar. At that moment a hand fell on his arm.

'Tom Grainger, isn't it?' a familiar voice said.

Tom turned and saw the red head, freckled face and gapped-tooth smile of Jack French. He hadn't seen him for years.

'Why, Jack,' he said, pleased to see a friendly face. 'How are you?'

'Never better,' Jack said cheerfully. 'Are you on your own?'

'For the moment.'

'Then you must join us.'

Jack led the way between the tables towards a corner where a young woman was sitting with her back to them. She was wearing a green dress and her dark shining hair fell to her shoulders. When she turned around Tom saw two brown eyes fringed by dark lashes and pale milk-white skin. He recognised her at once.

Jack was saying, 'It's Tom Grainger. You remember Tom, don't you, Lizzie?'

CHAPTER SEVENTEEN

A Ghost from the Past

'You look as though you've seen a ghost,' Jack laughed. 'It's only Tom.'

'I know,' Lizzie whispered.

'And I'm no ghost; I can assure you of that,' Tom said. He leaned forward and took Lizzie's hand. His long thin fingers caressed hers and wouldn't let go. 'See – I'm flesh and blood.'

'I didn't doubt it,' Lizzie said, managing to free herself. Her fingers felt tainted and she wanted to rub them. She knew Tom was looking at her and she wouldn't look up, afraid of what she would see in his eyes. Those cold grey eyes that had seen so much. She felt as if they'd seen into her very soul.

'Are you all right, Lizzie?' Jack was saying. 'You're very pale.'

'It's rather hot in here. I think I'll go out into the fresh air for a few minutes.'

'I'll come with you.'

'No. You stay and talk; you two must have a lot to catch up on.'

Leaving her drink untouched on the table Lizzie pushed her way through the crowd to the door. She'd felt cold and faint at the first sight of Tom Grainger, but now her face was burning and only the night air would cool it down.

She sat down on the low wall outside the pub and breathed deeply, slowly managing to regain control. Some youths were arguing outside a nearby house and opposite a queue had formed for a fish and chip shop, but Lizzie was aware of nothing but her racing thoughts. Tom! Tom Grainger, the man who she'd hoped never to set eyes on again, was only a few yards away, and by the look in his eyes he hadn't forgotten what had happened between them.

She'd been his victim and he'd used her cruelly, so why had her skin tingled when he'd touched her hand? She hated him for what he'd done to her all those years before, so why did her body come to life under his cold eyes and her heart beat faster with excitement?

And then there was Joey. Her son, and his son too, but she was the only person who knew that. She hadn't even told Jack who Joey's father was. How confident she'd been this morning when she'd given Joey the lucky charm she'd worn for so long around her neck. Now she regretted the impulsive action. Perhaps she should have kept it: she had the feeling she was going to need all the luck she could get.

'You've grown into a beauty,' a voice said behind her. 'I hope Jack appreciates you.' It was Tom, lolling against the wall, his eyes half closed in contemplation.

'Where is Jack?' Lizzie asked desperately.

'He's just coming. Don't look so scared.'

'I'm not.'

'You can't fool me, Lizzie. But don't worry, my intentions are completely honourable – for the time being.'

'Please leave me alone.'

'Of course. But how about a kiss for old time's sake.'

Before Lizzie could back away Tom put his arms around her, pulled her to him, and kissed her full upon the lips.

Frantically, she tried to push him away; she hated him reminding her of that awful occasion when he'd raped her in the red barn. So why did a flicker of excitement turn in her belly? Why did she close her eyes under the pressure of his mouth and feel as if she was going to lose consciousness? The kiss over, he let her go so abruptly that she almost fell.

'There, Lizzie,' Tom laughed. 'I could have sworn you liked it.'

'I didn't. I hated it – and I hate you!'

'Don't be so sure, darling. I haven't finished with you yet.' He walked away without looking back.

Lizzie watched until he'd disappeared and then she went in search of Jack. He was finishing his drink, and proudly accepting congratulations on his engagement from friends who knew them both. Lizzie shook his arm.

'I want to go home, Jack.'

'Of course. You look tired. Is it the excitement?'

'I expect so.'

Outside they walked slowly, Jack's arm around Lizzie's waist. 'Funny seeing old Tom again,' Jack said. 'We used to be such mates, although of course he comes from quite a well-to-do family. They own a gentlemen's outfitters. What did he have to say to you?'

'Nothing much.'

'I told him we were engaged. I suppose he congratulated you?'

'He didn't, as a matter of fact,' Lizzie said. She was looking at the ground, not able to meet Jack's eyes. What would he think if she told him about the kiss?

'He said we should have a party, or some sort of celebration, and let all our friends join in. What do you think, Lizzie?'

'I don't think we need any public celebration, Jack. I'm happy as we are.'

'You're a darling girl.' Jack squeezed her hand. 'But you deserve a party so that you can dress up. Mum and Dad would help, and the kids would love it.'

'Can you afford it?' Lizzie asked.

'It needn't be a posh affair. We could hire a room, and Mum would do the cooking. She hasn't had a chance to show off her fancies for ages. And it's you I want to show off, Lizzie. I want everyone to see how proud I am of you.'

'I could help your mother with the cooking,' Lizzie said. Jack's enthusiasm was making her warm to the idea. After all, it would only be a family affair, and Joey would love it. 'We'll have a party if you want one, Jack.'

'I'll have a word with Mum and Dad as soon as I get inside.' They were outside Mrs Marshall's house and Jack took Lizzie in his arms to kiss her goodnight. 'I was really pleased to see Tom Grainger again; and you should have seen his face when I told him about us. I think he was jealous. Anyway, I'd like to ask him to our engagement party, Lizzie, so you'd better put his name at the top of the guest list.'

In the darkness he couldn't see the expression on Lizzie's face or the apprehension in her eyes. In fact he was very pleased with himself as he let himself into his own home.

Half a mile away in Dyke Road, Tom Grainger was striding along whistling a gay tune between thin lips. He was also feeling pleased with himself. Lady Luck had dealt him a winning hand at last. So, his father wanted him to get married, did he? Well, so did he now. Lizzie Sargent was the only girl for him. So, she was engaged to Jack French, but he'd noticed that she wasn't yet wearing a ring, so there was still time for him to step in and win the prize. For Lizzie would be a prize. Sex with her had been crude, violent – and wonderful. She'd fought like a tiger but he'd mastered her. And she hadn't forgotten him. Only tonight he'd seen the fear in her beautiful brown eyes; but he'd also felt the trembling in her body when he'd kissed her – the trembling of desire. She'd wanted him at that moment as much as he'd wanted her. She hadn't forgotten. Lizzie Sargent was the girl for him – the beginning of the way to get his hands on his grandfather's money.

The day of the party dawned bright and sunny and there was much excitement in Coventry Street. The Frenches were up early because there was the baking to be done and sandwiches to prepare, so Grace needed to get things going early.

Next door Lizzie was just as busy. Gran Marshall had insisted on coming, so Lizzie had to get her clothes out of mothballs, shaken and pressed, as well as her own and Joey's things.

Fifty guests had been invited, including neighbours, friends, and relations of the Frenches who had grown fond of Lizzie over the years and accepted her. She had thought of sending an invitation to Greenlock in the hope that Aunt Hannah might pass it on to Billy. Her brother would be thirteen now, and it would be lovely to see him again and see how he'd grown. But she'd decided against it. When the time was right she'd return to Greenlock House and fetch Billy herself. But now wasn't the time.

Because of the size of the party the church hall had been booked. The elders were strict about what went on on their premises. No gambling or drinking of alcohol were permitted; but they did agree to a wind-up gramophone for playing dance music, as long as they chose only sedate waltzes and polkas. Ginger beer was the strongest drink that was allowed.

Gran said she would sleep all day to conserve her energy for the evening, which left Lizzie time to make her own preparations. She turned up in Grace's kitchen, with her face flushed from the hot oven, carrying trays of sausage rolls and jam tarts. Jack's mother was icing fairycakes with the help of Marjorie and five-year-old Eileen. The girls were laughing with merriment, and in the background Gracie Fields was singing on the wireless something to do with an aspidistra.

'Turn that down,' Grace instructed her daughters. 'I can't hear a word any of you are saying.'

When the room was quiet Lizzie was shown the food ready to be carried to the church hall for the party. Food in such quantities that she felt her mouth start to water. There were chicken patties and anchovy eggs, sandwiches of sardine and tomato, crab and cress, ham, tongue and cream cheese. As well as the fairycakes there were cream buns, chocolate éclairs, and fruit, madeira and cherry cake. There were bridge-rolls spread with Gentlemen's Relish, and mouthwatering jellies and sweets for the children. Enough food to feed an army.

'Do you think there'll be enough?' Grace asked, surveying her handiwork.

'More than enough,' Lizzie assured her. 'But if you're worried I can always make some extra sandwiches.'

'You'll do no such thing, Lizzie,' Grace said firmly. 'I think Jack has plans for you, and you've worked hard enough.'

Jack was summoned and immediately took charge. 'Go and get your coat,' he instructed Lizzie. 'We're going shopping. It's about time we sorted that ring out. I can't have my fiancée attending her own party with her engagement ring hanging around her neck.'

Lizzie dressed herself in a coat and skirt and her brown velvet hat with its blue ribbon and they caught a bus into town. Jack had bought the ring at a little antique jewellers in the Lanes, so they went there first and explained the problem. The shopkeeper, a small gnome-like man with rounded shoulders and an eye-glass, peered at the ring and then at Jack and Lizzie.

'Yes,' he said. 'I can have it made larger for the young lady, but it'll take time. Ten days – two weeks and it'll fit perfectly.'

'Oh dear,' Lizzie said, looking at Jack for guidance. 'I didn't realise it would take so long.'

'It's my fault,' Jack said, quick to take the blame. 'I should have brought you with me, but I wanted it to be a surprise.'

'What shall we do then?'

'I can always exchange it for you,' the jeweller said benevolently. 'I have many beautiful rings if the young lady would like to look at them.'

The young lady did, and soon Lizzie was poring over the most dazzling display of rings she had ever seen. Diamonds and pearls rubbed shoulders with rubies and emeralds; most of the prices well beyond Jack's reach.

'Do you see anything you like?' he asked anxiously.

'I don't want anything too ostentatious,' Lizzie said, shaking her head firmly at a heavy gold band with a Victorian cluster setting.

'You must have a diamond,' Jack said. 'It's traditional.'

But Lizzie fell in love with a dainty ring holding a single cultured pearl. It was quite small and much cheaper than Jack's original purchase.

'The price doesn't matter,' Lizzie insisted. 'That's the one I want. Look, it fits perfectly,' and she slid it easily on to her finger.

Jack smiled and accepted a refund of the difference in price. 'You certainly won't break the bank, Lizzie,' he said. 'You must spend the extra on something else. What would you like – a new hat?' and he indicated the battered brown velvet.

'I'm not throwing this one away,' Lizzie laughed, putting up her hands to protect it. 'It's special.'

'How about a new frock then? A pretty one to wear this evening.'

Lizzie agreed that a new dress would be nice; as long as it was a sensible one she could wear on any occasion. They went to Hanningtons, a fine department store in Castle Square, and she had a splendid time looking through the racks of ready-made dresses. Jack stood by and watched with amusement.

'What do you think of this one?' Lizzie asked, holding up a pearl-grey woollen dress with a white collar and cuffs.

'You'd look like a Quaker girl,' Jack laughed. 'Choose something with a bit of colour in it.'

There were autumn-weight dresses in all hues and fabrics: greens and blues, reds, oranges and browns, in velvets, cashmere and wool. So many to choose from that Lizzie's head was quite turned. She tried on a red velvet frock in the fitting room, and twirled in front of Jack hoping for his approval.

'Have it if you want it,' he said. 'It's your choice – but I like you in blue.'

'Have you got this one in any other colour?' Lizzie asked the assistant. She hadn't been sure about the colour herself. It was rather bright.

'No, madam. We did have it in brown, but it's a new line and so popular that we've sold out.'

'Have you anything similar in blue?'

'We have a blue wool that would suit you. I think it's your size. Wait a moment and I'll get it for you.'

Lizzie was shivering in her underwear when the assistant joined her in the fitting room with a blue dress draped over her arm. As soon as she held it up, Lizzie fell in love with it. The colour was perfect – not too pale to wear in autumn and not dark enough to be depressing. She held up her arms and the girl slid it over her head. The soft folds enveloped her body like a second skin, and she felt herself gently pushed this way and that while the buttons were fastened and the hem adjusted.

'It's lovely, madam – and a perfect fit. Look in the mirror and see for yourself.'

Lizzie turned and surveyed herself; she liked what she saw. The sweeping lines of the dress made her look taller than she already was, and the neckline was cut in a V, deep enough to be interesting but not immodest. The bodice was gathered into a wide waistband from which the skirt fell in flared panels, and the sleeves were long and full and gathered at the wrists. She pulled the curtain aside and stepped out on to the shop floor, walking towards Jack with pink cheeks, waiting for his reaction.

Jack looked up as Lizzie approached. The expression on his face didn't change and Lizzie thought she'd made a bad choice.

'Well, what do you think?'

'I think – I think, Lizzie Sargent, that you're the most beautiful woman I've ever seen, and I'm the luckiest man in Brighton.'

Of course after that there was nothing more to be said. The dress was parcelled into one of the store's distinctive bags, paid for, and Lizzie left the shop feeling as if she was walking on air.

'Are you looking forward to the evening?' Jack asked, guiding her through the shoppers in North Street.

'Of course I am.' Lizzie held out her left hand so that she could admire her ring. 'You are good to me, Jack.'

'Only because I love you so much. Never change, will you, Lizzie? And never leave me.'

'Never,' Lizzie promised, meaning it with her whole heart. Jack was a good man and she was lucky. So was Joey.

There and then, in the middle of the pavement, Jack took her in his arms and kissed her. The passers-by, instead of being annoyed, walked around them smiling.

Jack left Lizzie with her parcel outside her home, and she hurried inside to change and get Granny Marshall out of bed and dressed.

Someone had lent them an ancient basket chair on wheels, and padded with shawls and cushions it was waiting for the invalid. They made a stately picture as Lizzie pushed Gran towards the church hall: Lizzie in her beautiful new dress and a radiant smile on her pretty face, and Gran in a long black frock, with carpet slippers on her swollen feet, and a string of jet beads hanging around her neck and bouncing on her chest. Her skimpy hair was covered by a black straw hat trimmed with artificial flowers and fruit stitched around the crown, and from underneath the brim her aged eyes peered excitedly at the world she hadn't been part of for a long time.

'Don't put me in a draught,' she instructed Lizzie as her chair was carefully lifted over the step. 'But I want to be able to see everything.'

'Don't worry Gran. Marjorie's promised to look after you.'

A cheer went up as they entered the hall and Jack hurried forward. He looked awkward in a new pin-striped suit and with his hair slicked down with Brylcreem. Friends and neighbours offered their congratulations and gave them small gifts, and the children had made cards which they proudly handed to the engaged couple.

The hall, which was a barn of a place with a vaulted ceiling and dingy walls, had been made beautiful. Streamers and bunting were looped around, alternated with bunches of coloured balloons, and golden-rod and Michaelmas-daisies had been gathered from people's gardens and arranged in vases of all shapes and sizes to cheer things up. Two long trestle tables had been erected, covered with white cloths, and loaded with all the food Grace had spent so long preparing. The guests were turned out in their best clothes and in a party mood.

'Mum,' Joey said, tugging at Lizzie's skirt. 'Johnny says we're going to play games. Can I join in?'

'Of course you can,' Lizzie said, wiping a streak of green jelly from his cheek. Little fingers had been trying out the sweet-meats behind the grown-ups' backs. 'You're a big boy now.'

The children played Hunt the Thimble, Sardines, and Pass the Parcel to the music from an old upright piano. They were supervised by the choir mistress who made sure there was no cheating.

Granny Marshall clapped her hands and shouted 'Bravo!' when Joey won a bar of Cadbury's chocolate for finding the silver thimble hidden among a pile of hymn books. Then Eileen won a felt needle case for being the winner in a skipping race, so that was all right.

Then it was time to eat and everyone fell silent while the young people carried plates and cups of tea to their elders. Jack found Lizzie standing all by herself in a corner, with an uneaten cake in her hand and a faraway look on her face.

'I thought I'd lost you,' he said, taking her hand. 'What's the matter?'

'Nothing. I'm not very hungry.'

'Cheer up then; there's going to be dancing later on.'

Lizzie smiled and rejoined the celebrations. She couldn't tell Jack how she'd suddenly remembered Tom Grainger. She knew an invitation had been sent to him, and although they hadn't received a reply she'd feared that he may have taken it into his head to turn up. But there was no sign of his tall slim figure among the throng, so she managed to push the thought of him out of her head.

Someone put a record of the Laughing Policeman on the wind-up gramophone, and the children tried to join in with Charles Jolly's recorded voice. There was much merriment, and some of the smaller ones rolled around the floor and held their tummies with laughter.

'Someone's going to be sick in a minute,' Grace French said to Albert who was in charge of the music. 'Put something quieter on quickly.'

Then there was Victor Silvester, followed by Charlie Kunz playing Romona on the piano, and soon couples started dancing around the floor. Lizzie went in search of Jack, swaying her hips in time to the music. She found him replenishing Gran's plate with a huge slice of chocolate cake.

'Come on,' she said, pulling his arm. 'I want you to dance with me.'

'I can't dance,' Jack said ruefully.

'You only have to move around the floor in time to the music. I'll show you.'

They circled the floor slowly with Lizzie guiding Jack. He soon got the hang of things although he'd never make an expert dancer. He got on better when the record was changed to a lively dance. 'You can see me dance the polka', blared out noisily.

'Can I dance with you, Jack?' Marjorie asked, coming up behind her brother and tapping him on the shoulder. She was wearing her first grown-up dress: a pretty creation made of pale pink voile. She wanted to show it off, but was too shy to ask any of the boys to partner her. In the arms of her brother she would feel safe.

'Do you mind?' Jack asked Lizzie.

'Of course not. I'll find myself another partner.'

She was waltzing around the hall in the arms of Albert French to the voice of Al Bowlly singing 'Who's taking you home tonight?' when she was aware of someone behind her. A voice she didn't at first recognise said, 'Can I butt in? If you'll excuse me, of course.' She turned to find herself looking into the cold eyes of Tom Grainger.

'I'm sorry…' she started to say, but Albert released her.

'It's time I danced with Grace – you two young things carry on,' and he disappeared into the crowd.

'Don't look like that,' Tom said. 'Anybody would think you're not pleased to see me.'

'I'm glad you've managed to come to our party, Tom,' Lizzie said politely, 'but I think I'd better go and find Jack.'

'Jack's busy. You must dance with me. I am your guest, don't forget.'

Lizzie had no option but to let Tom put his arm around her and draw her into the dance. She held herself stiffly and wouldn't look at his face.

'Relax,' he whispered into her ear, and pulled her closer. She could smell his maleness and the smoky odour of his cigarettes.

'Please let me go,' she said, as he spun her so quickly she thought she'd lose her footing. 'You're making me dizzy.'

'That's my manly charm. I seem to have that effect on pretty girls.'

'Even ones who've just got engaged?'

'Especially them. Do you love Jack?'

The question was so sudden that Lizzie was caught off-guard. 'Of course,' she said. She found herself looking into Tom's eyes: the cool grey eyes that frightened but fascinated her at the same time.

'Once you loved me,' Tom said matter-of-factly.

'I never loved you.'

'Not even that evening in the red barn?'

'You forced me,' Lizzie whispered.

'But you enjoyed it, didn't you?' Lizzie didn't answer. 'Didn't you?'

'No! No, I didn't!'

'Well, perhaps my technique has improved since then. Wouldn't you like to find out?'

'Please let me go.' Lizzie struggled to free herself but Tom only gripped her more tightly. The music slowed and their movements slowed with it – became languid and sensual.

'Why do you think I've never married?'

'I don't know. I haven't thought about it.'

'Well, think now.'

'I suppose you've never met the right girl.'

'Wrong.' He was holding her so close that Lizzie could feel his hardness – his desire. If he didn't loosen his hold she feared she'd faint. 'I did meet the right girl once, but I let her go. We were both too young and I handled it badly. She was the most beautiful creature I've ever seen, before or since. She had long hair the colour of beechnuts and eyes like brown velvet. Her name was Lizzie Sargent.'

'You mustn't say these things, Tom.'

'Why not? They're true.'

They circled the floor again and Lizzie was aware of nothing apart from Tom's presence. Bravely she ventured to look at him and saw the same long brown face and thin quizzical lips, and the switch of dark hair that fell forward over his forehead. The eyes were as clear and grey as she remembered, but perhaps she'd made a mistake in thinking them cold. Perhaps they just showed youth and insecurity. Maybe she'd misjudged him, and in their innocence they'd blamed each other. And all these years she'd hated him.

'I thought I hated you,' she said softly.

'But not any more? Am I forgiven?'

'Of course.'

He smiled, and Lizzie suddenly realised how dazzlingly handsome Tom was. He looked rueful, like a little boy who'd been caught out in a wrongdoing and now regrets it. She wondered how many hearts he'd broken since hers.

'Mummy!'

Someone was tugging at her skirt. Lizzie looked down to see a small figure trying to attract her attention. It was Joey, tired and bored with the grown-ups dancing.

'Joey.' She struggled out of Tom's arms and bent down to her son. 'What is it, darling?'

'I want some ginger beer.'

'Go and ask Auntie Grace. I'm sure she'll find some for you.'

'I want you to get it.'

'All right. Will you excuse me, Tom.' And taking Joey's hand she led him to the buffet tables and filled a glass for him. Although her back was turned to the room she could feel Tom's eyes following her. Her cheeks were burning, and she tried to shield Joey with her body. Joey – her son – Tom's son.

'Would the little boy like a chocolate bar?' Tom was beside them holding out the wrapped sweet. Lizzie thought that ironically it was with a bar of chocolate that he'd tempted her.

'Can I, Mummy?' Joey looked at Lizzie for permission. She nodded, and he took the sweet eagerly and began to tear at the paper.

'Here, let me.' Neatly Tom folded back the silver paper and watched as Joey bit a piece from the corner of the bar. Then he looked at Lizzie and raised his eyebrows quizzically. 'He's your son?'

'Yes,' Lizzie said softly. Her cheeks were still aflame, betraying her inner confusion.

'And what's your name, little boy?'

'My name's Joey.'

Lizzie placed her hands on Joey's shoulders in an attempt to steer him away from Tom's prying questions. But Tom hadn't finished.

'How old are you, Joey?'

'I'm five. I've just started school because I'm a big boy.'

They were so alike that it was amazing. Apart from his eyes, Joey was a miniature replica of his father. The same wiry frame and long bony limbs, the same narrow face crowned by fine brown hair with the lock falling over the forehead. Only the eyes were different. Joey had inherited his mother's dark eyes, with their promise of tenderness and sensitivity.

'Why don't you go and join the other children,' Tom said. 'It looks as if they're going to play another game. I want to talk to your mother.' Joey trotted off obediently, his mouth smeared with chocolate. Tom took hold of Lizzie's arm, and the hard fingers pinched her flesh through the wool of her dress. 'Come outside.'

'I can't.'

'Why not?'

'Jack – he'll be looking for me.'

'And if he finds you you'll just be talking to an old friend. There's no harm in that, is there?'

Lizzie looked around quickly. Grace was bending over

the wheelchair, tucking a blanket around Granny Marshall's knees, and Jack was deep in conversation with a neighbour. No one was looking in her direction.

'All right,' she said. 'But only for a minute.'

Nobody saw them slip through the door. Just for a moment Lizzie paused and looked back, feeling she was teetering on the edge of a volcano. She looked round at all the familiar figures who had grown to be such an important part of her life. She saw Gran in her chair, half asleep but happy. And Grace, busy as always, with a frown between her eyes. Perhaps one day she'd want to be like Grace – worrying about everyone else, contentedly surrounded by her family – but not yet. Not while she still had her whole life before her. She saw Jack, his red hair standing on end and a happy smile on his face – little did he know that she, Lizzie Sargent, had the power to wipe that smile off his face for ever.

Then she looked for Joey but she couldn't see him. She wanted to call out but Tom was pulling her arm and she didn't have the strength to fight. Outside it was dark; just pools of light from the street-lamps, like amber lakes. They faced each other on the pavement with only the distant sounds of trains shunting on the nearby railway line disturbing the still night.

'Who is Joey's father?' Tom demanded without preamble 'Not Jack?'

'No.' Lizzie spoke so softly that Tom had to repeat the question.

'Answer me, Lizzie. Tell me Jack isn't Joey's father.'

'You know he isn't.'

'He's *mine*, isn't he?' The triumph in Tom's voice startled her. She wanted to see his eyes but they were in shadow.

'No, he ... he's ...' Lizzie stuttered, but the hesitation in her voice gave her away.

'Come on, Lizzie. He's mine, isn't he?'

Lizzie realised there was no point in denying the truth further. 'He's *ours*, Tom.'

'Yours and mine?'

'Yes.'

'And yet you were going to marry Jack French?'

'He's a loving man. Joey needs a father.'

'He's got one now – me.'

'But–'

'You can't marry Jack now, can you? And everyone will have guessed. I only had to look at that boy and I saw myself at the same age. Anyone with any sense will spot the resemblance at once. It's me you're going to marry, Lizzie, not that red-haired buffoon.'

'Don't call him …' but the words faded as Tom's arms went around her. He held her so tightly that she couldn't breathe. Her heart was pounding even before his hand slipped inside the V of her dress, slipping lower so that it cupped her breast, squeezing, bringing the nipple to life. Then his lips were all over her: on her neck, her cheeks and then her lips, biting and sucking, bringing her body to life like a wild thing possessed.

'Lizzie!'

She was only partly aware of Jack standing in the open doorway, his hair on end and an expression of utter despair on his face. She tried to pull away, part of her knowing she should and wanted to, but Tom's mouth was claiming hers. With a moan of despair she let him have his way.

CHAPTER EIGHTEEN

The Wedding of the Year

Thomas Stephen Grainger married Elizabeth Mary Sargent on the first Saturday in November 1936. The ceremony took place at the old Norman church of St Nicholas on a hill overlooking the town. It was voted the wedding of the year.

The day had broken on a damp and drizzly note, but just as the guests were deciding whether to carry mackintoshes and umbrellas the sun decided to shine. True, it was a watery sun, and did nothing to dry the raindrops dripping from the trees in the churchyard or make the pathway up to the church door easier to negotiate, but at least it was shining.

The bells were ringing as the white limousine drew up in Church Street. Lizzie got out of the back seat and took Victor Grainger's arm. She walked by his side with her head held high, just as she'd imagined the fictional Opal would have done, and looked neither to right or left as they passed the ancient graves of the female soldier: Phoebe Hessel, who joined the army to fight alongside her lover, and Martha Gunn, queen of the dippers. At the

porch door she paused for a moment to arrange the folds
of her dress, and the bystanders managed to get a good
view.

Lizzie hadn't wanted a traditional bridal gown. After
much deliberation she'd chosen a dress of ivory-coloured
lace and georgette, with a coatee of the same material.
The bodice was fitted into a tight waistband, and the lined
skirt flowed in alternate panels to her ivory satin slippers.
The coatee had long fitted sleeves and cape shoulders,
with a ribbon tie at the front. Her hair had been expertly
cut and waved so that it framed her face like a shining
cap. Instead of a veil she wore a wide-brimmed hat
trimmed with ivory ribbons. In her hands she carried a
posy of pink rosebuds. She looked fashionable and expensive, and no one was aware of the inner conflict she was
concealing, as she pushed away the thoughts that
plagued her – of the gentle red-haired man who had
become such an important part of her life – and forced
her mind back to the present. She must put Jack behind
her now. Joey came first and Tom was Joey's father. This
was her big day, she told herself, and she was probably
just nervous.

The organ started to play a voluntary and the one
bridesmaid, a cousin of Tom's, fell in behind. She was an
ungainly girl of fourteen named Doris; she wore glasses,
had straight brown hair and a permanent sniff. It was
obvious that she was bored by the whole occasion and
would probably have been happier riding her bicycle or
walking her dog – anything rather than be decked out in
a frock trimmed with frills and following a virtual stranger into the shadowy interior of a church.

Lizzie hadn't wanted to bother with bridesmaids; but
she would have liked Joey to have been a page-boy. He'd
have looked so sweet dressed in velvet shorts and a silky
shirt. But both Mr and Mrs Grainger had been adamant.
They were thrilled with the unexpected appearance of a
grandson, and didn't dispute the relationship, as Joey was

so like Tom in every way. Apart from his brown eyes, he was a miniature of their son at the same age. There was no doubting his parentage, even if his advent had been a surprise.

'He's even got a mole on his cheek,' Frances had cooed. 'And he's got Tommy's hands and long fingers. There's no doubt about it – Joey's our grandson.'

'Thomas is certainly a sly one,' Victor had said. 'I knew he had an eye for the girls, but he certainly made a better choice than I would have given him credit for.'

'And of course he couldn't tell us before because he wasn't married to Lizzie. You have forgiven him, haven't you, Victor?'

'I suppose I'll have to,' Victor Grainger had said grudgingly. 'And I think we should call her Elizabeth.'

'Oh no, dear. She says everyone calls her Lizzie, and she likes it.'

'Well, we shall see.' Victor smiled. 'Anyway the young Jack-a-napes has certainly surprised me. Of course he'll get his legacy now, as soon as he's married the girl. He'll need it to set up a comfortable home. But Joey mustn't come to the wedding – that would be rather tasteless.'

'Oh, dear.' Frances had flushed nervously. 'I think Lizzie has set her heart on it.'

'I said no, and I mean it. He can stay here and Mabel can look after him.'

There was nothing more to be said and Joey didn't seem to mind being excluded. He liked Mr and Mrs Grainger's house, or Granny and Grandad's as he was expected to call them. There were so many rooms and they were so big; and Granny had kept all his father, Tom's toys, and he was allowed to play with them. There were tin-soldiers that lived in a fort with a drawbridge which went up and down, games and puzzles, and a wonderful thing you looked through and saw pretty patterns inside. Granny said it was called a kaleidoscope. He'd rather stay with Mabel and play with the toys than be dressed up like a girl and made to go to church.

Lizzie came to give him a hug and a kiss before she left. 'I'll bring you some goodies,' she promised. 'What would you like – cake?'

'Yes, please.' Joey looked up. He held a tin soldier in one hand and Lizzie was transported back to the old days with Billy and his favourite story about the steadfast tin soldier. 'You do look pretty Mum,' he said.

'Do I?'

'Yes. Can I have chocolate cake?'

'Of course you can, my darling,' and she suddenly bent down and hugged her son close. Someone was calling to her from downstairs and reluctantly she walked to the door. 'I must go now.'

'Mum.'

'What is it?'

'Would you like your lucky coin back?' Joey was holding out the silver threepenny that he still wore around his neck.

Lizzie's eyes filled with tears. 'No, darling,' she said quickly. 'You keep it for me,' and she fled from the room before she broke down.

All eyes were upon Lizzie as she walked down the aisle, and everyone, Tom included, thought she was more than pretty. Tom was surprised at his own feelings as his bride stood smiling at his side; and if Lizzie's smile was somewhat fixed he didn't notice it.

He'd expected to feel pleased and proud because everyone had congratulated him on his good-fortune. He'd expected to feel triumphant at acquiring his inheritance and a beautiful wife and ready-made son, in that order. What Tom hadn't expected was a gut feeling of – could it be affection? It wasn't love because he didn't believe in the word; so affection or fondness was the nearest feeling he could acknowledge. But both were signs of weakness and must be stamped out. Tom Grainger had no intention of falling in love with anybody.

The ceremony went without a hitch. No one stood up to claim just cause or impediment. When Tom slipped the gold band on to Lizzie's finger she held her breath for a moment, remembering the time when Jack's ring had stuck so stubbornly. Had it been an omen? But the wedding ring slid into place, a perfect fit, and Tom kissed his bride.

Then there was the signing in the vestry, and the triumphant procession back through the church and out into the daylight. And the sun was actually shining so that the guests could forget their worries about umbrellas and show off their new wedding outfits.

The reception was held at the Grand Hotel, in a long room overlooking the sea. Victor Grainger had spared no expense, and a sit-down meal beginning with oysters, followed by Vienna steaks, and ending with ice-cream sundaes was enjoyed by the fifty guests. Most of them were strangers to Lizzie. She had no one to invite, so they were all friends and relations of the bridegroom. Toasts and speeches were made by Victor, and everyone sipped champagne as if they drank it with every meal.

Last, but by no means least, the wedding cake was wheeled forward on a decorated trolley. It was in three tiers and stood almost four feet high: a masterpiece of white icing-sugar and silver baubles. On the top stood a miniature bride and groom under a marzipan archway.

'Lizzie and Tom must make the first cut,' someone called out, and a silver-handled knife was passed to them.

Blushing, Lizzie took hold of the handle and pressed the tip into the frosty icing, and Tom placed his hand over hers. The pressure of his fingers sent shivers down Lizzie's spine and she looked up into the familiar grey eyes that gave nothing away. Then Tom smiled, and together they cut the first slice.

They were to spend a short honeymoon in London, and as Tom had passed his driving test only the year before, his father had offered the loan of his car. But they spent the first night of their marriage in a rented flat in Buckingham Road.

Finding a suitable house was going to take time so a flat was a temporary solution. When Lizzie first saw it she was awed at the size.

'It's simply huge,' she'd said in wonder as she wandered from room to room. 'Railway Cottage was like a doll's house compared to this.'

There were two reception rooms: a dining-room with a table long enough to accommodate ten people; and a drawing-room with deep armchairs and sofas, and high ceilings with ornate mouldings. The bedroom was also large, with the biggest bed Lizzie had ever seen and a pair of matching rose-wood wardrobes: one for her and one for Tom.

'I'll never have enough clothes to fill it,' Lizzie had said, peering into the empty depths which seemed to her the size of a small room.

'I'll take you shopping in London,' Tom said. 'You can buy some new outfits. What's the matter?'

Lizzie was looking around as if there was something missing. 'There's only one bedroom.'

'How many do you want?' Tom asked with a smile.

'At least one more – for Joey.'

'Ma and Pa have offered to keep Joey with them. You know how dotty they are over their grandson.'

'But I want him with me. Joey's always lived with me.' Lizzie was near to tears.

'He can live with us when we've got a house – I promise you. He can have a nursery, and a nanny to look after him if you want. But he's better with Ma and Pa for the time being. We don't want to take a five-year-old child on our honeymoon, do we?'

There was no answer to that. If Lizzie had been apprehensive about her wedding night, when it arrived she had nothing to fear. Tom was on his best behaviour;

he'd had only enough champagne to put him in a good humour and he wasn't drunk. When he saw Lizzie waiting for him in the big bed, the peach silk of her nightgown showing off the outline of her shoulders and breast, he thought he was the most fortunate man alive.

Even so, they were both tired so their lovemaking was languid, and they fell asleep without either of them reaching any great height of passion. Tom wasn't bothered: Lizzie was his now, and he had the rest of his life to use her in any way he chose. And when he tired of her charms there were plenty of other girls, girls like Milly, who he could pay to cater for his lusts.

In the early hours of the morning Lizzie was awakened by the sound of moaning. So used to sleeping alone, at first she thought it was Joey. She struggled to sit up, sleepily rubbing her eyes.

There was a weight on her chest, and when she looked down she saw a man's head. Then she remembered. She was a married woman and it was her husband, Tom, the father of her son. She put out her hand in the half-light of dawn and stroked the lock of hair away from Tom's forehead: the lock that Joey had inherited. Tom moaned again.

'What is it?' she whispered. 'What's the matter?'

'I can't breathe! I'm choking!' Tom seemed to be in some distress and for a moment Lizzie was afraid. But his eyes were closed and she guessed he was still asleep.

'It's all right. You're just having a bad dream.'

'Help me!' Tom started to struggle. 'I can't breathe, I tell you.' Suddenly his eyes flew open and they were filled with real terror. 'Where am I?'

'It's all right,' Lizzie said calmly, and she put her arms around him as tenderly as if he'd been Joey. 'You're safe. I think you were having a nightmare.'

'Oh, my god!' Tom sat up and Lizzie saw that he was pale and sweating. 'That awful dream again.'

'Do you want to tell me about it?'

'I've had it on and off all my life. It started after something that happened to me when I was little. Four or five I suppose.' Tom put his head in his hands and Lizzie waited patiently until he felt able to continue. 'Ma was such a fuss-pot,' he said at last. 'She wouldn't let me out of her sight, and I was never allowed to play with the other boys. She said we were too good for them, but I think she was just afraid I'd have an accident.'

'Go on,' Lizzie prompted.

'Well, one day one of the boys came knocking at the door. "Can Tom come out to play?" I heard him say. I was hiding behind the drawing-room door which was covered by a heavy velvet curtain to keep out the draughts. I remember it was maroon in colour. Of course she said "no" but I couldn't believe it. I was so angry that I started stuffing the material into my mouth. I think I expected Ma to be sorry when she found out what I was doing. The fluff got up my nose, and into my nose and eyes, and I thought I was going to die.'

'Was she cross, Tom?'

'No. It just frightened her, and after that she watched me closer than ever. I've had that dream on and off ever since.'

'I'm not surprised.'

Lizzie felt really sorry. That was the sort of childish trauma she could imagine following a child into adult life. An over-protective mother and a rebellious child. It explained a lot. But kind as Frances Grainger had been to her and Joey, Lizzie wasn't going to have her son growing up in the same stifling atmosphere. The sooner she had Joey back living with her the better. But the small event drew Lizzie closer to Tom. He needed her: he'd just proved it. Tom needed her just as much as Joey did – and Lizzie liked being needed.

'Do you have dreams?' Tom asked when he was feeling better.

'Only nice ones,' Lizzie admitted. 'I used to have day-dreams.'

'Tell me.'

'Well, when I was young I dreamed that the streets of Brighton were paved with gold, and if I ever came here I'd make my fortune. But of course it wasn't like that at all. Then I read this story about a girl called Opal who became a beautician and travelled the world.'

'Is that what your dream is – to travel?'

'Not really; although it would be nice. I'd just like to be a beautician – you know, learn about make-up and things.'

Tom was leaning on one elbow watching her. He could tell that she really meant what she was saying. 'You should have a word with Madame Yvonne,' he suggested.

'Madame Yvonne – who's she?'

'I've heard Pa talking about her. She runs a small beauty parlour next door to Grainger's, and she's retiring soon. Some of our customers bring their wives with them, and while they're waiting for their husbands they go and have a massage or their nails polished. Pa thought Ma might be interested in taking it on.'

'Isn't she?'

'She says she's too old, but I think she's just scared of anything new. But you, Lizzie – you could do it.'

'But I'm very ignorant. I'd have to learn.' Lizzie was certainly nervous of the idea. It was the sort of dream every girl has at some time or the other but doesn't expect to be fulfilled. 'Who would teach me?'

'Why not Madame Yvonne herself? Perhaps she'd train you as part of the arrangement.'

'I don't know.' Lizzie was still doubtful.

'Think about it. Otherwise Pa will only buy the business and open it as another department.'

Tom quite liked the idea of Lizzie becoming a working wife, although it was unusual. Most women were happy to stay at home and look after their homes and families. But he didn't want her turning out like his mother. No, if Lizzie became a business woman she wouldn't be so demanding of his time and attention. If her days were fully occupied she would be less likely to watch his movements. He would still be able to have a private life as well as a domestic one. In fact, he'd have the best of both worlds.

'We'll talk it over when we get back from London,' he promised, and gave her a quick kiss because she looked as though she expected it.

Their cases were already packed, so while Tom went to fetch the Bentley, Lizzie changed into her going-away outfit. She wore a new grey suit with a fox fur around her shoulders, and a little pill-box hat with a feather on the side. She was already waiting in the hall when a cab drew up and Tom jumped out and began lifting their luggage into the boot.

'What's happened?' Lizzie asked. 'Has your father changed his mind about lending us the car?'

'Get in and I'll tell you all about it on our way to the station.' Lizzie did as she was told, and then waited patiently while Tom explained the change of plan. 'It's good news,' he said excitedly. 'Pa's really come up trumps this time. He's bought us a car for a wedding present. It's one of those new Ford saloons with four doors. It's going to be delivered to our hotel. What do you think about that?'

'Your dad's a darling,' Lizzie said. 'And so are you.' She put out her hand to take Tom's, but drew it away when he ignored the pressure of her fingers. He didn't like shows of affection and she didn't want to upset him.

Lizzie felt childishly excited when they arrived at the station. The station-master, a fatherly figure with a drooping moustache and an important hat, actually greeted them personally. He called a porter forward to carry their cases.

The mighty steam-engine was like a home on wheels with its comfortable carriages. It was the first time Lizzie had travelled first class, and she felt like a film star as she sank into the soft seat with its starched linen headrest.

There were loud whistles and the clanking of wheels as the train started to puff its way out of the station and the view from the window was temporarily obliterated by steam. But it soon cleared, and then they were rattling out of the town, leaving behind the rows of terraced houses with their tiny walled gardens full of flapping washing. They were travelling through the green Sussex countryside where sheep dotted the Downs and black and white cows chewed the cud.

Tom sat back contentedly and lit a cigarette. 'This is travelling in style,' he said. 'Aren't you glad you married me and not that oaf Jack French?'

Lizzie coloured. The sudden mention of Jack's name jolted her. He had been a good friend – at one time her only friend – and she'd treated him badly and found she missed him – and his family – terribly. 'Jack's a nice man. You mustn't say such things about him.'

'Oh, Jack's all right. We were pals for a time,' Tom said airily. 'But he works at a greengrocer's, doesn't he? And he dresses like a workman.'

'There's nothing wrong with that,' Lizzie said faintly.

'A lovely woman like you deserves better; and I'm the one to give it to you. You're happy, aren't you, Lizzie? Say you're happy.'

'I'm happy,' Lizzie said obediently.

And most of the time she was. It was only sometimes when she allowed herself to stop to think, that she wondered if she'd made the right decision in marrying Tom. Then she thought of Joey and his need for a real father, one who had the same blood in his veins, and she knew that she'd had no choice. Her son's happiness came first.

And Tom was exciting. His unpredictability was a constant challenge, and she was proud to be seen with him. They made a handsome couple – everyone said so.

Her reflections were cut short by a white-coated steward passing the door with a brass bell to announce that refreshments were being served in the restaurant car. Tom led the way and they were soon being served tea, toast and jam, and Dundee cake by waiters in freshly starched coats. Outside the scenery sped past: fast or more leisurely, according to the times the train was expected to slow down at stations and halts.

As they approached the metropolis the scene changed. The buildings grew taller and closer together, and everything seemed to be coated with a film of dust. Even the washing in the gardens had changed from white to a dingy grey, and the chimneys from houses and factories belched black smoke into the air. Lizzie wasn't surprised that London was often nick-named The Smoke.

But when they came out of Victoria Station and Tom hailed another cab to take them to their hotel things changed for the better. True, the streets were still dirty and littered with steaming horse dung, but the shops were brightly lit and there were buskers singing at street corners.

They passed a one-legged man turning the handle of a barrel-organ, and the wailing strains of 'Lily of Laguna' filled the air. Lizzie found the sights and smells intoxicating: fish and chips, roasting chestnuts and the Cockney traders shouting their wares. They passed a ragged boy selling matches, and an old woman with a basket of wilting flowers on her arm and a care-worn expression on her face. London was exciting, but it was also a sad place. It depended on whether you had money or not – which side you were on.

'We're here,' Tom announced, as the cab slowed down outside a hotel with white marble pillars each side of the doorway and a flight of black and white steps leading up to the entrance.

A commissionaire in a uniform decorated with gold braid hurried forward to open the cab door. Lizzie found herself walking across red carpet towards a sweeping staircase. There was a lift but she wanted to walk and savour the hotel's interior. The striped wallpaper had the texture of silk, and the polished hand-rail was smooth to the touch. Their apartment was a suite of three rooms: a sitting, bed and private bathroom. Two huge windows overlooked a green park so that the dirty buildings of the city were at a distance. Lizzie sighed with pleasure as she fingered the silk of the bed-cover and the satiny feel of the polished dressing-table.

'No need to unpack,' Tom said. 'The chambermaid will do it while we're at dinner.'

True to his word, when they returned from the dining-room after a delicious three-course meal, all their belongings had been unpacked and neatly folded away, and the bedcovers turned down.

So followed days filled with delight and new experiences. They went shopping in Bond Street, and Tom bought Lizzie two sets of underwear so sheer that she could see her hand through the transparent material. Then she chose a winter coat with a lambskin collar, and a figure-hugging black evening gown with a flared panel of frills from knee to ankle.

Lizzie had only ever worn black when she was in mourning, but Tom insisted it was fashionable. He said it made her look older and more sophisticated.

They ate in expensive restaurants where Tom demanded good service and complained if everything wasn't to his complete satisfaction. When he reported a young waitress for clumsiness, Lizzie tried to intervene, fearing the girl would lose her job, but Tom insisted that if she were sacked it was entirely her own fault.

'But she might not be able to get another position,' Lizzie said, seeing the girl's frightened face.

'That, my dear, is her look-out,' Tom replied. 'It's nothing to do with us.'

There was no more to be said, but Lizzie kept worrying about the young waitress for the rest of the day.

In the evenings they had good seats at the theatres. Lizzie fell in love with the melodious voice of Jack Bucanan singing 'Goodnight Vienna', and the tunes from the new musical show by Noël Coward ran through her head long after the curtain had fallen.

Then the new car arrived. Tom had hoped for a Rolls-Royce, but he seemed quite pleased with the shiny black Ford with its sparkling chrome headlights. He couldn't wait to get behind the wheel and take Lizzie out to see the sights. They went to the Zoo and the Tower of London, and drove along the embankment to watch the Thames flowing past and ferrying little boats and pleasure steamers to their destinations. It was all too good to last – and of course it didn't.

On their last evening they were in the hotel bar having a late drink. Lizzie was sipping sherry and Tom was on his second double whisky. Lizzie was wearing her new black dress, which was much too dressy for the occasion but Tom had insisted. She'd noticed before that he couldn't take his drink and hoped he wouldn't order another. On the odd occasion alcohol put him in a good humour, but usually it shortened his temper which was quick even at the best of times. As a waiter passed their table Tom hailed him although his glass was only half empty.

'Another whisky, boy,' he ordered. 'And be quick about it.'

'Tom, please!' Lizzie put a restraining hand on her husband's arm. 'Don't you think you've had enough?'

Tom roughly shook her off. 'I'll decide how much I have to drink,' he said, so loudly that people at the next table stared in their direction. When the drink was brought he said, 'And bring me a bottle of Claret to take to my room, and a packet of Players Weights.'

'I'm sorry, sir,' the waiter said politely. 'We don't sell drinks by the bottle – only the glass.'

'Rubbish!' Tom said rudely. 'I want to speak to the manager.'

The manager, when he came, was servile but confirmed the waiter's words. 'Sorry, sir – we don't sell alcohol by the bottle.'

'What sort of hotel is this anyway?' Tom moaned, downing his third whisky at one gulp. 'Our early morning tea was late today, and there were no clean towels until we rang for them.'

'And you, madam,' the manager turned to Lizzie, a strained expression on his face. 'I hope you have no complaints?'

Lizzie wanted to calm things down. Tom would regret his fiery words when he was completely sober. 'None at all,' she said. 'I think the service has been perfect. Thank you very much.'

Tom gave her a fierce glance. When the manager was out of earshot he said, 'Really, Lizzie, that was extremely bad form – not standing up for your husband when he's in the right.'

'But, Tom,' Lizzie remonstrated, 'the tea was only five minutes late, and the girl apologised when she brought the towels. I don't know why you're making such a fuss.'

This set Tom off. 'Don't you? Then it just seems to me that you don't know anything.' And with this he slammed out of the bar; and out of the hotel, without stopping for his coat.

Lizzie waited, and then, as he didn't come back, called a cheerful 'goodnight' to the waiter and went upstairs to their room. She felt miserable and knew she wouldn't sleep, but when the bedside clock reached one o'clock and Tom hadn't returned she dozed from tiredness.

Tom in the meantime was walking the streets. Anger always made him want a woman – any woman – and he'd heard that prostitutes were two a penny on the streets of London.

However, his luck seemed to be out. He'd walked over two miles into a shabby district of mean streets and late-night clubs before he spotted a woman standing under a gas lamp. She was tall and thin with obviously dyed hair and a heavily made-up face, but she seemed willing. It was only as they walked away arm in arm, discussing terms, that Tom realised he had hardly any money on him: he'd left his wallet back at the hotel. He emptied his pocket of loose change – it came to about three shillings and six pence. He offered it hopefully.

'Who do you think I am?' the woman sneered sarcastically, pushing him away. 'I'm not *that* hard up, my lad. Fifteen bob or nothing. Take it or leave it.' She walked away to find a more generous client, her high heels tapping indignantly on the pavement.

By the time Tom returned to the hotel the rage inside him had fermented into a pain so great that it had to have release. He flung open the bedroom door, hoping that Lizzie was waiting up for him. She'd left a lamp burning and was sleeping peacefully on her side of the big bed. At once he put all the blame on her. She should have backed him in front of the management; she should have come after him, or at least waited up. Not gone to sleep as if nothing had happened. He had to show her who was boss.

Tom walked across the room, stripping off his clothing as he went and leaving it scattered on the floor. Without bothering to put on his pyjamas he pulled back the covers.

Lizzie lay there curled like a beautiful but innocent child. Her shining hair was ruffled and her shoulders and arms bare. Tom could see the outline of her slender body through the white silk of her nightgown. The desire within him was too much to contain. With one movement he tore the gown open and straddled her naked body. Her brown eyes flew open but he ignored their pleading as he repeatedly violated her tender flesh.

Only when he was exhausted did he bury his face between her bruised breasts and weep.

CHAPTER NINETEEN

Return to Greenlock

The following morning breakfast was a silent affair in the hotel dining-room. Tom seemed in deep thought and couldn't meet Lizzie's eyes, and try as she would Lizzie couldn't draw him out.

She'd been shocked and humiliated by her husband's actions the previous night, and when she saw the bruises on her white skin in the bathroom mirror a frisson of fear had enveloped her. On one breast there was a purple mark the size of a saucer, and her stomach and ribs were covered with scratches. There were teeth marks on her neck, extending from her shoulder almost to her ear, and her whole body ached. But the hurt Tom had inflicted reached much deeper than the surface scars. It brought back memories of that time in the red barn. She'd hoped that event would never be repeated. But even after all these years it seemed that Tom hadn't changed, apart from the fact that he was now her husband and so had certain rights over her body.

She'd dressed carefully, choosing a high-necked blouse to hide the ugly marks, and now sat opposite her husband toying with a piece of toast. Tom didn't seem to have much appetite either.

'I'm not hungry,' Tom suddenly announced, pushing away the plate of bacon and eggs which he'd barely touched. 'If you've finished we'll make a move before the roads get busy.'

'I'll go upstairs and finish packing,' Lizzie said minimally, getting to her feet.

Tom looked at his wrist-watch. 'We'll leave at ten then. I'll be outside with the car.'

True to his word Tom was waiting at the foot of the hotel steps with the Ford when Lizzie appeared. The porter followed behind with the cases, and she was relieved because her body still ached every time she moved. Even soaking in a hot bath hadn't helped.

Lizzie had been looking forward to the drive back to Brighton. Neither of them was in a talkative mood, and they sat side by side like strangers as the miles sped past.

'I think we'll take the longer route through the country lanes,' Tom suddenly announced. He turned left. 'I'm still not used to this driving business, particularly on busy roads.'

Lizzie didn't mind. The Sussex countryside, even in November, was charming. The trees were stripped and bare, and the woodland was covered with a carpet of brown and golden leaves. The fields were yellow and flat where the harvest had been gathered in, and even the birds were lazily silent. She waited for an opportune moment and then put out her hand, resting it on Tom's sleeve.

'Tom. About last night ...'

'What about it?' Tom asked roughly. 'Don't touch me when I'm driving. It distracts me.'

'Sorry.' Lizzie removed her hand. 'I just wanted to say that ... I think we should discuss it.'

She thought that if they talked about Tom's behaviour she might understand his actions. Lizzie had chosen to marry Tom and her natural optimism made her determined to make their marriage a success – if only for Joey's sake.

'What are you talking about?'

'It's just that although I've had a child I'm not very experienced. If you could be kinder to me – gentler…'

'We'll talk about it later. Have a look at the map, Lizzie, and see where we are. I think we've missed the turning.'

Lizzie sighed and unfolded the map. She knew they wouldn't talk about things later: by the look on Tom's face the subject was closed.

'I think this road leads to a place called Penbury,' she said.

'Never heard of it.'

Lizzie thought the name sounded familiar, but it was only when they drove into a small town and Tom parked the car opposite a green that she realised she had been there before. It was where she'd caught the tram to Greenlock after her mum and dad had died. She'd been heading for Aunt Hannah's house so that she could be nearer to Billy. Oh, how she missed her brother.

'I know this place,' Lizzie said excitedly. 'I've been here before. Look, there's the Market Cross and the bus stop. There should be a sign-post somewhere showing the way to Greenlock.'

'Never heard of it,' Tom said gruffly.

'I worked there for a while as a housemaid. I told you about my aunt and my brother. I'd love to see if Billy's still there.'

'Some other time, Lizzie. Give me the map.'

'No, Tom!' Lizzie said in desperation. 'I want to go there now. We're so near, and it shouldn't take long. Look, there's a sign; it's only three miles away. Please!'

Tom sighed; he needed a drink and the pubs would be open soon. He could ditch Lizzie for an hour or so and pick her up again later. 'I need some petrol,' he said. 'I'll take you to Greenlock, and you can go and look for your brother while I find a garage.'

'Oh, Tom, thank you!' Lizzie was so delighted she nearly flung her arms around him. She managed to restrain herself, and busied herself giving him directions instead.

Tom did offer to do his duty and take Lizzie right up to the door of Greenlock House, but she insisted on being dropped some way away. She needed to walk the last mile and compose herself – to be in the right frame of mind before confronting Aunt Hannah. Even after all these years the thought of the woman terrified her. And Billy, would he still remember her? Would he understand why she had to go away and leave him? Would he forgive her and welcome her, now that she could offer him the security she'd craved for them both?

She passed the churchyard where she'd picnicked, and the market where she'd delighted in her freedom on the day she left Greenlock House. She'd vowed then that she'd come back looking like a lady – and she had. The faded dress and battered straw hat had been replaced by a smart grey suit and hat and a fox fur looped across her shoulders. She felt prepared to meet her aunt on equal ground.

The tree-lined road was just as she remembered. When she stood on the pavement in front of the square red-brick house, the years fell away and she felt sixteen again. It was just the same: the four rows of windows and the iron railings. The little balconies framing the upper windows were rusted but still in place, and the ivy had climbed higher and hung in green blankets from the brickwork. Above it all, like a giant hat, sat the roof with its bulging outcrop of tiny blind windows, and the one tall chimney with a life-size stone griffin on either side. The griffins still looked like Hannah Seymour as Lizzie remembered her: grinning, malevolent and evil.

Lizzie tore her eyes away from the ugly house. Before she could change her mind she marched up to the front door. No side door for her now – she was a visitor. The bell-rope was still in place, and while she waited, brown curly leaves blew around her feet, making a rustling noise as if they were trying to tell her something.

There was no sound of footsteps approaching. She rang a second time and heard the distant clanking of the bell somewhere inside. After a few moments Lizzie put out her hand and turned the handle. It wasn't locked. The door opened easily over the red tiled floor that she'd had to keep polished as part of her duties. Ahead the inner door shone golden and red like the rays of a sun. This door wouldn't open – it was locked or bolted.

Lizzie had the sudden feeling that she was alone. Greenlock House was uninhabited and she had only her memories for company. The front door creaked behind her in the wind. Lizzie shivered as if someone had just walked over her grave.

'You can't frighten me,' she said aloud with more bravado than she felt. 'The side door will let me in.'

The dusty laurels almost obscured the pathway and Lizzie had to push them aside to reach the servants' entrance. This also was locked against her. When she banged the knocker the hollow sound it made was ghostly.

Lizzie was just about to turn away, defeated, when a piece of paper blew across her path. She picked it up idly, thinking to screw it up and throw it away tidily. There were bold letters printed on the white paper. It was a notice that had probably been fastened to the door; she could see the holes made by drawing-pins: IN EMERGENCIES PLEASE CALL ON MRS BUTTERY, MEADOW COTTAGE, GREENLOCK. Underneath was a little diagram showing that Mrs Buttery lived in a turning down by the market-place.

Lizzie had no option but to retrace her steps. She didn't know who Mrs Buttery was. Perhaps she was the disagreeable Ellen, married and in a home of her own. If so, Lizzie would be pleased to see her face to face.

Meadow Cottage was easy to find. It was a fat little house with pebbled walls and a thatched roof, set back from the road among a garden full of bronze chrysanthemums and bushes of lavender and rosemary. At the side was a vegetable patch and a wire pen where chickens scratched.

A black cat with golden eyes rose to its feet and ambled towards Lizzie. It rubbed itself against her leg in rumbling welcome. She bent down to scratch its neck and it rolled on its back and waved its paws in the air in ecstasy.

'I see you've found a friend, Sooty,' a pleasant voice said.

Lizzie looked up into a friendly face; the face of a stranger. It certainly wasn't Ellen: she'd been tall, thin and unpleasant. The woman standing in the open doorway of Meadow Cottage was plump, with curly hair and a welcoming smile on her face.

'Mrs Buttery?'

'Yes. I'm Gladys Buttery. If you've come about the room I'm afraid you're too late, I've already let it. You could try two doors down at Mrs Smithers. She lets rooms.'

'I don't want a room,' Lizzie said with a smile. 'I've just called at Greenlock House to visit my aunt – Mrs Seymour. There was no one about, but I found your name and address on a notice.'

'Oh yes, that explains it, dear,' Gladys Buttery said with a smile. 'So Mrs Seymour is your aunt?'

'Yes.'

'And you are …?'

'I'm – I was Elizabeth Sargent. But everyone except my aunt calls me Lizzie. But I'm Mrs Grainger now – Mrs Thomas Grainger.'

'Well, whoever you are, you're welcome. Why don't you come inside and join me in a cup of tea? I can hear the kettle singing, and I usually stop for a cup about now.'

Without waiting for an answer Mrs Buttery disappeared inside her cottage. Lizzie followed and found herself in the smallest, but neatest little living-room. A fire blazed in the grate, and deep, shabby, comfortable chairs were drawn up on a threadbare patch of carpet to catch the warmth.

Lizzie sat down and loosened her jacket and fur while her hostess busied herself over the tea-things. Gladys Buttery was a large woman for such a small room, but she'd learned to monitor her movements so that she didn't have any accidents. Only when Lizzie was sipping her tea from a delicate cup, with a fruit scone on a plate in her lap, did she speak again.

'So you're Lizzie?'

'Yes.'

'And Mrs Seymour is your auntie?'

'Yes. Greenlock House seems to be deserted. Is my aunt away?'

'You could say that – she's in the county hospital.'

'Oh dear!' Lizzie tried to sound concerned. 'What's the matter with her?'

'She's never been the same since the heart attack,' Gladys said, spreading jam on to a scone and taking an enormous bite. 'That was several years ago – soon after I started to work for her. She was poorly for a time and we all took turns looking after her. I'd some nursing experience, and she took kindly to me.'

'I used to work for her,' Lizzie admitted. 'She sent me away. We didn't get on very well although we were related.'

'So you're *that* Lizzie.' Gladys beamed as if she now understood things. 'Ellen told me about you.'

'She didn't like me either.'

'That Ellen didn't get on with nobody. She had a big row with your aunt and walked out soon after. That just left Daisy and me.'

A picture flashed into Lizzie's memory of the little scullery-maid with her misshapen body and overlarge head. 'What happened to Daisy?'

'She was a queer one and no mistake,' Gladys said. She was enjoying the chat about old times. 'She talked about you too, in her odd way. Said you were her friend. But she had a fit or a brainstorm, or some such thing, and your aunt had her put away. She hadn't any family, you see.'

'Poor Daisy.'

'As you say: poor Daisy. So that only left me. I did what I could; but my old man was dying so I couldn't give up this cottage although Mrs Seymour wanted me to. Then when she had another turn the doctor said she'd be better in the hospital. There's a private nursing wing so she's well looked after.'

'And Billy?' Lizzie was almost frightened to ask. 'My brother lived with Mrs Seymour. What happened to Billy?'

'I used to feel sorry for that poor little boy,' Gladys said with a reminiscent sigh. 'Shut up in that big house with only an old woman for company. It was better when he went to that school down the road; but he didn't have a chance to play like a growing child should. So Billy's your brother, is he?'

'Yes. What happened to him, Mrs Buttery?'

Gladys paused for a moment before replying. Then she said: 'I've often wondered that myself. All I remember is that he made friends with the headmaster's niece and went off with her for a holiday, or so Ellen said. That was the last I saw of him. Poor little boy.'

'But where did they go? Think, Mrs Buttery – think!'

'Sorry, I've no idea. But wherever he went it must have been better for him than Greenlock House. There's no use you asking at the school either; that closed down last year. Mr Bond, the headmaster, retired, and went to live in Scotland, so I heard.'

'But my aunt must know.'

'Probably; but she'll only tell if she feels like it. Why don't you go to the hospital and visit her? I'm sure she'll be pleased to see you.'

Lizzie wasn't so sure. Her last picture of her aunt had been of a formidable old woman with a hooked nose and a long black dress. But why should she be scared? She'd done well for herself, and surely she had every right to enquire about the whereabouts of her brother. Aunt Hannah would surely be impressed by her smart clothes and her wedding ring. She had nothing to fear.

'I think I will go and see her,' Lizzie said, getting up from her chair and smoothing the creases out of her skirt. 'Is the hospital far away?'

'No. I'll give you directions. And I think you'll find your aunt changed.'

'For the better, I hope.'

Gladys Buttery didn't answer. Instead she led Lizzie to the door and explained the way. The hospital was situated in a part of the town Lizzie didn't know, but it was a pleasant walk and gave her time to think.

'I must be firm but kind,' she decided. 'After all, Aunt Hannah is a sick old woman. She's also Dad's sister, and treated him and Mum badly. She deliberately separated me from Billy, and then when I tried to stand up to her turned me out of the house. But she's still a sick old woman,' her conscience argued, 'And Mrs Buttery says she's changed.'

Instead of frightening herself by letting her imagination run riot, Lizzie bought some fruit and a bunch of flowers to take to the invalid. By the time she reached the hospital she felt ready for anything.

It was a pleasant enough place, set in open ground on the edge of the town. The main building was large and grey, like a Victorian mansion, but the nursing home was situated in a more modern wing at the side.

Lizzie pushed open the main door and found herself in a bright comfortable foyer. There were chairs for visitors and low tables holding magazines. Behind a desk a white-coated receptionist was busy filing cards in a metal cabinet. She looked up and smiled pleasantly as Lizzie entered.

'Can I help you?'

'I'd like to visit one of your patients. Mrs Hannah Seymour.'

'Usual visiting hours are between four and six, dear.'

Lizzie looked at her watch. It was half past one – two and a half hours early. 'I'm only passing through,' she explained, 'and I wouldn't stay long. I really would be grateful.'

'Well, dear …' the receptionist looked Lizzie up and down and liked what she saw. 'Mrs Seymour doesn't get many visitors. Are you a friend or relation?'

'I'm her niece – Elizabeth Grainger.'

'If you'd like to sit down and wait I'll go and see what Sister says.'

Lizzie took a seat and leafed through a magazine. Part of her was curious to see what the years had done to her aunt; and another part couldn't help hoping that her request would be refused. She didn't have long to wait. When the receptionist returned she was accompanied by a uniformed nurse wearing a fancy head-dress that stood out around her head like the wings of a bird. She smiled kindly at Lizzie and shook her hand.

'How kind of you to come,' she said. 'The old ladies don't get many visitors, you know. The young are very selfish these days. They put their relatives away and then forget all about them. It's nice to meet someone who cares.'

Lizzie blushed slightly. 'I'm Mrs Grainger …'

'And I'm Sister Pierce. Now who was it you wanted to visit?'

'Hannah Seymour – if it's convenient.'

'I don't see why not, Mrs Grainger. Mrs Seymour's been a good girl and eaten all her lunch – even the rice pudding. She can have her rest later. Follow me.'

Lizzie wanted to laugh. The description of Aunt Hannah being a good girl for eating her pudding didn't fit in with her recollections. But there couldn't be two patients with the same name.

Sister Pierce walked briskly along the passage, her starched skirts rustling. She smiled at old people in wheelchairs, and nodded approval at the staff. It seemed a friendly place and Lizzie hoped Aunt Hannah was happy. They stopped outside a door with a little window set in the top panel. After a swift glance inside, Sister Pierce pushed the door open saying softly, 'She's awake. Now try not to tire her.' Then in a louder voice, 'It's a Mrs Grainger to see you, dear. Isn't that a nice surprise?' Then she quickly backed out of the room closing the door behind her. Lizzie was alone.

She'd somehow expected a long ward with rows of beds, but instead found herself in a small room with everything in it built to miniature scale. A small chest of drawers stood against one wall and a child-size armchair in the window. There was a wicker-work commode disguised as another chair, and a narrow bed in the middle of a strip of drugget. The rest of the floor was uncarpeted, but covered by shiny black and white squared linoleum. Everything was spotlessly clean and smelled of carbolic soap.

Lizzie walked a step or two forward and then froze. Surely that tiny figure tucked up in the bed couldn't be Hannah Seymour? Her aunt had been a big woman with dark hair and an upright carriage: the sort of imposing figure that had struck fear into the tender heart of the young Lizzie.

The woman in the bed was small and crooked, with rounded shoulders draped with a fluffy pink shawl. Aunt Hannah would never have worn such a garment. Lizzie had never seen her dressed in anything but funeral black. This woman's hair was so white and skimpy that she could see the pink skull shining through the fine gossamer threads. The cheeks were sunken, and the mouth stretched upwards in a permanent grimace as if she'd suffered a stroke as well as a heart attack. Only the eyes belonged to the old Hannah Seymour: small and sharp, darting here and there; and the beak of a nose, bonier than ever. The hands, threaded with purple veins, picked continually at the woollen bedspread.

'Come nearer – I can't see you,' Lizzie was instructed. 'I don't know anyone called Grainger.'

'It's me, Aunt – Lizzie.'

'Lizzie?' The voice was as frail as the body – an old woman's voice.

'Your niece, Elizabeth Sargent.'

'Then why did you say your name was Grainger? Are you trying to confuse me?'

'No, Aunt Hannah. My married name's Grainger.'

'Married, eh? More fool you. Nothing good comes out of marriage. Look at Ernest and Mary.'

'I've brought you some flowers and some fruit.' Lizzie placed her peace offerings on the bed.

Mrs Seymour stretched out a greedy hand towards the fruit. 'Grapes, eh? I hope there're no pips in them.'

'I'm sorry to find you unwell,' Lizzie said. 'I went to the house but there was no one there. Mrs Buttery told me where to find you.'

'Gladys Buttery was the only one who stayed.' Hannah Seymour leaned back against the pillows, the fruit forgotten. A tear coursed down her cheek. 'Everyone left me. Daisy went mad, and Ellen wouldn't do what I wanted. Even you left me, Elizabeth.'

'You sent me away – remember,' Lizzie said softly.

'I told Gladys I'd leave her all my money if she'd move in and look after me; but she preferred to stay with that husband of hers.'

'She had to stay; he was dying.'

'And what about me?' Mrs Seymour managed to pull herself upright in the bed so that she looked more like the woman Lizzie remembered. Her eyes flashed with anger and a trickle of saliva dribbled from the corner of her twisted mouth. 'I could have died, but no one cared. Gladys Buttery could have been a rich woman if she'd stayed. I'd have left her everything.'

'I thought Billy was going to inherit everything,' Lizzie dared to say.

'Billy – who's Billy?'

'My brother.'

'Oh, you mean *William*. He went away as well.' As if the subject had exhausted her, Hannah lay back again and closed her eyes.

Lizzie waited for a moment and then asked gently, 'I'd like to see my brother. Where is he?'

'I don't know and I don't care. I was planning to make him worthy of Greenlock House. I paid his school fees and gave him everything a boy could want, but he was weak, like his father.'

Lizzie ignored the slight against her father. 'Mrs Buttery says he went away with the schoolmaster's niece.'

'Did he? I don't remember,' Hannah said vaguely.

'I think you do remember.' Suddenly Lizzie lost patience and felt she was being played with; that her aunt wasn't as forgetful as she was making out. 'Please, Aunt Hannah, it's very important to me.'

'Go away! You're upsetting me.' Mrs Seymour sank down under the covers as if she was trying to hide.

'Not until you've told me where Billy is.'

'I told you I don't remember.'

Lizzie's temper snapped. She leaned over the bed and stared into the face she'd hated for so long. 'You don't want to remember, do you? You're an evil old woman and everybody's afraid of you. But I'm not. I'll find Billy some day, with or without your help.' Lizzie turned and marched towards the door. She wanted to get away, out into the fresh air.

'Stop!'

The sharp voice, so reminiscent of the old days, brought Lizzie up sharp. She turned and looked at the old woman in the bed and saw that a change had taken place. The eyes, sunk deeply in their sockets, were brimming with tears, and the sharp features and beaky nose had collapsed into a quivering travesty of the Aunt Hannah Lizzie hated.

'What is it?' she asked softly.

'Your brother made friends with Mr Bond's niece Caroline. They used to play together. When I was taken ill he spent more and more time at Mr Bond's school – Greyhaven. It lightened the load for Ellen. I missed him, because I really was fond of him, you know.'

Lizzie thought her aunt had a funny way of showing her affection, but she didn't say so. She waited because the old woman seemed to be struggling with her thoughts.

'What happened?' she prompted at last.

'Caroline's father came to take her home. The children were inseparable by that time; and when William was invited to join them for a holiday it seemed the ideal solution.'

'Where did they live? You must have known that.'

'I was ill – too ill to take notice. It was somewhere on the south coast. A little village by the sea, I think. He never came back. I haven't seen him since.'

'So Billy could still be with this family?' Lizzie said wonderingly. 'Surely it's not possible? I can imagine them accepting a strange child for a few weeks – but you're talking about *years*.'

'I know.'

'Didn't anyone make any enquiries?'

'Not that I know of. Ellen never said anything.'

'Ellen wouldn't,' Lizzie burst out passionately. 'She would have been glad to see the back of Billy; just as you were glad to get rid of me.'

'I'm sorry.'

'Sorry!' Lizzie laughed bitterly, but when she looked into Hannah Seymour's eyes she saw that they'd softened as if perhaps the old woman did mean it. Was it possible that after all this time her aunt was feeling the emotions that most people take for granted?

'I was jealous, you see,' Hannah Seymour whispered. She put up a hand to wipe away a tear from her withered cheek.

'Who were you jealous of?'

'Everyone. When we were children your father was always the favourite. The baby of the family, who was not only better looking but cleverer than me. Then I married a rich man and Ernest married your mother. If it hadn't been for the war he might have done better for himself; but with two children and a sickly wife he didn't have the opportunity.'

'Why didn't you help him?'

'Because it made me feel good to see him struggling while I was going up in the world. I had no children and I was jealous of him for having a son. I had nothing after my husband died – only money.'

'But the money didn't bring you happiness?'

'No.' Hannah looked at Lizzie, taking in her expensive suit and hat, her hand-made shoes and carefully set hair. 'You look as if you've done well for yourself, Elizabeth. But I hope you've chosen a good man, a man who'll make you happy, because that's more important than wealth – apart from sons.'

'I have a son,' Lizzie confessed in a low voice. 'He's five years old and his name's Joey.'

'Joey,' Hannah said softly, as if she liked the name. 'Then you must look after him, Lizzie. You must take care of him better than I took care of Billy.'

Lizzie's eyes pricked with tears. It was the first time her aunt had dropped William and Elizabeth and called them by the names they were used to. It could only mean one thing: that her sorrow was real. She put out her hand and took one of the bony claws lying on the coverlet.

'I will,' she said. 'And I'm going to find Billy somehow, even if it takes me the rest of my life.' Suddenly she remembered Tom waiting in the car in the centre of

Greenlock. She'd been gone for ages and he would be getting impatient. 'I have to go now, Aunt Hannah,' she said. 'My husband is waiting for me. But I'll try to come again.'

'Don't worry.' Hannah patted Lizzie's hand. 'I think we understand each other.' They smiled, as if for the first time in their lives they liked each other. 'You're an independent young woman just as I was,' she continued, 'so I'd like to give you a present.'

'There's no need,' Lizzie protested.

'But I want to. In the drawer of my locker you'll find a key. Sister Pierce is looking after the case it fits. On your way out she'll give it to you. What it contains is for you - only you.'

Lizzie tried to refuse but Mrs Seymour insisted, so when she left the room she was clutching a small metal key in her hand.

Sister Pierce looked surprised, but she handed over the case without argument. It was a brown box with a handle, like a small suitcase, and felt quite heavy as she hurried away from the hospital.

After worrying about keeping Tom waiting, Lizzie was the first to reach the place where he had arranged to collect her. To pass the time she slipped the key into the lock and lifted the lid, curious to see what Aunt Hannah's present could be. To her astonishment the case was full of money. Five-pound notes, one-pound and ten-shilling notes, all rolled neatly and fastened with elastic bands. Hundreds of pounds - a fortune in her hands!

'Come on, get in. It's time we were off.' It was Tom, leaning out of the car trying to catch Lizzie's attention. As she climbed in beside him she smelled beer on his breath and he looked in a bad temper. Suddenly she disliked him. 'What have you got there?'

'Just a present from my aunt,' Lizzie said. She slipped the key into the pocket of her jacket for safety.

'I hope she's been generous,' Tom said sarcastically.

'Not really,' Lizzie said airily. 'Just something personal.'

CHAPTER TWENTY

Lady Elizabeth's

'Well, what do you think, Lizzie?'
'I want to live by the sea.'

'Patcham is only a ten-minute drive away. Look at the brochure.' Tom pushed a green and blue booklet across the table in Lizzie's direction. She put down the leaflet she'd been perusing and opened the one advertising "Downland Homes". 'Look at the houses in Ladies Mile.'

Lizzie turned the pages and studied the houses and bungalows that had recently been built on the new estate. They were spacious properties with large windows and tiled roofs in various colours.

'They're very expensive,' she said doubtfully. 'The bungalows are nearly five hundred pounds and the houses are over six hundred.'

'How many times do I have to remind you that the price isn't important. Look, the deposit is only sixty-five pounds, and the repayments seventeen and three pence a week if we don't want to pay a lump sum at once.'

'That's an awful lot, Tom.'

'The entrance hall is ten feet square, and there's a large lounge and dining-room as well as three bedrooms. It's all electric as well so it will be easy to run. It's cheap at the price.'

'I'd rather live in Peacehaven,' Lizzie said. 'They call it the Seaside Garden City and the houses are only four hundred pounds. Think of the long walks we can take along the cliffs.'

'I hate walking.'

Tom scraped back his chair and walked across to the window. He stared out into the street, his hands in his pockets and his back turned to Lizzie. She knew what that meant: he intended being awkward.

'But the sea air would be so good for Joey. It says there is easy access to the beach and caves and sands for bathing.'

'It's not Joey you're thinking about – it's that wretched brother of yours.'

Lizzie didn't answer because what Tom had just said was true. Ever since Aunt Hannah had told her that Billy had gone to stay in a seaside village she'd felt nearer to finding him. She'd tried to locate Mr Bond and his family, placing adverts in local papers along the coast, but so far it had been to no avail. However, Lizzie remained hopeful. Perhaps he was now, this minute, in Peacehaven. Perhaps if they bought a house there she'd see him walking past or bump into him in the street. She knew it was unlikely but she had to have her dreams.

Tom turned; there was a set look on his face as if he'd come to a decision. 'I'm going to buy one of these houses in Patcham,' he said firmly. 'There'll be a spare bedroom so we can have Joey with us. That's what you want, isn't it, Lizzie?'

'Yes ... but ...'

'I know Ma and Pa will be disappointed at losing him – but he's *our* son.'

'Yes, of course.'

'So, that's settled.' Tom scooped up the pile of leaflets and put them to one side. 'I'll get on to the agent today.'

'If you say so, Tom.'

Lizzie got up and started to clear the table. She kept her head down so that he couldn't see her disappointed face. Tom frowned; he hated to see Lizzie doing domestic chores.

'Leave that,' he said sharply. 'I want to be at the shop early – it's stocktaking. If you need a lift I'll be leaving in five minutes.'

Lizzie looked at the clock. It was a quarter to nine and Madame Yvonne would be expecting her on the hour. Three days a week she worked in the small beauty parlour next to Grainger's, and she was learning fast. As an unpaid employee she watched Madame go through the routines of massage and manicure, and saw her apply make-up and nail-varnish. There was so much to learn, but some day soon she hoped to be able to practise herself. When Madame Yvonne decided to retire she might be able to take charge. Her dreams of following the fictional Opal into the beauty business would come true at last.

Before leaving, Lizzie had to give the daily woman her orders. Her name was Ada Hunt, and she was a widow with three young children to feed.

'I'd like the bed-linen changed,' Lizzie said, as she watched Ada wash the breakfast dishes. Once she'd attended to this lowly task at Greenlock House but now the roles were reversed. The difference was that Lizzie tried to be fair to her employee and not overwork her.

'Yes, madam,' Ada said with a cheery smile. She was fond of Lizzie and was aware of the way her husband treated her. She couldn't understand how such a nice young lady could have wanted to marry such an unpleasant man in the first place. 'It's a lovely drying day, so I'll have the sheets blowing on the line in next to no time.'

'Could you polish the silver in the drawing-room? Only if you have time, Ada. It's just that my husband mentioned that the candlesticks are looking dingy.'

'I'll make the time, madam,' Ada promised. 'What do you fancy for dinner? The butcher's calling this morning.'

'Lamb would be nice for a change,' Lizzie said thoughtfully. 'Telephone him and ask him to deliver a leg of lamb if he has one.'

'Yes, madam. I'll make some mint-sauce to go with it. There are peas and new potatoes, and a rhubarb pie to follow.'

'Thank you, Ada, that sounds lovely. I must go now or Mr Grainger will think I'm not coming.'

With a cheery smile Lizzie pulled on her gloves and picked up her handbag. It wouldn't be the first time that she'd kept Tom waiting and he'd left without her. The shop was only a fifteen-minute walk away but she was wearing new shoes and they pinched her toe. A lift would be welcome.

Tom was drumming his fingers impatiently on the steering wheel trying to decide how much longer to wait. Just then Lizzie appeared in the doorway so he leaned over and opened the passenger door.

'I thought you were never coming,' he said testily.

'Sorry, Tom. I was just giving Ada her orders. She's promised to clean those candlesticks.'

That calmed him down a bit. He liked to hear Lizzie apologise, and servants should be kept in their place. Sometimes he suspected that his wife was too friendly towards Ada Hunt.

But Lizzie was looking nice this morning, Tom acknowledged as he started the engine. She was wearing a navy-blue serge two-piece that he hadn't seen before. The gored skirt was high-waisted, and the top hip-length and loose like a Magyar blouse. The collar, cuffs, and floppy tie were bordered with matching navy-blue velvet. Her gloves and shoes were also navy, and on her shining brown hair was perched a small blue hat with a fringe of veil. Tom felt proud of her, and hoped the neighbours had noticed his beautiful wife as she ran down the steps and took her seat beside him.

It was only a short drive, but hazardous as Tom was an impatient driver. Everyone seemed to be in a hurry to reach the town centre and he hated any vehicle passing him. He had to take the last few yards at a crawl, but at least there was plenty of space: no lorries unloading or buses trying to drop passengers.

'Hop out then, Lizzie,' he said. 'I've got to park the old jalopy.'

'Shall I see you at lunchtime?'

'Don't know. Depends how busy I am. Morning, Pargeter – tell my father I'll be in in five minutes.'

'Yes, sir.'

Mr Pargeter had opened the double doors to Grainger's and was polishing the brass door furniture with quick circular movements of his large rough hand. He wore a stiff brown overall over his striped shirt and braces, and on his head was a check cap which he only removed out of politeness to his employers. He doffed it now – to Lizzie rather than Tom.

'Morning, Mrs Grainger.'

'Good morning, Mr Pargeter. Isn't it a lovely morning?'

'It is indeed; you can smell the spring.' Pargeter tipped back his head and sniffed the air like an elderly bloodhound. 'And you're looking very spring-like, if I may say so.'

The admiration showed in his eyes. Elderly men were the best admirers of youth, and their appreciation was based on memories of their own long-gone salad days.

'Thank you – and how's your wife keeping?'

'Very well, Mrs Grainger.'

'And your son?'

'The boy's growing into a fine young man. Thirteen he is now. He certainly keeps us on our toes.'

Lizzie smiled. She'd never seen the caretaker's son, but she'd heard from many sources how proud the Pargeters were of the lad they always referred to proudly as 'the boy'.

'And what does he want to be when he leaves school, Mr Pargeter? A train-driver, I suppose – or maybe a footballer?'

'Oh no, Mrs Grainger. The boy likes to kick a ball about like the rest of them, but he wouldn't want to make a career of it.'

'A fisherman then?' Lizzie often saw the local lads trooping off to fish from the pier with their home-made rods and lines. 'I suppose he dreams of catching the largest fish off the south coast?'

'No!' There was something about the way Mr Pargeter spoke that made Lizzie wonder what she'd said wrong. 'Don't rub against the brass, Mrs Grainger – you'll get polish all over that smart outfit.'

'Sorry.' Lizzie moved away.

'Old Mr Grainger has promised the boy an opening here when he leaves school. The wife and I are delighted. It'll be good for him to have a settled job with prospects.'

'My father-in-law doesn't make promises lightly. He must think your son has potential.'

'Oh, he has.' Mr Pargeter smiled. 'My boy could do anything he sets his mind to.'

'I'd like to meet him,' Lizzie said. 'You must bring him into the shop one day.'

'I will – when he's not so busy with his homework.'

Lizzie saw a tall thin figure approaching: a woman wearing a fitted lavender suit and a wide-brimmed hat. She walked with easy strides to the shop next door, produced a key from her square leather bag, and inserted it in the lock.

'I must go, Mr Pargeter – Madame Yvonne has just arrived. Give my regards to your wife.'

'I will, Mrs Grainger.'

Tucking his polishing cloth into the capacious pocket of his overall, Mr Pargeter picked up a broom and began to sweep the pavement. Lizzie hurried to the beauty parlour and followed Madame Yvonne inside.

It was a small salon consisting of three cubicles decorated with faded pink and grey Regency stripe wallpaper. Each cubicle was furnished with a dressing-table, a hanging mirror, a chair, and a narrow padded couch.

Lizzie's first job was to polish the mirrors and dust the work surfaces. She quickly changed into the pink housedress she wore for working; on the pocket was an embroidered monogram: a fancy 'Y' in deeper pink. Although she was unpaid because Madame Yvonne was teaching her the trade, she still liked to do the basic jobs to save the cost of a cleaning-lady.

'Mrs George is booked in this morning for a facial,' Yvonne Naylor said as she followed Lizzie around with a leatherbound day book open in her hands. 'Would you like to treat her on your own?'

'Oh, Madame!' Lizzie turned a delighted face to her teacher. 'Do you think I'm ready?'

'As ready as you'll ever be, Elizabeth. Cubicle two is empty so you can use that one. If you do well, and Mrs George is pleased with you, I'll pay you fifty per cent.'

'What time is her appointment?'

Lizzie had planned to clean and re-dress the windows. There was a dusty display of faded artificial flowers that had been there for ages, and she'd noticed the stiff carcasses of a couple of blue-bottles lying on the stained wood. The shabby frontage must put clients off. If she had her way Lizzie would have chosen something more eye-catching: she fancied a shop-dummy posed as the Sleeping Beauty, but Yvonne Naylor had laughed at the idea.

'This has always been a high-class establishment, Elizabeth,' she'd said. 'We don't want to attract the wrong sort of clients.'

Lizzie disagreed, but she wasn't in a position to argue. Madame Yvonne had been running a successful business for over twenty years, and didn't seem to mind that her regular customers were either dying or moving to more modern establishments. Some of the new salons were offering hair styling, and full body treatments, as well as manicures and facials. She was waiting to retire, and her hopes were banked on her pupil, Elizabeth Grainger. The young woman had talent and her father-in-law owned the shop next door. Yvonne knew he had his eye on her salon, but she didn't want it just amalgamated into Grainger's and becoming an extension of the bigger shop.

'Mrs George's appointment is for nine thirty,' she said.

Lizzie looked at her wrist-watch. It was already a quarter past so the window would have to wait. She had to mix the cleanser and astringents, and make sure there were plenty of warm towels. Mrs George was a fussy woman but she was also well-to-do. If she could be persuaded to have her nails attended to as well as the facial it would be worthwhile.

Quickly she added things up in her head. A facial was seven and six and a manicure four and six. That came to twelve shillings so she'd earn six shillings for a couple of hours' work. Mrs George was also generous with tips so with luck she might make a clear ten shillings.

It wasn't that Lizzie needed the money. Tom had received his grandfather's legacy and had a regular income from Grainger's, so if she needed anything she only had to ask. But the idea of actually earning her own money appealed to her. She could add it to the hoard Aunt Hannah had given her. She still hadn't told Tom about the five hundred pounds locked away in the case – it made her feel safe just knowing it was there.

There was a small room at the back of the salon where the stock was kept and tinctures and creams prepared. Lizzie spread a tray with a clean cloth and then arranged a jar of cold cream, rose and lavender water, cotton-wool rolled into small balls, tweezers for tidying the eyebrows and burned-cork to darken them. Then in a small glass bowl she measured elderflower water, adding a few drops of tincture of benzoin. In a second bowl she mixed almond oil with cold-cream and an ounce of ichthyol ointment, boric-acid and zinc-oxide, stirring in fifteen drops of lavender oil with a glass rod. By the time Lizzie heard the door open and Mrs George's loud cheerful voice, everything was prepared.

'How nice to be greeted by a pretty young face. Now, I want a facial. When I looked in the glass this morning I couldn't believe my eyes. Wrinkles, my dear, and the most awful eruption on my chin – look!' Mrs George turned her moon-shaped face up to Lizzie and pointed to a minute pimple. 'Ask Madame Yvonne what she recommends.'

After consultation it was decided that Mrs George needed a face mask, so while her client was relaxing on the couch Lizzie got everything ready. The masks were usually made of chamois leather but she had to make do with several layers of soft muslin. These were cut into shape and punctured with holes for the eyes, nose and mouth. A piece of elastic held it on. Then she mixed a paste out of fine oatmeal and egg-white and spread it on Mrs George's ageing skin, keeping the mixture in place with the mask.

'We'll leave it on for about three quarters of an hour,' Lizzie said, making sure her client was comfortable. 'It'll be dry then and easy to remove. It's good for closing the pores; and then a good cream will soften the skin and work wonders.'

'I hope so,' Mrs George laughed, her eyes twinkling at Lizzie through the holes in the mask. 'While it's working you can manicure my nails. I broke one this morning.'

With deft fingers Lizzie filed Mrs George's nails, gently easing back the skin so that the cuticles showed like pink half-moons.

'You have lovely hands,' she said in admiration. 'Would you like varnish or just a polish?'

Mrs George considered. 'My husband hates varnish,' she said at last. 'He says that if women were meant to have scarlet talons God would have seen to it. Just give them a polish and make them shine.'

Lizzie did as she was instructed and an hour later Mrs George was ready to leave. Her plump face was carefully made up, and she declared that she felt ten years younger as she screwed her hat to her permed head with a long steel pin.

'I'm very pleased, my dear,' she said as Lizzie made out the bill. 'You will be a good replacement for Madame Yvonne when she retires. Has she set a date yet?'

'Not that I know of,' Lizzie admitted.

'Well, if you succeed her I shall certainly recommend you to my friends. This place needs a fresh young touch.' She looked around at the faded drapes and fly-blown mirror. 'If you modernised things you could be sitting on a little gold-mine.'

Lizzie smiled. 'I'd certainly like to try,' she admitted. 'I'd have a new colour scheme for a start. Blue is relaxing – and I'd like a waiting area where clients can chat and drink coffee.'

'That sounds wonderful.' Mrs George sailed to the door. 'Why don't you suggest it to Madame?'

'Perhaps I will. Shall we see you at the usual time next week?'

'Yes, for my regular treatment. And don't forget what I've just told you.' Mrs George tapped the side of her nose with one manicured finger and was gone.

Lizzie busied herself cleaning the cubicle and leaving it neat and tidy for the next client. Ideas were buzzing around in her head: dreams of her name over the door – MADAME ELIZABETH. No – LADY ELIZABETH sounded better. Was it a possibility that some day she could be running a beauty parlour of her own? Even Opal hadn't achieved that.

'Elizabeth.' Yvonne Naylor was standing at her elbow, a large fluffy towel draped over one arm. 'Would you like to learn the basics of a good massage?'

Lizzie nodded and helped Madame Yvonne prepare the couch. First a firm pillow to support the head and neck, and a towelling gown to protect the clothing. Face and neck massages were the most they could manage, but Lizzie could see no reason why one day they shouldn't be able to advertise complete body treatments. But first she had to learn the rudiments.

'Mrs Smith is a regular client,' Yvonne Naylor explained. 'I've offered her a reduction if I can use her to demonstrate the principles. She likes the attention – not to mention the saving on her bill. Here she comes now.'

A small rounded woman bustled through the door. She was as plump as a chicken, with sharp eyes and a crest of dyed red hair that stood up from her head like a cock's comb.

'I thought I was going to be late,' she moaned as Lizzie took her coat and helped her up on to the couch. 'Now, I want you to pay special attention to my chin. I'm sure there's an extra layer of fat in that department.'

'I'll give it my special attention,' Madame Yvonne promised. 'But first I am going to concentrate on the delicate skin around your eyes.' Using the third finger of her right hand she commenced smoothing the skin with a gentle pressure. Then she stepped back so that Lizzie could try her hand, all the while explaining the basic rules of massage. 'It is one of the oldest forms of beauty culture, used by the Chinese over three thousand years ago. Hippocrates wrote "rubbing can make flesh, and cause parts to waste", so we must remember that the wrong sort of massage will only aggravate trouble. Now I will show you how to perform the movement called petressage, which is useful for decreasing the loose skin around the neck.'

Madame's hands worked quickly. First she used a kneading movement followed by circular pressure with the ball of her thumb. This, she explained, was for stimulating the skin and increasing a flow of blood. She finished by slapping beneath the client's chin and along the jaw line. Lizzie was allowed to perform this action after her.

'You have a natural flair, Elizabeth,' Yvonne Naylor remarked as Mrs Smith assured them of her satisfaction. She paid her bill, and departed to recommend the new young lady to her friends and acquaintances. 'There's not much more I can teach you. I think the time has come to see if your father-in-law is still interested in my business.'

Lizzie was pleased but the praise had gone to her head. Suddenly she wasn't so keen on managing a department under the name of Grainger's. She loved Tom's father dearly. He'd been very kind to her and Joey, making up for her husband's unpredictable ways. But she had a longing for independence. Madame Yvonne had achieved it, so why couldn't she?

'Can I speak to you, Madame?' she asked, following the older woman into the stock-room.

'Yes, of course, Elizabeth. Would you pass me those bottles of oil.' Lizzie waited until the vessels of perfumed oil were neatly stacked on the shelf. 'What is it?'

'I don't want you to talk to my father-in-law or offer him the salon.'

Yvonne Naylor looked surprised. Had she been wasting her time teaching Elizabeth the profession? Was the girl going to throw the chance of a career back in her face? Did it mean she was going to have to delay her longed-for retirement?

'Mr Grainger is waiting for me to give him the first offer,' she said. 'Perhaps you want to talk to him yourself?'

'No, Madame Yvonne. I want to take over the business myself.' Seeing the startled expression on Yvonne Naylor's face Lizzie added, 'You said you've taught me everything I need to know; and I'm sure I can soon pick up the business side. I'm good at figures.'

'But, my dear,' Yvonne Naylor put up her hand and patted her hair thoughtfully, 'even with your father-in-law's backing you would still be in charge.'

'I know.' Lizzie stood straight and tall and the older woman could see that her mind was made up. She'd never seen such a look of determination on the face of one so young – almost as if the girl had had such a bad time that life had hardened her. 'I know,' Lizzie said again, 'but it wouldn't be the same. I don't want anyone to back me. I want to do it all myself.'

'But, Elizabeth ... that needs money...'

'How much?'

'Well, to start with there's the lease, and the furnishings and fittings.'

'I would want to invest in everything new,' Lizzie said, looking pointedly at the faded drapes.

'And then there's the solicitor's fees and all manner of extras.'

'I'm well aware of that, Madame Yvonne. How much would I need to start with?'

'Several hundred at a guess,' Yvonne said sympathetically. The girl was so keen, but she obviously didn't realise what she was asking.

'Would five hundred be enough?'

'More than enough to begin with.' Madame Yvonne smiled. 'What are you planning to do – borrow the money?'

'I don't need to. I have five hundred pounds, in cash, and I want to take over the business as soon as possible.'

'But, my dear ...' Madame fluttered her hands helplessly. 'Your husband – your father-in-law...'

'What about them?'

'Surely you should discuss things with your family first?'

'Why?'

'Because you're so young and inexperienced. You know nothing about running a business, and you shouldn't make decisions like this on your own, because ...' her voice tailed off.

'Because I'm only a woman?'

'Yes. And a very young one at that.'

'I'm nearly twenty-three. You're a woman too, Madame

Yvonne. How old were you when you opened this salon?'

'Older than you, my dear. And I was unmarried. My father had just died and left me a small legacy. I spent it on training, and opening this salon. It was very hard work.'

'I'm not afraid of work.'

'No, Elizabeth, I know you're not; and I admire your determination. I just want you to be aware of what you're thinking of taking on.'

'So you'll give me the first offer?' Lizzie's cheeks were flushed with excitement and her brown eyes shone.

'But what shall I say to Mr Grainger? He thinks everything's settled.'

'Don't worry. I'll tell him myself ... and Tom.'

Lizzie's words were brave and she tried to ignore the stirrings of fear at the idea of telling Tom her plans. He was her husband, and Joey's father, but she was still afraid of him although she tried not to show it. He didn't seem to be able to help the black moods that descended on him more and more frequently. They changed him from a light-hearted man-about-town into a surly individual who was unnecessarily rude to his parents, critical of his small son, and unkind towards his wife.

At least he hadn't been violent towards her again; but their lovemaking had become a duty rather than a pleasure. Lizzie suspected that Tom was afraid of losing control – as if he might set free a sleeping tiger who would be unaware of its own strength. So their married lives were lived on the edge of a precipice, and she hoped the news of her intentions wouldn't hurtle them both over the edge into the unknown.

Lizzie bided her time, planning her actions carefully. She played the part of a dutiful wife to such a degree that Tom failed to suspect that she had anything up her sleeve.

One evening he was busy studying the property

columns in the evening paper while they waited for Ada to serve up their meal. He tapped his teeth thoughtfully with the end of his silver propelling pencil, and then made a rough calculation on the edge of the paper.

'I spoke to the agents again today, Lizzie,' he said at last. 'The ones dealing with the new houses on the Ladies Mile estate. There are only a few left because they're so popular.' Lizzie was unrolling her napkin and her fingers tightened, creasing the stiff damask with the pressure. 'I told them we're interested.'

'So you've made up your mind?' Lizzie said softly.

'Yes. The sooner we can move into a proper house the better. You'll be able to give up that silly job and learn how to be a proper housewife and mother.'

'It's not a silly job – and I am a proper mother,' Lizzie said slowly. 'Put the dish down there, Ada.'

'Yes, madam.'

Ada placed the plate of succulent meat in front of her mistress, and then uncovered a vegetable dish to show the tiny new potatoes and peas sprinkled with mint.

'You can leave us, Ada. I can manage.'

Ada bobbed and hurried away; Lizzie commenced dishing up the meal. She had to leave her seat to carry Tom's plate to him. He frowned.

'I don't know why you can't let the servant wait on us properly, Lizzie,' he said. 'That's what I pay for.'

Lizzie smiled. 'But you just said you want me to be a proper housewife.'

'You know what I mean.' Tom cut a slice of meat in half and inspected it closely as if trying to find something to complain about. 'I've asked the estate agent to send me the papers to look at. I don't want things hanging about too long. I want to be settled by the summer.'

'Won't you give the house at Peacehaven another thought?'

'No!' Tom slammed down his knife and fork, and glowered. 'Peacehaven is no more than a shanty town.

We're going to Patcham – I've decided.'

'Very well.' Lizzie resumed her seat and started to eat although she had little appetite. After a pause she spoke slowly and clearly so that Tom couldn't fail to hear. 'It doesn't really matter where we live because I shan't be there much.'

'What are you talking about?' Tom stared at Lizzie, his fork halfway up to his mouth.

'I shall have my time filled at the salon. When it's been refurbished I shall be there every day.'

'That, Lizzie darling, will be up to Pa and me. We may decide otherwise.'

'I don't think so, Tom. I've made my plans.'

'And so have I.'

Lizzie carried on regardless. 'I'm taking over the salon from Madame Yvonne. I'm buying the lease and intend turning it into a fashionable beauty parlour. I shall manage it myself with a small staff. It's what I've always wanted. I intend making a success of it.'

'Brave words, my darling – but just what are you going to use for money? *I* don't intend lending you any.'

'I don't need your money, Tom.' Lizzie placed her knife and fork neatly across her empty plate and folded her napkin. 'I told you Aunt Hannah gave me a present when I visited her at the nursing home. It was five hundred pounds – enough, and more, to set me up in business. I don't want your money, Tom. I have enough to take over the salon myself.'

Lizzie rose from her chair and crossed to the door. Tom watched her with his mouth hanging half open in astonishment. In the doorway she paused for a moment before turning back. 'By the way – I'm going to change its name. From now on it will be known as LADY ELIZABETH'S.'

She walked from the room, closing the door firmly behind her.

CHAPTER TWENTY-ONE

The Sleeping Tiger

'I always used to go to Reynard's in Ship Street.'

'So did I. But when I was playing Bridge at Mrs Delaware's she recommended Lady Elizabeth's. I've been coming here ever since.'

'My husband complains that it's expensive, but I tell him it's worth every penny. He admits that I look at least ten years younger since I've been coming.'

'And it's not only the treatment. It's the only place I know where you can get a decent cup of coffee and have a relaxing gossip.'

The three middle-aged matrons were lounging comfortably in the deep armchairs at the back of the salon. A low table in front of them was littered with cups and saucers, used ash-trays, and popular magazines such as *Good Housekeeping* and *Picturegoer*. The gossip turned to the novels recently borrowed from Boots Booklovers' Library, Greta Garbo's latest film and the new Paris fashions.

Lizzie, sitting at her desk where she could supervise the staff as well as the customers, smiled. She bent her shiny brown head over the open ledger in front of her.

Although the salon had been open for nearly two years she still liked to eavesdrop and make a note of clients' comments. If they were critical of something that could be improved she tried her best to put things right, but she usually heard only praise and then a warm glow of happiness would encompass her. She was still young enough to be proud of her achievement, which had taken dedication and hard work.

'Mrs Smith wants to know if we have that new shade of nail varnish she saw advertised?' Stella, the younger assistant asked, approaching Lizzie politely. 'She says it's pink with a special gloss finish.'

'I expect she means Damask Rose,' Lizzie replied. 'There's a bottle in the stock-room. It's a free sample sent by the manufacturers. Make sure you replace it when you've finished.'

Stella tripped away eagerly and Lizzie smiled her satisfaction. Stella Rogers was only fifteen and this was her first job after leaving school at the end of the Easter term. She was a pretty little thing and showed good potential in the beauty business.

The other assistant was called Julia Green. She was applying a face mask to an elderly actress who was performing that week at the Theatre Royal. Lizzie could just hear the soft murmur of voices through the drawn curtains of the cubicle.

Lizzie thought back over the two years since she'd invested Aunt Hannah's money in the beauty business. She'd made changes and the salon was barely recognisable from the shabby establishment Yvonne Naylor had run. The walls were painted dove grey and there was blue carpeting on the floor. The curtains and drapes were striped alternately blue and grey, and the assistants wore navy-blue dresses piped with grey. Lizzie herself wore a smartly tailored grey suit over a cream silk blouse, high-heeled black shoes, and sheer stockings on her slim legs.

The telephone at her elbow shrilled and she picked up

the receiver. 'Lady Elizabeth's Beauty Parlour. Can I help you?'

The woman's voice at the other end of the line was squeaky and eager. 'This is Marcelle Phillips. I need a manicure urgently because I'm holding an important dinner party tonight. Can you fit me in?'

'If you hold the line, Mrs Phillips, I'll look in the diary. We may have a cancellation.' There was a pause while Lizzie flipped through the pages. 'I'm so sorry, Mrs Phillips, but we're fully booked.'

'I'll pay extra,' Marcelle Phillips begged. 'My husband's bringing home an important client and he wants me to look my best.'

'Just hold on a moment please while I have a word with my assistant.' Lizzie beckoned to Julia Green who happened to be passing to collect more towels. After a quick exchange she spoke into the receiver again. 'I've just had a word with Miss Green. She can visit your home after we've closed and treat you privately if that would suit you. About six? That's perfectly all right, Mrs Phillips – we aim to please. I'm just glad we've been able to help you out.' Lizzie replaced the receiver and smiled at her assistant. 'Thank you so much, Julia. Marcelle Phillips is rather demanding, but she's a good customer and her husband is on the Town Council. It's good for business to keep her happy.'

After that the telephone never seemed to stop ringing. Luckily there were no more emergencies and clients were able to book appointments for the day they needed them. The last customer left at five o'clock which gave the staff half an hour to tidy up, prepare the cubicles for the following day, and add up the day's takings.

Lizzie sent Stella home. She gave Julia Mrs Phillip's address as well as her bus fare, then after a final look around let herself out into the street, making sure the shop door was locked securely behind her.

As usual she took a last admiring glance at the window

display. A female dummy was posed against a woodland background as the fairy-tale Sleeping Beauty. She lay on a gold couch, with her plaster face carefully painted with the latest cosmetics. Her long golden hair streamed over her gown of white lace, which was one of Lizzie's old night-gowns, and her daintily tinted fingertips rested on her breast. The message to potential customers was clear: pay a visit to Lady Elizabeth's Beauty Parlour and you can expect to look as desirable as the Sleeping Beauty.

Lizzie smiled. After two years in the business she had learned how women, particularly older ones, live in a world of dreams and promises.

She crossed the road, avoiding the traffic. Western Road was always crowded at this time of the day, with the shops closing and everyone hurrying home to their tea.

The first bus that came along would take her all the way home to Patcham so she climbed quickly aboard. The days of expecting Tom to give her a lift were over. The answer was to learn to drive herself; then she would be totally independent. She could well afford to buy and run a small car without getting into debt, and she planned to do so before the summer was over. There would of course be arguments; there always were these days. Lizzie had given up hope of a loving husband and a happy marriage, so she'd taken control of her own life and tried to ignore Tom's sulks and tantrums.

She'd had such high hopes in the beginning and knew she wasn't to blame. She had sacrificed so much for this marriage and intended making the best of things for Joey's sake. Tom's sexual advances had often been disturbingly violent, but they'd also aroused an excitement in her that she could neither explain or understand. She had mistaken this excitement for love.

Often Lizzie craved what she had lost: the warmth of Jack French's love, his friendly freckled face, his kindness, and the family that had taken her to its heart and embraced her as one of their own – and who she had let down. She had exchanged it all for a cold marriage; and her successful career only partly compensated for what she had lost. But for her own sanity, she didn't allow herself to dwell on what could have been, and kept herself so busy that it gave her little time to ponder her empty life or worry about the future.

The only times she felt close to Tom were when he suffered from one of his nightmares and turned to her for comfort as a child turns to its mother. She would cradle him in her arms and reassure him, and he seemed grateful, but in the morning it was all forgotten. He would be his usual aggressive self: selfish and uncaring.

The salon had done nothing to improve things. At first Tom had seemed delighted with Lizzie's success and even encouraged her. He'd expected her to fail and turn to him or his father for help. Instead, his jealousy and anger grew as Lady Elizabeth's became an important feature of the town, attracting celebrities with its good service and attractive premises.

Victor Grainger was extremely proud of his daughter-in-law and that enraged Tom even more. He'd soon tired of the daily grind in the shop, and now that he had his legacy only rarely showed up at Grainger's. When he did show his face he was rude and bossy to the customers and staff, and became increasingly unpopular. He preferred to spend his time at clubs or the nearby race-track, or picking up prostitutes in the sea-front pubs and bars.

Then one day things reached a turning-point. It had been a warm Sunday afternoon soon after they'd moved into the new house at Patcham. Joey had been spending the weekend with his grandparents, and as Ada Hunt worked only alternate weekends Lizzie had prepared the lunch. Afterwards she'd sat in the garden, which was a quiet peaceful place under the sheltering arm of the South Downs.

'Would you like to come for a walk, Lizzie?'

Lizzie had looked up in surprise, shading her brown

eyes with her hand. Tom was standing in front of her, smiling in a friendly fashion. She saw again how attractive he was at first sight, with his slender figure, and the boyish lock of hair falling forward over his narrow forehead. As Tom usually drove everywhere and didn't like the countryside, Lizzie was surprised at the invitation.

'That would be lovely,' she'd said quickly, slipping on her shoes and getting to her feet. 'We could walk down the road and through the village. There are some pretty cottages there that I'd like to look at.'

'No,' Tom had said firmly, taking her arm and guiding her out of the gate. 'Let's climb the hill and go past the farm.'

'Whatever you want,' Lizzie had said, anxious to please.

They'd strolled along arm in arm, just like any young married couple. Lizzie had felt almost happy. Perhaps Tom wanted to change – perhaps there was hope for them yet.

They wandered through a farmyard where chickens pecked on the cobbles and a tabby cat sunned itself on a wall; it was a warm sleepy afternoon and there was no one about to stop them. Out of sight of the farmhouse they came across a barn: a rambling structure made of corrugated iron, with weeds growing knee-high around the sides and a broken door hanging open on rusting hinges.

Lizzie felt out of breath after the up-hill climb and put her hand to her side.

'You're tired,' Tom had said, all concern. 'Let's sit down and rest.'

'It's only a stitch. It'll go in a minute.'

'No. Let's go inside out of the sun.'

Lizzie had looked at the open doorway with distaste. The inside of the barn looked dark and gloomy. Anything could be lurking there.

But Tom was insistent, and propelled her through the opening with his hand on her arm. A ray of sunlight that managed to penetrate a crack in the wall showed a pile of old sacks, some bales of hay, and an assortment of rubbish.

'It's cold in here,' Lizzie had said, shivering. 'Let's go back outside.'

Tom didn't answer. Lizzie could just see his face, a pale oval in the gloom, and his eyes staring at her in a strange fashion.

'No,' he'd said. 'Doesn't this remind you of anything?'

'No. Should it?'

'Gates Farm.'

Memory flooded back and Lizzie started to tremble. The horror of that time when she'd been only a young inexperienced girl had never completely left her, although she'd managed to dampen down the memories over the years. But now she was a married woman, and a mother, and the man confronting her was her husband. There was nothing to fear. So why was her heart beating so fast, and why did a chill of apprehension run up her spine?

'Let's go, Tom,' she'd said sharply. 'I don't like this place.'

'It's me you don't like – isn't it, Lizzie?'

'Don't be silly.'

'That time at Gates Farm was the best I ever had. You enjoyed it too, didn't you? That's when you fell with Joey – remember?'

'Yes, I remember,' Lizzie whispered.

'You don't seem so keen on me these days,' Tom went on. 'Perhaps you need a bit of excitement to whet your appetite. I think it's time Joey had a sister.'

'Not here!' Lizzie looked around desperately.

'Why not? Or is Lady Elizabeth too proud to open her legs for her husband?'

'Please, Tom …'

'I'm sick of your high-and-mighty airs, Lizzie.' Tom's

voice had become low and hard and she knew he was past listening to reason. The least she could expect was to do as he asked so as not to enrage him further. 'I'll get you pregnant if it's the last thing I do, and then you'll have to give up that wretched salon and become a full-time wife and mother. Take off your things – all of them.'

'What – *here?*'

'Why not? You're my wife, aren't you? I have a piece of paper to prove it. I own you. So you'll take off your clothes where and whenever I command you to.'

Suddenly a calmness overtook Lizzie. She would have to do as he asked, not because he was her husband, but because he was physically stronger than she was. But whatever he did to her he couldn't touch her heart, because she'd given that to another man a long time ago. It was safe in Jack French's keeping. If she kept her head there was nothing to fear.

Lizzie was wearing a crêpe de Chine dress in a delicate shade of apricot. It was fastened down the front by a row of tiny covered buttons. She slowly put up her hand and unfastened the top three.

'Faster!'

Lizzie's fingers felt clumsy but she continued sliding the buttons out of their holes until the front of her dress was open. Underneath she wore French knickers and a pink brassiere made of artificial silk. She slipped off her shoes and stood in front of Tom in her stockinged feet.

'Let's go home, Tom. We'll be more comfortable in bed. Joey won't be back for hours.'

'No.' Tom was fumbling with the buttons on his trousers. Lizzie could see the bulge of his erection through the grey flannel of his slacks. She would have to go through with it. 'Take off the rest of your things unless you want me to do it for you.'

She could see he was excited at the prospect of forcing himself on her, and also at causing her humiliation.

'All right,' she'd said, and slid the ribbon straps of her

brassiere over the pale flesh of her shoulders. The round-
ness of her breasts kept the cups in position, just showing
Tom the tantalising shadow of her cleavage.

'Hurry up!'

Lizzie put her hand to the waistband of her knickers
which was fastened by a pearl button. Her slowness
seemed to enrage Tom and he started forward. She knew
what he would do: tear the clothes from her body and
ravish her as he'd done at Gates Farm. Suddenly she
despised him and felt unafraid. He could kill her if he
wanted to, but he wasn't going to abuse her delicate living
flesh again – not now or ever.

He was closer now and she looked around for a weapon:
something to stop him. Just before Tom's outstretched
hands reached her, Lizzie bent down and picked up one of
her discarded shoes. It was made of leather, with a high
heel. It was unsuitable footwear for hiking through the
countryside, but the suggestion of a walk had been unexpected and she hadn't had time to change.

It was an unusual weapon but the only one within
reach. Lizzie gripped it firmly and swung it with all her
might in the direction of Tom's head. The sharp heel
caught him on the temple and brought him up with a
start. He put his hand up to his forehead in surprise as he
saw the blood on his palm.

'Why, you little bitch,' he said in a low, menacing voice.
'It's time I taught you a lesson.'

His hand reached for Lizzie again, but the trickle of
blood was half blinding him. Before he could grab her,
Lizzie brought up her knee and caught him a blow on his
swollen groin. He gave a grunt that sounded like the air
escaping from a punctured balloon, and bent over, holding himself with both hands and rocking backwards and
forwards in pain.

With a grim smile on her lips Lizzie picked up her frock
and slipped it on. 'Next time you try to touch me, Tom, I'll
kill you,' she said in a calm voice. 'I will remain your wife,

but not your lover. I hope you understand me.' And holding her shoes in her hand she left him to recover and ponder over her words.

That same evening Lizzie had moved her belongings into the spare room. Neither of them had referred to the occasion since. In public they seemed a devoted couple, attractive and secure, with all the money success could provide, but their private life was cold and sterile. Lizzie often wondered where and when it would end.

Every time Lizzie stepped down from the bus and saw the turning ahead that led to the farm she remembered that day. Today was no exception. She pushed the distasteful memory away and headed for home.

The house was only a few minutes' walk from the bus stop and Joey would be waiting with news of his day at school. In exchange she would entertain him with stories about the salon. He loved to hear tales about the more outrageous clients who expected miracles to happen after a visit to his mother's beauty parlour. Particularly if they were people he knew.

Usually he would be hanging over the front gate or swinging like a monkey from a nearby tree. He was small for his eight years, but strong and agile. Although his build and features were carbon-copies of Tom, his dark brown eyes were exactly the same as Lizzie's. His nature was inherited from the sensitive Sargent line on his mother's side.

Lizzie let herself into the house. The interior was smart, with highly polished mahogany furniture and thick rugs. Not a thing was out of place, as the master of the house demanded perfection. If Tom found a cushion crumpled or a picture crooked, someone would have to provide an explanation and apology. Lizzie had ceased to be afraid of him, but she liked a peaceful life when she came home from work. She encouraged Joey to be as tidy as she tried to be herself.

At first Lizzie thought the house must be deserted, it

was so quiet and still, but then she heard the faint chink of china from the direction of the kitchen. Ada Hunt was still working – preparing supper.

Lizzie removed her jacket and hung it neatly from the hall-stand. She patted her hair into place and then went to see if she could be of any assistance. Ada was bent over the open oven inspecting a bubbling pan.

'That smells delicious.'

'It's macaroni cheese,' Ada said, straightening up with the aid of a chair-back.

'Joey's favourite. Fancy you remembering.'

'I thought he deserved a bit of spoiling,' Ada said grimly. She started to shell peas into a bowl.

'You're always spoiling him,' Lizzie said, pinching the end of a pod open and eating the contents. 'Where is he anyway, Ada? He should be home from school by now.'

'He is. He came in over an hour ago – just before his father.'

Something in Ada's tone made Lizzie freeze. So Tom was home already and Joey was keeping out of the way. She suspected trouble.

'Where is he, Ada?' she asked softly.

'Mr Grainger's in the drawing-room. He said he wasn't to be disturbed. Joey's out the back somewhere.'

'I'll go and look for him.' Lizzie popped the last pea into her mouth. 'I expect he's playing with his rabbit.' When Joey was upset he usually retreated to the back garden to seek comfort from his pet, Smokey.

'There's some fresh carrot tops on the top of the bin,' Ada said. 'I saved them specially.'

'Thank you, Ada.'

Lizzie picked up the feathery greens and opened the back door. The garden sloped away gently, with a velvet lawn and flower-beds kept trim by a visiting gardener. It was as neat and tidy as the house.

She saw Joey before he saw her. He was sitting cross-legged in front of Smokey's hutch with the grey rabbit cradled in his arms. Lizzie's feet made no sound on the soft grass so he didn't hear his mother approaching and had no time to wipe the tears away from his cheeks.

'Hullo, Joey.' Lizzie pulled a wooden box forward and sat down beside her son.

'Hullo,' he grunted, and wiped his face with the back of his hand before turning a tragic little face up to her.

'What's the matter?'

'Nothing.'

'Is Smokey ill?'

'No.'

'Ada's saved him some carrot-tops.'

'Thanks.' Joey took the tit-bits and began to feed the rabbit, who wriggled excitedly in his arms. 'I'd better put him back in his hutch.'

'That's a good idea.'

When Smokey was safely back in his little house Lizzie said, 'Come and sit down beside me, Joey, and tell me what's wrong.'

'Mum …' Joey started, and then, 'oh, Mum!' and flung himself into Lizzie's open arms with noisy sobs.

'Hush.' Lizzie cradled him until he'd calmed down a bit and then kissed the top of his ruffled head. 'Now tell me.'

Joey looked at the ground and then said in a small voice, 'Father says Smokey has to go.'

'Why?'

'Because I took him into the house and he made a mess on the carpet, the new one in the drawing-room.'

'Oh, Joey,' Lizzie sighed. 'That was a silly thing to do. Rabbits aren't house-trained.'

'I know. I didn't think. I said I was sorry.'

'I'll have a word with your father – I'm sure he'll forgive you,' Lizzie said doubtfully.

'He says the butcher will buy Smokey. People eat rabbits, and then they make things out of their furry coats. I don't want Smokey to be eaten.' The tears had started again and Lizzie took his hand.

'I can't promise anything, but I'll do what I can.'

'Thanks, Mum. Father says the butcher will pay half a crown for a good rabbit. Half a crown is a lot of money, isn't it?'

'A fair bit.'

'Enough to have the carpet cleaned?'

'I expect so.'

'I don't want Smokey to die.'

'I'll talk to your father after supper.'

'All right. I don't want any: I'm not hungry.'

'It's macaroni cheese. Ada made it specially to cheer you up.'

'Perhaps I'd better have some then.'

'You can have it in the kitchen if you want.'

'All right.'

'I'll come up afterwards and tuck you in.'

Supper was a silent affair. No one seemed to have much appetite. Lizzie managed to force down half of her meal, but Tom said he hated macaroni cheese anyway and he wished he'd eaten out. The apple pie and custard that followed was his favourite so he ate two large helpings; then he wiped his mouth on his napkin before pushing back his chair and rising to his feet.

'Are you going out?' Lizzie enquired as she stacked the dirty plates on a tray.

'Perhaps later. I'll read the evening paper in the drawing-room first.'

'I promised to tuck Joey in. I expect he'll want a story. Then I'll make the coffee. Ada will be waiting to get away.'

Tom just grunted and left the room with the folded paper tucked under his arm. Lizzie carried the tray into the deserted kitchen. Ada had already left so she stacked the dirty plates on the draining board to be washed the following morning. Then she filled the kettle and placed it over a low flame before going upstairs and tapping on Joey's bedroom door.

'Can I come in?'

There was no answer. After waiting a moment Lizzie pushed it open and peeped in. Joey was kneeling in his pyjamas beside his narrow bed, his hands folded and his eyes tightly closed. He opened one eye when he was aware of his mother's presence.

'Amen,' he chanted. 'I've finished.'

'Would you like some hot milk? It won't take a minute.'

'No thanks.'

'Hop into bed then like a good boy.' As Lizzie tucked the bed-clothes around her small son she spotted something hanging in the neck of his pyjamas jacket. 'I see you're still wearing your lucky threepenny,' she said, remembering how the silver coin had been given to her all those years before by Mr Bennet.

'I wear it all the time,' Joey assured her, his fingers touching the coin for reassurance. 'Perhaps if God doesn't answer my prayers it will protect Smokey for me. Have you spoken to Father yet?'

'Not yet. But it'll be all right, I promise you.'

'Thanks, Mum.'

'Do you want a story?' Lizzie picked up a twopenny magazine from the table by Joey's bed. 'I'll read to you out of *Sunny Stories* if you like.'

'I'd rather hear the story you used to tell your brother.'

Lizzie smiled, remembering Billy's love for the Hans Christian Andersen tale about the steadfast tin soldier. He'd be too old for fairy tales now. Wherever he was his tastes for reading must have changed. He probably liked cowboy or Tarzan stories now.

But she still remembered the story well enough to tell it to Joey, and he seemed to enjoy it as much as Billy had always done.

'I wonder where Billy is,' he said sleepily when the tale was finished.

'I don't know, dear, but I think he's somewhere close. I can feel it.'

'I'd like to meet him.'

'You will one day – that's a promise.'

Two promises, and Lizzie didn't know if she was going to be able to keep either of them. 'Please God,' she prayed in her turn. 'Make Tom change his mind about getting rid of Smokey. It will break Joey's heart. And help me find Billy again. Joey and I both need him.'

Lizzie only left the bedside when her son was fast asleep. Now she had Tom to deal with.

She was dreading the confrontation; he was so unreasonable these days. The slightest thing would infuriate him, sending him either into hours of silence or slamming out of the house, when he could be away for days at a time. Lizzie didn't know which was worse.

The kettle was boiling so she made the coffee, carrying it into the drawing-room, where her husband was sitting smoking with the paper open on his knee. She pulled up a low table and sat down opposite Tom. The coffee smelled delicious as she poured it into tiny cups and added cream and sugar.

'Did you say you were going out?' she enquired when she couldn't stand the silence any longer.

'I don't know. I might later,' Tom answered. 'Why?'

'I want to talk to you.'

'Not tonight, Lizzie. I've had a long day.' He buried his nose in the paper again.

'A hard day doing what?' Lizzie asked herself silently. 'Drinking, betting and womanising no doubt.'

Tom always seemed to have plenty of money but Lizzie sometimes wondered how much of his grandfather's legacy was left. At least LADY ELIZABETH'S was doing well so they'd never be penniless.

'It's important, Tom,' she said now. There was something in her voice that made him look up.

'All right,' he said at last. 'Fire away.'

'It's Joey. He's upset.'

'What about?'

'Smokey. He thinks you're going to take him to the butcher – and sell him.'

'So what? He brought the wretched creature into the house when I'd strictly forbidden it.'

'He's sorry now.'

'I'm sure he is. But being sorry doesn't get the carpet cleaned or make me overlook his disobedience.'

Lizzie sighed. 'Oh, Tom! He's only a child. He loves Smokey.'

'So he learns a lesson by losing him. When he learns to obey me perhaps I'll buy him another rabbit.'

'He's your son, Tom. Don't you care about his feelings at all?' Lizzie's voice rose angrily and her face was pale.

'Yes, Joey's my son,' Tom said coldly. He stubbed out his half-smoked cigarette in a glass ash-tray with a vicious gesture. 'So, isn't it about time he started behaving like one, instead of disobeying me at every turn and then running to you? And while we're about it, isn't it about time you started acting like a wife?'

'What do you mean?' Lizzie felt her cheeks redden.

'You know what I mean.'

Lizzie did know. Tom was referring to her moving into the spare room; to her being a wife only in name. But after his last show of crudeness and brutality the thought of him even touching her had made her flesh crawl. And yet things could have been so different. If only he would show a little kindness, a little tenderness, some understanding of her and Joey's needs.

She asked herself again if it was too late? Should she give him another chance? For Joey's sake she must. His happiness came first – always. But could she put her pride in her pocket even for him? Lizzie didn't think so. But then the image of her son's tearful face as he hugged his precious rabbit came into her mind, and she saw the way his eyes had lit up with hope when she'd promised to try to intervene. She had no choice; she was Joey's mother and only she could stop his heart being broken.

Lizzie picked up the tray of dirty cups and walked to the door. She could feel Tom's eyes on her, watching her every move. When she turned in the doorway to face him she stood tall and proud, with her head held high and a half-smile on her face.

'If you promise to let Joey keep his pet, I ...' Lizzie paused before she forced the words out, 'I will share your bed again.'

CHAPTER TWENTY-TWO

The Tiger Wakes

Lizzie stood in the middle of the spare bedroom and looked longingly at her bed. Ada had turned down the covers and her simple cotton nightdress was folded on the pillow. She was weary and it would be so easy to undress, slip between the sheets, and try to forget her bargain with Tom.

But there was no getting away from it. At least for this one night she had to share her husband's bed and bear any insults and abuse he felt like forcing upon her.

'Please, God, give me strength,' she prayed silently. As if in answer she was filled with an inner calmness and peace. She felt she could cope – and it only had to be for one night.

Lizzie sat down on the stool in front of the mirror and surveyed her face. She was twenty-five years old, a successful business woman, a wife and a mother. But the last nine years had left their mark. There was a crease of worry between her eyes she hadn't noticed before, without the daily camouflage of cosmetics her face was paler than it should be, and only the other day she'd noticed a silver thread in her still glossy brown hair.

Apart from these things she was still the same Lizzie; her eyes as big and brown as ever, and her mouth full and generous. The years had given her an added dignity, but she was as quick-tempered and impetuous as she'd ever been.

However, tonight, she felt, she had to give the performance of her life, and she had to dress the part. The cotton nightdress she usually wore was much too simple for the occasion. Tom would expect her to look glamorous and sexy. In the past he'd bought her plenty of clothes, but most of them lay unopened in the cupboards and drawers. Surely she would find something suitable – something that would please him.

She settled on a black negligée he'd bought her on their honeymoon in London. She'd never worn it because, not only was the style too revealing for her taste, but the silk was so fine that it was almost transparent. The material slid like gossamer through her fingers, but to Lizzie's heightened senses it felt more like the clinging touch of a spider's web.

Slowly Lizzie removed her blouse and skirt and took her time hanging them in the wardrobe. Then, on a sudden impulse, she stripped off her underwear and stood naked in front of the long cheval-mirror.

She'd put on weight, but because of her height the extra pounds suited her. Her legs were long and slim like an athlete's and her waist was trim. But her breasts were heavier and her hips broader, and there were tiny silver stretch-marks under her stomach: the result of pregnancy.

Her eyes in the glass took in every pale inch. She wanted to remember this moment because in the morning she knew her white flesh would be discoloured with bruises, bite-marks and any other wounds Tom felt like inflicting on her. Perhaps this time he'd kill her and put an end to their misery. But to think that way was to give in and Lizzie wasn't a quitter.

She shook back her hair and picked up the black nightdress. It felt like a second skin as she slipped it over her head and felt the soft folds slide down her body. Then she pinched the flesh on her cheeks to redden them naturally, and dabbed cologne at the base of her neck and behind her ears. She was ready, and walked through the doorway of the master bedroom like a lamb to the slaughter.

The room was empty. The double bed had been turned down but was unoccupied. Lizzie's spirits rose slightly. Perhaps Tom had changed his mind and decided not to torment her with his lusts.

On bare feet she walked silently across the landing and leaned over the banister. The house was as still as the grave. Had he gone out after all? Just as she was about to relax she heard a cough and the rustle of paper – Tom was still downstairs, biding his time.

It was more than an hour before Lizzie heard footsteps on the stairs and movement in the bathroom next door. Then came the sound of water flushing and the click of the light-switch. Now he was in the doorway, looking the perfect gentleman in his silk pyjamas. Only the coldness of his grey eyes and the thin line of his lips gave away his inner feelings. In one hand he carried a bottle and in the other a glass.

'That's more like it,' Tom said as he crossed the room towards the bed. 'You're still beautiful, Lizzie. At least you haven't let yourself go.' Lizzie didn't answer. She just lay propped up against the pillows, silently waiting. Suddenly Tom burst out, 'For God's sake, smile at a fellow, can't you? I am your husband after all.' Lizzie managed a sort of smile although it was the last thing she felt like doing. Crying would have been more appropriate. 'I like your nightgown – there's something about a woman in black.'

'You chose it for me,' Lizzie reminded him.

'Did I now? Just shows I've got good taste, doesn't it?'

Tom pulled back the covers and climbed nimbly into

the bed beside her. His body felt cold and hard against Lizzie's softness. Although he was lean, the muscles in his thighs were hard and strong; the lifestyle he led hadn't affected him yet. Propped on one elbow he peered into Lizzie's face. She could smell the drink on his breath and longed to turn away.

'Shall we have a little drinky first, darling? You can have the glass because you're a lady, and I'll drink straight from the bottle because I'm no gentleman.'

He laughed as if the joke was a good one, but there was no humour in the sound.

Lizzie took the glass. She drank alcohol only rarely, but perhaps a couple of drinks would dull her senses and help her cope.

'What is it?'

'Gin – in other words, Mother's Ruin. What could be more appropriate?' He laughed again at his own cleverness.

Lizzie drank. 'I've had enough,' she protested when he tried to top up the glass.

When she'd finished Tom took the glass and placed it carefully beside the bottle. Then he touched the thin black material covering her modesty with one long bony finger. 'If I bought this for you I can do what I like with it, can't I?' he said harshly.

'I can't stop you,' Lizzie admitted.

'That's true.' With one swift movement he ripped the gown open, revealing the whiteness of her breast and belly. 'There!' he said with satisfaction, his fanatical eyes feasting on her nakedness. 'I always said you looked better in rags – or without them, as the case may be.'

'Please, Tom!' Lizzie begged. But she could see he was going to show no mercy so she closed her eyes tightly and waited.

The anticipation and coolness of the night air made her shiver, so it was almost a relief when she felt the weight of his body and the pressure of his lips. But when his greedy mouth found her breasts and he began to bite her aroused nipples she whimpered with pain. He put his hand over her mouth to silence her, at the same time whispering in her ear: 'Be quiet – or do you want to wake Joey?'

So Lizzie bit her lips until she tasted blood, and even when she felt Tom's nails on her flesh and the pressure of his grip bruising her she kept silent. She didn't utter a sound even when he wrenched her legs apart. Then she felt his weight straddling her, and his laboured breathing as he tried to penetrate her.

Silently Lizzie began to pray. 'Please, God, help me to bear whatever Tom does to me, but don't let him get me pregnant. I mustn't bear another baby conceived in this way.'

She was still praying when he released her. 'You bitch!' he muttered. 'It's your fault I can't make it. Your fault! Your fault!' At each rebuke he hit her around the face so that her head spun and she almost lost her senses.

Half-conscious as she was, she was aware of him struggling into his clothes and leaving the room, his footsteps on the stairs and the slamming of the front door, and then blessed silence.

'Mum, are you all right?'

The frightened voice brought Lizzie to her senses. Joey was standing in the doorway rubbing his eyes sleepily.

'I'm fine,' she assured him, hastily pulling up the bedclothes.

'I heard a noise.'

'I was just having a bad dream.'

'Like Father has sometimes?'

'That's right. Go back to bed, darling.'

'I'm scared. Can't I come in with you?'

Lizzie thought quickly, then she said, 'Why don't you get into my bed in the spare room. I'll join you in a few minutes.'

'All right.'

He padded away on bare feet and Lizzie got out of bed to inspect her injuries. They were all on the surface and not as bad as they might have been. One side of her face was discoloured by the impact of Tom's hand, and there were teeth-marks on her breasts and scratches around her ribs. Her body ached when she moved but that would pass.

She washed herself in the bathroom. Not because she was dirty, but because she needed to cleanse her body from Tom's touch. She didn't want to frighten Joey so she dabbed powder on her face to cover the bruising.

In the spare room Joey was already asleep, curled in a ball with his thumb in his mouth, a lock of hair stuck damply to his forehead. Lizzie stripped off the torn nightgown and replaced it with the cotton one, before sliding under the covers beside her son. He grunted and turned to her. She took him in her arms and stroked the hair away from his forehead.

'Good night, darling,' she said softly. 'Sleep well.'

'Good night, Mum. I love you,' Joey said without opening his eyes.

'And I love you,' Lizzie said.

It was only then that she allowed herself to weep. Silent tears that cleansed and healed as she cradled her sleeping son in her arms.

Tom bent over the steering wheel like a coiled spring. Every muscle in his body was on red alert; if he didn't get release soon he felt he would go mad.

Of course it was all Lizzie's fault. If she'd treated him right everything would have been fine. She'd even closed her eyes as though she couldn't bear the sight of him, and instead of fighting and helping him to keep an erection she'd lain there as coldly as a fish on a slab. Beautiful – but death to Tom's sexual advances.

Damn her! Damn her! Luckily there was little traffic on the road. Tom's mind was on his troubles and not his driving, which was erratic at the best of times.

He needed a drink badly; almost as much as he needed a woman. But it was nearly eleven o'clock and he doubted if any respectable pub would risk losing their licence by serving him so late. His best hope was a beer-house, but the landlord of the only one he passed was already sweeping the sawdust from the wooden floor.

He left the car in a turning off Church Street and, pulling the brim of his trilby low over his forehead, started to walk up the hill towards the Clock Tower. It was a favourite place for prostitutes to gather, either in the shadow of one of the clock's faces or in the shop doorways of nearby West Street and Queen's Road.

'Goodnight, guv'nor.' A man's voice greeted him out of the darkness. Tom jumped, but it was only a lonely Bobby on a late beat.

'Goodnight, constable,' he answered, without slowing down.

He stopped only to strike a match and light a cigarette, and was aware of the tap of feet on the pavement behind him. Perhaps he was going to be lucky after all.

"Ullo, darling – you're out late. Are you looking for a nice time?"

A hand clutched at Tom's sleeve and he saw red nails and cracked skin ingrained with dirt. There was a smell of unwashed flesh, and he found himself peering into a face so old and ugly that it looked barely human. Eyes sunk into dark sockets and a pock-ridden nose warned him of disease. He wasn't that desperate.

'Take your hand off me,' he ordered.

A peal of laughter greeted Tom's words. 'I've got a bottle of fizz in me pocket, mister. Give us a quid and we'll split it.'

'Leave me alone, you filthy tart, or I'll call a policeman.' Tom pushed the old hag so violently that she tottered back against the wall.

'All right – all right. Give us a tanner then out of the kindness of your heart.'

Tom scooped some loose change out of his trouser pocket and this seemed to satisfy the old crone. She vanished into the shadows, clutching her booty. Tom breathed a sigh of relief.

His chances of picking up a decent tart were sinking fast; but he was only a few minutes' walk away from Artillery Street – perhaps he could try his chances again with Milly Taylor.

Once, a long time ago, he'd been a regular customer, but he'd burned his boats with Milly one day when he'd lost his temper. Oh, Milly had forgiven him. He was generous with money and she was in business. But the friendliness had gone. Often now she refused to see him even when he knew she was alone. That only whetted his appetite for the black-haired beauty even more.

He hadn't been near Milly now for several months, and the thought of her plump white flesh made his mouth water with longing. Milly Taylor wouldn't dare to refuse him; and after a night spent in her arms he would feel like a new man again.

Tom knew his way blind-fold through the dark streets. It was so quiet he could hear the crash of waves on the shingle a few streets away, and somewhere close by the creaking of a gate.

Even in the darkness Milly's house stood out against its neighbours. There was a glowing light in the upper window, and a street-lamp illuminated the fresh paint-work and flower-filled window-boxes. The curtains were closed so Tom couldn't see the canary in its cage, or whether the noisy bird was covered or not. He hoped Milly hadn't got company.

Tom squared his shoulders and crossed the road, kicking out at a stray cat that dared to cross his path. The green door looked welcoming, but when he turned the handle he found it locked fast. He rapped impatiently on the knocker and waited, but there was no reply.

Tom frowned. Surely Milly wasn't against him as well?

He took two paces back and looked up at the brightly lit window. Was it his imagination or did the curtain move slightly as if he was being watched?

'Milly,' he called. And then louder, 'Milly!'

It was only when Tom picked up a handful of small stones and threw them against the glass that the casement shot up and a dark curly head looked out.

'Who is it?'

'It's me, Milly – Tom Grainger.'

'What do you want?'

'To come in.'

Milly paused as if she was thinking, and then turned to look over her shoulder. 'You can't, Tom – not tonight.'

'Why not?'

'I'm not alone.'

Tom thought quickly. 'Get rid of him, Milly. I must see you.'

'Go away, Tom. I'm not letting you in.' The window rattled down and the curtain swished into place, leaving him once more isolated in his loneliness in the deserted street.

'Damn the woman,' Tom muttered through clenched teeth. She'd pay for turning him away when he needed her. She'd pay as Lizzie had paid. Tom Grainger would show her who was boss.

Further down the street was a telephone box. Tom carried a list of numbers in his pocket book and Milly's was one of them. To own a private telephone showed how well she was doing. He dropped two pennies into the slot and waited for the operator to connect him. Then he heard Milly's voice.

'Milly – it's me – Tom.'

'Go away.'

'I must see you, Milly. Can't you get rid of the fellow who's with you?'

'No, Tom, I can't.'

'Why not?'

'Because he's my husband. I got married three weeks

ago. So you see why I can't see you, Tom – ever again.'

Tom put out his hand to stop himself falling. Milly Taylor married – she couldn't be! Who would marry a common prostitute? He forgot, or chose to overlook, that once he'd proposed marriage to Milly – and she'd turned him down.

'You bitch!' he said through clenched teeth. 'You bitch, Milly Taylor.'

'Not Milly Taylor any more, Tom,' the voice said in his ear. 'Milly Bartholomew – Mrs Milly Bartholomew. Goodbye Tom.' The line went dead.

Tom stared at the receiver as if he couldn't believe what he'd just heard. With a grunt he slammed it back in place and left the telephone box, striding away from Artillery Street towards the promenade.

The sea-front was quiet and deserted. Even the hotels were blacked out apart from their dimly lit reception areas. He had to wait to cross the road as a taxi cab cruised past. A lady dressed in a fur coat sat in the back giving instructions to the driver through a speaking tube. An old Morris with a low battery chugged past at about ten miles an hour. Then the road was clear. Tom strode across and leaned on the railings looking out to sea.

It was a dark night, the sea and sky so black that he couldn't make out the dividing line on the horizon. The waves below crashed relentlessly in upon the pebbles, drowning out the other night sounds. Tom shivered and pulled his collar up to his ears and the brim of his hat down. He felt cold and sorry for himself.

He hadn't realised how much he'd depended on Milly being available. Where could he go now, apart from back home? His face felt wet and he put up his hand in surprise. Was it spray or was it beginning to rain? Tom didn't at first recognise the tears he was wiping away – because Tom Grainger never cried. But then his throat felt tight and his nose started to run, and even his eyes felt sore. He had to pull his handkerchief out of his pocket to dry his face and blow his nose.

At first he was surprised at the show of weakness, although there was no one to see. Then he felt sorry for himself because life was so unfair, before a flicker of some strange emotion stirred in his chest. For the first time in his life Tom wondered if he was partly to blame for his own misery.

Had he been a hard father to Joey? He saw again the little boy's tragic face when he'd made the threat against Smokey. He recalled a time, long past, when his own beloved pet cat had died and he'd been heartbroken. His father had offered a replacement but he'd asked for a toy fort instead. He hadn't wanted to chance again feeling the pain of losing something he loved.

Then there was Lizzie. When he'd first married her she'd been so patient and caring, nursing him through his nightmares and never complaining. The salon had spoiled things, taken her away from him. Or had he driven her away? Lizzie – beautiful Lizzie – whom he'd lusted after when all she'd wanted was to be loved.

Damn it, his face was wet again. He mopped his eyes and swallowed hard.

And now Milly. What fun they used to have in the early days of their relationship. How she used to tease him about being the son of Victor Grainger. How he'd loved to wind her black hair around his finger and make up stories for her amusement. Then he'd grown tired of her and only used her when there were no better fish in the sea. Now he'd lost her.

Tom blew his nose again. He'd lost Milly, but was it too late for him and Lizzie? Could he make things up to her? Did he even want to try? What did life hold for him without Lizzie and Joey? So many questions and Tom didn't have the answers.

Suddenly Tom wanted to try. For the first time in his life he'd seen himself as other people saw him and he didn't like it at all.

He'd go home now; take Lizzie in his arms and tell her

he was sorry, that things were going to be different. Then he'd tell Joey that Smokey was safe; he'd even buy the lad another rabbit to keep Smokey company. And first thing in the morning he'd turn up at the shop and give his father a fit. He'd be a changed man. He had to change because he couldn't bear the feeling of emptiness that was all his old life had left him.

Tom felt different already. He wiped his face again and straightened his tie. If nobody had tampered with the car he could be home with Lizzie within the hour. What a surprise he had in store for her.

'You all right, love?'

Tom had been so deep in thought he hadn't heard the woman approaching. He nearly turned his back and walked away without answering, just in case there were traces of tears on his face. But the voice was warm and friendly, as if she was really concerned for him.

'I'm fine, thanks.'

The woman was leaning against the railings a few feet away. Tom could see the generous curves of her body under the green folds of her dress. Around her shoulders was draped a fox-fur, and there was a little pill-box hat perched jauntily on the side of her red head. She wasn't beautiful, or young, but her eyes were large and blue, and her rather large painted mouth had dimples in the corners as if she laughed easily. That was the thing about the woman that appealed to Tom; he needed someone to have a good laugh with.

'Would you like a cigarette?' She took a crushed packet of Woodbines out of the handbag that swung from her wrist on a gold chain and offered it to him.

'Thanks.'

She lit their cigarettes with a tiny silver-plated lighter. They stood side by side leaning on the railing, staring out at the sea.

'I thought you were going to jump.'

Tom laughed. 'If I'd intended that I'd have gone to

Beachy Head. If I jump over here all I'm likely to break is an ankle.'

There was a pause, then the woman asked, 'Had a row with the old woman then?'

'Something like that,' Tom answered.

'I should go home then, darling, before you get yourself into trouble.' The woman laughed: a loud, jolly, knowing laugh, that made her hat bob up and down and her red curls dance a jig.

Tom knew she was a prostitute: he'd had dealings with so many of them that he could pick one out a mile away. He'd known good and bad prostitutes, and this woman was a good one, like Milly had been in the old days.

'I'll go home when I'm ready,' he said brazenly. He had to show that he was still in control. 'What I want is a drink but the pubs are shut.'

'There's a club under the arches that could still be open. They might serve us. Want to give it a try?'

'Why not? Is it far?' Tom spoke lightly, but for a drink he would have followed the woman any distance.

She took his hand and led him. Before he knew it his arm was around her waist and he could feel the comforting warmth of her body. She smelled good too. Not of cheap Californian Poppy, but something more delicate that reminded him of a flower garden on a summer's day.

The club was small and dark, filled with cigarette smoke and late-night drinkers. 'Hullo, Rose,' the doorman said. 'Haven't seen you recently.'

'Willy's had a bad cold,' Rose said. 'He's better now.'

'Who's your friend?'

'This is Stanley. He's an old mate of mine, aren't you, Stan?' Rose nudged Tom in the ribs. He nodded, smiled, and followed her inside.

A whisky made him feel better, and a second one gave him back his confidence. Rose drank gin and chattered happily, and Tom soon felt so at ease that his old longings began to surface.

Of course, he told himself, he was still going to go home and make it up with Lizzie, but surely he deserved a bit of fun first. Rose was willing, she had her own place, and Tom seemed a nice enough bloke who would be able to afford her prices.

It was well after midnight when they left the club, both a bit merry, but not drunk. Rose took the lead. She told him she lived near the railway station, in Terminus Street. Her landlady would be asleep and there wouldn't be any trouble.

'I've got some cider, and bread and cheese if you're feeling peckish,' she told him. 'I always like a bit of supper to keep up my strength.' She laughed again, the loud throaty laugh that he found so attractive.

In daylight Tom might have hesitated, but the street lamp outside number ten was out of action so he couldn't see the broken windows or the dirty frontage. Anyway, his attention was on the woman on his arm and she was smart and fresh.

He followed her through a narrow hall and up the stairs. It was so dark that he almost lost his footing. The room Rose led him into seemed light in comparison, but there was only a shaded lamp by a large brass bed drowning the rest of the room in shadows. All Tom could make out were the humps of unidentifiable furniture against the walls. He thought he saw a movement in one dark corner but put it down to his imagination.

Rose removed her fur with a graceful gesture, and then the tiny hat, shaking out her hair. Tom put his arms around her waist and buried his face in her curls. He could feel passion in his loins and could hardly wait to take Rose to bed and satisfy his lusts.

'Wait – you're very eager.' Rose pushed away the urgent pressure of his body. 'I'm hungry after all that walking. Let's have something to eat first.'

She produced a loaf of bread and a knife, and then began cutting thick slices which she spread liberally with butter before filling them with cheese. It was only when she arranged the sandwiches on three plates that Tom looked at her questioningly.

'Why three?' he asked.

'One's for Willy.' Rose crossed the room to a dark corner and leaned over a makeshift crib. 'Supper, Willy. Who's a good boy then?'

It was only then that Tom realised that they weren't alone. The half-naked creature in the cot, with its humped back and balding head, snatched the food and crammed it into its dribbling mouth, all the while making moaning sounds. Tom was shocked and horrified, but Rose crooned to the monster and stroked its head tenderly.

'What the hell is that, Rose?' Tom burst out.

'This is my son, Willy. Willy, this is a new friend.' After the introduction she laughed at the expression on Tom's face. She'd seen it before on other men's faces. But if they wanted her they had to put up with Willy as well – and most of them found Rose worth it.

'Don't worry,' she said, crossing the floor and putting a reassuring hand on Tom's shoulder. 'Willy's used to me bringing my friends home; he'll probably go back to sleep in a minute.'

But the sight of Rose's son had dampened Tom's ardour. How could he even think of making love while that creature was in the room – asleep or awake? But he'd have to try. Rose had been kind to him, and she'd expect it.

He watched as she slowly unbuttoned her dress and let it slide to the floor in a billowing green heap. As she stood there in her underwear, Tom saw that she had a lovely figure. If he could only concentrate on Rose and forget the third occupant of the room perhaps everything would be all right.

'Come on – we're wasting time.'

Rose flung herself gracefully down on to the bed and held out her arms. Behind him Tom could hear the creaking of the crib and the whimpering and moaning of Willy. He crossed the room and feasted his eyes on Rose. Her hair was like a curling fan on the pillow and her body, rounded in the right places, excited him.

He lay down beside her and stroked her bare shoulder and breast, her rib-cage, and then the curve of her stomach. Everything was going to be all right. As he prepared to enter her, Willy began to mutter in his dark corner. Then the creature clambered to its knees and peered with vacant eyes at the lovers, the mutters turning to moans.

Tom's desire fled and was replaced by a rage, stronger and fiercer than anything he'd ever known before. Even here fate was dogging him and spoiling his chances. First Lizzie, then Milly, and now just as he'd found Rose, the perfect woman, fate had sent Willy to spoil things for him.

With a roar Tom leaped to his feet and charged across the room. He caught Willy by the shoulders and began to shake him so that his head lolled. But he still kept up the infernal moaning; even when Tom's hand found his throat and his fingers squeezed so that Willy's eyes rolled and his tongue swelled out between broken teeth.

'Leave him alone!' Rose screamed from the bed. 'Leave my baby alone!'

But Tom couldn't stop. The anger had made him insane. Half-naked, Rose ran across the room and tried to pull Tom away, but he was deaf to her entreaties. In desperation she saw the bread-knife resting by the remains of the loaf. She picked it up and thrust it once, twice, three times into Tom's back.

Willy moaned again, and Rose stepped over Tom's body to comfort him.

CHAPTER TWENTY-THREE

War

'PROSTITUTE KNIFES SON OF WEALTHY SHOPKEEPER TO DEATH', was the headline in the newspapers dated 1 September 1939. But by the Monday the murder of one Thomas Grainger by Rose Harrison was pushed into a small column on the centre page.

Rose escaped capital punishment because she had been defending her son. The judge, who was a compassionate man, decided the murder wasn't planned. Although Rose was guilty of taking a young man's life, she had been aroused by Tom's attack on her disabled son. She deserved punishment, but not a death sentence. She was imprisoned for three months because of the mitigating circumstances. The newspapers who had been planning sensational disclosures lost interest. The front pages were cleared for news of the forthcoming war.

On 3 September Britain declared that it was at war with Germany, and a sordid murder in a slum street in the centre of Brighton was of no more account.

Lizzie had no time to mourn, even if she'd wanted to. Changes to everyone's lives were inevitable, and the struggle to survive and protect one's nearest and dearest dulled the pain. Joey was now her life, and together the two of them would come through.

And yet Lizzie did not forget Rose Harrison. The horror of Tom's death, and the knowledge that a woman who had once been her friend had struck the fatal blow, had nearly made her lose her senses. But when the whole story had come out, and Lizzie had visited Rose in prison and heard her version, she couldn't help but understand and forgive.

They'd wept on each other's shoulders and Lizzie had promised to see that Willy was cared for while his mother was serving her sentence. They knew their paths would have to part, because of the painful memories, but they would always think well of each other.

The early days of the war progressed and people's lifestyles changed. Brighton became a friendlier place as the residents tried to help and comfort each other through the difficult times.

Grainger's Gentlemen's Outfitters sold siren-suits and balaclavas, as well as duffle-coats to beat the winter's chill, and surplus military great-coats. Next door, LADY ELIZABETH's also did its bit for the war effort, becoming a centre to distribute gas-masks, blankets and black-out material.

Twelve thousand evacuees arrived in the town. Mothers came with two or three children each, mostly from the London slums. Church halls were opened to accommodate them. They were given advice, free milk and orange juice, and the addresses of families who might be willing to take them in.

Many didn't stay more than a couple of nights. After the first air-raid alarm, which turned out to be a false alarm, people took themselves back to town, saying that if Hitler was going to get them they'd rather die in their own beds.

LADY ELIZABETH's soon became known as LIZZIE's and

started to deal in folding beds and second-hand bedding as well as clothing. Lizzie exchanged her smart suit for trousers and a Fair-Isle jumper, and tidied her hair away in a fashionable snood. The new outfit was warm and comfortable in the first bitterly cold winter of the war. Lizzie blossomed with her new lifestyle.

Joey revelled in the excitement. He rushed home from school with the box containing his gas-mask banging against his bare knees, to tell his mother about the air-raid shelters that were being dug in the play-ground, and how an enemy plane had been spotted over the Downs.

Even the promenade was a different place. The beach was cordoned off with barbed wire, and there were piles of sandbags outside the Aquarium and the Princes Hall.

The Germans were reported to be only a few miles away across the Channel in occupied France and there were fears of an invasion, so a gap was blown in the West Pier and signposts were removed to confuse the enemy. But no one took the threat of invasion to heart and people braved the beach until it was pronounced a prohibited area. Only when air-raids became a daily occurrence and bombs began to drop on the town did the people of Brighton start to take the war seriously.

Even the house at Patcham looked different. Brown paper sticky-tape was criss-crossed over the window-panes to lessen the risk of flying glass, and black-out regulations were brought in allowing no one to show even a chink of light. A stirrup-pump, bucket of water and sand stood nearby, ready to deal with incendiary bombs. And of course in the corner of the living-room stood a metal cage called a Morrison shelter, which also served as a table.

Through the disturbed nights Lizzie would huddle with Joey in the safety of the shelter, with biscuits, candles and, of course, a torch, in case it was going to be a prolonged raid. When Joey couldn't sleep she would tell him stories. The ones he liked most were about her life at Railway

Cottage, her lost brother Billy, and how she'd come by the lucky silver coin he still wore around his neck. And then he always asked his mother to tell again the story about the steadfast tin soldier, and how Billy had loved playing 'The March of the Gladiators' on the piano.

'How does it go again, Mum?' he'd ask sleepily, and Lizzie would hum the tune until he dropped off to sleep.

The house was too big for the two of them. Ada Hunt still gave her services willingly, but as she was also working part-time in a munitions factory her availability was limited. Lizzie had to juggle Joey's care, the home and the shop, as well as rolling bandages and making tea for the Red Cross. Because of her busy life she didn't notice that Joey had something on his mind.

It came to a head one tea-time. Eggs were in short supply, so Lizzie had used powdered egg and scrambled the mixture on toast. It was one of Joey's favourite meals, as long as he could cover it with plenty of tomato ketchup.

Not having the time to bake cakes, Lizzie had fallen back on the sweet ration of three ounces per head per week instead of a pudding. By Joey's plate was one of the new Rowntrees Kit-Kats. It had a blue wrapper to indicate that it was made with plain chocolate as full cream wasn't available.

Joey started his meal but Lizzie was so weary she rested her face in her hands and gave a big sigh. There was a clatter as Joey dropped his knife and fork.

'Don't cry, Mum. Please don't cry.'

'I'm not crying, Joey.' Lizzie sat up straight to show that she was telling the truth. 'Whatever made you think I was?'

'Eileen cries every day,' Joey burst out passionately. 'I can't bear it.'

'Eileen. Eileen who?'

Joey looked embarrassed and his cheeks flushed pink. 'I can't remember,' he muttered, picking up his knife and fork again and pushing the food around on his plate.

Lizzie was curious. After a minute she prompted, 'Is Eileen a little girl at your school?'

'Yes. She sits next to me.'

'And she cries a lot?'

'Yes. Every day.'

'Why?'

'Because she's so unhappy.'

'If she's your friend why don't you invite her home to tea?'

'I can't.'

'Whyever not?'

'Because … because …' Suddenly Joey burst into noisy sobs. Although Lizzie tried to comfort him it took a while before he could control himself.

'Come on, Joey,' Lizzie prompted. 'Tell me what's worrying you. You'll feel better afterwards, I promise. Who is this little girl?'

Joey swallowed, and then said in a small voice, 'It's Eileen French.'

Lizzie was dumbfounded. Eileen French – Jack's little sister! She hadn't seen any of the French family for over three years. Not since that terrible engagement party from which she'd run off to marry Tom for Joey's sake. She'd tried not to think about their kindness because to dwell on it brought a deep sense of loss and made her feel guilty.

Darling Jack, with his rough red hair and gentle ways, and his mother Grace who had taken her, pregnant as she was, into her home in Coventry Street.

None of the family had asked questions or condemned her. They'd shown her only love and understanding and welcomed her into their family. In return she'd walked out on Jack, although she'd loved him, and believed that he returned her love. She couldn't expect them to understand the reason behind her actions. And now here was little Eileen French, a ghost out of the past, becoming Joey's playmate again.

'But, Joey …' Lizzie said gently, 'Eileen French lives a long way away, in Coventry Street, and goes to Stanford Road School where you used to go.'

'Well, she doesn't any more. They moved into a bigger house. Then the war came and a nasty bomb knocked it down and killed Eileen's daddy.'

'Oh no!' Lizzie thought back to Albert French. He'd been an easy-going man with little to say for himself, but a steady rock for his wife Grace and family. 'Is that why Eileen cries, Joey, because she misses her daddy?'

'It's not only that, Mum. They didn't have anywhere to live, so they had to come to Patcham and live in one room in the village.'

'What, *all* of them?'

Lizzie thought of Jack who was all arms and legs, Johnnie who must now be a man, and Marjorie, not to mention their mother and Eileen. Eileen had always been a lively little thing who liked running around and needed plenty of space to play. There wouldn't be much space in one room.

'Eileen says Jack and Johnnie are soldiers,' Joey explained. 'So there's only Marjorie, Eileen and their mum. Eileen cries because she hates to see her mum so sad. She wants them to have a proper home again, so that when Jack and Johnnie beat Hitler and come back they can all be together.'

'Poor Eileen,' Lizzie said. 'No wonder she cries. But why did you keep this all a secret? Why didn't you tell me before about Eileen and her family?'

'Because … because, I didn't think you liked them.'

'Whatever gave you that idea?' Lizzie put her arms around her troubled son and held him close. 'Of course I liked the Frenches. They were the loveliest people – all of them.'

'Then why did you leave them – why did you take me away?' Joey's face was so tragic that Lizzie wanted to weep. 'You were going to marry Jack. I wanted you to;

because then he would have been my dad.'

'I wanted you to have your real father, Joey,' Lizzie said gently. 'Tom Grainger was your real father.'

'I know – but I didn't like him. I'm glad he's dead – aren't you glad, Mum?'

'Hush, darling, you mustn't say such things.' And yet in her heart of hearts Lizzie agreed with her son. Whatever complicated feelings she had for Tom, she'd never really *liked* him either.

Lizzie didn't sleep well that night, and when she did manage to doze in the early hours of the morning her dreams were full of memories. She lived again the time she'd spent in the little house in Coventry Street: the tender nursing care Grace French had given her, the birth of her son whom she'd nicknamed Silver Joey after the good-luck charm Mr Bennet had given her. The French children had accepted her as Jack's special friend, and her son as another brother. Even Spud, the little black and white dog, bounded through her dreams, pink tongue hanging out and tail wagging. And of course Jack, dear gentle Jack, who'd always been there to support her.

Lizzie woke with a start in the early hours, thinking about Jack fighting for his country. He'd be a brave soldier. Perhaps he'd be killed and never come back from the war. Perhaps she'd never see him again.

The next day was a busy one. Women still yearned to look beautiful, even in war-time when pretty clothes were in short supply. The salon was now open only one day a week and manned by a single assistant. Today it was being taken over by the baby clinic. The children of refugee mothers would be weighed, have their teeth examined and their heads checked for lice. They would be given vitamins, cod liver oil and orange juice, and coupons for milk. Lizzie had to be there to supervise things, console crying children with sweets, and listen to their mothers' problems. Homelessness abounded. The

French family certainly weren't the only ones living in one room.

Her duties were finished early and she was free to go. A siren wailed as she boarded a bus for home, but it must have been a false alarm because there was no sign of roving planes in the blue sky or any sound of gunfire.

For some reason Lizzie found herself getting down from the bus a stop early. It meant she had to pass Joey's school, although the children would have gone home long before. The building looked more like an army barracks with the windows criss-crossed with sticky tape and piles of sand-bags leaning against the wall. Some had burst open because the children liked to climb on them, and there was a loose trail of sand where it had been carried away to make sandcastles. The entrances to the underground shelters yawned like giant mouths trying to catch unsuspecting prey. Torn paper had escaped from a litter bin labelled 'Keep Britain Tidy' and had been blown against the railings.

The playground was deserted apart from one solitary figure perched forlornly on a dust-bin and trailing a canvas satchel from one hand. The head was bowed, and the girl in her grey cardigan and skirt, with T-bar sandals and white knee socks, could have been anybody. But there was something about the red curls that Lizzie couldn't fail to recognise.

The gate creaked rustily as Lizzie pushed it open; but the humped figure didn't look up even when she stood as close as could be.

'Eileen?'

Only then did the child slowly raise her head. Lizzie saw a tear-stained face, a freckled nose, and big blue eyes. Even after the passing of time it was Eileen French without a doubt.

'Hullo, Eileen,' Lizzie said gently. 'Don't you remember me? I'm Lizzie – Joey's mum.'

'Lizzie! Is it really you?'

'Of course it is. Joey's only just told me you're here.'

'I didn't think you wanted to see me.' The tears had turned to smiles. Leaping from her perch Eileen gave Lizzie a welcoming hug.

'How you've grown,' Lizzie marvelled. 'Nearly a young lady.'

Eileen giggled, and then her face straightened. 'I don't want to be a young lady; I want it to be like it used to be. Jack's a soldier, and so's Johnnie. Marjorie thinks she's grown up, and Mum's miserable all the time because of Dad...'

'Joey told me,' Lizzie said softly.

'And we live in one room because a bomb hit our house. We have to share a lavatory and a kitchen and there's nowhere to do my homework.'

'Eileen! How many times do I have to tell you not to talk to strangers?'

Neither of them had been aware of the woman approaching, but they both turned at the sound of the harsh voice. Dressed as she was in a shabby coat, with a grubby scarf bound turban-wise around greying hair and a face lined by worry, Lizzie didn't at first recognise Grace French. She remembered her as a plump, homely woman with a constant smile on her face; not thin and care-worn with a permanent frown etched between faded eyes as this woman had. She would only be in her fifties but could have easily passed for ten years older.

'It's Lizzie, Mum. Don't you remember Lizzie? She's not a stranger,' Eileen said excitedly.

'She's a stranger to me,' the hard voice continued. 'Come with me, Eileen.'

'But, Mum—'

'Do as I say, girl.'

'But, Mrs French,' Lizzie interrupted, 'Joey's just told me you're living close by and Eileen's at his school. I wanted to see you again.'

'Well, we don't want to see you.'

'Why not?'

'Because you broke my Jack's heart, that's why not. I don't mind our Eileen playing with Joey, it's not his fault, but we don't want anything to do with you.'

Lizzie's face flushed and she felt her eyes fill with tears. She could understand how Jack's mother had interpreted things and was full of sympathy.

'Would it help if I said I was sorry?'

'No, it wouldn't. You dropped Jack because there were richer fish in the sea. I'd never have believed you could be so cruel – not after all we did for you.'

'I know, Mrs French, but I'm a widow now...'

'So I read in the paper,' Grace French said bitterly. 'And now you want my Jack back.'

'No, I don't. I just want to be friends for old times' sake – to see if I can help you in any way.'

'We don't need your help.'

'If you change your mind, Eileen can give Joey a message.'

But Grace was dragging Eileen away. Although the child looked back at Lizzie longingly she had to comply.

Lizzie returned home sadly to a house that was too large for her and Joey, while Grace French was going back to one cramped room.

Over the next few days she thought constantly about Jack's family but knew she couldn't make them accept help. And why should they? They had their pride just as she had.

When food rationing became part of wartime Britain, all families had to register at their local shops. All the residents of Patcham did their shopping at the same store. Lizzie bought her groceries on a Saturday, and with a basket on her arm she joined the queue the following weekend to collect their weekly ration of 2ozs of butter and cheese, 4ozs of fat and margarine, 8ozs sugar and 2ozs of tea. Plus the one egg per person when it was available.

In front of her in the queue was a small figure with a familiar red curly head. The grocer in his white apron was weighing out sugar and pouring it into a cone of blue paper.

'There's three of you,' he was saying to Eileen, 'so you can have a pound. The butter's five pence a pound, cheese at four pence and five pence for tea. There are three eggs this week.'

'How much is that then?' Eileen asked, counting the money in her purse.

'That comes to one and six.'

'I've only got a shilling.'

'You'd better leave the eggs then.'

'Mum'll want the eggs,' Eileen said firmly, knowing how scarce they were. 'I'll only take half the butter and no tea.'

'All right, me darling – don't break them. Here's your penny halfpenny change.'

'Thanks.' Eileen put the coins in her purse and picked up her shopping. She passed Lizzie with an embarrassed smile.

'Next please,' the grocer was saying, and everyone moved up a place nearer the counter.

As Lizzie waited her turn she saw the ginger head bobbing about outside the shop-window between the packets of Oxydol and the bottles of Camp Coffee. Eileen was joined by two rough-headed boys who seemed to be larking about. After a few moments Lizzie heard a little cry of distress and the boys ran away laughing. Giving up her place in the queue she ran outside to find Eileen in tears and the three precious eggs broken on the pavement.

'Mum'll kill me,' Eileen sobbed. 'Mum'll kill me.'

'It wasn't your fault,' Lizzie assured her. 'Just tell her what happened.'

'She won't believe me. She'll say I was mucking about.'

'No she won't.'

'She will! She will! You tell her, Lizzie – *please*.'

'I don't think your mum will want to see me.'

'Please come and try.'

Eileen took hold of Lizzie's hand and began to pull her down the street. She stopped outside a cottage whose door stood ajar. It was a clean enough place, but by the number of children tumbling about in the hall, and the shouts of care-worn women, it was full to overflowing. A bit like the home of the old woman who lived in a shoe.

'We're in the back,' Eileen said.

She pushed her way through the milling children, dragging a reluctant Lizzie behind her. A door was standing ajar and Lizzie could just see a smallish room crammed with essential furniture.

There was a double bed that was probably shared by Mrs French and her eldest daughter, and a mattress rolled against the wall for Eileen's use. A deal table stood in the middle of the room, and the rest of the furnishings consisted of a couple of wobbly chairs and a pile of boxes. Grace French was sitting on the end of the bed staring at a piece of paper in her hand. She looked up as Eileen and Lizzie entered the room, but her face was expressionless.

'Eileen wanted me to come,' Lizzie said quickly. 'She's broken the eggs, but it wasn't her fault. I saw what happened.'

'It doesn't matter.' Grace pushed the straggly hair away from her face with a blind gesture.

'What's the matter, Mum?' Eileen asked in a frightened voice. 'Has something happened?'

'I've just had a telegram.' Grace stared at the piece of paper again to assure herself of the wording. 'It's about Johnnie.'

'Johnnie!' Eileen snatched the paper from her mother's fingers. 'He's not dead, is he?'

'No, but he's wounded.'

'How bad?'

'He's going to be okay – this time.'

'And Jack?' The words broke out of Lizzie before she could stop them. 'Is Jack all right?'

'Yes – Jack's fine,' Grace said. 'We had news yesterday. He's in the thick of the fighting, but he's all right.'

'Thank God! Oh, thank God!'

Before she could stop them Lizzie found her eyes streaming with tears of relief. She was sorry about Johnnie, but at least Jack was safe. She covered her face with her hands.

'So you *do* care about our Jack?'

Slowly Lizzie lowered her hands. Grace French was staring at her, and behind the lined, worried face she caught a glimpse of the old Grace, the tender motherly woman who'd cared for her so gently.

'Yes,' she said softly. 'I do care. I always have.'

'Then why did you do it? Why did you leave him and run off with that Grainger fellow? You broke our Jack's heart.'

'I did it for Joey. The last thing I wanted was to hurt Jack.'

'I don't understand,' Grace said, but the look on her face told Lizzie that she was prepared to try.

'Tom Grainger was Joey's father – his real father. I never told anyone – not even Jack – but Tom raped me. I thought I'd never have to see him again but then Jack and I bumped into him – and the memories came flooding back. Then as soon as Tom met Joey he knew he was his and he wanted to marry me. Naively, I thought it would be the best thing for Joey – to let him grow up with his real father. I was very young, and there was no one to advise me. It was the biggest mistake of my life.'

'Oh, Lizzie! If only you'd told us.'

'I know, but I thought I was doing the right thing for Joey. I regretted it very soon. Joey was never really happy and I missed all of you terribly. It was always Jack that I loved.'

'Oh, my dear, to think of both you and Jack living in

misery.' Suddenly Lizzie felt fond arms around her and she knew she was forgiven. 'And to think what that man put you through.'

'Even so I didn't wish Tom dead.'

'From what I read in the papers, seems to me he asked for it,' Mrs French stated bluntly. 'Now I'm going to make us a nice cup of tea. Go and fill the kettle, Eileen, while I light the oil stove and set out the cups. It'll be quite like old times, won't it?'

It was. Even with the shadow of Johnnie's injuries hanging over them, they managed to gossip about the old days in quite a cheerful fashion. Eileen was so pleased her mother was making Lizzie welcome that she even managed a smile.

By the time Lizzie left, Grace looked more like her old self, because she'd been invited to spend the following day with Lizzie and Joey. The thought of getting away from the crammed conditions she lived in, even for a few hours, had lifted her spirits.

It was a Sunday and the sun was shining; Joey was up early and shaking his mother out of bed to tell her his plans for the day.

'Eileen hasn't got any pets so I want to show her my rabbit,' he said. 'They had to find another home for Spud and she misses him, although he really belonged to Jack.'

'He must be very old now,' Lizzie said thoughtfully, remembering the little black and white dog who had been Jack's constant companion.

'He is, but Eileen said that an old man is caring for him. His wife has just died so they're company for each other.'

'That's nice,' Lizzie said. 'Come on now, we'll have a quick breakfast and then I want to bake a cake. I'm going to put caraway seeds in it because I know that's Mrs French's favourite.'

'And can we have corned-beef for dinner, Mum? That's Eileen's favourite.'

'I'll mix it with mashed potato and bake it in the oven. There'll be plenty of fresh vegetables to help it go round.'

Joey nibbled a piece of toast and poured himself a glass of milk. 'Do you think Marjorie will come?'

'Mrs French wasn't sure. She's training to be a nurse and may have to be on duty. But I know she'll come if she can.'

Grace had also confided that her elder daughter had a young man. Even if she wasn't working she might want to spend her free time with him.

Marjorie sent her apologies, but Grace and Eileen turned up promptly to find Joey waiting for them on the garden path.

'Mum's just made a cake – and ginger-bread men,' he informed them before ushering them through the front door.

Grace sniffed the air. 'I can smell them; they smell lovely,' she said as she followed the spicy aroma into the kitchen. Lizzie was bent over the stove, her face flushed and her hair untidy, and a large apron bound around her waist.

'Let's have a cup of tea first,' she said with a welcoming smile, 'and then I'll show you the house.'

Grace was impressed and tried not to be jealous, but Lizzie couldn't help but be aware of the envy in her eyes. She tried not to feel guilty as she displayed the spacious dining and drawing rooms with their thick carpets and polished furniture, and the bedrooms with comfortable beds and wardrobes. Not to mention the luxuries of the fitted kitchen and bathroom.

'You are lucky, Lizzie,' Grace said as she sat down at the kitchen table for another cup of tea and a slice of cake.

'I'm not lucky,' Lizzie said firmly. 'Money and possessions don't bring happiness.'

'No, but you deserve a nice home. If you'd married my Jack he would have done his best, but I doubt if he could have provided things on this scale.'

'I know,' Lizzie said reminiscently. 'But I think I would have been happy just being with him. He was always so kind – and made me feel safe.'

'Don't talk like that,' Grace said. 'Jack's not dead, or even wounded. He'll be coming back when this awful war ends.'

'Perhaps he'll have forgotten me,' Lizzie said wistfully.

'Never! Don't say such things. The last thing Jack said to me was that if he couldn't have you he didn't want anyone.'

A warm glow filled Lizzie's inside. Was Grace French speaking the truth or just being kind? She could hope – but she mustn't bank on Jack waiting for her after the way she'd treated him.

'It's been a lovely day,' said Grace, getting to her feet. 'I've enjoyed myself no end and so has Eileen. But we'd better be going now.'

'Do you have to?' Lizzie was bent over the sink, her sleek brown hair swinging forward.

'We mustn't outstay our welcome,' Grace said firmly. 'Or you mightn't ask us again.'

'I've been thinking.' Lizzie turned round to wipe her hands on a tea-towel. 'Why don't you move in?'

'What, all of us?' Grace laughed in disbelief, suspecting a joke.

'Why not? There's heaps of room. Joey and I rattle around this big house like two peas in a drum. It'd be company for us.'

'Well, I don't know…'

'Come on now, Grace. You know you want to get out of that poky room, and you'd be doing me a favour. I've got a woman who comes in sometimes, but it's difficult juggling Joey when I have to go out. We can help each other.'

'Well, I don't reckon Marjorie'll be around long, what with her nursing. She could be sent anywhere. And then, if she's serious about this young man she might want to get married. She's talked about it often enough.'

'Then you'll come?'

At that moment Eileen and Joey appeared in the doorway, chatting happily, one dark head pressed close to a ginger one.

'Eileen,' Grace said. 'Lizzie's asked us to come and live here. What do you say?'

The shout of delight and the two pairs of starry eyes were answer enough. The matter was settled there and then.

CHAPTER TWENTY-FOUR

Jack

Nineteen forty-three brought with it more shortages and restrictions for householders.

'How can they expect us to keep clean when we're only allowed one bath a week, and then we mustn't use more than five inches of water,' Lizzie complained. Before the war she'd enjoyed a hot soak every day.

Grace French smiled but didn't answer. After living in one room, any bath was a luxury. The children didn't seem to suffer; in fact they rather enjoyed the restrictions.

'And now I've got a two-pound fine to pay,' Lizzie continued. 'Someone tore the blackout and we showed a light last night. The ARP Warden woke me up at half past one in the morning.'

'I'll see to it,' Grace promised. 'After I've put the pig food out. They'll be collecting this morning.'

She picked up the metal pail of vegetable peelings and carried it outside. There were also bins for compost, waste paper and bones, as well as jars for milk-bottle tops and cheese-rind to feed the chickens kept by many householders. Eggs were now so scarce that sometimes there was only one a month each. She came back into the kitchen rubbing her hands.

'I had to put half a loaf of bread in the bin. It doesn't keep like it did before the war – it was all over mould.'

They switched on the wireless as they did every morning to listen to the nine o'clock news. In his upper-class accent the newsreader reported that the Eighth Army was doing very well against Rommel; Stalingrad was holding firm; and the Russians were gaining some ground. Nearer home, over fifty Nazi raiders had bombed Canterbury.

Lizzie listened avidly every morning, but Mrs French was more interested in trying to light a coal fire as it was a cold November day. She was using the recommended fire-bricks to cut down on fuel.

'I had a letter from Jack yesterday,' she said over her shoulder. 'I'd written and given him all the news. He sends his love.'

'I had one yesterday,' Lizzie said. She bent her head to hide her blushes. Grace had told Jack everything that had happened to Lizzie, and now that he understood the situation and knew Lizzie was free and still cared deeply for him he was writing regularly. At first his letters had been distant and cautious but slowly he was showing his feelings more and more. However, neither of them were rushing things. They both knew they had to put the past behind them and be gentle with each other if their future was to be secure. 'He says he has fourteen days' leave due to him.'

'Wouldn't it be nice if he was with us for Christmas?' Grace said. 'And Johnnie too. Then we would be a family again.'

Johnnie was in a Red Cross Convalescent Home. He'd suffered a wound to his leg, but although it had been fairly serious he was now receiving treatment to strengthen his weakened muscles. He was lucky compared to some of his comrades who had lost whole limbs and were hobbling around on crutches while they waited to be fitted with artificial legs. Johnnie loved being a soldier and couldn't wait to get back to the front.

Lizzie had gone to the hospital with Grace to visit him and she'd hardly recognised the big blond man propped up in the bed; but then she'd seen the resemblance to his father, Albert, and knew it was Johnnie French, the schoolboy she'd once known.

The fire was now burning merrily and Grace got to her feet. 'I thought I'd make the Christmas pudding today,' she announced. 'There's a recipe in *Home Notes* that doesn't need eggs. Did you know that you can use potato instead of flour?'

'I know,' Lizzie said. 'There's a Ministry of Food leaflet that tells you about it. That baked sponge pudding we had for supper last night was made with cold mashed potato.'

'Was it now? Well I never … you'd never have known, would you?'

'Will Marjorie be in to supper tonight?' Lizzie asked.

'No. Nigel's taking her to see that Noël Coward film about the Navy. It's called *In Which We Serve.*'

'Then I'll buy some fish and we'll make it into a cheap and filling pie. It'll be good for the children. Have you thought what we can have for Christmas dinner instead of a turkey, Grace?'

'I asked the butcher's advice and he suggested a plump leg of mutton. He'll bone it for me, and then you stuff it with a mixture of stale bread-crumbs, minced onion, suet and herbs. You cook it just like a bird and serve it with roast potatoes and sprouts. He says it's very tasty.'

'Sounds all right,' Lizzie agreed. 'Fancy planning Christmas when it's barely December.'

'Just as well to be prepared, I always say.'

It snowed early in December and everyone started talking about a white Christmas. Joey found an old toboggan in the shed and cleaned it up in readiness. But a steady thaw set in and to his disappointment Christmas Eve was mild.

There wasn't much in the shops even if one did have money to spend, so most of the presents under the decorated tree were home-made. Grace had made both the children dressing-gowns out of old grey blankets. They had cosy snug-fitting hoods, and would be perfect to wear when they had to run downstairs to the shelter during air-raids. Lizzie had bought them slippers to match. There was plenty of fruit, nuts and small toys to fill the stockings they would hang on the ends of their beds.

Grace had made Lizzie a blouse so she would have something new to wear on Christmas Day. It was made of pale blue crêpe de Chine and had long sleeves and a little pointed collar. It was plain, but dainty, and had a row of tiny pearl buttons down the front.

They sat down to an early tea. Eileen and Joey were too excited to eat much because they were waiting for the carol-singers to arrive. They were always invited in for a hot mince-pie and a glass of home-made ginger punch.

As usual they sang all the old favourites: 'We Three Kings', 'The Holly and the Ivy', and Lizzie's favourite, 'Oh Little Town of Bethlehem'.

Although their throats were sore they sang lustily, and then they stood about, filling the hall to overflowing as they chattered, laughed, and wished everyone a merry Christmas. They wore brightly coloured scarves and mittens, but their flickering lanterns, shaded with dark paper because of the black-out, cast ghostly shadows around the hall and staircase.

Lizzie was handing out glasses when she saw a taller shadow detach itself from the darkness of the open front door and enter the house. Then she saw it was a man in an army great-coat, with a kit-bag slung over one shoulder. She held her breath. She saw, as if in a dream, a freckled face, blue eyes fringed with spiky lashes, and a smiling mouth with a broken tooth at the front.

With a cry Lizzie would have dropped the tray if Grace French hadn't rescued it in time. Then she was in Jack's arms, feeling the roughness of his uniform coat, and his big hands stroking her so tenderly as he whispered, 'Lizzie! Oh, Lizzie!' into her tumbled hair.

He'd brought presents for the children: a doll for Eileen and a *Just William* book for Joey. They were soon hidden away with the other presents under the tree. He had a special present for Lizzie but that had to be concealed until the following day. Enough for them to hold each other close in the shadowy hall while the carol-singers slipped away to the next house. Grace shepherded Eileen and Joey upstairs so that the lovers could have privacy.

The evening wasn't long enough. They couldn't bear to be out of each other's sight or to be unable to touch. Jack helped Lizzie with the last of the decorations, and they both felt a spark of recognition as their fingers touched while they passed strings of tinsel or greenery. When Lizzie busied herself in the dining-room, folding serviettes and polishing silver so that it would sparkle under the flickering candles arranged as a centre-piece, Jack followed her.

'Mum wants to know if you need dessert spoons?' he asked by way of excuse.

'Yes, please – and teaspoons as well. The silver apostle spoons would be nice as it's Christmas.'

And then the children were in bed and the grown-ups gathered around the fire. There were chestnuts roasting in the ashes and the smell of apples and spice wafted out. Lizzie put her head on Jack's shoulder and his arm crept around her protectively.

'It's ten o'clock,' Grace said, looking pointedly at the mantel-clock.

'Christmas in two hours,' Jack said.

'I must fill the children's stockings,' Lizzie announced, stretching sleepily.

'I'll help.'

So they crept into the bedrooms and filled Joey and Eileen's empty stockings with nuts and raisins, not forgetting the sweets bought with the carefully saved coupons. There was a wooden whistle painted red and blue for Joey and a necklace of china beads for Eileen. The children didn't stir, even when Jack stubbed his toe against the dressing-table and let out a muffled curse of pain.

On the landing Jack took Lizzie in his arms to kiss her goodnight. 'You're tired,' he said.

'So are you.'

'It'll be morning soon.'

'Yes. Happy Christmas, Jack.'

'Happy Christmas, Lizzie.'

And then Christmas morning dawned with all the excitement of church and present opening. Jack drew Lizzie aside because what he wanted to say was for her ears alone.

'Do you remember the ring I bought you once?' he asked.

'Yes.' Lizzie had the grace to blush. What a happy day that had been, until Tom had come along and ruined things.

'Well, I've bought you another one – I hope you'll accept it.' From his pocket Jack produced a golden wedding band. It wasn't wide or heavy like the one Tom had bought her, but it had been chosen with loving care and paid for with well-earned money. 'Will you marry me, Lizzie?'

'Oh, Jack, of course I will,' and Lizzie kissed the rough cheek and was the happiest woman on earth. Somewhere the church bells started to chime, and Lizzie's heart rang with joy.

Jack obtained a special licence and the wedding took place at Brighton Register Office in January 1944. It was attended by only close friends and relations. All the Frenches were there: mother, daughters and sons. Marjorie, dreamy-eyed, brought her fiancé, Nigel. She'd also received a ring on Christmas morning and was now planning her own wedding.

Joey was present wearing his first suit with long trousers. At thirteen he was now tall, thin, and handsome. He was growing into a charmer like his father; but he had a soft heart as well as a conscience, and that would make all the difference.

Frances and Victor Grainger were there as well. Frances was in tears because of memories of another wedding, but her husband, smiling, wished Lizzie and Jack all the best. Victor had become the father figure Lizzie still missed. When she'd told him of her proposed marriage he'd kissed her warmly and wished her well. Tom had always been a worry and disappointment and he didn't blame Lizzie for the tragic happenings. He knew they'd been beyond her control. Now his hopes were on Joey joining him in the family business when he was old enough.

There weren't enough clothing coupons for Lizzie to have a completely new outfit, so she chose the material for a new dress and matched it with a coat she already had in her wardrobe.

The coat was made of navy wool with padded shoulders, no collar, but wide turned-back revers at the front. Underneath she wore a grey jersey dress cut in three flared panels, with long fitted sleeves and buttons from neck to waist. To finish she wore a small grey hat with navy trim and a feather at the side, and navy shoes and bag.

Jack wore his uniform, and they were a proud and happy couple when they were pronounced man and wife. They'd both suffered so much and waited so long that everyone felt they deserved happiness.

There wasn't time for a proper honeymoon as Jack

was due back to his regiment in a few days, so they chose to have two nights away from home at a local hotel. Jack suggested the Metropole on Brighton's sea-front but Lizzie preferred something more homely. Her days of wanting to be like the fictitious Opal were over, and the Metropole was the sort of place Tom would have taken her to.

In the end they settled on a modest boarding house in Manchester Street. Although they couldn't see the sea from their bedroom window, the view wouldn't have been all that good on a foggy January day because the beach itself was a tangle of barbed wire.

After a tasty meal of liver and bacon, followed by suet pudding, served in the small dining-room that smelled of starched table-linen and beeswax polish, they went upstairs early to the best bedroom. Lizzie thought it delightful. There was a large oak bed covered by a crocheted white spread, and hand-made rag rugs on the polished linoleum. As she unpacked her nightdress she wondered why she was feeling so scared; and then she saw Jack's reflection in the dressing-table mirror and was surprised to see that he appeared as nervous as she was.

'What on earth's the matter with me?' she chided herself. 'You're thirty years old, you've already had one husband and a child, and yet you're frightened of sex with darling Jack. What do you think's going to happen? Do you imagine that Jack's going to turn into some cruel monster and abuse you like Tom did? You know he won't.'

Seeing her nervousness Jack disappeared into the bathroom carrying his striped pyjamas. Lizzie quickly slipped out of her clothes and into her nightgown. When he returned, with his red hair sticking up in spiky tufts, she was sitting in front of the mirror brushing her hair.

He came up behind her and put his large rough hands on the softness of her shoulders.

'Happy, Lizzie?' he asked.

'It's the happiest day of my life,' she answered honestly.

'Why are you looking so scared then?'

'I don't know.'

'I wouldn't hurt you for the world, Lizzie, you must know that. We've waited so long – I don't mind waiting a bit longer if that's what you want.'

Lizzie turned to him, her big brown eyes wide and honest. 'You're as nervous as I am, Jack, aren't you?'

'Yes.' Jack's neck coloured red as if he was embarrassed at the admission. 'You see, compared to me you're quite experienced. Oh, I had a few girl friends when I was young, but it never led to more than kissing and canoodling in the back row of the pictures. But then I met you, Lizzie, and I knew that if I couldn't have you, I didn't want anybody else.'

'That's a lovely thing to say,' Lizzie said softly.

'It's the truth.'

'Let's just take it slowly.' She took Jack's hand and kissed the palm. 'We've got the rest of our lives to discover each other. I can wait if you can.'

'But you'll lie with me, won't you? You don't expect me to sleep on the floor?' He looked so worried that Lizzie struggled not to laugh.

'Of course we'll lie together. I want that more than anything.'

Jack bent over and picked Lizzie up in his arms. He was so broad and she was so slender that it was like carrying a child. He could feel the warmth of her body through the cotton of her nightdress, and her head rested trustingly against his shoulder. He would have carried her to the ends of the earth if she'd asked him to.

The covers had been turned down by the landlady and he laid her down gently and climbed in beside her before pulling up the crisp linen sheet and white spread. In the dim light she smiled at him, her eyes dark as chestnuts and her hair fanning the pillow like glossy silk thread.

'You're beautiful, Lizzie,' Jack said.

'So are you.'

They both laughed. The nearness of Jack's body warmed Lizzie. Her limbs felt languid and a small glow in the pit of her stomach started to grow and spread so that she felt light-headed. She felt so strange that for a moment she wondered if she had a temperature. Perhaps she was sickening for something. But then an overwhelming desire to touch Jack came over her. She put out her hand, and her fingers trembled slightly as she slipped them between the buttons of his pyjama jacket and stroked his chest which was covered by a mat of rough hair. An electric shock exploded somewhere in the centre of Lizzie's brain, making her weak with desire. Her insides were melting, and she knew that if Jack didn't touch her soon she'd die of longing.

'Touch me,' she whispered, and her voice was low and urgent. She took his hand and placed it on her breast so that he could feel her heart-beat through the nightdress and the budding of her aroused nipple. 'Touch me here,' she instructed. 'And here,' and she guided his hand downwards so that he could feel the smoothness of her belly and the soft moist hair between her legs.

Jack groaned, and Lizzie knew that he desired her as much as she wanted him. They were so in tune that they didn't have to speak. Everything happened naturally. Jack gently removed Lizzie's night-clothes as if he was unwrapping a precious jewel. His hands and lips aroused her until she was mad with desire, and when he finally entered her, hard and strong, it was so beautiful that she thought she was melting. Jack's manhood soon pierced the barrier Lizzie had built to protect herself from Tom's cruel advances. She was all liquid love and femininity.

Afterwards they slept in each other's arms, Lizzie curled as tightly as a kitten with Jack's hand cupping her breast. When they woke it was daylight. Sunshine had replaced the mist and it was the dawning of a beautiful winter's day. Lizzie stretched languidly.

'What's the time?' Jack asked.

Reluctantly Lizzie turned away from his embrace and peered at the clock on the bedside table. 'It's nearly nine o'clock. Do you think we've missed breakfast? I'm starving!'

'So am I.'

Hurriedly they washed, dressed and, hand in hand, crept down the stairs like two naughty children. The dining-room door was open and they could see their landlady, Mrs Piper, clearing the tables. Apart from her the room was empty, and there was a sign on the door saying that breakfast was served between seven and eight-thirty.

Mrs Piper saw them hovering in the hall and beckoned them in with a beaming smile. She'd recognised them as a newly married couple and hadn't expected them to surface early.

'Good morning, dears,' she said cheerfully, immediately putting their minds at rest. 'Come in and sit down. There's a table in the window all laid ready for you.'

'I'm sorry we're late,' Lizzie said. 'I'm afraid we overslept.'

'It doesn't matter,' Mrs Piper assured her. 'There are some kippers keeping hot, or I can make you some fresh porridge.'

'Porridge sounds lovely.'

Jack said he'd like porridge as well as kippers, and Mrs Piper said it would be no trouble. She bustled off to the kitchen leaving them alone to chat over a pot of tea.

The breakfast when it arrived was so enormous that Lizzie vowed she wouldn't need anything else to eat for hours. Jack agreed with her.

'What are you planning to do this morning?' Mrs Piper enquired when their plates were empty and they'd pushed back their chairs. They'd booked in for two nights, and much as she liked the look of them their room needed cleaning and the bed straightening.

'We're going for a walk, aren't we, Jack? I fancy a brisk walk by the sea.'

'You won't get far,' Mrs Piper said. 'They've closed off the sea-front from Newhaven to Lancing. It's full of tanks and soldiers in uniform – anyone would think Hitler's about to land. If he does, there's no use him expecting breakfast here. I can't bear men with moustaches,' and she hurried away with her loaded tray, chuckling at her own wit.

'Let's walk inland then,' Lizzie said, when they were wrapped up in scarves and coats. The sun was shining but it was still only January.

They strode out briskly, Lizzie hanging on to her husband's arm. She was so happy she felt like singing.

Her wedding night had turned out to be wonderful and she'd had nothing to fear from her darling Jack. His lovemaking had transported her to heaven, and although he would soon be back fighting the Germans she would be left with a host of happy memories. Where in the past she'd feared pregnancy, now she prayed that soon, God willing, she would bear Jack a child. A brother or sister for Joey. Perhaps she would manage to conceive before he left, and she would have the joy of writing him the good news while he was at the front. Wouldn't that be wonderful? Enough to take his mind off the war and make sure he came home safe and sound. Lizzie smiled at her thoughts, and the way she was planning their future and looking forward with anticipation.

'What are you smiling at?' Jack asked.

He guided her along the road past the glorious Royal Pavilion, the former home of the Prince Regent. Hitler was boasting that when he won the war he was going to live there, but the Brightonians said that would only be over their dead bodies. Then they passed the Dome. There was a poster outside inviting people to 'Dance away their dumps' to the music of Douglas Reeve on the organ.

'I'll tell you one day,' Lizzie said, and quickly changed the subject.

They were almost opposite the tall grey church of St

Peter when Lizzie suddenly stopped so that people had to walk around her. Ahead stretched the road to London, bordered by shops and buildings, wide and straight. Jack looked at her in alarm.

'What is it?'

'Look!'

'Where?'

'Straight ahead.' Lizzie was staring, her eyes wide as if she was in a dream. 'The road is made of gold.'

'No, it's not, you chump,' Jack said. 'It's just the sun shining on the tarmac. It makes it look as if it's paved with gold.'

But Lizzie didn't want to be disillusioned. Her dream of finding the streets of Brighton paved with gold had finally come true, even if it was only all in her mind. A fairy-tale made up by her imagination. Her dreams were coming true, thanks to Jack; now all she had to do was find Billy and life would be perfect – war or no war.

Soon they came to Marshall's Row where the blacksmith was busy hammering a nail into a horse's hoof. Sparks flew, and he was always surrounded by bystanders who enjoyed watching a trade that would soon be part of the town's past.

But it was too cold to stand still for long. Ahead was the Open Market, with its striped awnings to ward off the chill, and its stalls heavy with local grown vegetables. Fruit was in short supply but one stall had had a small delivery of oranges and was allowing one per person. There was a queue waiting patiently, with mouths watering at the thought of the juicy fruit.

'Carrots – a penny a pound,' a stall-holder called, deafening the passers-by. 'Home grown. Fill a bag, ladies – juicy carrots, only a penny a pound.'

Now it was Jack's turn to stand and stare. He wandered from stall to stall as if in a daze. Lizzie followed, but he seemed to be in a world of his own making. In the end she put her hand on his arm.

'Jack?'

'What is it?'

'Can we go now? I'm cold.'

At once he was all concern, pulling her towards him in a clumsy embrace and rubbing her cold fingers. 'I'm a thoughtless fellow, Lizzie. It's just that I love markets, ever since I worked in the greengrocer's. If I hadn't worked at Staggs I'd never have met you again. I just love the smell of fruit and vegetables and serving the public.' He looked around at the passing crowd. 'These are the real people; this is the real world. Flesh and blood, pain and suffering, love and laughter, that's what I want, Lizzie. Do you know what my dream is?'

'Tell me,' Lizzie prompted.

'I want to have my own shop. I've wanted it ever since Mum sent me out with a basket to get the vegetables when I was only knee high. Do you think that's silly?'

'Not at all. No more silly than my dream of being a beautician. Even then I never thought I'd have my own salon – even if the war has slowed things down a bit.'

'Well, perhaps when it's all over, and we get back to normal, you'll be able to pick things up again; and I'll have my dream – even if it's only a market stall.'

'You will, Jack,' Lizzie promised. 'You will.'

They continued their walk, but although she held tightly to Jack's arm Lizzie's thoughts were far away. Not in the past but in the future, where all their dreams would come true and they'd live happily ever after.

'Are you tired yet?' Jack asked, when they reached Preston Circus.

'Not a bit.'

'Then let's go to see George.'

'George?'

'George Stagg. My old boss. I promised to drop in and see him when I was home on leave.'

'That's a good idea.'

If it hadn't been for George she might never have met up with Jack again.

So they climbed the steep hill under the railway arches until they reached the part of the town known as Prestonville. It was just like a village on the top of the world, with its panorama of streets and the view over Preston Park. In summer the giant horse-chestnut trees veiled the scene with a curtain of luxurious greenery, but on a winter's day the park was easy to see through the stately tree trunks with their delicate bare branches like lace against the sky.

Staggs was one of a parade of small shops serving the local community. There was a chemist's, a newsagent's, draper's, butcher's and baker's, not to mention the hardware store and the fish and chip shop. Lizzie's mouth watered at the smell of hot fat and vinegar.

'You go and talk to George,' she said. 'I'm going to buy some chips.'

'After that enormous breakfast?' Jack joked.

'That was hours ago, and we've walked miles. I wish we still lived around here, Jack. Apart from Railway Cottage, the happiest time of my life was spent in Coventry Street.'

Jack handed her a sixpence and Lizzie disappeared into the chip shop while he greeted his old employer with a friendly handshake. When he rejoined her she was sitting on a garden wall licking salt from her fingers.

'I've saved you some,' she said, and passed over a greasy newspaper parcel.

'Thanks. They smell good.'

'You've been a long time. What have you been talking about?'

Jack concentrated on eating for a few minutes before saying, 'I was telling George how you'd like to live around here again. Did you mean it, Lizzie?'

'Yes. I suppose we should have talked it over earlier, but the house at Patcham was where I lived with Tom. It has so many unhappy memories. I think I should sell it.'

'What about Mum and Eileen?' Jack asked thoughtfully.

'They must come with us. So we'll need somewhere quite large.'

'George was just saying there's a house in Chatsworth Road for sale. It's quite big – five bedrooms. It sounds interesting.'

'Where's Chatsworth Road?'

'Just around the corner. Number twenty-nine used to belong to a doctor and his family.'

'Let's go and have a look,' Lizzie said excitedly.

They found it in a few minutes, and stood on the pavement in front of a red-brick house with a deep porch and big bow windows. It had probably been built at the turn of the century, when families were large and people could afford space and quiet areas to live. There was coloured glass in the front door and a creeper climbing bravely up the wall. Lizzie liked it at once. She knew she could be happy living there.

'It's empty,' she said, peering through the curtainless windows.

'I'll go to the agent's tomorrow and get the keys.'

But Lizzie couldn't wait. She was off around the side of the house. There was a narrow alley leading to the back door which was blocked by a battered dustbin.

'The lock's broken,' she called over her shoulder. 'It will be easy to get in.'

'We ought to wait – come back tomorrow.'

'I can't wait. Come on! I want to see inside.'

The passage they found themselves in was dark and gloomy; but then they pushed open a door and found themselves in a big airy kitchen with old-fashioned fittings and a floor of red tiles. Jack looked doubtfully at the chipped butler-sink, but Lizzie was already out of the room, eager to inspect the three large reception rooms, and the back garden that boasted a small conservatory and a rusty swing.

Then they climbed a wide curving staircase with its newel post in the shape of an acorn. Upstairs they found three bedrooms and a spacious bathroom, and a narrow circular stair that wound up to the attics where there were two smaller rooms with tiny windows in the eaves and a view of the sea.

After exploring every nook and cranny they stood in the master bedroom and looked at each other.

'We can sleep in here,' Lizzie said. 'And your mother can have one of the rooms across the hall.'

'Eileen and Joey will want the little rooms in the roof,' Jack said. 'That leaves a spare room for visitors.'

'We may not have room for visitors,' Lizzie said with a secret smile. 'I want a child, Jack. Your child. I want us to be a real family.'

'So do I,' Jack answered.

Standing in the window with its view of the sea, Jack took Lizzie in his arms and kissed her. Around them the empty rooms settled comfortably as if making them welcome. As if they had been away a long time and had come home at last.

CHAPTER TWENTY-FIVE

A New Home

'What on earth are you doing, Lizzie?'

'Digging for victory, like they tell us to do on the wireless.'

Lizzie leaned on the handle of the heavy spade and grinned at Grace French's shocked face as she stood in the kitchen doorway wiping her hands on a tea-towel.

'You'll hurt yourself – or the baby. Put that spade down at once and come indoors, girl.'

'I wish you wouldn't fuss,' Lizzie said with a sigh. But she did as she was told and followed her mother-in-law into the kitchen.

'Now sit down and rest yourself while I make us a nice cup of tea.'

Grace busied herself at the cooker and Lizzie sank gratefully down on a chair by the table. Perhaps Grace was right; but although she was eight months pregnant she didn't feel ill. Just tired sometimes. But that was to be expected with the extra weight she had to carry around all the time.

Her wishes had come true, and she'd conceived during their two nights of passion at the boarding house before

Jack had returned to his regiment. She'd saved the good news until his next leave, which turned out to be only forty-eight hours.

'It's a good thing it is only two days,' Jack had said wryly, leaning on one elbow to look into Lizzie's flushed face after they'd spent the first night making love almost continually. Now that they were man and wife they couldn't get enough of each other and separations were increasingly painful.

'Why do you say that, Jack?'

'Because I don't want to harm our baby.'

'It's all right, you won't,' Lizzie had reassured him, holding out her arms. 'I asked the doctor and he said it won't do any harm, particularly as it's so early in the pregnancy. Anyway, I want you, darling.'

So he'd made love to her again, tenderly, showing all his love, and then, finally exhausted, they'd slept in each other's arms.

Lizzie missed Jack when his leave was over but luckily there was a lot to keep her busy, and Grace French had been a tower of strength. First there had been the sale of the house at Patcham and that had turned out to be more difficult than she'd expected.

With the war struggling into its fifth year people had more important things to think about than moving house, even those who could afford to, but at last a buyer had come forward, someone who wanted to move his family south thinking that Brighton was a safer place to live than London. So Lizzie had the money to buy the house they'd set their hearts on in Chatsworth Road, although sometimes she felt uncomfortable about using Tom's money to set up home with Jack.

Victor Grainger had stepped in and tried to set her conscience at rest. 'You were a good wife to my son,' he said, 'and he didn't deserve you. And Joey is Tom's boy and needs a happy home. I know you and Jack will give him one, so you must do what you want – with my blessing.'

So the move had taken place and Lizzie had never regretted it. She tried to make her new home as different as possible from the old one. The smart expensive furniture Tom had insisted on was sold with the house, and Lizzie toured the second-hand furniture shops for good old-fashioned pieces to grace the tall old rooms with their ornate mouldings and original fire-places decorated with coloured tiles.

The finished house was full of warmth and charm: antique pieces brushing shoulders with more modern ones. Nothing matched, but that was the way Lizzie liked it. There were plenty of cupboards and drawers for the children's clutter, although Grace still complained when they continued to leave things about. But she smiled at the same time. Lizzie was delighted to see that she'd put on weight and looked more relaxed – in fact she looked more like the Grace French she'd first known.

Even so, Grace thought Lizzie had gone mad when a furniture-van drew up outside the house one morning to deliver a piano. 'I'm sorry,' she'd said firmly to the driver. 'You must have come to the wrong address.'

'Number twenty-nine?' the driver asked, taking off his cap and scratching his balding head.

'That's right.'

'Name of French?'

'Yes – but there must be some mistake.'

'It's all right.' Lizzie pushed past Grace and beckoned the driver and his mate. 'You've come to the right place. Can you carry it down the passage, please? It's to go in the drawing-room between the French windows.'

Grace waited until they were alone and then she looked at the instrument with a puzzled frown. Lizzie had opened the lid and was running her fingers over the ivory keys. 'I didn't know you could play,' she said at last.

'I can't.'

'Then why …?'

'It's for Billy – my brother. I told you he could play the piano. Mum taught him before she died. His favourite piece was called "The March of the Gladiators".' She hummed a few bars dreamily. 'I promised Dad I'd look after Billy – but somehow I lost him. But I'm going to find him again someday. The piano is for him.'

'How old would he be now, Lizzie?' Grace inquired gently.

'Twenty-one.'

'Do you think you'll recognise him after all these years?'

'Of course I will. He's my brother and we were always very close.'

But Lizzie's eyes had filled with tears because sometimes she wondered if she would know Billy if she passed him in the street. He'd be a man now, and when she'd last seen him he'd been a little boy.

So the piano stood waiting for Billy Sargent to come and claim it, polished and tuned regularly, keeping Lizzie's hopes alive.

It was Jack's mother who saw the advert in the paper.

> To whom it may concern. If anyone knows the whereabouts of Elizabeth Mary Sargent (Grainger) and William Sargent, will they please notify the firm of Butler, Mason and Kent. Solicitors.

'There's a telephone number,' Grace prompted when she showed it to Lizzie. 'Why don't you phone now?'

Lizzie guessed what it was about. It must be something to do with Aunt Hannah. She'd probably died in the nursing home and they were trying to trace her relatives. Lizzie had already received her unexpected legacy in a cardboard suitcase but her aunt had always said the bulk of her fortune would go to Billy, so she supposed the solicitors hoped she would know where he was.

'What's the point in my phoning?' Lizzie asked. 'I don't know where Billy is – I only wish I did.'

'I still think you should contact them. Your aunt might not be dead, you know. She might be feeling better and asking for you.'

'That's true, I hadn't thought of that.'

So Lizzie dialled the number. She was put through by the operator and was soon speaking to a receptionist who told her that Mr Mason, who dealt with Mrs Seymour's affairs, would be very pleased to hear from her. An appointment was made for her to visit his office the following day.

So once again Lizzie found herself in the town of Greenlock.

The surprise came not when a business-like Mr Mason informed her that her aunt had indeed passed away, peacefully and in her sleep, but when he told Lizzie her aunt must have been aware of her imminent demise because she'd changed her Will only days before. Instead of naming Billy sole heir, her house and belongings were to be sold and the money divided equally between her niece Elizabeth and nephew William.

'But what made her change her mind?' Lizzie couldn't help asking.

Mr Mason polished his spectacles and smiled. 'I understand that you visited her in the nursing-home,' he said. 'She was quite impressed by you, and I think she felt guilty for not helping you earlier. Of course, she was a very proud woman so wouldn't admit it. Have you any idea of the whereabouts of your brother William?'

Lizzie shook her head. 'What will happen if he can't be found, Mr Mason?'

'We will open a trust fund and the money will earn interest while we continue our inquiries. We will advertise at home and abroad until we find out whether William is alive or dead.'

Lizzie shuddered. 'He's alive, Mr Mason. I don't know why I'm so sure, but I just know he's alive.'

'I wish I was as convinced as you are, Mrs French. In the meantime you will receive a cheque for …' and he named a sum that made Lizzie stagger. 'Mrs Seymour was quite a wealthy woman, you know.'

Lizzie had travelled back to Brighton in a dream. Aunt Hannah had finally relented and treated her more than fairly. She was now financially comfortable, even without the money she'd inherited from Tom and her income from the salon. Joey would never have to worry about money, and neither would Billy when she found him.

But there was still somebody on Lizzie's conscience, and one of the first things she did was send a large cheque to Rose. It was intended for the care and upkeep of Willy, and to give her friend security so that she wouldn't have to worry about money ever again. Perhaps, Lizzie hoped, Rose would settle down and give up her old dangerous ways, although somehow she doubted it. Rose Harrison had liked her way of life and was probably too old to change. But at least Willy would be safe.

Lizzie never received a reply from her old friend; but the cheque was cashed and that was enough. She didn't want thanks.

'What are you thinking about, Lizzie?' Grace asked, leaning across the table to refill her cup.

'The past,' Lizzie replied with a smile, 'and the future.'

'I'll get Joey to finish that digging in the garden. He's a big strong lad even if he is as thin as a rake. Where's he gone? He's not with my Eileen, I know. She's gone out with her girlfriends.'

'He's gone with his grandfather to help out at Grainger's.'

'What, again?'

'He loves it, Grace. He can't wait to leave school and spend every day there.'

'Funny job for a young lad.' Grace sniffed her disapproval. 'Serving behind a counter and measuring people for trousers.'

Lizzie laughed. 'Someone has to do it.'

'I suppose so.'

'And he gets pocket money for helping; that's part of the attraction. His grandfather says Joey's very useful, and he loves showing him off to customers.'

'I still think it's not a career for the young. There's someone coming in now – Joey by the sound of it. He can't do anything quietly.' Grace opened the back door and peered down the side path into the street. 'Mr Grainger's car's outside. I don't know where he gets the petrol from. Most people have hidden their cars away in their garages until the war ends, but not Mr Grainger – oh no!' and she tutted disapprovingly.

'Hi, Mum. Hi, Auntie Grace. Grandpa's just coming in.' Joey bounced into the room, his cap at a rakish angle and his eyes sparkling. 'I'm starving – is tea ready yet?'

'Not yet young man,' Grace said. 'Help yourself to biscuits from the barrel. I was going to make a cake but your mum and I got talking.'

'Did you have a good time, Joey?' Lizzie asked.

'It was super. I've been helping Mr Pargeter. Can I have six biscuits, Auntie Grace?' Joey turned from the biscuit barrel with his hands full.

'Don't fill yourself up and then pick at your tea,' Lizzie warned. 'And take your cap off in the house.'

'You sound just like Grandad.' Joey grinned and crammed a whole biscuit into his mouth. 'Mr Pargeter wouldn't let me stop for lunch because we had to clear the stock-room out. He bought me a bar of chocolate though with his own money and sweet coupons.'

'I thought Mr Pargeter was off sick. Didn't he have a bad back or something?' Lizzie asked.

'That's *Old* Mr Pargeter,' Joey said. 'I'm talking about *Young* Mr Pargeter.'

'You mean Mr Pargeter's son?'

'That's right.'

Lizzie thought back and remembered Mr Pargeter, Grainger's caretaker, talking about a son. He'd spoken with pride, and like her father-in-law had plans for the young man's future. She'd never met the lad but he must be in his twenties now.

'Hasn't he been called up?' she asked, suddenly interested. 'Or is he home on leave?'

'He was in the RAF but he had something wrong with his ears so they invalided him out. He's a Warden now, and belongs to the Home Guard. He's very disappointed that he can't fly planes any more.'

'He must be.'

'He's ever so nice. Talks to me just as if I'm as grown up as he is and not a kid. I had to do the interesting things like climbing up the step-ladder to clear the top shelves. Young Mr Pargeter said he couldn't have managed without me because if he climbs his bad ear makes him dizzy.' Joey related this information with pride.

'I'm glad you're making yourself useful,' Lizzie said, and then, when she saw her son's hand reach towards the biscuit-barrel again, added, 'Don't eat any more. You've had enough.'

'But, Mum...'

'Do what your mother says, lad,' and there was Victor Grainger standing in the doorway, a big grin on his plump pink face and his white moustache bristling. 'You've behaved well all day; don't spoil it now.'

Joey smiled sheepishly. 'Young Mr Pargeter said I was a great help to him. He said he couldn't have managed without me.'

'I said you were going to be an asset to the firm,' Victor

said, accepting a cup of tea from Grace French. 'Just a quick one then. Mustn't be late or Frances will be fretting.'

'How is she?' Lizzie inquired.

'Not too bad.'

Frances Grainger's health had been a source of worry ever since Tom's violent death. He'd been her whole life for so long that even Joey couldn't fill the empty place in her heart. She liked Lizzie and didn't blame her, but her nerves had suffered and she had bad days as well as good ones.

'Tomorrow Young Mr Pargeter is going to let me paint the stock-room ceiling,' Joey said proudly.

'Who said anything about tomorow?' Lizzie said with a smile.

'I can go tomorrow, can't I, Grandpa?' Joey asked with a worried look on his face.

'If your mother agrees.'

'I can, can't I, Mum? Young Mr Pargeter will be expecting me.'

'I suppose so,' Lizzie replied. School didn't re-open until the following week and at least if Joey was at Grainger's with his grandfather he'd be out of trouble. She turned to Victor Grainger. 'And what's all this about "Young Mr Pargeter"? Hasn't he got a proper name?'

Victor laughed. 'I knew it once: when he was a slip of a lad and came to the shop with his dad. Jimmy I think it was – but it's a long time ago – I may have forgotten. Now what about your wages, Joey? I told you to remind me.'

Joey looked up eagerly and caught the spinning coin his grandfather tossed in his direction. 'Gosh!' he said. 'Half-a-crown. Thanks, Grandpa.'

After Victor Grainger had left, the women started to prepare the evening meal. It was sausages and tinned beans, served with a helping of mashed potatoes. While the sausages were sizzling in the pan, Grace sent Joey outside to continue the digging his mother had started. After a few minutes, raised voices alerted her. She looked out of the kitchen window to see what was amiss.

'It's Joey and Eileen,' she reported over her shoulder to Lizzie. 'They're arguing about something.'

'That's unusual.'

'They usually get on so well. I wonder what it's about. Come in, you two,' she called. 'The sausages are just about cooked. And don't forget to wash your hands.'

Joey and Eileen trooped into the kitchen. They both looked sullen and argumentative. But they were hungry and soon tucked into the food, until Joey passed the bottle of OK sauce and accidentally jogged Eileen's elbow so that a brown sticky stream splashed on to the tablecloth. She scowled.

'You did that on purpose.'

'I didn't.'

'Yes you did. Say you're sorry.'

'I won't. So there.'

'Stop it, you two,' Lizzie interrupted. 'Whatever is the matter with you both?'

'Nothing,' Joey said, but his ears gave him away. They went quite red which was always a sign that he was either angry or upset.

Mrs French turned to her daughter. 'What's the matter, Eileen? Come on, out with it.'

'Joey doesn't keep his promises,' Eileen muttered. She put down her knife and fork as if she'd lost her appetite. 'He promised to come blackberrying with me tomorrow, to the copse, and now he's going to the shop with his grandad instead.'

'I forgot,' Joey protested. 'We can go blackberrying any old time.'

'But I wanted to go tomorrow.'

'Well, Young Mr Pargeter wants me to paint his ceiling; that's more important.'

Eileen picked up her fork again and thoughtfully scooped up some beans. Then she looked at Joey slyly. 'All right then, I'll come with you and help you paint the ceiling.'

Joey looked horrified. 'You can't do that.'

'Why not? I can paint just as well as you.'

'But Grandpa hasn't asked you. And it's a man's shop; girls aren't allowed.'

'Why not?'

Eileen looked near to tears so Lizzie thought it was time to intervene. 'I'll take you blackberrying tomorrow, Eileen,' she said. 'If you really want to go.'

'Will you?'

'Yes. That's a promise.'

'At least your mum will keep her promise,' Eileen said archly to Joey. But she seemed to have forgiven him because they went off together to play Snakes and Ladders quite amicably.

Grace turned to Lizzie when they were on their own again. 'Do you think it's wise, Lizzie?'

'What?' Lizzie was busily rinsing plates under the cold tap and then stacking them to be washed.

'Going blackberrying.'

'I go every year. You'd better find some empty jars, and see if there's enough sugar left to make jam.'

'Do you think it wise in your condition, I mean?'

Lizzie ran her hands over the large lump protruding under her apron and smiled. 'It can't do any harm and I promise to be careful. We'll take the bus up Dyke Road and then the copse is a gentle downhill walk. Eileen can do the bending and stretching and I'll just do the easy picking and carry the basket. Then we'll catch the bus back.'

'What if there's an air-raid?'

'They'll be aiming at the town, not the open countryside. Anyway there haven't been any raids for ages. Don't worry, Grace.'

'Well, I still don't like it…'

But Lizzie wouldn't be swayed. She felt strong and healthy and her pregnancy wasn't a burden. The baby wasn't due for another month, and the thought of a day in the open air picking berries for home-made jam was very attractive.

Grace French was still worried, about bombs and babies, and an unexplained fear about something she couldn't put her finger on. She just knew, as she tossed and turned in her bed that night, that she would be glad when the next day was over and her fears proved to be groundless.

But Lizzie slept peacefully. She dreamed that the war was over, Jack was home, and the baby safely born. She woke up smiling. Although it had only been a dream the joy stayed with her and when she looked out of the window at the new day and saw the sun shining and the blue sky with just a scattering of fluffy white clouds, she wanted to sing.

She washed and dressed quickly, and then went to wake Joey. Victor Grainger was calling for him early and would be impatient if he was kept waiting.

Joey slept curled up like a snail under the lightweight summer quilt. He was a handsome boy, and his long dark lashes fanned his cheek, and his hair, even with its quiff, lay sleek and silky against his small neat head.

Lizzie thought it a shame to disturb him, but she put out her hand and shook his shoulder gently. 'Joey, wake up. It's nearly half-past.'

Joey groaned and sat up, sleepily rubbing his eyes. He smiled when he saw his mother, and then lay down again as if he was going back to sleep.

'Joey, you must get up and have your breakfast. You don't want to keep your grandfather waiting, do you?'

'Grandpa! I'm going to the shop with him, aren't I?'

'Yes.'

'I'd almost forgotten. I'm going to paint the ceiling for

Young Mr Pargeter. I'd better hurry.' Suddenly wide awake, Joey leaped out of bed and reached for his clothes.

'Don't forget to wash.'

Laughing at her son's eagerness, Lizzie left the room to see if Eileen was awake.

The young girl was lying on her back, her big blue eyes wide open as she watched the sunlight flickering through the branches of a tree outside her bedroom window. She was growing into a pretty young woman. Her curly red hair fanned around her head, and her white skin was sprinkled with freckles like fairy-dust. As a child she'd been plump, but now the puppy-fat was a thing of the past and she had the beginnings of a bust and a shapely figure.

'Is it time to get up, Lizzie?'

'Yes. Joey's up already.'

'We are going blackberrying, aren't we?'

'Of course. I promised, didn't I?'

Downstairs, Grace French already had the kettle boiling and they were soon all gathered around the table drinking tea and eating toast spread with margarine. Eileen and Joey were friends again, and when Victor Grainger called for his grandson, on foot as even he had run out of petrol, they parted amicably.

'We'll have another game of Snakes and Ladders tonight,' Joey promised.

'All right. This time I'll beat you,' Eileen laughed.

By mid-morning Lizzie and Eileen were ready to leave. They both wore summer frocks although it was early September, but took cardigans in case it turned chilly. Lizzie carried an open basket over her arm for the fruit. She also had a bottle of cold tea to quench their thirst, and a packet of biscuits because Eileen was a growing girl and permanently hungry.

They boarded a bus and sat on the lower deck because Lizzie didn't feel like climbing the steep stairs. The sun was warm on their faces as they were transported up Dyke Road, past the park whose green lawns had been dug up and converted into allotments to help the war effort. In the distance they could see the sea glinting blue and silver. It could have been any summer's day, and if you closed your eyes you could have forgotten that there was still a war on.

When they disembarked they found they weren't the only ones out to take advantage of the free fruit. Whole families were gathered in the copse stripping the bushes of their purple offerings. Some had come armed with baskets, like Lizzie, but many made do with paper-bags, or even jam-jars with string handles. But there was plenty for all, and a spirit of comradeship enveloped everyone.

Someone started to sing 'Sonny Boy' and soon others joined in: men, women and children. And then it was 'With a Song in my Heart', followed by 'Beyond the Blue Horizon'. Everyone felt safe on that glorious day, with the sun shining down out of a cloudless sky and a feeling of friendship surrounding them.

It was a small boy who saw the planes first: three of them, flying high above the town towards the Channel. 'They're Jerry planes,' he shouted excitedly. 'I can tell.'

'I didn't hear a siren,' someone else said, carrying on picking. Planes overhead were an everyday occurrence and people were used to them.

'We wouldn't hear the warning out here,' somebody else ventured.

'I can see a bomb dropping,' a woman shouted hysterically. 'Take cover, everyone!'

'We're safe,' a man's voice called. 'They shed their load before going home. They'll aim at the town; probably the railway line. We're safe enough out here.'

'We might be safe but what about people in the town?' thought Lizzie, remembering that Joey had gone in to work with his grandfather. She wanted to get home as quickly as possible. A panicky feeling began to spread through her.

They watched another bomb dropping down and the distant thud of explosions before the planes flew away towards France, getting smaller and smaller until they were no bigger than toys.

'They've gone.'

Everyone breathed a sigh of relief but few people wanted to carry on with their picking. The magic had gone out of the day and they all wanted to head for home to make sure their friends and families were safe and their houses still standing.

'We're going home now,' Lizzie said to Eileen. 'We've got enough, and I have to make sure everything's all right at home.'

'I can see some really big ones further down,' Eileen argued. 'Just let me pick those.'

'Leave them for someone else,' Lizzie said. 'We just have time to get the bus. I don't want to have to wait for the next one.'

'But …' Eileen was just going to argue. Then she saw Lizzie's face, pale and worried, and changed her mind. 'All right. I'll carry the basket. You can take my arm if you're tired.'

Silently they retraced their steps and were soon riding back towards the town. Everyone was asking where the bombs had dropped and if any house had been damaged, but no one knew any details. It was a relief when they turned into Chatsworth Road and found everything looking normal. Lizzie let out a long sigh: her fears had been without foundation.

Grace was folding newly washed sheets ready for ironing. She smiled with relief when she saw the wanderers safely home.

'I found some empty jars,' she told them. 'And I've managed to get some extra sugar. How many blackberries did you get?'

'Pounds and pounds,' Eileen told her mother. 'I was ever so careful so they shouldn't need picking over.'

'Wash them and put them to cook then,' Grace said. 'But mind the washing: we don't want purple stains all over the sheets.'

'Is Joey back yet?' Lizzie asked as she lit the gas.

'Not yet. But it's still early and they're on foot. Don't worry, Lizzie, Mr Grainger will make sure Joey gets home safely.'

'I know,' Lizzie said. 'But I can't help worrying.'

'We saw the planes and the bombs dropping,' Eileen said excitedly. 'Do you know where they fell, Mum?'

'No idea. We'll ask Mr Grainger – he's sure to know.'

The time crept on, and when it passed six o'clock Lizzie began to panic. 'They should be back by now even if they're walking. Something *must* have happened.'

'No news is good news,' Grace said calmly, although she was also beginning to feel apprehensive. 'Calm down, Lizzie, and test that jam. It looks as if it's at setting point.'

Lizzie dipped a spoon into the mixture and poured it on to a cold saucer. A skin formed almost immediately. 'It's ready,' she announced. 'Hold the jars for me, Eileen.'

Her hand wasn't quite steady as she poured the jam, and when she looked at the clock and saw that another half-hour had passed and Joey still wasn't home she had to fight down a feeling of fear.

'What can have happened, Grace?' she asked.

'I don't know, Lizzie. Why don't you go upstairs and lie down? I'll let you know at once if there's any news.'

'I can't,' Lizzie said, pacing up and down. 'I wouldn't get a moment's peace. I'll just go outside and see if they're coming.'

'Don't go far,' Grace warned.

'I'll just go to the corner.' She didn't take a cardigan because she didn't intend going far, but when she reached the crossroads and there was still no sign of Joey and his grandfather, Lizzie decided to walk a little further towards the Seven Dials. That was the most direct way home.

'Are you all right, Mrs French?'

Lizzie hadn't seen the woman approaching. It was a neighbour, but one she didn't know very well. 'I'm fine,' she said, trying to smile.

'I should go home if I were you. You shouldn't be out on your own in your condition.'

'I just needed a breath of air.'

'Terrible about the bomb, isn't it? Landed right on a shop in the town centre. Near the Clock Tower, so I heard. People trapped in the rubble ... Where are you off to?'

But Lizzie was running. She surprised herself at how fast she could run with the bulk of the baby to carry. She had to know the worst. Grainger's was near the Clock Tower, and Joey had spent the day there and hadn't come home. In her mind's eye Lizzie pictured him lying crushed under fallen masonry, calling for her. 'I'm coming, Joey,' she panted as she ran. 'Don't worry – I'm coming.'

The road had been closed to traffic, but bystanders stood in groups watching the rescuers at work. The frontage of the shop and the neighbouring salon were still standing but a Warden told Lizzie to keep well away. The bomb had dropped on a house directly behind, destroying an adjoining wall, so that the back area of Grainger's had collapsed into the basement like a pack of cards. Joey had been working in the stock-room – and that was in the basement.

'Joey!' Lizzie shouted, pushing her way through the milling crowd. 'Joey!'

'Get back, lady. They're doing the best they can.'

'But my little boy's in there. I must get him out.'

'They won't let you near; it's too dangerous.'

And then Lizzie saw Victor Grainger walking slowly towards her. He looked old and his face was grey with fatigue and brick-dust. She ran to him.

'Where's Joey?'

'He's trapped in the basement, my dear. With Mr Pargeter's son. They're doing all they can to get them out.' He put his arms around Lizzie and held her tightly.

CHAPTER TWENTY-SIX

Two Silver Joeys

'You look much too smart to wield a paint-brush, Joey. I'll have to find you something more suitable to wear.'

Joey looked at Young Mr Pargeter and grinned. He was dressed in a cotton shirt, tie and grey trousers. 'I never thought,' he said.

Mr Pargeter looked much more workmanlike in a navy-blue boiler suit, a one-piece garment with a zip-fastener up the front.

'Wait there a minute and I'll see what I can find.'

Joey looked around the stock-room which was cleared of goods and ready for redecoration. The shelves were empty, and there were just some boxes and metal clothes racks stacked in one corner. In the middle of the floor stood a step-ladder and some tins of paint and brushes. Joey tested the bristles on the biggest brush; he couldn't wait to start work.

Young Mr Pargeter came back. He was a tall, handsome young man, with light brown hair and clear grey eyes. He was gentle and kind and Joey loved being allowed to work with him. He held out a white cotton garment to the boy.

'Here you are. Try these overalls on for size. The sleeves and legs will be too long but you can roll them up. I should take that tie off if I were you, and loosen your shirt. You'll be more comfortable.'

Joey was so eager he was all fingers and thumbs. 'Can you help me?' he asked.

Young Mr Pargeter's fingers were nimble and he soon removed the boy's tie and undid the top button of his shirt. 'There, that's better. What's this you're wearing around the neck?'

'It's a silver threepenny piece,' Joey said. 'I wear it for luck. I don't know whether it works or not.'

Mr Pargeter laughed. 'It does, I assure you,' he said, and unzipping the top of his boiler suit he pulled out an identical coin. 'I've worn one for years. I found it on the beach when I was a boy, younger even than you, and I've worn it ever since.'

'My mum gave me mine,' Joey said. 'The day I started school. She called it a lucky Joey. She said she didn't need it as well as me, because I'm her lucky Joey.'

'Your mum sounds nice,' Young Mr Pargeter said.

'She is. She's the best mum in the world.'

'Take care of her then, lad. My mum's dead and I still miss her. But my lucky Joey found me a new mum and dad, almost as good as the real ones.'

'Isn't Old Mr Pargeter your dad then?'

'No - but don't let on to him that I've told you. He likes people to think he is.'

'I won't say a word,' Joey promised. 'Isn't it exciting?'

'What?'

'You not really being Old Pargeter's son. Like me. My dad's name's Jack French, and he's not my really true dad either. I didn't like my real dad; he was cruel and unkind to my mum. I was glad when he died.'

'Don't say that.'

'All right – but I can't help thinking it. What's your real name, Mr Pargeter?'

'Most people think of me as Jimmy. There was a son called Jimmy who died, you see. I've sort of taken his place.'

'I didn't mean that …'

'I know you didn't. You can call me Bill if you want to, young Joey.'

'All right, Bill.'

'And now we'd better get on with some work or we'll have your grandad after us.' Bill opened the steps and made sure they were safe. Then Joey, clad in his work-manlike overalls, climbed to the top and Bill handed up the paint and brush. 'Now take it slowly. Don't put too much paint on the bristles or it'll drip. Here, wear this old cap to cover your hair. That's fine. You all right up there?'

'I'm fine, Bill,' Joey called down. 'What are you going to do?'

'I'm going to make a start on the walls. Tell me if you get tired.'

Joey nodded, but he was enjoying himself so much he didn't think he'd ever get tired. There was something so satisfying slapping away with a brush and seeing the dingy ceiling transformed until it was shining white. It was a bit streaky in places but that was all to the good, an excuse to give it a second coat.

'Grandad wants me to come into the business when I leave school,' he confided to his new friend. 'But I may decide to be a painter and decorator instead.'

'If you do, you'll be a good one,' Bill said. 'You're certainly making a good job of that ceiling.'

Bill Pargeter had brought a flask of hot tea with him so they stopped work mid-morning and shared it, sitting side by side on the boxes and chatting about this and that. Joey told Bill about his mum and his Auntie Grace who lived with them, and about his best friend Eileen who was his auntie's daughter and the same age as himself.

Bill, in his turn, told Joey about his life in the little house off Elm Grove. How he missed the Air Force, but how he liked his job as a Warden.

'I like music,' he confided. 'We have a little harmonium, but it's very old and some of the keys don't work properly. I'm saving up to buy a piano but they cost a lot of money.'

Joey thought of the piano sitting forlornly between the French windows in their drawing-room. His mum had bought it for her long-lost brother, but sometimes Joey wondered if he would ever be found. Perhaps Mum would let him bring his new friend home for a visit and let him play a tune for them. He'd suggest it that evening and see what she said. It seemed silly to have a piano when there was no one who could play it.

Bill decided that they deserved a break at mid-day. 'I bet you're hungry?' he called up to Joey.

'I am a bit,' Joey admitted. 'I should have brought some sandwiches.'

'I'll pop out and get us some bread and cheese. Want to come with me?'

'I think I'll just stay and finish this bit.' Joey didn't want to stop until he'd finished the first coat. He'd rest then and start the second coat that afternoon.

'Rightio. Won't be long. Mind you don't fall off the ladder.'

Joey grinned. What did Bill think he was – a kid? But he could see by the wink they exchanged that he was only joking.

Bill ran up the basement stairs two at a time and walked through the shop. It was quiet at that time of day and he stopped to exchange a few words with one of the assistants before hurrying through the front door into the sunny street. He bought a crusty loaf of bread and some cheese. The grocer slipped him a tin of Spam and they winked like conspirators. At least Joey wouldn't go hungry after his morning's work.

He'd almost completed the return journey, and was

only a few yards away from Grainger's, when the first plane droned overhead. Bill looked up idly, not hearing a siren, and saw the sun glinting silver on the wings. Then a second plane appeared and he saw the bomb.

'Take shelter!' he yelled at passers-by. Everyone threw themselves into doorways or on to the ground.

Bill sprinted for Grainger's. He'd just made it through the door when the bomb struck. There was a loud explosion and the whole building shook with the impact. The back wall caved in, sending clothes-racks tumbling and shirts and trousers flying across the floor in the blast. Hats rolled everywhere: panamas, top-hats and trilbys, spinning on their brims in a wild dance. One hat, a brave straw with a ribbon band, tried to trip Bill up, before careering away across the shop floor and teetering a moment on the top step before somersaulting down into the basement. The basement, where he'd left Joey innocently working only a short time before!

'Joey!' Bill took the steps four at a time. 'Joey!'

The light was still on in the stock-room and he could hear a high boyish whistling. Joey obviously hadn't been aware of the explosion over his head, the thick walls protecting him from the vibration. But he must have heard Bill's warning shouts because there was a sudden silence as if he was holding his breath. Then the silence was broken by a terrible rumbling as part of the roof caved in, filling the basement cellar with broken masonry and brick-dust.

Bill stood aghast, wiping his eyes on his sleeve to clear his vision. Where once Joey had been working there was now only a pile of debris.

'Joey, where are you?' Frantically Bill pulled away part of a door that, ripped from its hinges, had plunged down from the floor above. 'Joey – if you can hear me call out.'

Bill's hands were soon torn and bleeding, but he couldn't, wouldn't, give in. He'd grown fond of Joey, as fond of him as if he were his own flesh and blood. If the boy was still alive he was going to find him and get him out. The basement was now in darkness because the lights had blown and he had to feel his way, slowly, inch by inch, dreading what he might find crushed under the broken stones.

'Bill! Is that you, Bill?'

The voice was so small and weak that at first he thought he was imagining things, but he stopped and listened, and then it came again, a young boy's voice, full of fear.

'Bill – is that you?'

'Yes, Joey. Don't be afraid. I'm going to get you out.'

'I'm not frightened, Bill. Not now you're here.' Guided by the small voice Bill edged his way across the floor, but when he reached Joey's side a thrill of fear went through him. 'I can't move, Bill,' Joey said.

Using his hands to explore, Bill soon found out why Joey couldn't move. He was lying on the floor where he'd been thrown and was pinned down by a slab of concrete that had fallen across his legs.

'Lie still, Joey, don't try to move.'

'What are you going to do, Bill?'

'I don't know yet. Can you feel your legs?'

'I think so – they hurt. But I can't move them.'

'I'm going to try and lift this piece of masonry off you. It's very heavy so I may be able to lift it only a few inches. Then see if you can pull your legs clear.'

'All right.'

'That's a brave boy.'

'I'm not brave,' Joey said matter-of-factly. 'I just know everything will be all right because my silver joey will protect me. You've got one as well, Bill, so we'll both be safe.'

Bill wished he could be as trusting, but there wasn't time to ponder on the merits of the lucky coins. He had to work fast in case there were going to be other falls of rock from above. Putting his hands under the stone block he tried to lift it. He thought he'd succeeded when he managed to raise it a few inches off Joey's legs.

'Try to wriggle free, Joey,' he instructed.

'I can't.'

'You must try.'

'My leg won't move. I think it's broken.'

'Lie still then. I'll try to wriggle underneath and lift the slab off you.'

It was all he could do. Inch by inch Bill crawled under the stone slab until he managed to take the weight on his shoulders. He froze in that position, not daring to move further, lest it topple back and crush the boy completely. In the silence that followed they could hear each other's breathing: Joey's quick and light, Bill's deep and laboured with the weight he was carrying.

Joey spoke first. 'Do you think they'll find us?'

'Of course they will – any moment now. We must both be very patient.'

'Shall we call out?'

'That's a good idea, Joey.'

They shouted at the tops of their voices but the sound just seemed to vibrate around the walls and echo back at them.

'They can't hear us, Bill.'

Hearing the quaver in Joey's voice, Bill tried to think of some way of distracting him. 'Do you like stories, Joey?' he asked.

'Yes.'

'Shall I tell you one to pass the time until we're rescued?'

'Yes, please.'

Bill thought quickly but he could only remember one story – a special story he'd liked when he was a boy. 'Once upon a time,' he started, 'there were twenty-five tin soldiers ...'

'I know that story.' Joey's voice came out of the dark. 'My mum tells it to me. It's called "The Steadfast Tin

Soldier". It's about the adventures of a brave one-legged soldier who falls out of the nursery window and gets swallowed by a fish.'

'That's right,' Bill said. 'My sister used to tell me that story when I was a boy. She said I had to learn to be brave like that toy soldier and then everything would be all right.'

'And were you brave? And was everything all right?'

'I tried to be brave, Joey, but I was only a little boy and it was hard. Things never got completely right because I lost my sister – I still miss her.'

'That's sad,' Joey said.

'Yes, but I tried to be brave, and that's what we have to be now; brave and steadfast, until we're rescued.'

'And we will be rescued,' Joey said firmly. 'Because we've both got lucky silver threepenny pieces. Shall we shout some more?'

'If you like,' Bill said. His back was hurting with the weight of the stone slab.

They shouted some more and then Joey said, 'I'm tired of shouting – let's try a song.'

'I don't know any songs.'

'Then a tune. Let's whistle a tune, Bill, to show we're brave.'

Bill could think of only one tune: a march he liked to play on Mr Pargeter's old harmonium. He started to whistle and was surprised when Joey joined in, high and shrill with clear boyish tones.

'That's called "The March of the Gladiators",' Joey said proudly when they reached the end. 'Mum says her little brother Billy used to play it on their piano. He loved that march. She's bought a piano so that when she finds him again he'll be able to play it for her.'

There was a silence, and then Bill asked in an odd voice, 'What's your mum's name, Joey?'

'Mrs French – she used to be Mrs Grainger, like me; but now she's married to Jack she's Mrs French.'

'I meant her Christian name. What's your mum's Christian name?'

'It's Elizabeth really – but everyone who doesn't call her Mrs French calls her Lizzie.'

Bill let out a long sigh. Joey asked, 'Are you all right, Bill?'

'Yes, Joey. I'm all right,' came the answer. Joey wondered why his friend suddenly sounded so excited. 'More than all right. Do you know the first thing I want to do when we get out of here?'

'No.'

'I want to meet your mum.'

'She'll like that,' Joey said. 'She'll want to meet you to thank you for rescuing me.'

'That's not why I want to meet her.' Bill thought carefully before adding, 'I want to meet her because I'm sure she's my sister.'

'The one that you lost?'

'Yes. Her name was Lizzie. She had dark brown hair and eyes.'

'So you must be ...'

'I'm Billy – the brother who likes Hans Christian Andersen stories and played "The March of the Gladiators" on the piano.'

'But you're a man,' Joey said in wonder.

'I've grown up, Joey. I'm your Uncle Bill now; and we're going to get out of here, so take a deep breath and start shouting.'

With renewed gusto they shouted at the top of their voices and were rewarded when an answering hail came from above. 'We know you're down there. Don't worry, we'll soon get you out.'

This turned out to be easier said than done. The sudden removal of any piece of masonry could start an avalanche of bricks and plaster, enough to fill the basement and crush Joey and Bill to death. So the job was long and painstaking, but when the first flicker of light penetrated their prison they felt like cheering.

'Won't be long now,' Bill said in what he hoped was encouraging tones. He prayed that his back and shoulders would hold out.

'Does your shoulder hurt, Bill?'

'A bit - but not more than your leg, I shouldn't think.'

'We're coming down,' a voice called from above, and two feet and legs appeared clad in navy blue, and then a reassuringly broad chest, and a cheerful face topped by a tin hat. 'There's a doctor on his way down,' this welcome apparition told them. 'Now, which of you's hurt?'

'The lad,' Bill said. 'His name's Joey.'

'What about you, young man? You look as if you're at the end of your tether. Let me give you a hand,' and the warden leaned over to help take the weight of the plaster beam.

'No!' Bill said quickly. 'See to the boy first. He's my nephew. I can hold on a bit longer.'

A doctor came next, with his dark suit covered with a film of dust and a tin hat protecting his bald head. He quickly confirmed that Joey's leg was broken and made a temporary splint from a wooden beam, strapping the limb in place with a torn scarf. Only then did he and the warden gently move Joey from under the beam. Then, as helping hands carried him safely to the surface, Bill was able to let go of his burden.

'You all right, mate?' the warden asked as he saw Bill stretch his aching limbs with difficulty.

'A bit sore,' he admitted.

'We're taking the boy to the hospital to have his leg set. You'd better come as well.'

'I'm all right.'

'Better to be on the safe side. They'll just want to check you over.'

They'd placed Joey gently on a stretcher and when Bill stepped forward to lift one end he was waved away. 'You all right, Joey?' he asked softly.

'Yes,' Joey said. 'I feel like one of those Indian princes.'
He tried to sit up so that he could wave in a royal fashion
but he was told to keep still or he would be tipped off on
to the ground. The bystanders let out a cheer when they
saw his grinning face and knew he was safe. Then he saw
a face in the crowd that he knew and let out a yell. 'Mum!'

'Joey!'

Lizzie was struggling with a policeman who was trying
to control the crowd.

'Keep back, lady,' the policeman was saying. 'Or I'll
have to arrest you.'

'But that's my son. I thought he was dead. Let me go to
my son!'

'Your son, eh? That's different,' and he let go of Lizzie's
arm so that she could run forward to meet the stretcher.

'Joey – are you hurt?'

'I've broken my leg, Mum. They're taking me to
hospital to put some plaster on it so that I can walk.'

'Oh, darling, I'm so sorry. I should never have let you go
with your grandfather.'

'But, Mum,' and Joey looked at Lizzie and his eyes were
sparkling, 'if I hadn't gone with Grandpa I'd never have
found him for you.'

'Found who? What are you talking about?'

'Billy. I've found Billy for you! The little brother you lost.
Only he's not a little boy any more and he likes to be
called Bill now.'

Lizzie looked into Joey's shining eyes and immediately
decided he must be running a temperature and should be
humoured. 'If you say so,' she said.

'And he's got a silver threepenny just like the one you
gave me – and he still remembers "The Steadfast Tin
Soldier". And we sang "The March of the Gladiators" until
we were rescued; and I've told him you bought him a
piano.'

'Oh, Joey,' Lizzie said, 'you mustn't make up stories.'

'I'm not,' Joey said indignantly.

Victor Grainger suddenly appeared beside them. 'Thank God the boy's safe!' he said. 'I've been almost out of my mind.'

'He's all right,' Lizzie said. 'Only a broken leg. That'll mend – but he's imagining the most strange things.'

'What things?'

'He thinks he's found my lost brother.'

'I have found him,' came an indignant voice from the direction of the stretcher. 'Here he comes now.'

Lizzie and Victor turned to look where Joey was pointing. They saw a tall young man striding towards them. His hair was light brown and his eyes grey. He was rubbing his arms as if they pained him, and wriggling his shoulders to loosen the muscles.

'The pain of his broken leg must be affecting him,' Victor said softly to Lizzie. 'That's young Mr Pargeter – Jim Pargeter.'

But Lizzie wasn't listening. She was staring at the young man as if she was seeing a ghost, and her face had turned so pale she looked as if she was about to faint. She took a step forward, and then another, and then she was running with her arms extended. And the young man didn't see a heavily pregnant woman with a careworn face: he saw a young girl with shining brown hair and big brown eyes and he started to run to meet her. They stopped a few feet apart and stared into each other's faces, and the years fell away as if they'd never been.

'Billy?' Lizzie gasped. 'Is it really you?'

'Yes, Lizzie.'

'You've grown.'

Bill laughed. 'I was barely eight when you last saw me. I'm twenty-one now.'

'Fourteen years,' Lizzie said. She put out her hand and touched him as if in a dream. But he was real flesh and blood and his face was warm and rough. 'You need a shave,' she laughed, as if it was a miracle that her little brother needed the use of a razor.

'And you're going to make me an uncle,' Bill said, as if
that was miraculous as well.

'For the second time.'

And then their arms were around each other and they
were hugging, their faces wet with tears. It was only
because the ambulance man was anxious to be off that
they managed to separate and climb in beside Joey who
was lying in state.

At the hospital the patient was carried away to have his
leg put in plaster. Bill was given a brief examination and
declared fit, and then he joined Lizzie in the waiting-room
where they attempted to catch up on the years that had
passed. Lizzie skipped over her brief marriage to Tom, just
declaring herself a widow, and assuring Bill that her
marriage to Jack French was an ideally happy one.

In his turn Bill related the events that had ended in him
finding new parents. He emphasised how happy he'd
been with the Pargeters, although he'd never stopped
missing Lizzie.

'And Aunt Hannah? Whatever happened to Aunt
Hannah?' he asked at last.

'She died, Billy. But she remembered us both at the end.
Your legacy is safe. You only have to claim it.'

'I never wanted her money,' Bill said. 'It wasn't important. I wanted her to love me – but she wasn't able to do
that.'

'She relented in the end,' Lizzie assured him. 'I think she
was sorry.'

'I vowed I'd never forgive her for the way she treated
you, Lizzie,' Bill said passionately. 'My biggest fear was
her finding me again and taking me away from the
Pargeters.'

Lizzie took Bill's hands and looked into the clear grey
eyes she remembered so well. 'You must forgive her,' she
said. 'She was a lonely old woman and she treated us fairly
in the end. So you must try to use her legacy wisely.'

'Don't worry, I will,' Bill said, and his face lit up as an idea occurred to him. 'I don't need the money; I'd rather work for my living. But the Pargeters do. They've never had much and yet they shared what they had with me. So I shall do the same. Aunt Hannah's money will make life easier for them. They deserve it.'

'That's a lovely idea.'

After that they talked not about the past but the future. But much as Lizzie tried, Bill couldn't be persuaded to make his home with her. He said he longed to meet the French family who'd been so kind to his sister; particularly Jack.

'When this war ends and he comes out of the army Jack wants his own greengrocery business,' she told him. 'He says that's where you meet the real people.'

'I agree with him,' Bill said approvingly. 'If he does, perhaps there'll be a place for me. I'd like to learn a trade.'

'I know the two of you will get along famously. I've talked about you so much he must feel he knows you already.'

'I hope so.'

'And you'll come to tea tomorrow and meet Jack's mother, and his sister Eileen?'

'Can I bring Mum and Dad?'

'Who?' For a moment Lizzie looked puzzled – then she smiled. 'You mean Mr and Mrs Pargeter?'

'Yes. I know they're not my real parents, they'll never fill that special place in my heart, but I've called them Mum and Dad for so long that it's become a habit. I can't change it now.'

'Of course you can't. You can bring them and they'll be made welcome.'

'Thanks, Lizzie.'

'How do you think they'll take it?' Lizzie asked suddenly. 'Your finding a new family I mean. Will they be upset?'

'No, I'm sure they won't. They'll be pleased for my happiness. Mum's always said she wanted a daughter, so now she'll be able to have an adopted daughter as well as an adopted son.'

'And grandchildren,' Lizzie said with a smile.

'And grandchildren,' Bill repeated after her.

They didn't want to part, but it would only be until the following day. Anyway, Lizzie couldn't wait to get Joey safely back home and impart the good news to Mrs French.

She was as excited as they were. She'd heard so much about Lizzie's lost brother and couldn't wait to meet him.

'And he's bringing his adopted parents to meet us all? I think that's lovely,' she said. 'The house'll be bursting at the seams, and that's the way it should be.'

'I wish Jack was here,' Lizzie said, suddenly looking sad.

'He will be soon. The news from the Front is better every day. The war will come to an end and Jack will come home safely – you'll see.'

'I hope and pray so.'

'Now, what shall we have for the tea-party?' Grace's eyes shone. She loved planning things. 'There's some sausage-meat left over so I can make some sausage-rolls. There's a tin of Spam in the larder, and sardines, so they'll do for sandwiches. I was planning on baking cakes tomorrow morning anyway.'

Everyone was up early the following day. Lizzie was full of energy and set to work tidying the house, while Grace started on the baking. Joey was installed on the drawing-room sofa with his leg supported on a footstool. Eileen kept him company.

'What's your Uncle Billy like?' she asked for the tenth time.

'I told you – he's nice. And he wants to be called Bill.'

'Is he handsome?'

'I suppose so.'

'Do you think he'll like me? Will he find me pretty?'

Eileen's head was full of romance and the film stars she saw at the pictures. Joey's Uncle Bill sounded a romantic figure. After all, he'd been invalided out of the Air Force, and then he'd saved Joey's life. He sounded terribly brave.

'You are pretty,' Joey said generously. He grinned as Eileen preened herself. Why were girls always so obsessed by their appearance? He couldn't understand it.

The door bell rang to announce the arrival of the visitors. Bill put his arm around Grace and gave her a kiss saying that Lizzie had told him all about her. Then he kissed Eileen who blushed scarlet. Mr Pargeter, whose back was still bothering him, was installed by Joey's side on the sofa; and Mrs Pargeter insisted on helping Grace in the kitchen as if she'd known her all her life. Lizzie looked around happily. Everything was going fine; it would be perfect if only Jack were here.

After tea they played games, the sort that Joey could join in from the sofa. And then during a lull in the conversation, Bill suddenly got to his feet and walked over to the piano standing between the two windows. He lifted the lid and ran his fingers gently over the keys. Then he sat down on the stool and began to play 'The March of the Gladiators'. He played it for his mother, and for Lizzie and young Joey, as well as for the new baby that was due shortly. Lastly he played it for himself. It was a brave tune, a soldier's march, that had carried him from the trials of childhood into manhood.

As if knowing it was welcome, Lizzie's baby couldn't wait for its father to come home. It was born that night: a little red-headed girl who Lizzie called Mary after her mother. Grace declared her the living image of Jack; and the baby, feeling the love surrounding her, nestled trustingly against her mother's breast.

Lizzie looked down at the small face and prayed for peace so that Jack could come home and see his baby daughter.

CHAPTER TWENTY-SEVEN

Peace

The war in Europe officially ended on 8 May 1945, although the nation had been expecting the good news for some time. The people of Brighton had got their Union Jacks ready and started collecting food and drink so that they could have a big celebration. For Lizzie the highlight was the lifting of the black-out restrictions, but the youngsters were looking forward to the street parties that were being planned.

On Monday 7 May it was reported on the news that crowds had assembled in Piccadilly, Trafalgar Square, and outside Buckingham Palace for the official bulletin. They had a long wait. A cheer went up when it was announced after several hours that the following day would be celebrated as Victory in Europe day and it would be a national holiday.

The whole country turned their wireless on at three o'clock the following afternoon to hear Winston Churchill's speech, in which he confirmed that the surrender document had been signed by the Germans at 2.41 a.m. the previous day.

Brighton had seen nothing like it before. Church bells

rang out joyfully and people sang and danced the night away. Pianos were dragged into the streets, lights turned on, and celebration bonfires lit in the parks and fields. After almost six years of worry and shortages everyone was determined to make it a day to remember. Of course, there would still be years of rationing and other hardships but at least people could go to bed easy at night without fear of bombing.

Winston Churchill summed it up well when he wrote: 'Weary and worn, impoverished but undaunted, and now triumphant.' That's how everyone felt – triumphant.

But the French family living in Chatsworth Road still had to be patient as they waited for their menfolk to come home. Johnnie arrived first: big and blond, with barely a limp to show he'd been wounded. He was proud of his scarred leg and had great plans for the future. He wanted to live in London and become a reporter. He'd written some poetry about his experiences and intended to write a book. Grace was proud of him.

It took longer for Jack to be demobbed. He was sent to a Military Dispersal Unit, which was the official name for a series of warehouses, where he would exchange his uniform for a civilian outfit. This turned out to be a three-piece suit of inferior quality and cut, a hat, tie and shirt, as well as two pairs of socks and one pair of shoes.

Jack chose a plain navy-blue double breasted suit with a matching tie, a grey striped shirt with two collars, and a trilby hat, commonly known as a pork-pie.

When Lizzie opened the door to him she didn't know whether to laugh or cry – but ended up crying with relief. It didn't matter what he looked like; her man was home safe and well and she was never going to let him go again.

Seven-month-old Mary had seen her father only once before. She'd been barely a month old at the time so obviously didn't remember him. Now, fat and curly-haired, red-faced and round-cheeked, she sat in her high-chair and laughed at the big burly stranger.

'Do you think she knows who I am?' Jack asked, smiling down at his daughter.

'No,' his mother said. 'She laughs like that at everyone. She's a real clown.'

'She's fat, isn't she,' Jack said, who'd imagined a dainty little daughter. 'And her nose is squashed.'

Grace French thumped her son good-naturedly. 'She's the spitting image of you and Eileen at that age. You haven't changed much, son, but look at Eileen...'

Fifteen-year-old Eileen had the grace to blush. She'd changed overnight from a gawky schoolgirl into a tall pale swan. Her red hair fell in silky curls over her ears, and her freckled nose was pert and pretty. She'd left school at Christmas and was a counter assistant at Boots the Chemists in Western Road. While she was waiting to train as a pharmacist she sold aspirin tablets and bandages to customers with such a lovely smile that they immediately felt better and often left without handing over their prescriptions.

The reason for the transformation was that Eileen was in love. She'd lost her heart the year before to twenty-two-year-old Bill Sargent, Lizzie's brother, and although he hadn't declared it, her love was returned.

Bill was in no hurry, and to him Eileen was still a delightful child. He was prepared to wait and watch her grow up and then he would claim his prize. And what a charming prize it would be. In the meantime he petted and played with her, took her dancing and to the pictures and anywhere else she fancied going. He'd comforted her when she cried her way through *Gone with the Wind*, *Mrs Miniver* and *Brief Encounter*, and smiled secretly as he watched her try to copy the alluring charms of Vivian Leigh, and the more homely ones of Greer Garson.

He planned to wait until Eileen was eighteen before declaring himself, and a couple more years until he stood beside her at the altar. There was plenty of time and he knew their future together was secure.

Lizzie would be pleased, and so would Grace French, because her elder daughter, Marjorie, had married a bounder who'd left her after only a few months of marriage. She was now back with the family, working as a nurse and trying to make the best of things. Her corn-coloured hair and sweet disposition wouldn't leave her single for long – or so the family hoped.

The months passed quickly, and by the time the country had been at peace for a year many changes had taken place in the town. There was scaffolding around the buildings that had suffered only minimal damage, and others had been razed to the ground. It was usual to see the skeletons of houses with only one or two surviving walls. Wallpaper, carefully chosen and hung before the war, now faced the elements, and fireplaces and gas-fittings hung from walls without any means of support.

The less badly damaged buildings were being restored, and among these were Grainger's and Lizzie's salon. The frontages were complete, and although Victor Grainger had ideas about expansion, Lizzie was happy to settle for a smaller salon with just one cubicle and a small reception area. During the war her young assistants had led different lives: Stella making ammunitions, and Julia working on the land. Lizzie had lost touch with both of them so she was on her own.

Joey had left school and joined his grandfather in the newly refurbished shop. Victor reported that he was settling in nicely and had the makings of a competent member of staff. He was helpful and friendly, and regular customers were already asking if Young Mr Grainger was free to serve them.

He went off to work every morning wearing a charcoal grey suit, with a neatly folded handkerchief peeping out of the breast pocket. His dark tie was kept in place by a tiny gold pin: a present from his grandfather. He was waiting eagerly for the day when his head was large enough to fit one of the smart trilbys in the hat department. He was a handsome lad but didn't chase the girls like his father had done. In fact, he was devoted to a solid schoolgirl of fourteen called Jennifer. She wore spectacles and cut her hair in a straight unbecoming fringe, but Joey was enamoured by her. He declared that she had a kind heart, made him laugh, and her nature was lovely even if her face wasn't.

Old Mr Pargeter's back was better and he'd returned to work, so Bill was temporarily without a job. Lizzie was thinking about this one Sunday afternoon as she walked with Jack along the promenade pushing Mary in her pram. She was wearing a new outfit: a grey woollen two-piece consisting of a fitted jacket with padded shoulders and a tight skirt with a pleat at the back. With it she wore a saucy hat set at a jaunty angle, nylon stockings and platform shoes. During the war Lizzie had become so used to wearing loose clothing or slacks that in comparison the new fashions were uncomfortable. But she had to get used to looking smart again because the salon was re-opened. She would soon spoil her reputation if she happened to meet one of her customers when she wasn't looking her best.

Mary was fast asleep in the high black perambulator. It rocked slightly on its big wheels as they crossed the road and paused in their walk to look at the sea.

'Let's sit down for a moment,' Lizzie said. She parked the pram by a bench and sank down on to the seat gratefully.

'Are you tired?'

'It's these shoes and this skirt. They're both too tight.'

Jack grinned. 'Why do you wear them then? When I first knew you, you wore a faded cotton frock and broken shoes. I still thought you were beautiful.'

'You sound just like Joey when he talks about his Jennifer.'

They laughed, and then gazed out to sea, each deep in their own thoughts. Then Lizzie asked, 'Can you look after Mary tomorrow, Jack? I've got a busy day at the salon and your mother wants to go shopping with Marjorie.'

'Of course.' Jack paused and then said, 'Lizzie, I want to talk to you.'

'What is it, darling?'

'I think it's time I started working.'

'You don't have to,' Lizzie assured him. 'We're comfortably off with the house and the salon. And then there's Aunt Hannah's money. I only keep the salon going for an interest.'

'But don't you see, Lizzie, that's what I want – an interest – a purpose in life. I can't keep living off your money.'

Lizzie was immediately contrite. She knew she would have felt the same if she'd been born a man. 'Then you must get a job,' she said. 'If you feel like that. What do you want to do?'

'You know what I want – to be a greengrocer again.'

'To serve the *real* people?'

'You remember.'

'Of course I remember.' She took his hand and kissed it. 'I'll buy you a shop.'

'No, you won't.' Jack pulled his hand away quickly. 'I won't take your money. I have to do it myself. I'm going to rent a stall at the Open Market and Bill's coming in with me. He's getting a van so he can collect supplies and make deliveries. Don't look like that – or will you be ashamed of having a stall-holder for a husband? Will it degrade Lady Elizabeth?'

'Jack,' Lizzie said, and her voice was soft with love. 'I shall be proud to have a stall-holder for a husband – and hang Lady Elizabeth's.'

'Oh Lizzie,' Jack breathed. 'Do you really mean that?'

'Mean what?'

'That my market stall will be more important to you than Lady Elizabeth's.'

Lizzie didn't answer for a moment. She knew she had to make a choice: the answer she gave now would be the pathway she'd have to follow for the rest of her life. But it didn't take long to make up her mind. She turned to Jack and took his hands again between hers, and the smile she gave him was the smile of a young girl on the verge of a great discovery.

'Jack, all these years I've had my priorities wrong,' she said. 'I thought the salon and having all the good things in life would bring me happiness. But I was mistaken. I know that happiness for me will be working beside my husband on a market stall – that is if you'll have me.'

They looked deep into each other's eyes, and then Jack's arms were around Lizzie and she was more content than she'd ever before been in her life. At that moment the sun came out from behind a cloud, streaking across the pebbles on the beach and the paving stones on the promenade and, just for a second, Lizzie saw that Brighton was indeed paved with gold.